THE SOUND OF Silence

by Dakota Willink

Library of Congress Cataloging-in-Publication Data
ISBN: 978-1-954817-19-7
The Sound of Silence | Copyright © 2020 by Dakota Willink

Praise for The Sound of Silence

*"Raw. Inspired. Invigorated. Empowered. This book will leave
you reeling with emotion as Willink's heroine scrapes herself off
and embarks on a tumultuous journey to finding herself once
again. It is a story of strength despite fear, of resilience despite
the chance of failure, of freedom and rediscovering oneself."*
— **Carey Decevito, Author**

*"A 5 star page turner that is so much more than just an edge of
your seat romantic suspense. It's an emotional roller coaster that
perfectly mirrors the silent struggles of too many women. Beyond
pure entertainment, it is a plea to open our eyes, to realities that
are often right in front of us."*
— **Cassidy London, Author**

*"I was completely robbed of breath, gulping in desperation and
taken by fits of adrenaline. This is an in-your-face, heart-
pounding story that is so vivid, you feel as if you're living it."*
— **Not Your Moms Romance Book Blog**

*"I was blown away by this inescapable page turner! The
powerful emotions that spiral throughout will have a lasting
effect on me for years to come!"*
— **2 Vixens Book Blog**

*"Dakota Willink's latest dark romantic thriller is a chilling and
heart-stopping romance that's guaranteed to keep you on the
edge of your seat!"*
— **After Fifty Shades Book Blog**

TRIGGER WARNING

This story contains situations of domestic violence and abuse. Some aspects may be sensitive for some readers.

Me too.

PART I

GIRL MEETS BOY

1

Gianna

Cincinnati, Ohio

I slid my palms over my black apron, smearing the sticky remnants of vermouth over the gold embroidered Teddy's Tavern logo. I surveyed the long row of customers sitting at the polished mahogany bar of the upscale restaurant in Hyde Park. Most were dressed in business attire, having just come from work to hit happy hour. They chatted away with their colleagues, all seemingly satisfied—for now. It wouldn't be long before I was flagged down to make another martini.

"Gia!" Theodore Reeves, also known as Teddy, called out to me from the door leading to the kitchen. "Nat is swamped since the new girl called in. Can you do a sweep of the tables over in section A?"

I glanced over at Natalia, my co-worker and best friend. She definitely looked frazzled.

"On it, Teddy," I replied with a little salute.

"Thanks, doll. It's impossible to find good help these days."

I moved around to the end of the bar and waved him off.

"Come on now. You know they all can't be perfect like me," I joked as I headed over to my friend. When Natalia saw me, I watched her shoulders visibly sag with relief. "What can I help you with?"

"Table seven and nine need drink refills. Table five's food should be ready in the kitchen. Take your pick. Grab the drinks or get the food," she said in a rush. A strand of jet-black hair fell loose from her ponytail and she hastily tucked it behind her ear.

"I'll get the drinks. That way I can keep an eye on the bar customers too," I suggested.

"Good idea. I can't believe how slammed we are today! With the Danbury Musical Festival going on, I thought it would be slower."

I cocked one eyebrow and leaned in closer to her so I wasn't overheard by any of the patrons.

"Seriously, Nat? What you see here is Cincinnati's most prestigious yuppie crowd. Do you honestly think any of them would be going to see Fall Out Boy or Sublime?"

She smirked, then pinched up her face as though she was trying to picture it.

"No, I suppose you're right. I can't imagine this swanky bunch anywhere near a mosh pit."

I laughed, patting her shoulder, then headed in the direction of the tables needing drink refills.

Five hours later, the restaurant had cleared out and there were only a few stragglers left at the bar. I leaned on the back counter watching Natalia as she counted our tips for the night. She handed me a stack of cash totaling six hundred dollars.

"Good night for tips," I mused, grabbing my purse from under the bar. Separating the money, I put half in my wallet and the rest into a worn, tattered white envelope. After I put my purse back under the counter, I glanced up to see Natalia staring at me with a sad look on her face.

"What?" I asked.

"Just thinking, toots. That's all."

"Thinking about what?"

"About how long it's going to be before your mom's bills are paid off," she quietly replied.

Emotion scorched my throat and I tried to ignore the stab of pain I felt whenever I was reminded of my mother. Natalia was referring to the credit card debt I racked up trying to help my mother pay for the prescription drugs she needed to survive the death grip cancer had ensnared her in. She'd had decent health insurance, but sometimes it wasn't enough. At the end of the day, nothing I did mattered. No amount of money spent was enough to save her. I lost her to ovarian cancer nearly a year ago and I still missed her something fierce. Unfortunately, the small life insurance policy she had was only enough to cover the burial expenses and I was stuck paying off the mountain of credit card debt.

"I only owe another few thousand," I said with a shrug.

Four thousand two hundred ninety-eight to be exact, but who's counting?

"After they're paid, what comes next?"

I pursed my lips and contemplated her question. I knew what she was asking. Both of us frequently talked about our bucket lists and all the things we wanted to accomplish before we turned thirty. The only thing holding me back from scratching things off my list was the credit card debt. Once that was paid, I could begin to really live my life for the first time.

"I know we talked about traveling but I think I want to go to college first," I blurted out.

"College? You've never mentioned that before."

"Yeah, well... the money might be good at Teddy's, but I don't want to work here forever."

"Hey, I heard that!" shouted Teddy. "What's wrong with being a lifer?"

I looked up to see him sitting at a table near the far side of the restaurant with Ben Santos, the unofficial bouncer at Teddy's Tavern. The stack of leather-bound books in front of Teddy told me he was tallying up the weekly numbers. He winked at me and I smiled.

"Being a lifer means I won't be able to take a month off to backpack across Europe. Mark my words—I will do that one day. But," I drawled out in a teasing voice, "maybe I'll stick around part-time just for you, old man."

Ben snorted a laugh which earned him a scowl from Teddy.

"This place wouldn't be the same without you," Teddy grumbled.

"And what about me?" Natalia asked accusingly.

"Alright, you too," Teddy begrudgingly admitted, but we could all tell it was in jest. "You girls keep this place running like a well-oiled machine, and the customers love you too."

I was about to respond but the sound of a glass being slammed down on the bar stopped me.

"Hey, if you can wrap it up anytime soon, I need another drink down here!" yelled a man sitting five stools to my left.

I straightened quickly and headed his way. He was scowling, but I simply plastered a sweet smile on my face and reached for his glass—which I had literally filled just ten minutes before. I tossed Ben a sideways glance to signal we might need to keep an eye on the guy.

"Sorry to keep you waiting, sir. Another Jameson? Neat, right?"

"That's right," he confirmed, watching me through narrowed eyes. The guy wasn't a regular customer, of that I was sure, nor did this seem like a place he'd frequent. Almost everyone who came to the upscale tavern looked like they just stepped off the pages of a Nordstrom catalog. The five-star restaurant reeked of class—but definitely not this guy. He was sloppy in an unbuttoned plaid flannel with a faded concert tee underneath. His hair was a mess and he desperately needed a shave. He appeared more suited for the crowd at the music festival than Teddy's. Still, he was handsome in a rugged sort of way.

I grabbed a napkin, placed the drink on top of it, and slid it across the bar to him. I was about to ask if he needed anything else when he grabbed hold of my wrist. I tried to tug my hand free but he held firm as his gaze roamed up and down my body. I fought the urge to roll my eyes. When you worked behind a bar, getting hit on by guys who overindulged in their booze tended to be a nightly occurrence. Nine out of ten times, the best thing to do was kill them with kindness and move along.

"Would you like something to eat? The kitchen is technically closed but I'm sure I can get the cook to throw something together for you," I told him with a sugary sweet smile on my face.

"I don't want nothin' to eat," he slurred. "I heard the customers here love you. I can see why. What's not to love about that tight little ass of yours? Gia, that's your name, right?"

The smile I'd plastered on fell. When my strategy of killing them with kindness didn't work, a blunter approach never failed.

"Gianna, actually. Only my friends call me Gia," I pointed out, making it clear he was very much *not* my friend. When I tried to pull my hand away again, he only squeezed tighter. I took in his glassy eyes and a chill raced down my spine. He most likely started drinking well before he wandered into Teddy's and he was giving me a serious case of the creeps. "Sir, please let go of me."

"What if I don't wanna?" he sneered.

Out of the corner of my eye, I saw Ben jump from his chair. Before he could get to the creepy guy, another man with dark, wavy hair abruptly stood up. He'd been quietly sitting two stools down and I'd nearly forgotten he was even there. The dark-haired man grabbed the drunk guy by the front of his scruffy t-shirt and spun him around. Everything happened so fast yet it unfolded like a slow-motion video replay at the same time.

"The lady said let go of her," the man growled.

Startled, my very drunk customer swayed slightly as he put both hands up in the air.

"What the fuck, man! I was only jokin' around with her."

"Take your jokes elsewhere. They aren't funny here."

I saw Ben slowly moving toward the two men, braced for a potential fight. Teddy wasn't far behind him, both looking like mountain lions stalking their prey.

"You heard the man. Take your jokes elsewhere," Ben reiterated, stepping between the two men in an attempt to defuse things in a non-violent way. The entire situation was bizarre. Altercations like this just didn't happen at Teddy's Tavern.

His glazed eyes landed sluggishly on each of the men surrounding him. Then he looked at me, scowled, and took a step back.

"Alright, alright. I get your point. I'm goin'," he said. Without another word, he not-so-gracefully sauntered out of the tavern, defiantly tipping over every empty chair he passed on his way to the door.

"Asshole," Natalia muttered.

"I'm sorry. I shouldn't have interfered like that. It's instinct I guess," said the dark-haired man. I turned my attention back to him and watched as he pulled out his wallet to flash a shiny badge at me. Apparently, my rescuer wasn't just a nice guy—he was a cop too.

I shook my head and rubbed my wrist.

"No, it's okay. I'm just glad he left before things escalated. Um... thank you for your help," I said with a small shrug. "How about a drink? On the house," I offered.

"Maybe another time. I need to get going," he said. Reaching into the pocket of the leather tri-fold wallet, he tossed a fifty on the table. "That piece of shit didn't pay for his drinks but that should cover it. Enjoy the rest of your night, Gianna."

I paused at the way my name sounded coming from his lips. I knew he must have heard my conversation with the drunk guy, but there was just something about the way it rolled off his tongue that made me flush. I took another look at my rescuer. He was attractive—very attractive actually. With all the commotion, I hadn't taken a moment to appreciate his sculpted cheekbones and full mouth. He appeared older than me but still had a youthful look that made me think he wasn't more than thirty. His eyes were a deep brown, nearly matching the dark waves on his head. His crisp white shirt stretched over the wide span of his shoulders, tapering down to tuck into the trim waistline of his khaki pants.

He flashed a crooked grin, completely captivating me. Whether he knew it or not, he was charming—but not in an obvious sort of way. When he started to walk away, I impulsively called out to him.

"Wait! I don't know your name!"

He glanced over his shoulder and afforded me another sexy, crooked smile.

"It's Ethan. Ethan Walker. Maybe I'll see you around, Gianna."

Then… he left.

As soon as the tavern door closed behind him, Natalia pounced.

"Gia, oh my God! That guy was fucking gorgeous! And he's clearly into you!"

"Nat!" Teddy hissed. "Keep your voice down. There are still customers here."

"Sorry," she whispered and grabbed my arm. "Gianna Valentini! For crying out loud! He's a hot cop! You need to go after him. You'd be crazy if you didn't."

"Go after him? And say what?" I asked, the flush I felt a few moments before deepening.

"I don't know. Ask him out for coffee or something!"

I stared at her, then looked back at the front door. He was probably long gone by now.

But if he wasn't...

I hadn't dated in over four years. College wasn't the only thing I missed out on when my mother got sick—dating was another. Her illness didn't allow me any time. As a result, I was probably the most inexperienced twenty-four-year-old on the planet. I had no idea how to ask a guy out. Well, maybe I did, but I was incredibly rusty.

Natalia was persistent, shoving me in the direction of the door with repeated statements about how this would be good for me. Perhaps she was right and I should go after him. I needed to start moving forward with my life. Life is about the living after all. Finally, I turned my head toward Natalia and grinned.

"Wish me luck!"

"Luck!" I heard her say as I hurried to catch up with him.

I pushed open the front door of the tavern and looked around. A few cars whizzed by, breaking through the silent night air. Other than that, all was quiet. He was nowhere to be found. My shoulders slumped, awash with disappointment at missing my chance at a possible real date in years.

I huffed out a frustrated breath. I was being ridiculous. For all I knew, the guy was married. Maybe that was why he turned down the drink I'd offered. I never once thought to check his hand for a ring. If he was interested in me like Natalia thought, surely he would have stuck around to talk. As I was about to turn around to go back inside, I spotted a familiar form climbing into a late-model BMW parked down the street.

It was him.

"Ethan!"

He paused and looked up, a slow grin spreading across his

beautiful features. I hurried across the street, trying not to appear too terribly obvious.

Just play it cool. You can do this.

"Hey," he greeted as I approached.

"Hey," I repeated like a freaking parrot. This was going to be harder than I thought. "So, um... I feel like I owe you for what happened back there. What do you say? Want to grab a cup of coffee sometime?"

Ethan's sexy grin widened, although he didn't answer right away. The grin was a good sign, despite the fact his hesitation made my insides twist with apprehension. I was practically bouncing on my toes waiting for him to answer. After what felt like forever, but was probably more like three seconds, he responded.

"Okay, I'll go for coffee, but only on one condition."

"What's the condition?" My brow furrowed in confusion.

"I get to call you Gia."

2

Ethan

I watched her walk back into Teddy's Tavern, carefully balancing the door with her delicate little hand so it didn't slam closed. She tossed me a quick smile before disappearing inside, giving me one last look at her perfectly shaped ass when she turned.

Her body was tight and compact, like my very own Scarlett Johansson. Their likeness was uncanny; she could easily pass as the actress's double. Still, I couldn't help but notice no panty lines were visible through Gianna's black pants. I wondered if she was wearing a thong. Or maybe she wasn't wearing underwear at all. I hoped it was the latter.

Then again, maybe I didn't want that.

I chewed my lower lip as I started the car and pulled away from the curb. I wondered if Scarlett Johansson went completely without. As soon as the idea popped into my mind, I chuckled. How stupid of me? Of course a refined beauty like her would choose a thong over nothing at all. A woman who went commando would definitely classify as sexually immoral, sinning against her own body.

And it was dirty.

Did I want my girl to be dirty?

No.

Hopefully, Gianna had class like Scarlett. I thought she did, but I'd need to make sure. If she didn't, I could adjust to the changes if needed. Intelligent men like me adapted. Hadn't I proved as much tonight? My original plan had been to stage a run-in with my girl. It would have been brilliant and romantic—a love at first sight sort of thing.

But love was hard work and it was never predictable.

So, when a different opportunity presented itself, I took advantage. Casually mentioning the pretty bartender who worked at Teddy's to the drunk loitering outside of the music festival had been all too easy. He took the bait—and the fifty-dollar bill I slipped him—allowing me to become her knight in shining armor. And the rest, as they say, was history.

Or at least it will be.

A few minutes later, I pulled into the parking lot of a run-down apartment building in Avondale. I grabbed the duffle bag I'd hidden away under a flannel blanket in the backseat and climbed out of the car. I grimaced as the smell of urine from the nearby alley assaulted my nose. The area, in general, was the definition of urban decay. With the rising crime rate and deteriorating housing, the absentee landlords neglected their properties, and tenants often abused the buildings. I scowled at the surrounding rot.

Why would anyone actually choose to live here?

The only reason I rented this particular flat was so I could have a safe place to stash my earnings. It was cheap, and it worked. I never planned to spend any amount of time there. I much preferred the pristine and orderly space of my inherited condo over on West 4th Street.

Then I wandered into Teddy's Tavern two years and seventeen days ago. From that moment on, everything changed —that's when I saw my girl for the first time.

In an instant, I knew I could love her. We were meant to be together. She didn't have to smile or be polite as I sat at a table all alone that day at Teddy's. Sure, she may have acted like I was any other customer as she jotted down my order for a bowl of baked potato soup and a craft beer, but it was obvious we were experiencing our first date.

She knew it.

I knew it.

I remembered the special day as if it had happened only yesterday. A nearby customer had spent a small fortune on eighties tunes at the jukebox. I hadn't minded because Sade was piping through the speakers.

And it was our song—mine and my girls.

And that was me.

I was a smooth operator.

We'd been so close, I could have reached out and touched her, but had refrained. It wasn't the right time, even if I knew the truth. She couldn't hide it from me. I could see it in her eyes.

She wanted me as much as I wanted her.

What we had right from our very first moment together was real. True. Authentic.

She changed my life.

She was the reason I didn't find an alternate, less putrid location for what had come to be the home for my most sacred belongings. Instead, I continued to renew the lease every six months to stay close to my girl—my Gia—at all times.

"My Gia," I whispered as I inserted the key into the doorknob of the flat. She was different from the others. She was special. After more than two years of watching, learning, and biding my time, I had finally moved to 'friend' zone. If all went as planned, it wouldn't be long before she was officially mine.

All mine.

No more fucking my mattress. No more watching her through a telephoto lens. She would be with me always.

I flipped on the overhead light and closed the door behind me. Pausing at the small table next to the door, I looked down upon the statue of the Virgin Mother, surrounded by seven unlit votive candles inside little red glass jars. Pride, greed, wrath, envy, lust, gluttony, and sloth were artfully etched into the glass of each jar. A framed photo of my own mother sat beside the Virgin, their presence here giving life to an otherwise lifeless room.

"Hello, Mother." I lit the candle that represented lust, then leaned down to kiss my mother's portrait. "I had a very interesting day today. I can't wait to tell you all about it."

I smiled when I thought about how pleased she would be to hear my news, then stepped away from the table. Walking passed the threadbare couch and large fish tank that covered the far wall, I headed to the kitchen pantry. Opening the door, I slid open the fake wooden wall hidden behind a few boxes of dried pasta to reveal a combination lock safe. I spun the dial until the cams aligned and I could open the latch. Removing the duffel bag from my shoulder, I unzipped it and removed my take from the day's bust.

The department seized fifty-two thousand in cash and sixty-eight pounds of cocaine in a raid today—or at least that's what they bragged about to the local newspapers. Little did they know, I skimmed fifteen grand and a brick off the top.

I didn't sniff the stuff personally—drugs clouded the mind, and intoxication led to sin. However, the street value for one brick was over thirty thousand. I never knew when I might need a bunch of cash in a pinch, and I just happened to have the connections to move it.

Did that make me a dirty cop? I didn't think so. As far as I was concerned, it was my right. If the other cops in my unit didn't think to do the same, that was their loss. We put our lives in jeopardy every day because of the scum who roamed the street —and the paychecks we received to do it were a joke. For me, it was a matter of survival, whereas the dealers and the traffickers were driven by greed. It was the deadliest of all cardinal sins but I had faith in Him. He would not let them go unpunished if they didn't repent.

"Be assured, an evil person will not go unpunished, but the offspring of the righteous will be delivered," I recited, having committed Proverbs 11:21 to memory years ago while still under my mother's teachings in the White Room.

After the cash and plastic-wrapped brick were placed neatly inside, I locked the safe and put everything back to the way it had been. Walking to the corkboard hanging on the wall above the rickety kitchen table, I smiled and pulled a pin from one of the pictures I'd placed there a few months back. It was one of my favorite pictures of Gianna and I didn't even have to use the zoom on my Nikon D850. I'd caught this one with my cell phone.

The sun and slight breeze had caught her blonde hair just right. When she raised a hand to push a wisp of it from her forehead, a shadow cast in a such a way that she appeared to have a halo. That was the moment I'd captured the photo. Who knew the iPhone camera could be so good?

She had been heading to work fifteen minutes before the start of her shift. I recalled thinking she'd be getting to work much too early, but that was just her way—always punctual and hard working.

I scowled. She was too good for a place like Teddy's Tavern and all the drunks who harassed her every night. The asshole who bothered her tonight should be thanking his lucky stars. It didn't matter if I'd set him up to do it, he'd gone too far.

I should have killed him for what he did to my girl.

I sighed and shook my head, knowing I'd have to repent for

even thinking about going against one of His most important teachings, "Thou shall not kill."

Be steadfast. It won't be long now.

She'd officially be my girl soon enough, and I would no longer have to bear the burden of coveting what wasn't mine. When that happened, she wouldn't have to work at Teddy's anymore. I would take care of her. She would be all mine, and my sins shall be forgiven.

I pinned the picture back on the corkboard alongside the rest. My gaze scanned the many images of her covering the board. I knew every single one of them by heart. She was so beautiful and she didn't even know it, but it wasn't because she was insecure.

No, not my girl.

She didn't know it because she was unassuming. She was even beautiful when she was sad, as she had been when her mother died. Others didn't see it, but I did. She looked so tired in the pictures taken during that time. The sparkle in her eyes had been absent.

I raised a hand to one of the sadder pictures and ran a finger over the outline of her cheek. The skies above her were gloomy as she stood over her mother's grave. I knew how upset she had been. I'd read about it on her Instagram account—long, descriptive captions underneath picture after picture of my girl with her mother. It was a tragedy, really.

"I wish I could have helped you then but I will soon. You won't have to worry about those medical bills for much longer. I'll take care of everything. I know it's hard, but you'll see. I've been in your shoes. Your mother's death was for the best." I paused and glanced at the picture of my mother before looking back to Gianna's image. "Mothers complicate things and I don't want any complications for us."

Cancer was a horrific disease but I understood He worked in mysterious ways. Everything happened for a reason. My mother was gone as well. To me, the death of Gianna's mother only strengthened the connection between me and my girl. We were both motherless souls, too old to be young and had nobody to love us as we once did. It was another a sign of how she and I were meant to be together—a sign she was meant to be my girl.

I glanced down at my watch and noted the time.

My girl would be returning home soon.

Killing the lights, I walked to the folding chair near the window, picking up my Nikon and a pair of binoculars. Then I waited as I had that morning.

Gianna always left the blinds for the balcony door open, giving me the ability to see most of her apartment. I didn't like that. It made me nervous. I mean, didn't she watch the news? Anybody could have climbed the fire escape up four stories and snatched her. Still, her lack of precautions worked to my benefit, so I didn't want to complain. It's how I'd come to know her routine so well.

She started her day with yoga and granola. While many people strived to be better, most took the cheater way out.

But not my girl.

She took care of herself, which was more than I could say for the vast majority of the delusional, over-medicated, take-a-pill-to-fix-my-problems people of America. My girl only took vitamin C when she felt the onset of a head cold. As far as I was concerned, that didn't count as medication since its effectiveness was only a myth, anyway.

After she finished with my favorite yoga stretch, the downward dog, she'd sit on the tan sofa and read a book. A bit of time would pass, her body cooling down from the yoga routine, and I'd see her nipples pebble beneath her tank top right before she'd cover herself with the pink-and-yellow afghan her mother knitted for her when she was just a child. She never read on a Kindle. No, my girl refused to cheapen literary brilliance by reading on an electronic device. She read paperbacks like smart people—but none of those trashy Harlequin things. Classics were much more preferable like *The Catcher in the Rye* or *The Great Gatsby*.

The stereo would go on after about an hour of reading time. Her taste in music left much to be desired, but we would fix that once we were officially a couple. In time, my girl would come to appreciate the works of Johannes Brahms and Ludwig van Beethoven. I just needed to show her the way.

After she picked a song, she'd disappear into the bathroom. That was the only time I couldn't see her. As much as it annoyed me, I realized using my imagination was probably for the best. My mother used to say, "Why buy the cow when you can get the milk for free, my boy?"

She was right—just as she almost always was—but the mere thought of my girl showering and rubbing soapy hands over naked breasts made my dick twitch. I would need to be punished for lusting, but at that moment, that was of little concern. I unzipped my pants at the exact moment the lights for Gianna's fourth-floor apartment across the street came on.

She was right on time.

"Gianna Valentini," I said in a hushed tone, her name rolling off my tongue like a damn poem. "Now, let's solve the mystery of whether you're wearing panties, shall we? Are you or are you not a dirty girl?"

Raising the binoculars, I watched as she launched into her nightly routine. It always began with the removal of her shoes, and tonight was no different. After placing them neatly by the door, my girl placed her hands on the small of her back and gave in to a good stretch. When she bent over to rub her toes, I knew her feet were aching after working a long shift. Even though she loved wearing those useless, non-athletic sneakers, I wished she would wear shoes with more support.

She walked through the family room into her bedroom. I watched her through the open bedroom door as she unbuttoned her black trousers and let them fall to the floor. Pulling her shirt over her head, she dropped it on the floor as well. I never liked to see her display such sloth. However, this time, I couldn't help but smile when I saw the strappy lines of a red thong wrapping around her hips.

"I knew you weren't a dirty girl, Gia," I murmured, pleased to see she was, in fact, wearing underwear. Scarlett Johansson would be proud. "I guess I can forgive you just this once for leaving your clothes on the floor. Besides, I know you'll pick them up later."

I began to stroke myself, anticipating what I knew would come next. She would disappear into the bathroom, then reappear wearing pink shorts and a tank top. If it was winter, she'd be wearing purple flannel pants with the same tank top.

Thankfully, it wasn't winter.

Pajama shorts hugging my girls' hips was always a treat—especially when she sat on the couch with her legs bent and ankles crossed as she watched reruns of *Friends*. What did kids call that sitting position nowadays? Apparently, it was no longer PC to say someone was sitting Indian style. All I knew was, whenever my girl sat that way, I was able to justify the cost of the Nikon. Just as I predicted, she went into the bathroom and reemerged a few minutes later, wearing my favorite little pink shorts.

"That's it, Gia. Now sit down on the couch. Go ahead and bite the sparkly polish off your fingernails. Yes, it's a gross habit, but we can work on that later as long as you cross your legs just the way I like. Go on now…"

Through the binoculars, I watched as she picked up the television remote. The pinky finger on her left hand went to her mouth while the thumb on her right hand pressed down on the remote-control buttons. She channel surfed for what seemed like eons.

Click, click, click.

"I don't know why you bother, Gia. Let's get real. We both know Ross & Rachel always win."

After a few minutes of futile searching, *Friends* appeared on the television. I was right again. I saw her smile, and I smiled, too. I knew she was probably giggling that adorable little giggle over something Chandler had said. I knew her so well, it was almost scary.

Pulling her knees up, she let them fall to the side and crossed her ankles. The shorts naturally parted to the side, giving me a small peek at naked lips and light brown curls.

"Criss-cross applesauce! That's what it is!" It was a stupid fucking name, but I didn't dwell on it, too busy wondering how loud my girl would scream when she orgasmed for me for the first time. Picking up the Nikon, I zoomed in on the area between her legs. "Good girl. Stay sitting just like that."

I snapped a few pictures, then went back to using the binoculars. Leaning back in the chair, I squeezed my cock tighter and imagined it was my girl's mouth, sucking me dry.

PART II

UNTIL DEATH DO THEY PART

3

Gianna

One Year Later

I stared up into Ethan's eyes as we swayed to the slow, harmonious voices of Ed Sheeran and Beyoncé. I wanted to pinch myself to make sure the moment was real. I was officially Mrs. Ethan Walker, the happiest woman on earth. If anyone had told me a year ago someone like me, a penniless girl from a run-down neighborhood in Cincinnati, would have landed the man whose arms were wrapped tightly around me, I wouldn't have believed it. That first coffee date turned into a dinner date, then quickly became so much more.

Four months later, after a whirlwind romance, Ethan proposed. He chose to do it on the night he was appointed the youngest Chief of Police for the Cincinnati Police Department. I had originally thought we were going out to celebrate his new title. Little did I know he'd pop the question.

"How did I get so lucky?" I asked my new husband.

"I don't believe in luck, Gia," he said, pulling me tighter to his chest. "We all make our own destiny. And you? You were destined to be mine."

"I'm yours forever," I whispered, smiling wistfully, and rested my head against his broad shoulder. He stroked my back softly with his fingertips, caressing the skin left bare by the V-shaped open back of my wedding gown. When the song ended, Ethan pulled back and took my face between his palms.

"I have a surprise for you."

"Oh? What kind of surprise?" I asked.

"Do you remember the house we drove by a couple of months ago in Indian Hill? The secluded one with the pond, surrounded by the tall pines."

"Of course I remember." I recalled the way I gaped at the large ranch-style home when we passed by it. With its stone exterior, picturesque dormers, and perfectly trimmed hedges, it looked as though it had come straight out of a fairytale. There had been a for sale sign staked in the front lawn. However, when I looked it up online, it was well out of our price range. "I really loved that house, especially the wrap around porch."

"I know you loved it, so..." A mischievous glint came into his eye.

"So, what?"

"I bought it."

"Ethan!" I gasped. "We can't afford that house. I looked it up. It was—"

"Shhhh," he said, placing his index finger over my lips. "I have my ways. Trust me. I wanted the house as much as you did. Didn't I say we make our own destiny? I'm the Chief of Police now, honey. I can make anything happen, and I can't wait to carry you over the threshold tonight."

"Tonight?"

"Yes. The movers were at your apartment today. My girl doesn't have to worry about a thing. All of your stuff is already in the new house."

"It is?" I blinked, not sure how I felt. I was still reeling from the idea I would be living in a storybook home. I was like Cinderella—a girl who dared to dream and had all of her wishes come true—however, the idea of a stranger being in my home, going through my personal things without my knowledge, was unsettling.

"Gia, what's wrong?"

Ethan's hands slid from my face to the crook of my neck and I felt him tense. I blinked again, unsure what to say. If I told him my thoughts, I would sound ungrateful, and I didn't want anything to spoil this moment. It was my wedding day, and I just found out my prince had bought me a castle. Instead of voicing my concern, I smiled up at him.

"Nothing is wrong. I'm just happy, that's all. Thank you, Ethan."

"Anything for my girl. I know you don't like city living. If a quiet suburb is what you want, that's what you get," he murmured. He tucked a blonde curl behind my ear, but I reached up to put it back.

"Those curly wisps are supposed to be there." I smiled and pointed to the matching curl on the other side. "See? Lisa did my hair that way on purpose."

"I wish you'd gone to the stylist I suggested." Ethan frowned and took a step back as the song ended.

He looked genuinely annoyed, and laughter bubbled from my lips. For some unknown reason, I found his displeasure with my hairstylist to be quite humorous. Most men I knew couldn't care less about such things, but then again, Ethan wasn't like most men.

"What's wrong with Lisa?" I asked with amusement.

He opened his mouth to respond, but whatever he was about to say was interrupted by Natalia.

"Gia, this wedding cake is the bomb! I'm completely addicted to the frosting. Where did you get it from?"

"Oh, um…" I couldn't remember and had to think about it. We tried so many cakes from various bakers, but Ethan ultimately made the final decision.

"Marcella's Bakery," Ethan answered without looking at her. His response was somewhat curt, and he was looking at something over my shoulder. I turned and saw a group of men lingering by the bar, recognizing them as officers from Ethan's precinct. When I looked back at Ethan, his jaw was tense. "Gia, there are some people I have to talk to. I'll be right back."

Ethan walked away, and I pressed my lips into a frown. Something was upsetting him. He'd been just fine a few minutes earlier. I looked back at Natalia. The music had transitioned to a catchy tune that had her tapping a pale pink, high heeled foot in time to the beat. She smiled at me as she licked icing from her fingers. After dropping her cake dish onto a nearby table, she flashed me a playful smile.

"I'm going to yank Teddy and Ben out onto the dance floor. The two of them have been sitting in the corner like a couple of duds all night. Come on! Let's get them up and moving," she said, waving for me to follow her.

Natalia was always the life of the party, whereas I was the one who loved to be in bed before ten. We were like night and day, yet somehow managed to balance each other out. Tonight, her energy was just as contagious as always, but I knew my limitations. I needed a quick time-out from all the festivities before I crashed too early.

"Actually, it's warm in here, Nat. I'm going to pop into the lady's room and freshen up first if that's okay. I'll meet you on the dance floor in a bit."

"Sure thing, toots. See you in a few."

Ten minutes later, I exited the restroom and returned to the reception. When I stepped over the threshold into the large hotel banquet room, my ears were assaulted by loud music. I glanced around for Ethan. He was still deep in conversation with the men at the bar. I spotted Natalia on the dance floor with Ben, but I didn't see Teddy. I knew I should join them, but just the thought of going back into a room where the air was thick and heated from all the dancing bodies made me hot and tired all over again. I needed to get away for a bit of fresh air—even if it was only for a few minutes. Turning away from the crowded room, I walked down the corridor to the outside hotel courtyard.

As soon as I stepped outside, the cool early September night air washed over me. It felt good on my skin and seemed to loosen the heavy satin dress sticking to my body. I spotted a wrought-iron bench a few feet away, walked over to it, and sat down to toe-off my heels. Leaning back, I closed my eyes and breathed deep.

"Runaway bride?" said a deep voice.

Startled, my eyes snapped open. I thought I was alone but standing in front of me was a man wearing frayed jeans and a fitted black t-shirt. Clearly, he was not one of the guests from the wedding, but rather someone who happened to be staying at the host hotel.

"Sort of, I guess. Although, I can assure you—I'm not running from my husband. I'm just taking a break from the stifling heat in the room," I admitted with a small laugh.

"I can appreciate that. I'm not one for crowds, either."

"Oh, I don't mind crowds, but being the center of attention for hours on end is exhausting. All the pictures, people clinking their glasses trying to get me to kiss the groom every thirty seconds… stuff like that. I know it's well-intended, but it can be suffocating. Does that make sense, or do I sound like a brat?"

He chuckled.

"I hear you completely. And no, you don't sound like a brat. You sound like a bride who just wants to take a few minutes to recharge. Mind if I sit down?"

"Oh, um… sure." I moved to gather the many layers of my wedding dress to make room on the bench. Every time I thought

I had them all, another one would spill free. I'd love to know who thought crinoline was a good idea. I huffed out a breath in frustration, and the stranger laughed again.

"It's okay, I can stand."

"Don't be silly. This bench has to be eight feet long. There's room if I can figure out where this damn dress ends." After another few seconds of rustling and gathering, I had the dress piled onto my lap, leaving plenty of space on the long bench for the man to sit. "There, see? Please, have a seat."

He nodded his thanks and sat down. Leaning back, he stretched one arm over the back of the bench.

"So, I suppose congratulations are in order," he said with a wink. "He's a lucky man."

I blushed from the indirect compliment.

"And I'm a lucky girl."

"I guess you have a big party inside," the stranger mused.

"You could say that. We have three hundred guests in attendance, but I only know about twenty of them," I added with a light laugh.

"Oh?"

"Yeah. Most of them are my husbands' friends, family, and colleagues. I don't really have any family and only had a handful of friends to invite," I said with a small shrug. "I'm the belle of the ball, yet I barely know anyone at my party."

"Well, parents should count for something."

"Not for me. I don't know my father. Well, I did but he left when I was just a little girl."

"Oh? That's too bad."

"Not really," I said, shrugging with indifference. "My memories of him are limited but I don't remember him being a very good father. He and my mother... well, they didn't really get along. I don't even know why he left. My mother never offered an explanation, and I never asked. Time passed, and asking her about him just didn't seem important until it was too late. She died a few years ago. Cancer won the fight."

His hand reached out, almost as if he wanted to place a comforting hand on my shoulder, but he pulled back at the last minute.

"I'm sorry to hear that."

"I wish she was here. I miss her," I said, unable to mask the melancholy that settled over me. My mother was an only child like I was. My grandparents had passed before I was born, and I had no aunts, uncles, or cousins to speak of. Until today, I never really appreciated what it meant to have a big family—to be surrounded by loved ones on one of the biggest days of your life.

"It's natural to miss her—especially on a day like today, but I wouldn't worry about not knowing anyone else. These big weddings are really all about how much is in the gift envelopes, anyway."

I looked at him in surprise.

"Well, that's a callous way to look at it."

"Is it? I mean, today is really all about you and your new husband. Tomorrow, none of those people will matter. It's all about you and the life you're going to build together. I don't think that's callous but knowing what really matters."

"I suppose," I said contemplatively.

"Perhaps someday, I'll find the right person. I want a woman who I can cherish—where the sun rises and sets on her happiness, you know? I was once told I'd meet the woman I was meant to be with when I least expected it." He paused and stared at me intently, curiosity clouding his eyes. "Maybe I already met her and just don't know it yet."

A flush began to rise up my neck, unsure of the meaning behind his words.

Did he mean me?

Surly, that's not what he meant. We'd only just met. Nevertheless, I couldn't deny the peculiar way he looked at me

—or the unexplainable butterflies that danced in my stomach at his words.

I watched him carefully, taking in his features for the first time. His sandy brown hair was wavy, bordering on curly, and cut short as if he thought he could tame the unruliness by shortening the length. His skin was the color of golden honey, like a Coppertone beach tan, from spending a healthy dose of his time outdoors. Although the lighting was dim, I could almost make out the color of his eyes. They were light brown, hazel perhaps, but I wasn't close enough to distinguish the color of the little flecks that glinted when he smiled... at me. It was a roguish grin, like he had a secret only he knew.

As if there were a magnet between us, our bodies turned toward each other, and we shared a held breath. The force of the pull blocked out the crickets, the faint music from the banquet room carrying through to the outside, and all the other sounds of the night. My stomach clenched again with those mysterious little butterflies. They swirled deep in my belly. He was looking at me so intently, his gaze traveling from my face to the curve of my breasts rounding above the sweetheart neckline of the strapless dress. The heat that had begun to rise up my neck flooded my cheeks.

Clearing my throat, I quickly shifted my body back to face forward and gave myself a reality check. I was only hours into my marriage. I had no business looking at another man like that. He was a total stranger. I sure as hell didn't know what had come over me. I wasn't the type to have a wandering eye. Perhaps it was just the fatigue I felt from an emotional day.

"Yes, well... um," I stuttered. "Maybe whoever told you that was right. After all, I met *my husband* when I least expected it." I emphasized my words in a way that would remind him, and me, I was very much a married woman.

"Is that so?"

I chanced another look at him to see he had one curious brow raised as he waited for me to continue.

"Yeah, I did. I was being harassed by a drunk customer at the restaurant where I used to work," I explained, then went on to tell him how I met Ethan. I gave him the abbreviated version of course, but he listened attentively, nonetheless. "On that first coffee date, he asked questions and wanted to know all about me. I told him my favorite color was pink and that I loved daisies. From that day forward, right up to the day he proposed, a pink daisy would be waiting for me at the beginning of every shift. He said the flower was to remind me he'd always be looking out for his girl."

The stranger cocked his head to the side curiously.

"You said until the day he proposed. What happened after that? Did he stop giving you the daisies?"

"Oh, no. I still received them, just not at work. My husband didn't want to wait long to get married, and putting on a large wedding is no easy task. He talked me into quitting my job, so I could focus on all the planning. Once that happened, he sent the daisies to random places. Sometimes they were at my apartment, and one time, there were daisies waiting for me with the seamstress who was altering my wedding dress. It was places like that." I paused to gaze out across the courtyard. Of course, there were pink daisies in the clay pots lining the wall of the building. They weren't in season, and I half wondered if Ethan arranged for them to be there. I smiled and looked down at the gold band interlocking with my engagement ring as I wrapped up the story of my fairytale romance. "We are a tale as old as time."

"I'm waiting for you to add the words 'happily ever after' somewhere in there," he teased.

"Well, things are pretty perfect," I admitted.

"Then I'll say it again—he's a lucky man."

We both fell silent for a time, the space feeling awkward. The bewildering spark that had flickered between us instantly extinguished after I told my story, and for that, I was relieved. After a few moments, he spoke again.

"So that's it for you? I know we just met but you don't strike me as the type to be content with being a kept woman."

My head snapped up to look at him, annoyed at the implication.

"Who said anything about being a kept woman?"

"Well, you quit your job, right? Do you plan to go back to work, or do you want to be a kept woman?" he asked with a what-the-hell-shrug.

I bristled at his use of the phrase for a second time. I wanted to be offended, but I understood how he drew his conclusion.

"I know how it probably looks, but actually, I do have plans. I'm going back to school for interior design, something I enjoy and have an eye for. I hope to enroll for the spring semester at the University of Cincinnati."

"Good for you." He nodded his head and smiled in admiration.

"Taking on the role of Suzy-homemaker is far from what I want in life. After watching my mother struggle for years to make ends meet by working two, sometimes three, jobs, I vowed to take my life in a completely different direction. To do that, I need to secure an education. Yes, my plans were put on hold for various reasons, but it's always been a temporary thing."

I fell silent, unable to believe how open I was with him. I rarely mentioned my mother to anyone besides Natalia, yet this was the second time I'd brought her up in less than fifteen minutes time. I didn't even talk much about her to Ethan. It was just too painful—a wound that would never quite heal. For some reason, I wasn't holding back with this man. My brow furrowed in confusion as I studied the stranger. For a moment that seemed to stretch on for hours, he simply stared back at me. Eventually, he placed his hands on his knees and slowly stood.

"I hate to end our conversation, but I need to get back up to my room," he said with obvious reluctance. "I have to be up before the sun rises in the morning."

"Thankfully, I don't have to be up that early. My husband was smart when he booked our honeymoon to St. Lucia. We don't leave until Monday morning, so I can sleep all day tomorrow if I want. What's dragging you out of bed so early?"

"My flight. Apparently, I wasn't as smart as your husband when I booked it," he joked. "I'm only here for the weekend. I'm headed home in the morning."

He shoved his hands into his pockets and rocked back on his heels.

And damn...

If that wasn't the sexiest thing I'd ever seen, I didn't know what was. Now that he was standing, I was able to take in his full height. I estimated him to be a couple inches over six feet tall and he was built—very built. His thick biceps grabbed my attention, and I didn't know how I'd missed them earlier. His black t-shirt stretched wide across his chest and I could easily make out very defined pectoral muscles. When my gaze traveled down to his narrow hips, I froze.

What am I doing? I should be dancing with my husband, not out here, gawking at a man I just met.

Despite my internal lecture, I was clearly a glutton for punishment. Instead of letting him walk away as he should have, I compulsively asked an open-ended question that would further our conversation.

"Were you here visiting family? Or was it something else?"

"No family. I was here on business. I had to meet with a silent partner about a business I'm starting."

"Oh, well, that sounds fun. What's your business?"

Another question—undoubtedly, I had lost my mind.

"Fitness."

My gaze skimmed over his hard, muscular biceps once more.

Of course, fitness was his business.

"Interesting," was my only reply. I was afraid to say more and risk embarrassing myself by saying something inappropriate. I really needed to get back inside.

"Yeah. I was tired of working for others and wanted to branch out on my own. In a few months, I'll be opening my own gym and training facility. A friend of mine agreed to help finance it, and we met this afternoon to finalize the contract. I will admit, though, it's scary as hell. Working for a gym is one thing, but owning one yourself is a risk. I already have an established client base and the expertise needed, but the market is competitive. I know I can do it, but there's always that little seed of doubt, you know? For the first time in my life, I'm afraid of failure."

His raw vulnerability was unexpected, and not something I was used to. Ethan was always so confident and never second-guessed going after what he wanted. Yet here this man stood, telling a woman he barely knew about his fears. I found his honesty endearing and considered him with new respect.

"I'm sure you'll do just fine. In fact—"

The slam of a door cut off my words and caused me to jump. I looked toward the sound. Ethan was striding toward me, looking frantic.

"What are you doing out here? I was looking all—" He stopped short when he saw I wasn't alone. Something flashed in his eyes but I couldn't quite place it. Anger? Jealousy? Whatever it was, he masked it quickly and reached out to take my hand. "Come back to the reception, honey. Our guests will be missing you."

I stood and slipped my arm through Ethan's. He pulled me close possessively, and I could feel the hard tension in his muscles. I looked back at the man who had kept me company for the last thirty minutes and realized then I didn't even know his name. When I thought about it, I never told him mine, either.

"It was nice chatting with you," I said.

"Likewise. Congratulations again… to both of you."

"Thank you," Ethan responded tersely, then coaxed me back toward the door to the hotel. Once we were inside, I felt his stiff body relax slightly. "Don't do that again, okay?"

"Do what?"

"Disappear on me. I didn't know where you were. When I found you..." He trailed off and raked a hand through his hair. "It didn't look good, Gia. You're my wife, dammit! *My* fucking wife. How would you feel if you saw me talking to another woman like that on our wedding day? I saw the way he was looking at you and you let him do it. I should have pounded him for having the balls to even talk to you—a woman who is clearly another man's bride. For fuck's sake! You're still in your wedding dress!"

His sudden outburst shocked me but he was right. It didn't matter that I didn't do anything wrong, or if it was an innocent conversation. Guilt took over my rationale, knowing no matter how innocent things appeared on the outside, there was no denying the flicker of *something* between me and the stranger—and that was not okay. My guilt didn't come from the words I'd exchanged with him, but from how I felt for even the briefest of moments.

Ethan, the man I loved with my whole heart, stared at me with accusing eyes, and a wave of shame came over me. This was on me, and I had to make it right.

"I just stepped out for some air, Ethan. I'm sorry. Honestly, I don't even know the guy's name. It was just... ouch!" I looked down at his hand wrapped around my arm. He was squeezing me so tight, I was sure he would leave a mark. "That hurts! Let go—"

"Not again," he repeated sharply, his stern interruption slicing through the air like a thousand knives.

I was no stranger to violence. I had seen it before with my mother and father. When I'd told the stranger they didn't really get along, it was the understatement of the year. I was barely five years old when my father finally left for good, but there was one thing I'd never forget—volatile, unhinged madness in the eyes of the abuser.

At this moment, I saw that same look in the eyes of my husband. At first, my instinct was to run, but as fast as the look in his eyes had appeared, the madness was gone. It was as if I'd imagined it.

"Not again. I promise," I whispered.

"Good. Now, no more fighting." He let go of my arms and softly stroked my cheek with a fingertip. Moving to touch my ear, he frowned. "You're missing an earring."

"I am?" I automatically reached up to touch my ears and glanced around on the floor. When I didn't see it, I glanced down the corridor that led to the courtyard. "Maybe I lost it outside."

Ethan's eyes darkened again and a shiver raced down my spine.

"It doesn't matter, Gia. It's only junk costume jewelry. Leave it. We need to get back to the party. We're being rude to our guests."

Shaking off my fears, I allowed my husband to take my hand and lead me back to the reception.

4

Derek

I'd gotten little sleep the night before, having stayed up most of the previous night fretting over the pitch for the biggest undertaking of my life. The weight I felt was odd since I was normally a pretty laid-back guy. I'd read somewhere, running a small business was one of the most stressful things a person could do. Nobody told me the stress would begin before the business even got off the ground. I was exhausted, anxious, and excited, all at the same time.

I should have been in bed hours ago, but restless energy had propelled me to go for a stroll in the hotel courtyard. Little did I know, I'd come across a captivating runaway bride who'd unexpectedly make me feel all kinds of things I never should have felt for a newly married woman. Now, all the edginess I'd felt earlier was more comparable to pre-match jitters, like the kind I'd get before stepping into a boxing ring to spar with an intimidating opponent. There was no way I could go to sleep anytime soon.

I paced the now empty and silent courtyard, contemplating

the conversation I'd had with the mystery woman. I should have been thinking about the contract I'd just signed with my silent partner, Ryder Malone. Ryder believed in me and my vision for The Mill, a state-of-the-art fitness center in the heart of Queens, New York. He agreed to invest a lot in this venture, so I owed it to him to keep my eye on the prize. Allowing myself to be distracted by a woman, even if it was only for the briefest span of time, was the last thing I should be doing when so much was at stake.

Still, the conversation with her reminded me I didn't have anyone to celebrate one of the most exciting and nerve-wracking times of my life. I didn't want our talk to end. There was a spark to her, kindling an underlying confidence and strength just beneath the surface. Despite my teasing about her being a kept woman, I could tell there was more to her—much more.

Her voice, smooth as silk with unabashed innocence, would not soon be forgotten. Her striking features were a combination of fierce and delicate, with high cheekbones and a straight nose, her full lips the color of pink roses in the sunset.

And her shape…

Lord have mercy, there was no denying the curves that punctuated the tight little body hidden beneath all that white satin and lace. The fullness of her breasts teased above the neckline of her dress, making me want to lean in and nibble on her neck as I pulled out every pin securing all that glorious blond hair. The indentation of her tiny waist gave way to the rounded curve of her hips, defining what it meant to be a woman. When our bodies had turned to face each other, it was as if a magnetic center pulled us toward one another. All sounds of the night had fallen away, and for the briefest of moments, it was as though the two of us were the only two people in the world. We'd barely had a second to acknowledge the humming electric current between us when the reality came rushing in to hit us with the force of a freight train.

She belonged to another man—a fact glaringly obvious the minute he showed up and wrapped a possessive arm around her waist.

I never shied away from a challenge, but she was one challenge I could never take on. There were unwritten rules about not going after another man's wife—rules and standards I'd always respected and followed—but for some reason, those rules didn't seem to apply here. I'd never felt so envious of another man.

So, why was this woman so different? I barely knew her. Hell, I didn't even know her name.

A sparkle near the leg of the bench where I'd been sitting on caught my attention. I bent over to see what it was and realized it was an earring. Picking it up, I turned it between my fingers, recognizing it as the earring worn by the captivating bride who'd made my heart skip a beat with just one glance. It twinkled like a diamond, reflecting at various angles under the dim lighting. For the second time that night, I was reminded of something my sister, Isabella, had once said to me.

"You'll find the girl who's right for you, little brother. Your diamond in the rough is out there somewhere—probably in the place you'll least expect her."

When life spiraled and changed, I could always count on my sister for support. She was my rock, anchoring me when I needed it most. When I was bullied for being overweight as a kid, my sister took me to the YMCA and bought us a membership. Together, we ran the track and swam in the pool until my pudgy pre-teen body became hard and lean. Her decision shaped my life for years to come, and I credited her for the scholarship I received to attend Syracuse University for Sports Management.

We were close, and I was there for her as much as she was there for me—especially when we got older and she started dating Christopher, her longtime boyfriend and now husband.

They were good together but had their ups and downs, just like all relationships. However, the good far outweighed the bad. Christopher cherished my sister in ways that mirrored my father's affection for my mother. They shared an unexplainable connection that anyone around them could feel. After years of watching that kind of devotion, I wanted to experience it for myself.

At twenty-nine, I still hadn't found what I was looking for. After a while, I gave up on chasing it, choosing to focus on my vision for The Mill instead. It worked for a time. I'd given up on the one-night stands and had only been with a handful of women over the past couple years. I didn't look for anything serious, but let things happen naturally. Unfortunately, things never worked out and often ended before they really began—whether their fault or mine.

Then tonight, I'd met the runaway bride, and all of those old desires came rushing back. She was everything I'd ever dreamed of and all the things I never knew I wanted. I didn't know how I could feel so strongly about a woman who was practically a stranger. I only knew the intense emotions were there. I wanted her, but I couldn't have her. Just like the misplaced earring, my feelings for her were misplaced, and I found myself disappointed over the lost possibility. I was mad some other lucky bastard got to her before I did. It didn't matter if she was the first woman to really stir my senses in a very long time. Fate was a capricious bitch, teasing me with a mystery bride who could never be mine.

I rolled the sparkling earring between my thumb and forefinger, watching the way the subtle lighting in the courtyard reflected off the sides.

"I should probably get this back to her," I mumbled aloud to no one in particular. Slipping the orphaned piece of jewelry into my pocket, I headed back inside. Finding the banquet room for the wedding reception was no trouble. I simply had to follow the music and the sounds of happy chatter from the guests. Walking down the corridor toward the sounds, I paused when I heard shouting coming from around the corner.

"For fuck's sake! You're still in your wedding dress!"

Slowing my steps, I approached the vestibule at the end of the hall, stopping short when I saw it was the runaway bride. Her husband looked enraged as he grabbed hold of her arm. Unsure what to make of the situation, I took a step back and partially hid from view behind a tall, leafy planter.

"I just stepped out for some air, Ethan. I'm sorry. Honestly, I don't even know the guy's name. It was just—ouch! That hurts! Let go—"

"Not again," her husband barked.

What an asshole.

My eyes widened in surprise at his rough handling. Instinct propelled me to step forward, intending to come between them, but just before I revealed my presence, I paused.

Is this really any of my business?

I quickly ran through the options in my head. If I did nothing, it would be as if I condoned his actions and that would make me no better than him. If I interfered, it could result in an altercation. I certainly wasn't afraid of that but I also didn't want to be the jackass who ruined someone's wedding. Or maybe I wouldn't ruin it—perhaps she'd want me to. Visions of the bride ditching her husband for me flashed in my mind.

Get a grip. That's never going to happen.

I studied the bride's face, hoping her expression would help me decide what to do.

"Not again. I promise." Her quiet whisper wavered. If I wasn't mistaken, she looked terrified. My blood started to boil. I knew his type—asshole pricks who got off on making women feel small.

"Good. Now, no more fighting," he cajoled, his tone now remarkably calm. He let go of her arm and seemed to relax but I still didn't trust the bastard. When he raised his hand to her face,

I nearly jumped out from my hiding place to get between them. Thankfully, all he did was touch her ear. "You're missing an earring."

"I am?" she replied. "Maybe I lost it outside."

I reached into my pocket. Looking down at the earring now resting in my palm, I wondered if now was the right time to make my presence known.

"It doesn't matter, Gia. It's only junk costume jewelry. Leave it. We need to get back to the party. We're being rude to our guests."

Gia.

So, that was her name.

Wrapping an arm possessively around her waist in a steely grip, the two walked away and entered the reception hall. When the doors closed behind them, I stepped out from my place behind the planter. Next to the door where the newlyweds had disappeared, a black and gold sign with glittery writing rested on an A-frame stand. The scrolling font read:

Wedding reception for Ethan & Gianna Walker
Happily Ever After Starts Here

I FROWNED. They didn't appear to be a happy couple. The girl I'd barely got to know deserved better. She had so much spirit and all he seemed to want to do was extinguish her spark.

A strange feeling of melancholy settled over me. My fingers clenched around the earring in frustration before I stuffed it back into my pocket once more. I turned away from the glittery sign boasting of happily ever after and headed to the elevators that would take me back to my room. My chest was heavy with an odd sense of loss for a girl who was never mine to begin with.

For the first time since I laid eyes on her arresting face, I wished I'd never met her.

It had been better not knowing there was a girl out there, who just might be my perfect match, than knowing she was unobtainable because she was committed to a guy like that.

PART III

SURVIVAL OF THE FITTEST

5

Gianna

Indian Hill, Ohio
Two Years Later

Of all the reasons a woman could miss her period, I prayed this wasn't the most common one. Yet here I sat on the bathroom toilet, my entire future in the hands of a little plastic stick. I opened my legs and raised the urine-stained stick to eye level. The gray moisture line moved across the little window until one pink line appeared. I held my breath and watched as a second line appeared.

I was going to be a mother.

Absently bringing my hand to touch my stomach, I blinked back the tears forming in my eyes. I didn't know if I should be happy or sad about the results. My stomach roiled and it wasn't because I was pregnant, but because I wasn't sure what I was going to do.

Ethan and I had barely sex at all over the past few months. In fact, it was only twice. We were still considered newlyweds by some standards, yet both times we were intimate was because I'd practically thrown myself at my husband. Family planning hadn't really been discussed outside of the occasion 'when we have kids' comment here or there. I wasn't on birth control, but Ethan almost always used a condom—almost being the keyword. I thought back to the last time we had sex and couldn't remember if he'd used one.

The churning ball of anxiety intensified. Pregnancy meant I would continue to be dependent on Ethan and wouldn't have the chance to go back to school and fulfill my career dreams. Deep down, I knew it was so much more than that. College and a job, while still very much important to me, were the least of my concerns at that moment.

A year ago, I might have been ecstatic about a baby, but things had changed—Ethan had changed. He hadn't been himself for over a year, and I didn't know what was wrong. I had asked him about it several times, worried I'd done something to upset him, but he insisted everything was fine. He said it was just work stress. When I pressed him to tell me about it, he told me he couldn't talk about ongoing investigations in the department.

While I knew he couldn't talk about certain aspects of his job, my insecurities had been working overtime as of late. He frequently went out in the evenings, returning late in the night or not until the next day. More than once, I'd considered the possibility there might be another woman. My heart didn't want to believe it, but my suspicions had become all-consuming. Perhaps it was my hormones going haywire since I was pregnant. Maybe the changes in my body were making me paranoid for no reason at all. I knew Ethan loved me as much as I loved him.

So, why was I afraid to tell him about the baby?

I ignored the worrisome thought and stood up. With a shaking hand, I placed the pregnancy test on the bathroom counter, turned on the faucet and splashed cold water over my face. Looking at my reflection in the mirror, I practiced a smile. *Happy—I needed to be happy when I told him.*

When we spoke over dinner just an hour earlier, Ethan seemed distracted, I assumed because of something to do with work again. He frequently came home agitated from the stress of his job, and it was something I'd just grown accustomed too. My only hope was news of a baby on the way would brighten his sour mood. It might even rekindle something that had been lost between us.

I exited the bathroom to find him on the sofa, leaning over to tie his shoes. I frowned. He'd pulled a twelve-hour shift and had barely been home for two hours. He couldn't possibly be leaving again.

"Are you going somewhere?"

"Yeah, honey. Work," he responded in the dismissive tone he often took with me whenever I asked him where he was going.

"Oh. I was hoping we could talk," I said softly.

"Now's not a good time. And by the way, I'm not going to ask you again. You need to remember to put the toothpaste away in the bathroom drawer. You always leave it on the counter, and I'm sick of having to put it away."

My eyes widened in surprise. Clearly, his mood over dinner hadn't improved. Now, he had to go to work—again. Or so he said. We needed to talk about what was going on between us. I needed to know if my fear I felt about his possible infidelity was all in my head.

He stood and walked to the front door. I hurried to catch up with him.

"Ethan," I pleaded, placing my hand on his shoulder. He pushed it away forcefully and I staggered a few steps back, my knee smacking against the hard, oak end table.

"Ouch!" The pain stung, but I ignored it. "Ethan, stop. Please. Where are you really going? I need the truth."

He turned to face me, his impatience evident as he ran his eyes over me unsympathetically.

"What truth?"

Tears burned the backs of my eyes but I refused to let them fell.

"I don't think you're going to work. I've been able to hear your police scanner most of the evening, and it's been quiet."

He glanced behind me at the little black box sitting on the end table next to the sofa. Taking a few steps toward it, he reached down to silence the quiet chatter between dispatch and patrol, then walked over to me and placed a placating hand on my shoulder.

"Gia, don't try to be smart. It doesn't suit you," he cajoled as if I were a child he needed to appease. My head snapped back from the insult.

"What is that supposed to mean?" I challenged. "Listening to the scanner, then putting two and two together isn't exactly rocket science."

The subtle grin that twisted the corners of his mouth was condescending, mocking, almost. I wanted to scream. Instead, I shrugged out of his grasp and turned my back to him. The man standing behind me felt more like a stranger every single day. I wanted him to be the man I married, the man I fell in love with, who brought me daisies. I wanted to feel cherished again. The idea of Ethan cherishing anything or anyone other than himself made me pause and think back on our relationship.

Have I ever felt cherished by him?

Not really. If I were honest with myself, I'd never felt truly respected or valued. Ethan had always doted on me in a placating way—like a child who was given a present for behaving.

I felt his hand come up to touch my shoulder. It was strange —a part of me longed for his gentle touch, but another part of me wanted to recoil from the contact.

"Come on, Gia. I don't like to see my girl all worked up over nothing. You know I'm the brains in the house. We both know that."

My eyes widened, and I spun to face him once again.

"You're the brains? Why? Because you have an expensive college degree, and I don't?" I snapped. "I wanted to go to college! You pushed me into the role of the police chief's wife, with me on your arm for various functions and photo ops. You convinced me of the demands and talked me into staying home to take care of the house. Don't you dare try to make me feel insignificant. I did exactly as you asked me to do!"

My lack of a college degree had always been a sore spot. It was something I yearned for—a longing deep in my belly that always seemed out of reach. Saying those words aloud made me realize what I had slowly become—a kept woman, the very thing I'd once told a stranger I didn't want to be. I pushed away the memories of a conversation from years long past and took a deep breath, unsure if I was overreacting.

"Honey, you aren't insignificant. You do a good job. The house looks great. Well, most of the time."

I stared at him and processed the negging comment. That was just his way—backhanded compliments that never ceased to make my confidence waver and make me worry if I was a good wife. I was tired of being spoken to that way, tired of being made to feel small. Still, I was too exhausted to fight, and we'd been doing so much of it lately. Sometimes, letting him go to wherever it was he went in the evenings was just easier.

Tonight, processing the implications of being pregnant, was one of those nights. If he had to go, so be it. Arguing with him rarely got me anywhere, and I'd learned to pick my battles long ago. Besides, if there was one thing I knew about being the wife of a police officer, it was that life was short. You never knew what could happen in the line of duty. If something had happened to him while we were on the outs, I'd never forgive myself.

Glancing down at the black sport coat he'd tossed over the arm of the sofa, I picked it up and moved to hand it to him. I intended to apologize for losing my temper but stopped short when a whiff of sweet-smelling perfume filled my nose. Raising the jacket to my face, I inhaled.

Roses.

It smelled like jasmine and roses.

I crinkled my nose in disgust, certain it wasn't the scent of any perfume I would wear. When my eyes found his, there was a curious expression on his face as if he knew what I was thinking before I even said it.

"Don't go there, Gia. Just don't," he warned.

All the emotions from the past year seemed to well up inside me. I was always so quick to roll over—to be the peacemaker. And for what? Didn't I deserve better?

I felt something inside me snap. I wouldn't be dismissed anymore. He needed to stop treating me as nothing more than an afterthought. I was pregnant, and we should be celebrating together as husband and wife. I was owed an explanation for why he'd turned so cold—for why his jacket smelled like another woman. Unable to hold back the hurt any longer, I exploded, the questions and demands pouring from my mouth before I could even think twice.

"Don't go where? Don't go after the truth? Tell me now, damn you! Who is she?"

He shook his head, almost as if he were resigning himself to the situation. When he fixed his eyes on me, his expression was as hard and cold as granite.

"She's an attorney—a prosecutor for the City of Cincinnati. Her name is Cynthia. There. Are you happy now?"

My eyes widened, unable to believe what I was hearing. I wanted him to deny it. No... I *believed* he would deny it. I thought he would tell me I was imagining things. Never did I expect him to admit it the very first time I asked. The sport coat slipped from my fingers and fell into a crumpled heap on the floor. Instinctively, I dropped my arms to my sides and balled my hands into fists, white-hot fury burning deep in my belly.

"No, I'm not happy!" I hissed through gritted teeth.

"Well, I don't know what to tell you then. You asked for the truth, and against my better judgement, I gave it to you." He shrugged as if it was no big deal.

"How could you do this to me?" I asked, my voice cracking as it raised to a dangerously high pitch.

"There are things I need," he said calmly. "Cynthia gives them to me."

I brought a hand to my mouth and shook my head. Angry tears stung my eyes and I blinked them back.

"You bastard! I love you! I'm your wife, and I deserve better than this!" I pointed my finger and jabbed him hard in the shoulder. Without warning, he grabbed my wrist and twisted it back so far, I yelped in pain. His dark brown eyes darkened until they were almost black.

"I don't understand what you want from me, Gia. I've given you everything. You have the house you wanted, money to spend, and a closet full of brand-new clothes you barely wear. Most women would love to be in your position."

I didn't dare tell him that I didn't want all the clothes. They were clothes he'd picked out as though I was his own personal Barbie doll. The clothes weren't even my style. Instead, I jerked my hand away and stepped back.

"Do you know what I want, Ethan? I want a husband—a real husband. I want someone who wants me to be his equal partner. I want to be truly loved. Cherished. I don't want some lying, cheating son of a bitch! And that's exactly what you are!"

His eyes flashed and before I could even think to react, the back of his hand slammed against my face, the blow forcing my head to whip to the side.

I cried out, not so much from the pain, but from the surprise of being struck. I'd never been hit before, not even when my mother disciplined me. I'd seen my father hit her when I was young, but that's as far as my knowledge about the pain went. There was no way I could have known the pain was so much more than skin deep. I felt this hurt in the depths of my heart, so shocking it rattled my soul. I reached up and brushed a finger over my lower lip. When it connected, I felt something warm and sticky beneath my fingertips. I poked out my tongue and swiped, the metallic taste of blood coating my taste buds.

Rage built up inside me, an instinctive need to fight back. Yet... somehow, I knew I couldn't. Ethan was so much bigger and stronger. I wouldn't stand a chance.

"Calm yourself down, Gianna! You're hysterical," he snapped, then took a deep breath and adapted a softer tone. "I'm sorry it had to come to this. You just say things you shouldn't. You need to learn to hold your tongue. Behave like you should, and this won't happen again." He spoke so calmly as if he hadn't just slapped me at all.

Visions of my mother rushed to the forefront—I saw her sad, tear-filled eyes as she apologized to me after my father had hit her. *"I'm so sorry, my sweet. You shouldn't have had to see that. I won't let him do it again. I promise."* But he did hit her again, and again... and again.

I still didn't know why my father eventually left. Did she throw him out? Did she press charges and force him away? My mother and I never talked about it, and I never wanted to ask. All I knew was that I never had to see that sad look on my mother's face again. I had often wondered why she didn't leave after that first blow, but I dismissed it as being a complicated situation, one of my faint childhood memories I couldn't quite piece together. I loved my mother deeply, but I didn't want to become that woman with the sad eyes.

I wanted to be stronger.

I glared at Ethan and took in his words as time passed. It

could have been seconds, minutes, or hours. I wasn't sure. All I could do was stare. Things hadn't been good between us, but I had no idea how bad things really were beneath the surface. He had hit me—actually hit me—and somehow thought it was my fault. A bitter cold seeped into my bones, a cold so chilling, my heart turned to ice.

"Don't do that ever again," I stated, my voice matching the calm tenor of his despite the fact every part of my being was shaking.

"Don't do what? Are you saying I can't hit you?"

"No. You. Can't."

I should have seen it coming, but I didn't until it was too late. The fist he landed on my face made me see stars. I fell back, landing on the hardwood floor with a crunch. I laid there in shock, disbelief rocking me to the very core. Slowly, I turned to look up at him. He stared down at me with disgust as if I was a misbehaving child who he didn't want to deal with.

"I pay for this house; therefore, it's mine. My house, my rules. And if I want to hit you, I will."

No. No. No. This isn't happening to me—it can't be happening.

I would never allow myself to be somebody's punching bag. Rolling to the side, I slowly got back to my feet. He took a threatening step toward me. I braced myself and put up my hands in a fighting stance. Ethan began to laugh.

"Oh, my girl. My silly, silly girl. Don't be foolish. Do you honestly think you can fight me? Come on now. I'm a man. It's basic physics. You can't overpower me."

"You are *not* allowed to hit me," I reiterated, trying to summon all the courage I could muster amid the implausible situation. He took another step toward me. I stepped back. This continued until my back was against the doorframe leading to the basement. My body shook in terror.

How could I be so afraid of the man I'm supposed to love?

It was as if I was living in a dream. Everything was surreal. My stomach rolled as I battled with the urge to vomit. I breathed deeply, in and out, focusing on the rise and fall of my chest. Once. Twice. Three times.

"That's my girl. Deep breaths. Don't you see? It's better that you know the truth. I was getting tired of hiding it anyway. Going forward, instead of telling you I'm going to work, I'll just tell you I'm going to meet Cynthia. Now there's no need for me to sneak around," he said softly.

His hand came up to caress my cheek, and I flinched. Pure instinct drove me to push it away, unable to stand his touch any longer—a foolish move, given my situation. It only angered him once again. He grabbed my arms, squeezing them so tight I thought the bones would break.

"Let go of me!" I yelled. "I'm done, Ethan! I'm leaving!"

His demonic laughter filled the room before he leveled a glare at me, and his eyes turned black as midnight.

"Do you honestly think I'd let you leave me?"

"I said let go of me, you bastard!" I repeated frantically. I fought him, struggling to free myself from his vice-like grip. The man before me was a stranger—a wolf in sheep's skin. How could I have been so blind? How did I not know he was capable of such cruelty?

I stepped back to get away, completely forgetting I was so near to the basement stairs. My foot caught nothing but air and I began to fall. My back hit halfway down the stairs, knocking the air from my lungs as I tumbled the rest of the way down. Sprawled at the base, I couldn't breathe.

And the pain.

Pain rocketed through my body, over my skin, until it felt like my internal organs were on fire.

"Ethan, I..." The whisper trailed off and I clutched my abdomen. That's where the pain was the worst. It took me a minute before I remembered.

The baby.

My eyes slowly moved to the top of the staircase. Ethan stood there with a disgusted look, shaking his head.

"I'm going to meet Cynthia. Don't do anything rash while I'm gone because I'll know. Remember, I'm the Chief of Police. All the cops work for me. They won't help you, Gianna. You and I both know it. You'll only embarrass yourself."

He disappeared from my line of sight, and a few seconds later, I heard the front door open and close. Wrapping my arms around myself, I curled into a fetal position and cried.

I DIDN'T KNOW how long I stayed on the basement floor. Time ceased to exist as warm blood pooled between my legs. Was it bad a part of me would be relieved if the blood meant a miscarriage? How could I feel that when there were so many women who wished to be blessed with a baby? I knew no child should be brought into my world—at least not right now. Anxiety, hope, fear, confusion, and anger consumed me, the emotions swirling as I clung tight to the pain, unable to move.

Eventually, I crawled up the stairs. My vision was hazy and I wondered if I had hit my head on the way down. Sliding my broken body across the kitchen floor, I reached up to feel for my cell phone I'd left on the center island. Once I had it in hand, I propped myself up to a sitting position and leaned against the base.

I dialed the only person I knew I could trust.

"Nat, I need your help."

6

Ethan

The moonlit night was unforgiving as I sat in my BMW parked across the street from my house. I watched the windows for any sign of movement inside. After about forty minutes, I saw Natalia's car pull into the driveway.

So predictable.

I knew Gianna would call her, I just wasn't one hundred percent sure what she would do next. I was fairly certain she wouldn't call the police. They wouldn't have believed her if she did. Convincing my guys at the precinct Gianna had mental issues would be a walk in the park. They'd seen all kinds of crazy females in their line of work. I just didn't want the embarrassment or have to make pointless explanations. After tonight, I would have to monitor her better. I made a mental note to put a tap on her phone, so I never had to worry about such things down the road. I honestly couldn't believe I hadn't thought to do it sooner.

Natalia would probably tell her I was an abusive asshole.

That was also predictable. Most people would agree with her on that front.

Most people were fucking idiots.

They didn't know anything about me or my relationship with my wife. Too many drank the Kool-Aid, believing in this new-wave idea that men and women were created equal, having so easily forgotten how Eve was the one who led Adam to sin. It wasn't Adam's fault. For him, evil came when the path to good was so hidden, there was no other way.

Still, I thought it best to make a few calls to cancel Gianna's credit cards in case she got any crazy ideas. Pulling out my wallet and cell, I dialed the first credit company.

"Thank you for calling Capital City Visa. This is Donna. How can I assist you today?"

"Hi, Donna. My name is Ethan Walker. My wife is a signer on my account and it appears she was a bit careless and lost her purse while out shopping this afternoon. I need to cancel her card just to be safe. You never know what kind of person may have picked it up."

"I completely understand your concern, Mr. Walker. Give me just a moment and I'll take care of that for you."

Once I finished my call to Visa, I repeated the same story to American Express and Master Card. After completing the calls, I took one more glance at the house. All seemed quiet. I imagined my wife sitting at the kitchen table, complaining to Natalia about me. The mere idea of her saying anything negative about me caused my muscles to tense. Tossing my wallet and cell phone onto the passenger seat of the car, I gripped the steering wheel until my knuckles turned white.

"Fucking bitch!" I hissed and started the ignition. Pulling away from the curb, I sped through the dark streets of Indian Hill toward Avondale.

After the long day, all I wanted to do was to come home, eat a quick meal, then head out to meet Cynthia at the condo I still kept on West 4th. I was glad I kept the place after my mother's death. It had more than served its purpose. It had been weeks since I'd last felt Cynthia's punishing strokes of ecstasy in the White Room, and I was long overdue. I just hadn't planned on Gianna's smart mouth to get in the way. Now my evening was ruined, having had to cancel with Cynthia in order to keep an eye on my foolish wife.

Twenty minutes later, I arrived at the tiny flat in Avondale. A homeless man laid on the steps leading up to the building. His presence pissed me off. Shit like that was the reason why Avondale had a bad reputation among most Cincinnatians—that and the higher than average crime rate.

"Get the fuck out of here!" I growled at the filthy lump. He was wearing tattered army fatigues—but that didn't make him a soldier. Oh, no. I knew this type—always looking for a handout. He probably got the outfit from the local AMVETS thinking the garb would gain him sympathy from strangers.

Most likely, he was richer than I was.

Giving him a hard, swift kick, he grunted. I kicked him a second time, this time even harder. Slowly, the man collected his sack of God only knew what and got to his feet. I nearly vomited from the smell of him. Pulling out my wallet, I flashed my badge. The sight of it made him move a little faster.

"I'm going, man," he slurred. He mumbled something that resembled an apology and staggered a few steps. If he didn't stink so bad, I might have driven my boot into him a third time.

"Go find a job, you worthless piece of shit! And I'd better not catch you on these steps again!"

Needing to get away from the putrid smell, I hurried past him, went inside, and climbed the stairs to my fourth-floor flat. I opened the door and slammed it closed behind me, the impact causing dusty drywall bits to fall to the dingy floor. I looked up and saw a crack in the ceiling caused by water damage.

"Great, just what I fucking need!"

The lowlife landlord had better fix the roof soon. My day had been terrible enough as it was. Keeping three residences wasn't cheap and money was tight this month. I wasn't able to pocket the cash I'd hoped to gain from today's crack house raid when Police Commissioner Greyson decided to show up on the scene. He said he wanted to see how we were bagging evidence but I smelled his bullshit. Greyson suspected someone was skimming, and I'd be damned if I was going to give him a reason to think it was me—even if I was low on cash.

Instead, I planted a few stacks of hundred-dollar bills under the front seat of the new rookie's cruiser. When it was found after an 'anonymous' tip, it would be enough to take the heat off of me for a while. Besides, the rookie was soft. His spirit may be willing, but the flesh was weak. He would never make it in this line of work.

I glanced down at the picture of my mother set among the candles on the table by the door. Ignoring the image, I lit seven wicks in preparation for later. Still, I could feel her eyes searing into me, burning my skin with accusation.

"Don't look at me like that, Mother. It was her fault. She needed to be taught a lesson."

There was nothing I could do about it. Gianna couldn't be allowed to challenge me. No. She had to be obedient. My girl knew how to listen. Tonight was just an off night for her. Perhaps I took things a little too far, but she had only herself to blame. It wasn't like I wanted to hit her.

Walking over to the corkboard covered with pictures of Gianna, I skimmed a finger over her unmarred complexion. She was so beautiful, but my mind couldn't erase the image of her battered face. Her eye had swelled more than I'd expected from where I'd hit her. Her lush, full lower lip had split and was caked with blood right before she went backward down the stairs. That was her fault as well. However, leaving her there brought on a twinge of guilt. I should have checked on her. Instead, I'd just left her there.

Now I deserved to be punished.

My gaze traveled to the neighboring corkboard, this one filled with pictures of Cynthia. She had a harder edge, a complete contrast to my wife, and that edge was more than skin deep. Cynthia understood me in ways Gianna never would. She knew when I needed punishing and never held back. She was more ruthless in the bedroom than she was in the courtroom. Next time I was with her, she'd know what to do. Until then, I would just have to take care of matters on my own.

Turning away from the wall of corkboards, I walked back over to the table with the statue of the Virgin Mother. I turned the statue to face the wall and flipped the framed picture of my mother so it was face down on the table. They knew I needed to be punished—but that didn't mean they had to see it.

I stripped out of my clothes, folded my pants and shirt, and placed them in a neat pile on the floor. I eyed up the tiny bottle of Chantilly that I kept on the table with all of my mother's special things. She loved the perfume. She had thought it smelled nice and it was much cheaper than the fancier shit. I was happy when Cynthia agreed to wear it for me too.

But I couldn't be with Cynthia today.

I scowled and tried not to think about it.

Picking up the tiny bottle, I removed the gold cap and spritzed the rose damask and jasmine *eau de parfum* three times over my naked body. My cock hardened as I inhaled the scent, the anticipation of what was to come almost unbearable. I replaced the cap and set the bottle back down, exactly where it had been. My eyes roamed over the seven candles burning inside red glass votive holders, each one a representation of the seven deadly sins.

Moving slowly, so as not to extinguish the flame, I picked up the candle representing pride and brought it closer. Cream colored, hot wax pooled around the flame. Leaning back, I poured the burning liquid over my chest, purging myself of all prideful desires and urges.

"God opposes the proud but shows favor to the humble."

I hissed from the brief sting as it dripped down and hardened before reaching my navel. My cock stood at attention, just tempting the wax to meet its mark. Next, I picked up the candle that embodied greed and repeated the process to eradicate all need for material wealth.

"Neither their silver nor their gold shall be able to deliver them on the day of the wrath of the Lord."

I relished the contrasting sensations of pain and pleasure, a representation of how the seven deadly sins can bring both.

After my chest was coated with the wax from all seven candles, I went to the television set and turned it on. Grabbing the remote, I aimed it at the DVD player until an overly made up brunette woman entered stage right, wearing a black leather trench coat. I'd seen this particular X-rated film before, so I knew what she wore underneath. My cock grew impossibly hard, thinking about the crotchless leather pants and matching bustier with holes cut out to reveal her pierced nipples.

"You've been a disobedient client. You need to be punished," she tsked. She played the part of a lawyer—a dominatrix lawyer —who had to punish her insubordinate client, a submissive male who already ready for her, naked on his knees in front of her desk. The woman's likeness to Cynthia was uncanny. Perhaps that's why I was partial to this particular porn skit. Cynthia had the same allure as the woman on the screen. She was my addiction, my very own Mary Magdalene.

"Pick up the flogger, then hand it to me!" the dominatrix ordered her submissive.

As the man bent to retrieve it like she commanded, I mirrored his actions and reached for the cattail whip resting on the floor in front of the television. It was time for my punishment to begin, as well. To rid my soul of its sinful nature once again, I had to repent for my sins. Mortification of the flesh was the only true way to drive out evil.

Every time she struck her slave, I brought the knotted cords over my shoulder, meeting her lash for lash and reciting the words, following the example of Father Peter Damien, just as my mother taught me.

"My punishment was good for me, because it made me learn your commands…"

Father Damien said self-flagellation should always be accompanied by the recital of psalms. Mother said many people didn't understand Father Damien, just as they would never understand me, and was the reason I was taught to never leave a permanent mark during my rituals.

"Be steadfast, my boy, but never leave lasting marks."

I remembered her words and began my session slowly, with only light thumping on my back until I increased the intensity. Eventually, I lost all touch with time and space. What were only moments seemed like hours, months, or years. It wasn't the same as when Cynthia punished me. No. when she did it, my understanding of space was completely destroyed until my body was the only connection to the physical world—where I needed to be to most clearly hear His word. It was the only way I could properly repent for my sins.

A vision of Gianna crumpled on the basement floor filled my mind.

My girl.

I had done that.

Now, I had to beg for His forgiveness, or I'd become the unrepentant wicked and suffer the fate of those who do not accept Him.

"I know that your judgments are righteous, Lord, and that you punished me because you are faithful… Have mercy on me, and I will live because I take pleasure in your law."

I continued to recite the psalms, one for every lash, needing Him to forgive me for what I did to Gianna. I shouldn't have left my wife on the floor, all alone.

Hurting.

Suffering.

All by my hand.

I was a sinner who had succumbed to the temptations of wrath.

Using all the energy I had left, I squeezed my cock and gave myself a final burning lash. Then I cried out, a humble penitent seeking His forgiveness for my transgressions.

"Bless me, Father, for I have sinned!"

Collapsing down to my hands and knees, a single tear slid from my face, onto the floor. My act of contrition was complete.

7

Gianna

I staggered into the emergency room with Natalia supporting
most of my weight. The throbbing in my head and cramping
in my stomach was close to unbearable as I struggled to stay
upright on my own. A nurse who was passing by saw us and
gasped. I could barely contain my relief when she rushed to
place a wheelchair under me. Collapsing into it, I smiled faintly
at her.

"Thank you."

"Of course." She paused and studied my face, smiling
sympathetically. I wasn't sure what I looked like but her kind
eyes embarrassed me. I felt my face flush with a shame I knew I
shouldn't feel. "Let's get you over to the registration desk, so
you can be seen by a doctor."

"She's pregnant and bleeding pretty bad," Natalia told her.

The nurse looked to my lap, and her eyes widened, seeing
the bloodstain on the denim between my thighs for the first
time.

"On a scale of one to ten, what's your pain level?" she asked, her tone taking on a sense of urgency that hadn't been there before.

"Um, maybe around a seven. Just really bad cramping." It was hard to tell. The throbbing in my head was so bad, I wasn't sure if it was masking the pain in my abdomen.

"Okay, then. I'll page OBGYN while you get registered. What's your name, hon?"

"Gianna. Gianna Walker."

"Well, Ms. Walker, don't worry. We'll take good care of you."

Once she stepped away, Natalia wheeled me over to the registration desk. The receptionist behind the counter took my information quickly and efficiently. When she needed to collect the co-payment for the emergency room visit, my hands shook as I fumbled with trying to get my wallet out of my purse.

"Here, let me help you," Natalia offered. Plucking the wallet free, she unclasped it at the front and opened it. "Which card?"

"The Visa is fine."

Natalia slid the plastic through the card reader and we waited while it processed.

"I'm sorry, Ms. Walker. The payment was declined," the receptionist said awkwardly.

"That's strange. There's always money in that account." I shook my head in confusion. "Nat, can you pull out the American Express? I'm not sure why the Visa isn't working."

Natalia swiped once again, only for that card to be denied too.

"That son of a bitch," Natalia cursed under her breath. Reaching into her own purse, she hastily pulled out her own credit card and slid it through the card reader. Her card went through without a problem. I looked up at my friend in disbelief.

"You don't think..." I trailed off.

"That he canceled your credit cards? Yeah, I think that's exactly what he did."

Before I could process her words or what it could potentially mean, the nurse who greeted us at the door poked her head around the corner.

"The doctor can see you now, Ms. Walker. If you're finished here, the two of you can follow me this way."

***

AN HOUR LATER, Natalia and I sat in silence as a stream of doctors and nurses bustled passed my cordoned off area in the ER. I'd been examined, had a pelvic ultrasound, and was now just waiting on the doctor to return. As it turned out, I had been about eight weeks pregnant.

But not anymore.

I felt empty, drained, and hollow, but even more so, I felt confused. I was brokenhearted over the baby I'd barely had a minute to love, but I also felt relief, no longer being pregnant. I needed to sort out my feelings. My marriage was in shambles. I couldn't even begin to wrap my head around what happened. I didn't know if Ethan and I should seek counseling to try to repair our broken marriage, or if I should leave him. I entered into my marriage knowing it was for better or for worse. After tonight, things had definitely crossed over to worse—much worse. Just thinking about it brought on a fresh wave of tears.

"Shh… It'll be okay," Natalia whispered softly as she rubbed her hand up and down my back.

"Will it?" I sobbed. I looked up at her through my tear-filled eyes and saw worry lines marring her pretty face.

"Gia, tell me what happened… everything. I know you didn't get that shiner from falling down the stairs."

I unconsciously reached up to touch the tender spot around my eye. Shame blossomed on my cheeks again, and I glanced away, unable to look at my friend. When I called Natalia, I planned to tell her everything, but Ethan's words about not doing anything rash rang in my mind. Instead of telling her the truth, I told her I'd just found out I was pregnant and, in all of my excitement over the pregnancy, I wasn't paying attention to what I was doing and had fallen down the stairs. When I choked out the words about a possible miscarriage, she was at my house within ten minutes to bring me to the hospital.

When she arrived on my doorstep, I knew she immediately saw through the façade. Natalia was far from naïve. My split lip, the spreading discoloration on my face, and the bruises already forming and wrapping around each arm didn't tell the story of a careless fall. Nonetheless, she temporarily let me have my lie and didn't question me when I told her I didn't want to call Ethan about my supposed accident.

However, when my credit cards were declined, it wasn't hard to connect the dots to form a perfect picture of my fucked-up situation. I owed her an explanation. Yet here I sat, staring at the one person I could always count on and I couldn't find the words.

"I don't know what happened, Nat. I can't explain it. He just…" He just what? Lost it. Belittled me. Beat me. Cheated on me. Became a stranger before my very eyes. I couldn't bring myself to speak any of those things out loud. I let my statement trail off, hoping Natalia would fill in the blanks. However, I knew her better than that. I could feel her probing eyes and wasn't shocked when she came right out with it.

"Ethan did this to you, didn't he?" she asked quietly, but I could hear the venom in her voice. I could only nod my confirmation. "Has he ever hit you before?"

"No." I shook my head. "I mean, he's lost his temper and shoved me before, but it wasn't anything that really hurt me. He almost always apologized and said it wouldn't happen again." Even to my own ears, my words sounded weak and pathetic.

"But it did, didn't it?"

"I know what you're thinking, but it wasn't as bad as it sounds. If he pushed me or something like that, there was always a reason—stressed from work or tired from a long day." I defended, avoiding her question. I didn't know if I was trying to defend Ethan or myself. "He's never actually hit me like this before, Nat."

"Well, the bastard certainly did this time. What are you going to do? Or should I ask, what do you want to do?"

I stared blankly at the light blue polka-dot pattern of my hospital gown.

What do I want to do?

"I'm not this woman, Nat. I'm not the kind of woman who lets her husband beat her."

"Do you love him?"

My head snapped up to look at her.

"What kind of question is that? He's my husband."

"That's not an answer, Gia."

"Yes, I love him. And he loves me. I know he does."

"What he's doing isn't love," she said and shook her head sadly. "There are other men out there—kind and good men—who wouldn't treat their wife this way."

I thought back to my brief encounter with the stranger in the courtyard on my wedding day. It was odd for that to come to mind right now, for the second time that day, when my world was literally crumbling to pieces all around me. Our brief interaction should have been inconsequential, especially after all this time, yet the details from that night collected, pulled from the deep recesses of my memory.

I wished I could tell Natalia how I was completely at ease under the kind gaze of a stranger in ways I'd never been with Ethan. I rarely kept anything from my best friend but this felt too personal to share for unexplainable reasons. Nothing happened that night so long ago. It had only been a brief, casual conversation, but it felt significant—almost seismic, even now. I should have forgotten all about it, but I couldn't stop myself from remembering. I wondered if he ever found that special woman to cherish.

"I don't know what you want me to say," I eventually said.

"You should go to the police."

"Nat, Ethan *is* the police," I scoffed.

"So what? There are laws, Gia! He can't get away with this."

More of Ethan's words from earlier crashed into my consciousness.

"Nat, I don't think you understand. My reality definitely has its challenges because Ethan is the chief of police, but the reality for the average woman isn't much better. You hear about it on the news every day. A woman can walk into a police station, file a complaint and have her abuser arrested. After that, he can get out on bail and go after her again."

"That's what restraining orders are for," Natalia quipped.

"What? That flimsy piece of paper? A woman can have all the restraining orders she wants, but it won't stop her abuser if he wants to get to her. If he comes around, the only thing the woman can do is call the police again. My case is so much worse because I just happen to be married to a cop. If I called for help, a report wouldn't even get filed. No cop in their right mind would want to take down a chief."

"So, forget the report. Just leave him. You can come stay with me."

I looked at her, finding myself at a loss for words once more. I was too embarrassed to admit I didn't know if I could leave him. I still loved him, despite everything that happened tonight, and I couldn't turn my feelings off that easily. I didn't dare tell Natalia about Cynthia. It was bad enough that she knew he beat me. Admitting his infidelity to her would be a blow to my pride that could very well be worse than any physical strike Ethan could dole out. My best friend would never accept a single excuse from me if she knew he was cheating.

Emotional confusion aside, there was also the money situation to consider. I didn't have a pot to piss in—as was proven an hour earlier when my credit card wouldn't go through. Ethan said he wouldn't let me leave him. I didn't know for sure, but every aching bone in my body told me he canceled them just to remind me, he financially controlled me. In fact, he controlled everything. He held all the cards in a deck he'd strategically stacked against me.

"I should have seen this coming," I whispered. "There were signs right from the beginning, but I just didn't see them. Or maybe I didn't want to see them."

Natalia shifted her position to sit next to me on the hospital bed.

"What do you mean there were signs?"

"Signs of how controlling he was. It started right after our very first coffee date. We began texting and I thought he was amazing—perfect boyfriend material, you know? But the texting alone should have been a huge red flag. Some days, I'd receive over fifty messages—really long ones too. At one point, he told me, 'I send you really long messages, but you only send one sentence back.' It really bothered him, so I tried to make more of an effort. After our third date, he said he loved me."

"I remember when you told me. You said you loved him, too, and I was worried about how hard and fast you were falling for him. Your whole life became him in just a few weeks' time. Outside of our shifts together at Teddy's, I barely saw you."

"No, but Ethan knew that." I smiled ironically. "Remember my birthday that year? We had a girl's night out. He encouraged it, and said it was good for me to hang out with my friends. I think it was just another way for him to fake how perfect he was, so he could make his next move. Just a few nights after that, as I neared the end of my shift at Teddy's, he came by the bar. He told me how much he wished I was going back to his place after work. I said I felt the same way, and he asked me to move in with him, just six weeks after we'd met."

"And you said not until you were married," Natalia mused, her eyes narrowing as she recalled the distant memories. "He brought you a gift that night, a scarf or something, right?"

"Maybe. I don't really remember because he was always buying me something. If it wasn't a daisy, it was a trinket of some kind. Gifts had always been important to him, although they would rarely be things I actually wanted or needed, but something expensive he wanted me to wear. It was almost as though he wanted to mold me into this idea he had in his head about what a girlfriend should look like. It bothered me a bit but I told myself I should be more appreciative of his sweet gestures."

"If you saw all those red flags, why did you say yes when he proposed?"

"I don't know. I think I was in love with the idea of what could be, I guess. Or maybe I was just tired of being alone. I'm not really sure of anything anymore..." I trailed off as I recalled memories that seemed to take place a lifetime ago. After we were married and moved into our house, I had immersed myself in his life even more. He took care of everything, and I let him, allowing him to provide for me in ways I'd only imagined to be possible. Natalia didn't know the half of it. "In hindsight, every step in our relationship was made to draw me in, creating a world I'd never want to leave."

"But now you want to leave?"

I shook my head.

"It's not that simple, Nat. Ethan clearly needs help—our marriage needs help. I have to think this through. Leaving him was never on my radar until a few hours ago. I have to be realistic. I have no money, no job, and no education. As it stands right now, I don't even have access to money. I'm not on any of the bank accounts. He just gives me a monthly allowance to pay for groceries and other household expenses."

Natalia's eyes widened in surprise. I knew why she was shocked. I had always been fiscally responsible, even when I was up to my ears in credit card debt. I was never frivolous and always had money saved in case of an emergency. The fact I didn't have a cent to my name shocked even me.

"Jesus Christ, Gia. He gives you an allowance?"

Dr. Murray came back into the room and interrupted any defense I may have had.

"Okay, Gianna. You are free to go. I've written you a script for a mild pain reliever. That should help you get through the cramping while your body goes through this process." She handed me a stack of discharge papers and the script.

I glanced down at them and noticed a few colorful brochures sticking out between the pages. Curious, I reached up and slid them out. The first was for a support group for women who've experienced a miscarriage. Another was for a new form of birth control. When I saw the third brochure, it caused me to stagger under the cumulative weight of the past few hours.

It was for a battered women's shelter in the city.

I glanced back up at the doctor. She was smiling at me with kind and sympathetic eyes. I knew she thought I was one of *those* women.

Was I?

If I stayed with Ethan, I would be. The right choice would be to leave. I knew it with every bone in my body. Actually verbalizing all the warning signs Ethan displayed over the years should have said enough, but I couldn't leave him, not yet—and it had nothing to do with money.

The dream of the fairytale life held me back. Despite the emotional and physical pain, I still believed I could have it with Ethan. It's what he had promised me, and I didn't think we were beyond repair. I wanted to hate him for what he did today—for breaking my heart with his infidelity and cruelty, but for some twisted reason, I couldn't. As messed up as it was, I still wanted to love him.

However, today had been a wakeup call. At the very least, until I could figure out the next chapter, I needed to take precautions to make sure a child didn't complicate my situation further. Blinking back more threatening tears, I hastily shoved the brochures down between the papers. Before the doctor left, I called out to her.

"Dr. Murray? Would it be possible to get another prescription?"

"For what?"

"I need birth control."

8

Gianna

One Year Later

Men and women were so profoundly different. The old adage, men are from Mars and women are from Venus was true. Men were tough, resilient, and smart. They were the providers, responsible for working to pay the bills and fixing the plumbing. Whereas women were soft and delicate. They should manage the household, raise the kids, cook, and do the cleaning, but most importantly, her duty was to please her husband.

That's what Ethan believed, and he found a way to make me believe it, too—at least for a time. I had lost myself for a while, but I knew better than to believe that load of bullshit now. Even though the wool Ethan had pulled over my eyes was long gone, I was smart enough to know I needed to survive. It's what I'd been doing for just over a year.

I didn't live each day—I survived.

On the outside, people thought I lived an idyllic life. I was the wife of the police chief and I'd mastered the role. On Ethan's arm, I'd attended countless high-profile events and even volunteered to chair the most recent Policeman's Ball. Working with the wives of politicians and high-society financial influencers, I'd put together a fundraiser for charities favoring disabled officers and families who'd lost someone in the line of duty. The women I worked with had fawned over my organizational skills almost as much as they fawned over my husband. They thought Ethan was perfect in every way—from his polished exterior to the smooth way he spoke. But they didn't know about the monster who lived beneath the façade.

I glanced at the digital clock on the stove. Ethan would be home from work in an hour. The latest from John Legend played quietly from the stereo mounted under a kitchen wall cabinet. The song and the butcher knife slicing along the wooden cutting board were the only sounds that could be heard in the sprawling ranch. As I tossed pieces of carrots and celery into the pot of soup I'd started for dinner, I basked in the last bit of quiet solitude I might have for the day.

I didn't know what his temperament would be like when he got home. I rarely did. If he came home in a foul mood, he'd probably leave shortly after, so he could go fuck Cynthia. I stopped caring about that long ago because his leaving to go to her usually meant my ribs got a break from his vile temper. If he came home in a good mood, that was almost worse because there was a high probability that he'd want to fuck me instead. Just the thought of it caused acid to rise in the base of my throat.

Ethan had always been a determined person, and always got what he wanted. It didn't matter what it was. He wanted me—I had given myself willingly. He wanted to be the chief of police —he schmoozed his way into the position. He wanted the house —he found a way to afford it, even though the means to pay the astronomical mortgage was still an unsolved mystery to me. He wanted a mistress—I stopped arguing with him about her.

But now... now he wanted a baby. The bastard even kept

track of my cycle, so he knew exactly when to stick it to me. Having a child had been his focus ever since he found out I'd had a miscarriage.

His controlling nature didn't end there. Ethan had a tap on the phone lines—an actual tap, like the kind only seen in movies and cop shows on primetime. He listened to every single phone conversation I had over the past year. I only knew because he'd slipped up and told me about the tap during a fit of rage, fury sparked after hearing me accept Natalia's offer to move in with her. I should have been outraged over the invasion of privacy, but I wasn't given the opportunity to feel anything but fear.

My fractured wrist had taken months to heal after that.

Since then, I'd been cautious and never said too much over the phone. I didn't try to move out again, knowing he'd just track me down. If I wanted girl talk, Natalia and I met for lunch at a restaurant Ethan approved of. We used code words to hide the true meaning of things in the off chance someone was listening. I knew these things weren't supposed to happen in real life but they were happening in mine. I had no privacy, no time I could call my own. His spying made me feel violated in ways I couldn't even describe. There were days, I felt like even my thoughts didn't belong to me.

By some miracle, I'd managed to hide the fact I was taking birth control. I never told him about the pills prescribed to me by the doctor one year prior—the ones I kept safely hidden under a floorboard I'd pried loose on my side of the bed. I had no intention of having a child with him. Whatever delusions I had about fixing our broken marriage had long died. I loathed Ethan with every fiber of my being.

My true feelings were another thing I managed to keep hidden. I could have been an Academy Award winner for my performances. I played the part of the perfect wife from sunup until sundown. My stellar performance meant I didn't have to feel the sting of his belt or the blunt force of his boot nearly as often—it also meant he wouldn't suspect when I planned to leave him. I just needed a little more time to get the cash I needed to escape.

Using the increasing cost of groceries as an excuse to get more money, I'd been slowly stashing away portions of my so-called allowance. It was the only way I could do it. Buying fresh from local produce stands and small, family-owned bakeries meant there were often no receipts for the purchases. Ethan never even questioned it.

Hearing the familiar click of the deadbolt on the front door, I silenced the radio and glanced at the clock.

Shit!

He was home early, and that wasn't a good sign. Home early equated a good day at work. That meant only one thing for me. As if they had a mind of their own, my thighs squeezed together, my body instinctively wanting to protect the part of me I didn't want to give.

Shoving the worry aside, I quickly looked around the kitchen for anything that might be out of place. There was a dishtowel balled up on the counter. I quickly shoved it in a drawer so Ethan wouldn't be upset I hadn't hung it back up after use. I glanced at the pink daisies, the flowers I'd come to loathe, in the vase on the center of the island. They would need freshwater tomorrow but were okay for now. Any cloudiness to the water would upset Ethan because he thought it meant I wasn't grateful for his gift. On the other side of the kitchen, the bread box was open. I cursed myself for forgetting to close it after I made myself lunch earlier that afternoon. I crossed the kitchen in three long strides and slid the door closed just as he entered.

"You're home early," I said as casually as I could, despite the fact my heart was racing. "Did you catch all the bad guys?"

"Yeah, actually. We raided a meth house today. There are eight fewer scumbags on the street now." He bypassed me and went straight for the safe hidden behind a large picture in the living room. After he spun the dial, he deposited his department-issued gun and a large duffle bag inside, then locked it again. I frowned, curious what was in the bag. I'd seen him come home with it on a few other occasions. Whatever the contents were, he always kept them locked tight in the safe I didn't know the combination to. Later in the evening, he'd return to the safe to remove the same bag, then leave with it and come back hours later empty-handed. I suspected it was something illegal. Ethan may think I was stupid, but I had always excelled in math. I knew his salary alone wasn't enough to cover the mortgage payment.

"Fewer drug dealers are always a good thing," I said lightly, still trying to gauge his mood.

"It is." He stepped up to me and placed a light kiss on my forehead. Pulling out skills even Meryl Streep would be jealous of, I leaned in and accepted his embrace. "Dinner smells good, Gia. I'm just going to wash up. I'll be back out in a few."

He pulled away, gave a little tap to my ass, then disappeared into the bedroom. When I heard the shower turn on in the master bath, I inwardly groaned in misery. Sex was almost guaranteed to be on the menu tonight. I was nothing more than an object to him. He took everything while I got nothing. I had faked more orgasms than I could count over the past year—not that I cared much about that anymore. It was easier to 'behave' than deny him his needs. Tonight would be no different.

Fifteen minutes later, he returned wearing jeans but no shirt, tiny beads of water dripping from his hair and onto his broad, muscular shoulders. Once upon a time, the sight of him wet from a shower would have turned me on, but there was no thrill or excitement to see him naked or bare-chested anymore. There hadn't been for a long time. Now, I just found him repulsive but still managed to put on a fake smile as he approached. However, my smile faltered when I saw the look on his face. I knew that look.

He was angry—very angry.

"What the fuck is this, Gia?" The tone of his voice caused shivers to race down my spine all the way to the tips of my toes.

Raising his hand, he held his palm open to reveal a pink plastic case. The round lid was unlatched, revealing the circular arrangement of birth control pills set in foil. I felt all the blood drain from my face. My mind raced, trying to recall my steps from earlier that morning. I had no idea how he found them. I was careful, always ensuring the floorboard was back in place. There was no way he could have found them by accident.

I discretely shifted my eyes toward random places throughout the kitchen, half wondering if he had installed cameras without my knowing. It wouldn't have surprised me. I didn't see any at a quick glance, but it didn't matter. He'd found the pills and now he was waiting for an answer. Somehow, I managed to keep my voice steady and cocked up one brow in mock confusion.

"I have no idea," I said with a shrug. Denying they were mine was the only thing I could think to do.

"Don't lie to me."

"No. Honestly, Ethan. I don't know what that is."

He took a step closer. I stepped back. My shoulders squared, and survival mode kicked in. I'd been here too many times before. Reaching behind me toward the counter, I tried to inconspicuously shove the butcher knife I'd been using to cut vegetables out of sight.

No weapons.

If he got his hands on an object that could hurt me, he would. I may have recovered from a beating with a metal spatula but I didn't want to chance a knife.

I was too late.

Tossing the packet of pills onto the counter, he grabbed hold of my arm and reached behind me for the knife. It all happened so fast, I had no time to react. I stayed perfectly still, too petrified to move a muscle. His hand slid up from my arm to wrap around my neck and pulled me close, squeezing until I could barely breathe. Bringing his lips to my ear, he pressed the flat side of the knife against my cheek.

"I told you I wanted a baby, Gia," he whispered. "The psalms teach us, 'Behold, children are a heritage from the Lord, the fruit of the womb a reward. Like arrows in the hand of a warrior are the children of one's youth. Blessed is the man who fills his quiver with them!'"

"The psalms?" I asked. His quote confused me. I'd never known Ethan to attend a single Mass, let alone quote scripture. While we had both been baptized Catholics, neither one of us was practicing—or so I thought. Religion was rarely discussed between us, but apparently, my husband was more devout than he let on. Bewildered, I could only remain still under the cold edge of the knife blade.

"Yes. Psalm 128:3 says, 'Your wife will be like a fruitful vine within your house; your children will be like olive shoots around your table.' You've been deceiving me all this time, Gia. I should have known you would deny your duty to me." His voice was eerily calm. Goosebumps raced over my body and my heart began to thud loudly in my ears. I knew what this false calm meant. When he sounded this way, it was nothing short of terrifying.

He grabbed hold of my hair and jerked my head back with a sharp tug. I sucked in a huge breath, not sure how long I had before his hand returned to crush my windpipe. That was his favorite method of punishment—cut off my air supply until I was begging.

"Ethan, please. Let's talk about this," I whimpered.

His next words made my pounding heart still and my blood turn cold.

"You've defied me for the last time, Gia. Things are going to get much worse for you now. You will get pregnant. If it means I have to tie you down to the bed and fuck you bloody raw for days, I will. I'll get what is owed to me. One way or another, I'll get it."

I'd seen many sides to Ethan, but this maniacal look on his face was something entirely new. I had never before seen him this angry—this enraged. For the first time, I felt genuinely afraid for my life. Fear slithered over my skin until an all-consuming calamity of terror began pounding in my skull.

"Ethan," I tried to plead again, my voice barely a whisper.

"Take your clothes off."

"It doesn't have to be like this."

"Having a baby was supposed to be the beginning of our future. You sabotaged that. Don't you love me, Gia?"

"Of course, I love you," I lied.

"Then prove it! Take off your clothes. I won't ask you again."

With shaking fingers, I began to unfasten the buttons of my silk blouse. Once the blouse fell open, Ethan took the knife and slipped it under the silky edge near my shoulder. Using the blade to push the material from my body, the blouse fell to the floor. Not bothering to wait for me to take off my jeans, he impatiently unzipped them himself and shoved them roughly down my legs. Too afraid to do anything other than comply, I stepped out of them.

Tears spilled down my cheeks, but he was completely immune. He pushed my panties down my thighs next, then unfastened the clasp of my bra. He didn't skip a beat, even when I whimpered from the violation that came from being so exposed. I could see the vein in his neck throbbing as he appraised my naked body. Even though he had seen me bare more times than I could count, his hungry, savage stare felt different this time.

"Turn around and bend over the counter," he said gruffly. I hesitated, not wanting to lose sight of him for a single minute. I would rather he told me to drop to my knees and suck him off than turn my back on him.

"Ethan, please. Don't do this."

He smiled, the curve of his lips a gleeful sneer as he traced the blade of the knife over my collar bone. I gasped as he slipped it down ever so slowly to my right breast. My nipple pebbled under the cold metal. His grin widened with delight as if he thought I was turned on, rather than experiencing a natural reaction to the cold against my bare skin. My stomach turned, and I had to fight a wave of nausea. After briefly tracing the tip of the knife over my nipple, he continued down. To my horror, he slid the blade against the most intimate part of my body. Although I wasn't a religious person, I found myself praying to anything or anyone who would listen.

Please...save me from this monster.

"I'm not going to tell you to turn around again," he warned.

I choked on a sob and did as he wanted. Terrified any sudden movement would inadvertently mutilate me, I slowly turned around and bent at the waist until my torso was pressed against the cool marble kitchen counter. I heard the clanging of his belt buckle, then the thud of his pants as they hit the floor. He grabbed a fistful of my hair once more and turned my head to the side. His free hand brought the knife down on the counter, his fingers still wrapped around the hilt, placing it directly in my line of sight, so I didn't forget it was there.

"I hold all the cards, Gia. It's about time you remembered that. I've warned you to behave far too many times. I don't like to hurt you but you don't know how to just fucking listen to me. Or maybe that's why you don't listen. Does my girl like it when I hurt her?"

"No," I whispered, unable to take my eyes off the razor-sharp edge of the blade mere inches from my face.

"No, what?" He yanked hard on my hair, pulling my head

back before slamming it down against the counter. A sob rattled in my chest as I tried to bite back my tears.

"N-no! I-I don't like it when you hurt me!" I stammered.

"Hmmm… I have a hard time believing that. I think you like pain. Have you ever been fucked in the ass, Gia?" He pushed forward, and I felt his erection press hard against the place no man had ever been. It didn't matter that I couldn't get pregnant this way—he didn't give a flying shit about that—it was all about control, and this was a power play. I tasted my own fear sliding down my throat. I wanted to scream, but I didn't dare. Instead, I began to beg.

"Ethan, please. No. Don't do this. You can't. I'll do whatever you want me to do."

"I don't believe that. You know why? You broke the trust, Gia. You thought you could outsmart me with those pills. For all I know, you have a plan to leave me too. Well, I'm going to make sure that doesn't happen. Like I said, I'll get you pregnant one way or another. You won't be able to leave me then. And if you try, well… I guess I'll just have to kill you."

He pressed forward, seeking the pathway to satiate his lustful desires. His arousal was thick when he met his mark. The sting of him trying to force his way inside triggered a fight-or-flight response.

No. No, no, no!

I couldn't think beyond my current situation. All the reasons why I had delayed leaving him fell to the wayside. All that mattered was stopping this from happening. I couldn't allow him to violate me in the worst, most demeaning way. My mind raced with ways to escape.

With every ounce of strength I possessed, I brought my elbow back to meet his face. I heard a faint crunch but I didn't think I did much damage. The plan wasn't to take him out but buy a few precious seconds to get away. I hadn't fought back since the day he first hit me, so when his hold on me slackened, and the knife went clanging to the floor, I knew my action caught him by surprise.

It was all I needed.

I wrenched myself free from his grasp and kicked the knife across to the other side of the kitchen. However, my actions weren't fast enough.

"You fucking, bitch!" he roared, his fury seeming to make the walls quake. The monster from my hell had lost all restraint. Grabbing hold of my hair, another favorite method of subduing me, he ripped back with such a force my naked body was sent sprawling to the floor. In an instant, he was on my back.

I screamed as loud as I could. The house was secluded, shrouded by tall pines, our nearest neighbor an eighth of a mile down the road. Nobody would hear me, yet a small part of me desperately clung to the hope, maybe a passing car or a random person walking their dog might hear my cries. I continued to scream and struggled to get him off my back, only to be silenced when his hands wrapped around my throat.

"Stop!" I squeaked, fighting for air as he squeezed tighter and tighter. Air. I needed air. "E...Eth...Ethan, I can't..."

This was it. Surely, he was going to kill me this time.

He began to laugh as if my grappling and begging pleas were an aphrodisiac to his madness. I clawed at his hands, to no avail. He was too strong. I was helpless as he tried to penetrate my resistant barriers.

"Fuck, Gia! Stay still!" he cursed, squeezing my throat so tight stars dotted my vision. I was afraid I might pass out—but Ethan wasn't that kind. Pressing his lips close to my ear, he whispered, "For he is God's servant for your good. But if you do wrong, be afraid, for he does not bear the sword in vain. For he is the servant of God, an avenger who carries out God's wrath on the wrongdoer."

I didn't have time to question why he was quoting bible

scripture yet again. With one ruthless thrust, he invaded the virgin space of my body.

The pain knocked the wind out of me, silencing the weak cries falling from my lips. He repeatedly shoved himself inside the dry, unprepared space, quenching his demonic pleasures. All sense of time ceased to exist. I kept waiting for the pain to stop but it seemed endless. The only thing I could do was lie still and wait for him to tap himself dry.

As the minutes passed, my mind took over and somehow distracted me from the pain of being ripped in two. It became a safe haven when the hurt seemed unbearable. Memories of my mother before she got sick flooded my consciousness, my thoughts of her just as clear as if they happened yesterday, thoughts of happier times before she got sick. I wondered what she would think of me now.

Then I remembered the piercing, hazel gaze of a stranger—kind eyes that made me feel at ease and comfortable in my own skin. I remembered his words about wanting to find a woman to cherish. My heart ached. I ached for the stranger I barely knew. I ached to be cherished by someone—anyone. Had I missed my window of opportunity? Was I now damaged goods? I didn't want to believe that.

When Ethan finally rolled off me, panting with a satisfied grin as if he'd just experienced the best sex of his life, I knew what path I had to take. My only hope was that it wasn't too late —that I would survive long enough to escape this.

9

Gianna

Just as he always did after he attacked me, Ethan turned apologetic. He lifted my lifeless body from the floor and carried me to the bed. As I laid under the blankets next to the man I hated all the way down to the depths of my soul, my body ached in places I hadn't even known existed. However, mentally I was numb. I pretended to be asleep, afraid to move for fear I'd do something else to enrage him. He spoke softly and calmly to me as if he didn't know I could hear him.

"I love you, Gia. I wish you could understand that. I just wish you wouldn't say and do things to upset me. You knew how important starting a family was to me. Why did you make me hurt you?"

It was incredibly bizarre. If I hadn't heard it all before, I'd almost believe the confusion and remorse in his tone. I might have even cried silently into my pillow. But I *had* heard it all before and knew my narcissistic husband was certifiably insane.

I tuned him out, completely withdrawn from my reality.

While he rambled, I contemplated life and how things came to be. I even questioned my very existence.

Was I born to suffer this way?

I thought about what I knew of sex—from my knowledge of it as an adolescent to how I understood it as an adult. I loved my mother, God rest her soul, but she came from a different generation where sex wasn't talked about. In fact, it was practically forbidden. Anything sexual or private in nature tipped her right off the scale of awkwardness. MTV and VH1 were never allowed in my home when I was growing up—heaven forbid I be corrupted by Madonna's *Like a Virgin*. I managed to not-so-accurately learn about the birds and the bees by sneaking reruns of *Beverly Hills 90210* while my mother was at work.

As an only child, I had no older siblings to learn from. My mother worked three jobs to send me to a small, private elementary school. The kids there were definitely not talking about sex, which only added to the reasons I was so utterly clueless as I grew older. Even my period talk was non-existent. At school, when we had *the* class, a ninety-something-year-old nurse came in and told us that tampons were dangerous. She said the string could break off, and the tampon would get lost "up there." And if that wasn't enough, all her talk about toxic shock syndrome was more than enough to make every girl in the classroom terrified of using a tampon.

The awkward silence about such topics meant I didn't know what sex actually entailed until I was ready to have it for the first time. I had no idea penetration was involved—yes, at seventeen-years-old, I really was that naïve. It's no wonder why today, at twenty-eight, I'd never really contemplated what it meant to be raped.

When Ethan took me tonight, he snatched a part of my soul I was afraid I'd never get back. I should have reported him to the police a year ago. Instead, I believed him when he said the police wouldn't help me and chose to stay silent. The sound of that silence had become deafening. The man I'd once trusted, for better or for worse, had tried to break me.

He failed.

My time with Ethan had made me harder and more resilient. I was no longer a naïve teenager who knew little about sex. I was no longer a woman blind to a man who wanted to control me in every sense of the word. I didn't want to be on the bad end of a statistic. I wanted to be one of the survivors. I had been waiting for the right time—to have enough money to start over again. I'd spent months plotting but none of that mattered now. My choice was made. The illusions I had over my level of preparedness fell away—I couldn't stay here for a minute longer.

It was time to take my life back.

Ethan's ramblings about loving me had fallen silent some time ago, so I chanced a glance in his direction. He was fast asleep. As quietly as I could, I gingerly slipped naked from the bed, desperately trying to ignore the pain from his assault, and awkwardly tiptoed around to his side of the bed. Without making a sound, I slid open the drawer to his nightstand and removed the COP .357 he always kept there. Knowing his department-issued sidearm was already securely locked in the safe, I hid the .357 in an old boot and shoved it in the back corner of the closet where it was out of sight.

Now that the potentially deadly weapon was safely tucked away, I pulled out a large garment bag hanging in the closet. The bag had once held my wedding dress. Months ago, I had removed the dress and burned it—literally. The corners of my mouth twitched up at the memory. I had picked a day when I knew Ethan would be working late and invited Natalia over. The two of us had a bonfire in the backyard and watched my dress go up in flames while we split a bottle of sauvignon blanc. We had laughed about our ever-growing bucket lists, and although leaving Ethan was far from being a joke, it had moved up to become my number one thing to do. I didn't burn the gown out of spite. I did it because I needed the garment bag. It was a step I needed to take in order to complete bucket list item one—leaving my husband for good.

The day after the dress burning, I packed the large garment bag full of clothes I'd need when I finally made my escape. I was careful to make sure the puffiness of the bag matched the way it had looked when it held the wedding dress. I couldn't pack a regular duffle bag—that would be way too telling on the off chance he found it. So, I'd kept the white garment bag hidden in plain sight inside my closet where it had hung since our wedding day. It seemed like I'd packed it a lifetime ago, but it also felt like yesterday.

As I tucked the bag under my arm, a sense of nervous trepidation crawled over my skin. I shook it off and tiptoed silently to the master bathroom to get dressed. Once the door clicked quietly closed behind me, I flicked on the light. It took my eyes a moment to adjust, but when they did, my hand flew to my mouth and I had to stifle a cry.

Dark purple lines snaked around my neck. There was a small knot on my forehead, and bruises covered my arms. My gaze traveled south to find the evidence of Ethan's sadism. Dried semen mixed with my blood caked the inside of my thighs. Angry tears flowed as I dampened a washcloth to clean myself. When I was finished, I unsuccessfully attempted to pull my blonde hair back into a ponytail but my head was too raw from where Ethan had pulled out chunks of hair. Leaving it as is, I wiped my tear-stained face and quickly threw on jeans and a teal, loose-fitting t-shirt.

Once dressed, I grabbed a few basic toiletries and tossed them into the garment bag with my clothes. The tube of toothpaste was lying on the counter. Instinctively, I placed it in the drawer before Ethan could get mad about it being left out, then thought better of it. Pulling it back out from the drawer, I put it back on the counter. The tube had been rolled up from the bottom, something Ethan always did, so I unrolled it with a feeling of great satisfaction.

Screw you and your damn toothpaste obsession.

I left the bathroom and silently made my way through the sprawling ranch into the living room. Crouching down to reach under the ottoman, I unpeeled the masking tape that secured a nondescript Tracfone under the base. Natalia had bought it for me months ago, part of the plan I'd concocted with her. After powering on the phone, I typed out a single message: BUCKET LIST #1.

Some might think I was going through ridiculous measures just to leave my husband but they didn't know Ethan like I did. He was always one step ahead of me, and as a result, I'd brutally paid the paid the price many times. I knew when the day came to leave, it would have to be well thought out. I'd have to run and never look back. After what happened tonight, I was grateful for the measures I'd taken. If I were caught leaving him now, there was no doubt in my mind—Ethan *would* kill me.

I heard a quiet moan, then a stirring. My heart began to race. Glancing up, I looked down the long hall toward the master bedroom. I could still see the outline of Ethan's body on the bed. He had rolled over but still appeared to be asleep. I closed my eyes and sighed with relief. I needed to move faster.

Pocketing the phone, I went into the kitchen and opened the freezer door. Using the masking tape I'd peeled off the phone, I quickly taped down the button that triggered the interior light for the freezer. Working in the dark, I felt for the empty Lean Cuisine box near the back. When my fingers made contact, I pulled it out. Inside the box was a roll of cash I'd been saving. I removed the cash and put it in my pocket. It wasn't much. A thousand dollars wouldn't get me very far, but at least it was something.

Having everything I needed, I positioned myself near the front window, making sure to keep the bedroom door in my line of sight. I took one last look at the walls that had defined my existence. Regret and self-blame gnawed at me, knowing I stayed when I should have left long ago. I smiled bitterly, happy to finally say goodbye to my prison, even if it was too late to save my dignity.

Fifteen minutes later, a black, late-model Buick, headlights off, slowly approached the house.

Teddy's car.

Natalia had gotten the message to him.

I slowly walked to the front door, careful not to step on any floorboard that might creak. I placed my hand on the door handle but froze when a light behind me turned on.

"Gia, where do you think you're going?" I heard Ethan say from behind me. I nearly jumped out of my skin, my heart beating overtime, and my breathing coming out in rapid succession.

"Fuck, no!" I cursed quietly as I fumbled with the door lock.

"Gianna!" Fury resonated in his voice. "Do you have a death wish? I told you what would happen if you tried to leave!"

His voice was coming closer—he was coming closer. I heard the lock click but before I could wrench the door open, I was hauled backward and thrown to the floor.

"No! You fucking bastard! Teddy! Nat!" I screamed as loud as I could, hoping and praying they'd be able to hear me through the walls.

I scrambled to move and get up from the floor. If I stayed down, he'd kick me. I got to my knees, but my recently battered body was too slow to react. A backhanded fist slammed into my cheek and I flew backward. Then the kick came.

I groaned in pain. The impact of Ethan's foot connecting

with my back stole all the air from my lungs. I tried to scream
for Natalia and Teddy again but all that came out was a gasp as I
struggled to find my breath. One more blow to the kidneys and
this would be all over.

Get up, get up! Don't let him win!

I silently repeated the chant over and over again as I
struggled to breathe. He moved to kick me again, but I rolled just
in time, and he missed me. Eyes raging like a category five storm
came for me but stopped short when the front door crashed open.

Natalia, Teddy, and Ben burst through. I'd never been
happier to see anyone in my life. Ethan spun around just as
Natalia rushed to my side.

"Oh my God! Gia, are you okay?"

I nodded weakly and looked away, sure she was examining
the swollen landscape of my face. Inside, I knew my appearance
wasn't my fault, but shame overtook any rationalization as I
moved to a sitting position. I winced, already feeling the bruises
blooming over my ribs.

"Get out of my house!" Ethan roared. I glanced up and
watched him reach into the couch cushions and pull out a gun I'd
never seen before. I silently cursed, unaware there was a third
gun in the house. It made me wonder how many more there
were. Ethan had the black barrel trained on Teddy as he stepped
toward him, moving the gun back and forth between Teddy and
Ben to show he had the upper hand.

"What are you going to do? Shoot us?" Teddy asked. "Be smart
about this, Ethan. I don't think you want to go to jail for murder."

"This isn't murder. You broke into my home. It's self-
defense," Ethan challenged.

"Gia, come on. Let's go. I need to get you out of here, toots,"
Natalia whispered.

"No, wait," I said, gingerly getting to my feet. I was afraid
Teddy would underestimate how violent Ethan could be, and I

didn't want him to get hurt. "Ethan, it's over. I'm leaving. Put the gun down."

"Shut up, Gianna! I need to handle these intruders," he snapped, never once turning his crazed eyes away from Teddy or Ben. "That's right, boys. Did you hear me? You're all intruders in my home and I have a right to defend it. Nobody will question that."

"Are you really willing to test that theory, Ethan?" Teddy gambled, then turned to me. "Gia, it's time to go."

The demented grin spreading across Ethan's face was bone-chilling. He knew people in powerful places. Teddy's gamble might be a mistake. We needed to move quickly. Standing in front of me, Teddy and Ben formed a human shield for me and Natalia. We moved together in unison toward the door.

"Don't do this, Gia," Ethan warned. Desperation was in his tone, and I chanced a look at his face. Sadness and something like regret flashed before turning hard and cold once more. When he spoke again, it was more like a snarl. "You'll regret this."

I hoped to God I wouldn't.

We ignored him and kept moving cautiously toward a front door that felt miles away. My lower back screamed in pain but I knew I had to keep putting one foot in front of the other. Natalia sensed my struggle and wrapped an arm around my waist for support. I winced from her touch, not sure if it was easier or harder to walk with her assistance.

I heard the sound of Ethan's heavy footsteps crossing the room. I tensed, bracing myself for what was to come. In the span of a heartbeat, everything seemed to move in slow motion before speeding up to meet real time.

A shot was fired.

There was a crash.

Natalia and I screamed.

All at once, our wall of protection was gone. I closed my eyes, terrified, unable to look at the scene unfolding around me.

"Gia, it's okay," Teddy said. I slowly opened my eyes and met those of my former boss. Daring a glance at Ben, I found him standing over Ethan with a table lamp in his hand. Ethan had been knocked out cold. "Come on. We need to get you to the hospital."

I shook my head. I couldn't trust my life to a system that favored men. The corruption in the police department only tipped the scales further in Ethan's favor. I couldn't risk doing things the right way—hospitals included.

"No. No hospitals. He'll know to look for me there. Just get me as far away from here as possible."

"Gia, are you sure?" Nat asked.

"I'm sure. Wait… I need to do one more thing."

Stepping away, I held out my left hand to look at my wedding ring. Pressed next to it was the engagement ring I foolishly accepted a lifetime ago. Together, they were supposed to be a symbol of eternal love, the circle signifying infinite devotion. When Ethan chose the design, I wasn't a huge fan. Now, I detested the rings more than anything. They didn't carry the meaning of a love everlasting but symbolized the shackles which held me down for far too long.

Tears blurred my vision as I ripped the rings from my fingers and took a few steps closer to where Ethan was sprawled on the floor. I didn't know why tears spilled down my cheeks. I wasn't sad. I didn't feel guilt over his motionless body. I wasn't even numb—although I wished I was. Numbness would have been better than the unadulterated hatred boiling my insides as I stared down at my husband—the Hyde disguised as Jekyll, who had damaged me beyond all repair. The hatred I felt surrounded me in shadows that were black as night, pulling me down until all I could see was red.

I didn't like feeling like that, but in some ways, it gave me solace. I knew hatred would be the driving force behind my survival, and I would hold on to it for as long as I lived.

Tossing the rings, they bounced and rolled until coming to a stop near Ethan's head. Turning back to my friends, my gaze landed on three sets of sad and worried eyes. Squaring my shoulders, I walked toward them, reaching deep into my soul to find the strength I would need for the road ahead.

10

Gianna

I couldn't go to Natalia or Teddy's house. Ethan knew where they lived and would expect that. Instead, Teddy drove me deep into farm country until we found a cheap hotel where I could grab a room for the night. I was about fifty miles from Indian Hill—not nearly far enough away from Ethan—but it would have to do for tonight. I hated putting my friends out, but I didn't have much of a choice. Fleeing in my own car was out of the question since it was registered to the chief of police. Ethan only had to flag the car as being stolen and every law enforcement agency in the country would be looking for me.

After much arguing, I convinced Teddy, Ben, and Natalia, I would be fine alone in the hotel, and they should head home. Teddy agreed to come back tomorrow to drive me wherever it was I needed to go. The only reason Natalia conceded was because Teddy said she could come back with him. The plan was for me to stay here overnight while I figured out what to do next. Perhaps it was foolish of me not to have planned for it, but I never once thought about anything past getting out. I assumed I would have more time to figure out the rest.

Flipping on the television, sounds from a vacuum infomercial filled the silence. I flipped through the channels and settled on a live concert, featuring Halsey and another band I wasn't familiar with. I didn't particularly care about watching anything on the screen, I just wanted the background noise.

I gingerly stretched out onto the bed, wincing as pain lanced over my ribs. My body hurt right down to the marrow of my bones, covered with a patchwork of bruises reminiscent of a Picasso painting. Once I was as comfortable as I could be in my current state, I stared at the yellowing ceiling and contemplated where I should go in the morning. I'd always liked the waterfront in Cleveland, and housing was affordable there. Perhaps I'd look into catching a Greyhound and head there.

The Tracfone rang and I recognized Natalia's phone number on the screen.

"Hey, girl," I said.

"Hey, yourself. I'm back in Cinci now. Teddy just dropped me off. You doing okay?"

"I don't know. I'm hanging in there, I guess. It's hard to articulate how I feel. Numb? Lost? I think I just need time to heal, you know?"

"And you will, Gia. You'll overcome this and be stronger than ever. Mark my words!"

I smiled softly, appreciating the fierceness in Natalia's tone and wishing I could channel some of that ferocity into myself.

"Thanks again for paying for my room. You didn't have to do that."

"Don't sweat it. It's like I said when we checked you in— you need to save your cash to get yourself back on your feet. Helping you out today was the least I could do. Any thoughts on where you're going next?"

"I was actually just thinking about that. I thought maybe Cleveland. It's affordable and only a few hours away."

"I'm surprised you didn't say someplace further," she observed.

"Oh, I definitely thought about it. I like the idea of being near the ocean, but that usually comes with a hefty price tag. That's why I'm thinking Cleveland. Lake Erie is going to have to be my ocean," I joked, although nothing about the situation was remotely funny.

"Going to make your own beach, huh?" Natalia kidded back.

Natalia and I chatted for a while longer about Cleveland, before reverting back to my physical well-being. Her repeated concerns about me going to a hospital to be checked out were well intended but she just didn't understand. I had patched myself up enough to know the drill. I was finally free of Ethan's clutches, which was all that mattered. I wouldn't do anything to jeopardize that. After thirty minutes of reassuring her I was fine, I heard her yawn. Glancing at the clock on the nightstand, the red digital numbers told me it was going on three in the morning.

"I should let you go. It's late."

"Alright. I'll see you in the morning when Teddy and I come to pick you up. He said we should be there around ten o'clock."

"Thank you for everything. Good night, Nat. I love you, girl."

"Love you too."

I placed the phone on the nightstand and got up from the bed to change into pajamas. Just as I unbuttoned the fly for my jeans, the hotel room phone rang. I froze. Natalia, Teddy, and Ben were the only people who knew where I was, and all three knew to call me on the Tracfone. The hotel phone continued to ring, the sound loud and intrusive. My heart raced.

Relax. It's probably just the hotel front desk.

I took a step toward it and hesitantly picked up the receiver.

"Hello?" I said cautiously.

"Gianna," said my husband's familiar voice on the other end of the line. My stomach dropped.

No. There was no way... impossible.

Without thinking, I slammed the receiver back onto the cradle. The phone rang again—and again, and again. With every ring, my heart thrummed louder in my ears. Snatching up the receiver once more, I skipped the pleasantries.

"How did you find me?" I demanded.

"Oh, honey, haven't I told you before that you shouldn't try to be smart? Finding you was way too easy. Natalia used her credit card to pay for the room. I'm a cop, remember? Finding out that information is like child's play. You can't hide from me."

I silently recited a whole slew of profanities and pinched the bridge of my nose. It never occurred to me he'd somehow found a way to track Natalia credit purchases, too. I knew better than to be so stupid.

"Leave me alone, Ethan. Don't make this more difficult than it needs to be."

"Leave you alone? Oh, I can't do that. I'd worry too much about my girl," he said in a sugary sweet voice. "Especially with your plan to go to Cleveland. I heard there's a lot of crime on the waterfront."

I stilled for the briefest of moments, my eyes growing wide, then threw the phone against the wall as if it had burned me. Blood pulsed in my temples and I broke out into a nervous sweat. The only way he could have known about Cleveland was if he heard the conversation I'd just had with Natalia. It had never been discussed before then.

I glanced around the room nervously, then ran to the window. Pulling open the curtains, I peered outside. Looking past the fire escape, my gaze went to the parking lot. My view from the second floor revealed a few cars but that was it. There wasn't anyone there.

A loud bang on the door caused me to jump a mile.

"Gia! Open up!" I heard Ethan yell. There was another bang, then a thud from his body—or perhaps his foot—slamming into the door to try to get in. The cheap frame on the old hotel room door splintered.

Shit, shit, shit!

Without thinking, I ran to the window and slid it open, then glanced back. The garment bag with my clothes was still in the room. So was my purse with all the cash, the phone, and my shoes. I looked at the door that was barely still intact as Ethan continued to pound. He'd be through it any second now. The clothes would just weigh me down, but I needed my purse and shoes.

"My girl! You're fucking my girl!" he roared. A deafening crack sounded and I watched as Ethan tried to wedge himself into the room through the now busted door frame. His eyes were crazed and dried blood caked the side of his head from where Ben had hit him with the lamp.

Moving as fast as I could, I snatched my purse from the floor. To my horror, the phone and wad of cash spilled out on the floor. Twenty-dollar bills seemed to unfurl in the air in slow motion just as Ethan burst through the door. He looked murderous. If there was any doubt in my mind about what Ethan was capable of, that doubt was gone now.

He would surely kill me this time.

Abandoning the cash and the phone, I spun and raced back to the window. I pulled the latch to release the fire escape ladder, then scaled down the rusty metal until my bare feet hit the broken asphalt driveway.

Then I ran.

And ran.

Ignoring the pain in my ribs, I ran until my feet were raw and bloody and I could run no more.

staggered up to a gas station located in the middle of nowhere.
The bottoms of my feet were torn up, my body screamed in pain,
and I couldn't stop trembling. I needed help. I had no phone and
no money. The only thing I had were the clothes on my back and
my purse—devoid of all the cash I'd squirreled away over the
last six months. I didn't even have shoes. My only saving grace
was a payphone at the gas station. I almost couldn't believe my
luck. I hadn't seen a payphone in ages and prayed it still worked.

As I dialed the operator and requested a collect call, I fretted
over whether or not this was yet another stupid move. Calling
anyone was risky—everything would be a risk from now on but I
didn't have a choice. When Teddy's voice finally came through
the line, I couldn't disguise my relief. I was stranded, and since
finding out Ethan was somehow tracking Natalia, I needed
Teddy like I'd never needed anyone else before.

"Teddy!"

"Gia! What's wrong?"

"Ethan found me," I choked out. Just verbalizing it caused
the trembling in my hands to worsen. "I was afraid to call Nat
because I think he's watching her."

"What do you mean? How the hell did he find you?"

"Look, I can't explain how or why, but I had to leave quickly.
All of my stuff is still at the hotel. My clothes, my phone, my
cash…"

I couldn't continue. The sobs I'd swallowed before making
the call burst forth.

"That fucking bastard is crazy. Where are you? I'm coming
to pick you up. I knew we shouldn't have left you at that damn
hotel. You can come back to my place and—"

"No. Not your place. He'll know to look there too."

"Gia, what do you want me to do?" He sounded exhausted. It
was understandable after the night he'd just had because of me.

"I'm so sorry to drag you into this further…"

"No, no, don't say that. That son of a bitch will never hurt you again. Where are you? I can't help you if I don't know where you are."

Despite the fatigue in his voice, there was also an urgency that gave me the strength to carry on. I took a deep breath.

"Near some random highway," I said, suddenly afraid because I truly had no idea where I was. It was dark and I wasn't sure if I'd run north, south, east, or west. I just ran in a zigzagging path in case Ethan followed in the direction I took off. I quickly looked around for identifying landmarks.

"What highway, Gia?"

"Route 71, I think. Yes, I can see the road sign. I'm at a gas station with a convenience store. The sign just says mini-mart and has a huge chicken on it. It's the only thing around as far as I can see. I can't be more than four or five miles from the hotel where you dropped me off."

He was quiet for a moment, as if he were trying to picture what I was describing.

"Okay, I should be able to find it. My ex-wife still has some clothes kicking around here and you're about her size. I'll bring what I can as well as some cash."

"You don't have…" I almost said he didn't have to bring money but stopped myself. I literally had nothing. I had no choice but to accept. "I'll pay you back."

"Don't worry about it. It's only money. Just lie low. It shouldn't take me too long to find you, then we can figure out a safe place for you to go. But Gia… Nat is going to ask questions when she can't reach you on the Tracfone. What do you want me to tell her?"

"Tell her the phone's gone and not to attempt to contact me." I paused, took a deep breath, and thought about how easy it had been for Ethan to track my location tonight. "That means you too, Teddy. It's too risky. Once I figure out where I'm going, there can't be any more contact. I need to disappear for a while. I'll call you both once I think it's safe."

He sighed and fell silent.

"Okay," he eventually acquiesced.

Tears pricked the corners of my eyes. The thought of giving up the only family I had was soul crushing.

"Thank you, Teddy. For everything."

"I'll see you soon. And Gia?"

"Yeah?"

"You will be okay. I promise."

PART IV

A FRESH START

11

Gianna

Queens, New York
Two Weeks Later

The water began to run cold and I turned off the faucet. Squeezing out my hair, I watched the clear droplets rain down onto my feet. Satisfied all the hair dye was completely rinsed, I stepped out of the shower. My eyes absently roamed the small bathroom as I pinched up my nose from the chemical smell of ammonia lingering in the air. Cream ceramic tiles in desperate need of fresh grout climbed the backsplash above the sink. Faded peel and stick tiles had begun to curl up around the edges of the floor, revealing another layer of graying linoleum. I wouldn't consider the tiny room dingy, but it wasn't anything like my bathroom in Indian Hill. Nevertheless, it was clean and that was all that mattered.

After wrapping a towel around my head and another around my body, I caught my clouded reflection in the steam coated mirror. I wiped the fog away and blinked harshly at the person staring back at me. I thought the deep chestnut brown hair dye would be enough of a disguise, but now I worried it wasn't. I still looked too much like me.

I twisted my hair up to visualize what I'd look like with a shorter style. I frowned and tried to decide if a short bob would give me more protection. Impulsively, I ran to the kitchen and grabbed a pair of scissors. When I returned to the bathroom, I separated my hair into four sections and began to cut.

Ten minutes later, I stared down at the long locks piled on the bathroom floor. Slowly, I brought my gaze back up to the mirror. The woman who stared back looked nothing like me. It almost hurt. I realized then, I might never see the old me again. The blonde was now gone, replaced by a dark brown that made my brows seem sharper. My eyes were hollow, my face sunken. With the short haircut, no one would ever recognize me without a double-take. It was unlikely I'd be spotted on a CCTV or street cam, either. Knowing Ethan and the lengths he would go to, there was no such thing as being too careful. I was a nobody hiding in disguise, no longer recognizing myself, but that was the goal. This was my life now, no matter how depressing it might sound.

I may look different but the change started well before the purchase of a box of cheap hair dye. It had been a gradual change—little pieces of myself slowly getting lost every day I'd spent with Ethan. The denial had won before I could think to stop it. I had learned a hard lesson and vowed to never lose myself that way again. My years with him had made me stronger, harder, and more resilient—but I was still very much afraid.

After I threw on a t-shirt and jeans, my stomach began to grumble. I went into the kitchen to fix myself lunch, but it was slim pickings. I knew I needed to get more groceries, but the thought of leaving the safety of these walls terrified me—hence the reason for the cut and dye. I hoped the changes would make me feel more comfortable venturing out.

Deciding on canned tomato soup, I poured it into a pot and set it on the gas stove. The old grandfather clock in the living room chimed noon as I waited for the soup to heat. I smiled to myself and looked around the sparsely furnished apartment. The well-worn plaid couch, faded curtains, and coffee-ring-stained end tables left much to be desired but I was thankful for a place to call home. It was the best I could do on short notice. I wouldn't have been able to do it at all if it weren't for the fat envelope of cash Teddy had given me the night I ran from the hotel. He had also arrived with a brand-new pair of Nike sneakers and a large duffle bag of clothes. Most were hand-me-downs from his ex-wife, but some still had the tags on them. Anything was better than nothing, and I'd forever be grateful to him.

On the night I made my escape, my old boss had come through for me in ways I never could have imagined. Once I'd stopped shaking enough to clean myself up in the bathroom of the run-down gas station, Teddy had driven me to the bus station and told me to pick a place. I had decided to scrap Cleveland. It was too close to Cincinnati and the city wasn't big enough. I needed some place I could truly hide. I picked New York City for no other reason than its vast size. The dense population would better allow me to blend in. Plus, I was banking on the fact Ethan knew I hated city living and probably wouldn't think to look for me here. It gave me a better sense of security.

Luckily for me, Teddy was able to hook me up with more than just cash and clothes. He also happened to have an old friend in New York and was able to get me an apartment relatively quick. My new landlord, Oscar Tomasz, used to be a poker buddy of Teddy's. They hadn't spoken in years, but Teddy said I could trust him. That was all I needed to hear.

Cash payment of the first and last month's rent was all Oscar required. The fully furnished apartment was on the ground floor, an added bonus I hadn't counted on. Not only did it eliminate the burden of getting furniture, but first-floor living meant I had more options in case I had to escape quickly. One could never have too many windows.

The building itself was sandwiched between a fitness center and a nightclub. I liked that people were always coming and going. It meant I wasn't isolated like I had been at the house in Indian Hill and someone would most likely hear me if I ever had to cry for help. The only downfall to the location was the pulsing bass from the nightclub late into the night on Fridays and Saturdays—something I discovered on my second night here. However, beggars couldn't afford to be choosers. I'd get used to it, eventually.

I was glad Oscar didn't ask questions about the bruise on my left cheek or the fingerprint marks on my neck. He also didn't ask why my ID didn't match the name I wrote on the rental application. During the bus ride to New York, I made the decision to combine a shortened version of my maiden name with my mother's maiden name. I was no longer Gianna Valentini Walker. From this point forward, all who met me would know me as Val Bonetti.

As I blew on a spoonful of soup to cool it down, I recalled the conversation with Oscar after the rental agreement was signed.

"I'm happy to have you here, Val," he'd said earnestly. "Teddy said you're going through a rough time but he didn't say exactly what was going on. No need to tell me—it's not my business to know—but I want to assure you, my apartment is right down the hall if you need anything. I'm number seven."

Oscar, with his kind eyes and hair just beginning to gray at the temples, seemed nice enough. His words had given me comfort but not enough to calm my frayed nerves. That would take time. Still, I couldn't begin to do that by staying holed up in the apartment all day. I had to stay productive or risk shutting down for good.

I rinsed my bowl and placed it in the tiny dishwasher that always made a loud, angry groan when running. Then I wiped down the counters with the lemon scented anti-bacterial spray the previous tenant had left behind. When I began to scrub a few spilled droplets of soup from the stovetop, I froze as a sudden realization washed over me.

I didn't have to clean. I could leave the mess for days if I wanted to—whole days.

I wouldn't, of course, but the simple fact was, I had options now. I no longer had someone looking over my shoulder, judging whether I had missed a speck of dust on the mantel or a crumb on the floor. And I had nobody to yell at me about leaving the damn toothpaste out on the counter.

I smiled to myself as I abandoned the sponge and went in search of my sneakers. I would clean up the stove and counters later—when I was good and ready. Feeling more confident about my venture out, I laced up my shoes and headed for the door.

12

Val (Gianna)

No one looked your way in New York City—even if you were doing something crazy. They just kept their heads down and kept walking. Knowing people didn't stare too long, or not at all, helped reduce my paranoia. The small grocery store was conveniently located only a block away. I knew I had to figure out the subway system, so I could venture out farther, but today was not that day. For now, it was all about taking baby steps. Once I was more comfortable out in public, I'd think about doing more.

As I walked down the aisles, perusing the organic cheeses and free-range poultry, I forced myself to feel normal. I wanted to feel like I belonged here—to embrace the trendy foods and eclectic styles. Unfortunately, all those things were well outside my budget. The ninety-nine-cent box of spaghetti and a generic jar of tomato sauce would have to do.

On my way out, I grabbed a free newspaper, hoping it would have a section with help wanted ads. I didn't have a laptop to browse job listings, nor did I know how to get to the public library. I hoped to get there eventually but the vastness of the city was too overwhelming to even think about it.

Traveling on foot meant I could only buy as much as I could carry, so I had asked the cashier to pack everything into two bags. I was beginning to second guess the bag of clementine oranges I'd tossed in at the last minute. The bags were heavy, and I worried about the strength of the cheap plastic handles under the straining weight. Surprisingly, they held out okay—until I reached the front door of my building. Just as I opened the door to step inside, one of the handles ripped. Of course, it had to be the bag with the jarred sauce in it.

"Damn it!"

Glass shattered, and red tomato sauce splattered all over the floor, covering my jeans and sneakers. The bag of oranges busted open as well, following the path my Granny Smith apples were taking down the hallway. Stunned, I could only watch as the fruit I'd purchased rolled.

I wanted to cry. My funds were limited until I found a job, and I couldn't afford this kind of waste. Forcing back tears that would get me nowhere, I got down on my hands and knees and began to collect the scattered fruit.

"Need some help?" asked a male voice. I startled. I thought I was alone in the dimly lit hallway.

"No thanks. I've got it," I mumbled without looking up. I just collected my groceries and fretted over how I was going to clean up the sauce on the carpeted floor. Oscar was not going to be happy about this.

There goes my security deposit.

I paused when a pair of blue-and-white Reebok running shoes blocked my path, and an orange was placed in front of my face. I glanced up, annoyed the man was still there after I told him I had things handled. When my eyes met his, I felt all the air leave my lungs.

"You sure you don't need help?" The man asked again and

gestured to the mess in the hallway. I couldn't speak or take my eyes off his face—I knew the man standing before me. It seemed like our chance meeting was a lifetime ago, but I'd never forget those kind, hazel eyes—eyes I'd found comfort in remembering during some of my darkest moments but never understood why. Every detail was the same as my memory—only better.

He was my stranger.

Quickly, I stood and tried to act nonchalant, although I wanted to run as fast as I could and never look back. The chances of seeing a familiar face in a city exceeding eight million people had to be slim to none. I couldn't afford to be recognized. Then again, maybe he wouldn't remember me. Our meeting was a long time ago, after all. I forced myself to take a few calming breaths.

"It's okay. I..." I began.

"Hey, don't I know you?"

My stomach sank.

"No, I don't think so," I said hurriedly and tried to move past him.

"No, we've definitely met before." He snapped his fingers. "Your hair is different but I'd never forget that face. You're the runaway bride!"

I closed my eyes and cursed my shitty luck. Every instinct I possessed was being questioned by the conflicting synapses in my brain. I should deny who I was—pretend I didn't recognize him and tell him he had the wrong girl. Then there was another part of me—a very small part—that was genuinely curious about the stranger with the hazel eyes who had haunted my consciousness for years. That small part of me overruled any rational judgment I may have had.

There was no use denying who I was now. It was better to acknowledge his memory of our brief encounter, then move on and hope to never see him again. Slowly, I turned. Focused eyes roamed over me head to toe. I crossed my arms self-consciously.

"That's right. I sort of remember you now. Funny running into you here," I said with a weak smile.

"Yeah, it sure is. Since you only 'sort of' remember me, allow me to introduce myself. I'm Derek Mills. Pleased to meet you... again," he joked and held out his hand for me to shake.

Panic washed over me as I tried to recall the conversation details from all those years ago.

Had I told him my name?

I didn't think I did.

"I'm Val. Val Bonetti," I said quickly, trying to portray confidence I didn't feel. He cocked his head to the side, almost as if he were confused.

Shit. Did I tell him my name back then after all?

No, I was sure I didn't. He was probably looking at me curiously because I was acting like some kind of loon with this false sense of bravado. I knew using a fake name was necessary to stay hidden from Ethan, but actually saying it out loud felt awkward and foreign on my tongue as I accepted his handshake. When my palm met his, my stomach lurched with anxious butterflies that had nothing to do with worry about my true name being exposed. The dancing wings weren't qualmish or uneasy. They were fluttery and excited—and exactly how I'd felt during our first meeting. That mysterious something, I couldn't quite place—that inexplicable spark.

His fingers skittered lightly over mine and another peculiar, questioning look flashed across his face before he seemed to reluctantly pull away.

"Well, um...Val Bonetti. I have just the thing to clean up the sauce from the carpet before Oscar sees it. He's a good guy, but this is sure to get a rise out of him. Wait right here for a minute."

As I watched him hurry away, attempts at ignoring all six feet of that rugged gorgeousness were futile. His grin had been wide with an excess of both cuteness and suggestiveness when he shook my hand. The combination caused a jolt of electricity to zap me, provoking exhilarating goosebumps to pebble all over my body. I absently rubbed the hand he'd momentarily held and shook off the unwarranted feelings.

When he returned, he was holding two bottles, a bunch of rags, and a plastic garbage bag. To my surprise, he got down on his hands and knees near the stain, wiped up the excess sauce, then tossed the soiled rags into a trash bag. Taking one of the bottles, he then dumped a pungent liquid over the carpet.

"Oh, that stinks! What is that?" I asked, crinkling up my nose.

"Hydrogen peroxide. It cuts through the oils. Don't worry. It won't smell for long. I'll spray it down with an Ivory soap concentrate and all will be good. You'll see."

I just nodded and furrowed my brows. It was strange watching him scrub the carpet. Being married to Ethan, a man who never cleaned anything, made me forget men were actually capable of doing household chores. A part of me wanted to take the rags from Derek and clean it myself—but not because I felt it was my duty as a woman. I was done being a man's doormat. I wanted to take over the task because it was my mess and I should be the one to clean it. However, stopping him might entail inadvertently touching him, and after the tingling I felt from our brief skin-to-skin contact a few moments earlier, that was dangerous.

After he finished, he threw the remaining rags into the trash bag and stood. Miraculously, the carpet looked cleaner than it had before the sauce spill.

"Wow! That sure is a magical home remedy you've got there! Here," I said, extending my hand to take the bag. "Let me take those rags and get them washed for you. It's the least I can do."

When I took the bag, our hands briefly touched. Energy snapped in the air, and once again, I was reminded of the night we first met. The contact was like elastic stretching taut with unspoken words. And just like a rubber band, it snapped back as if the moment hadn't happened at all.

"Thanks. Ah...Lisa will appreciate that," he said awkwardly. Whatever this was, it was clear he felt it too. It took me a second or two to process what he'd said.

"Lisa?"

"One of the ladies who works for me at The Mill."

My ears perked up and I pushed away the strange feelings. I needed to focus. The Mill sounded like it might be a restaurant or local bar. I had experience waitressing, even though it had been a while, and bartending was like riding a bike—one never forgot. Maybe they were hiring.

"I just got here a few weeks ago. I haven't heard of The Mill. Is it nearby?"

"Yeah, it's attached to the building. It's where I grabbed the cleaner. Lisa takes care of washing the used sweat towels."

I frowned.

"Now, I'm confused. Sweat towels? I think my assumption about The Mill is incorrect. I thought it was a restaurant or a bar," I admitted. Derek laughed.

"No, not at all. Do you remember me telling you about the gym I was going to open?"

"Yeah, I remember."

"That's The Mill. I own the one on the property as well as a few more in other areas of the city. There's a side entrance off of this hallway I usually use when I want to sneak in unnoticed," he explained and pointed to a glass door about twenty feet behind him.

Realization dawned.

"Oh, I gotcha now. I knew a gym was next door, but I never paid attention to the name."

"I give discounts to building tenants on this block. I live in the building across the street so it's my way of getting in good with the neighbors," he teased with a wink. "If you and your husband are interested in joining, I can hook you up."

"Oh, no, there's no husband," I said in a rush. When he raised his eyebrows in question, I explained. "We're divorced."

The lie caused a pang of guilt to stab at me. Then again, what was a piece of paper? To me, Ethan and I were divorced in every sense of the word. There was no need to go into all the sordid details.

"Well, just you then," he offered with an easy smile. He stuffed his hands in his jean pockets causing the dark blue denim to stretch across his legs.

I stared back at him, unsure how to respond. I couldn't figure him out. He was just as kind and charming as I remembered, but there was something else. I'd found him attractive when we first met, and time had been good to him—very good. He was distracting, to say the least, and I didn't mean that in a simple sense. His tall, broad build would make most women drool. He wore his sandy brown hair cropped short in the back with long, tight waves left on top to frame his tanned forehead. He had an easy aura that made me feel at ease—a feeling I couldn't afford to have. I still needed to be cautious.

"Thanks for the offer, but I'm going to have to pass," I told him. His smile loosened, but he nodded.

I stepped away, meaning to retreat back to the confines of my apartment, yet found myself hesitating. I didn't want to walk to my door with him watching. I didn't really know him and didn't want him to see which apartment was mine. Perhaps I was being ridiculous, but my past proved I had a poor track record when it came to sizing up a person's character. I couldn't trust my judgment about anyone.

"Are you sure?" he pressed. "It's a great way to get to know people since most who live in the surrounding area are members of the gym."

I was at a crossroad, conflicted about whether or not I should be getting to know anyone right now. A part of me wanted the security of friends and I'd been missing Natalia so much. If anything bad ever happened, I was truly alone here. Another part of me was terrified. Allowing people to get too close to me meant the web of lies surrounding my identity could be jeopardized. Then there was the issue of money. At this point, there was no way I could afford a gym membership.

"Yeah? Well, I suppose I can think about it." I shrugged my shoulders in a noncommittal way.

"Well, if you want to come by," he began and took a step closer to me. Reaching into his pocket, he pulled out a small card. "Here's a coupon for a free month just to try it out. If you decide to join after that, you'll get the neighborhood discount."

I took the card and forced a smile. Without another word, he turned and walked out the front doors of the building. I stared after him for a short moment before carting my groceries and the bag of soiled rags back to my apartment.

Once inside, I closed the door with a sigh, let my head fall back, and closed my eyes. I'd been here for only two weeks, and my situation was already complicated.

13

Derek

I opened the door to my apartment, and Maisie, my ten-month-old Cavalier pup, immediately began scratching in her crate to be let out.

"There's my pretty girl! Are you hungry?" I crooned in a not-so-masculine voice that I'd never dare use in public. I bent over to unzip the mesh door, and she came bounding out, her nails scraping on the wood floor as she jumped up to greet me. Picking her up, I allowed her to lick my face, knowing she was equally happy to see me as she was eager to be fed lunch. "Okay, girl. Let's get you some food."

After my little companion scarfed down her kibble, I took her up to the building's rooftop garden, where a section was cordoned off to create a mini dog park for residents with pets. Normally, when I stopped home mid-day, I'd feed her lunch then head back to The Mill until six. As Maisie sniffed around for the perfect place to do her business, I realized I had no intention of going back to work anytime soon. Before I did anything, I had to get over the shock I felt after reconnecting with the runaway bride who'd haunted my dreams for too many years.

She was here—she was actually here.

I paced the perimeter of the manmade greenspace and tried to wrap my head around what happened. Never did I expect to see Gianna—or Val as she was apparently calling herself now—scrambling to collect runaway fruit in the hallway leading to The Mill. It had been three years since our last meeting—three long years. During that time, I'd been with a lot of women. Yet despite a few one-night-stands and many relationships that fizzled out to be nothing more than casual flings, I'd never stopped thinking about the one who got away. I had thought of a million questions to ask if I ever saw her again, but when I finally had that chance, my mind came up blank.

Recalling what she looked like all those years ago in her wedding dress, I knew then she had a great body, but seeing her again put my memory to shame. She had been wearing a cropped top today, just short enough to reveal the creamy skin near her belly button. Her jeans sat low on her hips, molding to her ass and shapely legs. Her cropped dark hair, once a luxurious golden color, had initially thrown me off. However, the moment she looked up at me, I knew it was her. I could never forget those rose-colored lips, the splash of pink on her cheeks, or the flecks of gray in her deep blue eyes. My heart had felt like it momentarily stopped from some sort of power surge, a lightning strike straight to my soul.

She was absolutely gorgeous.

And when our hands briefly touched? Hell, there was no way I imagined that pull—the invisible energy snapping and sizzling between us. It had been there three years ago, and there was no denying it was still there. Had she felt it, too? I couldn't be sure, but one thing was certain. She was different from how I remembered—and it went well beyond her hair color. Something inside her had dulled, and there was a measure of fear in her eyes that wasn't there before. She was clearly a woman hiding from something—or someone.

I recalled seeing her with her husband on her wedding night. My jaw clenched from the memory of how rough he'd been with her—how mean.

Was that why she divorced him?

Is that why she told me her name was something other than what I knew it to be?

Was she hiding from him?

So many questions and possible scenarios swirled in my mind. Mixed emotions consumed me, and I couldn't figure out why. After all, I barely knew her, but there was no denying the intimacy we shared that night, no matter how subtle, so many years ago. It was a moment in time I'd never forgotten but always looked back on as the age of innocence.

She wasn't the only one who had changed. I had, as well. We were both different now. Back then, she was just a bride with fairytale dreams, and I was still carefree and full of hope, unable to fathom the responsibility I now carried. I'd since learned some dreams were the sweetest before they came true.

While I couldn't be happier about The Mill's success at all four locations, the attention I'd received on the road to achieving that success had been unforeseen. Despite being in a city as large as New York, I'd become fairly well known in a very short period of time, thanks to Ryder Malone's decision to have The Mill become a sponsor of the New York City Marathon. Neither of us could have predicted the amount of recognition I'd receive as a result of that sponsorship, and I had no idea my face would end up plastered all over billboards advertising the marathon sponsors.

Since Ryder was nothing more than a silent partner, he simply rode the wave while I was labeled most eligible bachelor by a local fitness magazine—hence the reason I'd experienced so many empty, casual flings. Too many women believed me to be a wealthy person of importance. As soon as they found out I was just an average guy living an average life, they showed themselves the door. While I welcomed and appreciated every minute of my success, I could live without the notoriety. Still, I counted my blessings every day. I had built nothing into something, and I was proud.

I let out an audible sigh, knowing I needed to get back to work soon. Shift change at The Mill was only an hour away. I whistled for Maisie.

"Come on, girl! Time to get going. Duty calls."

All in all, I was happy with my life—at least I thought I'd been. I may never have found that special woman who I wanted to cherish the rest of my life but, that was okay. My business was thriving and I'd become independently wealthy, practically overnight. I had Maisie for companionship, and I truly believed I was content.

Somehow, all of that seemed to change in the blink of an eye. Seeing Gianna—or Val—brought back the old wants and desires. A connection I thought I'd only imagined was suddenly back again, pulling me toward her. In a matter of minutes, my content life was upended, and I was trying to figure out how Val fit into the mix. I needed more answers.

"What do you think, girl? Should I play hooky today and do a little research?" I asked Maisie as she and I got on to the elevator that would take us back to my apartment. She wagged her tail in response. "You're right. We'll let Lisa run the floor today."

Once inside my apartment, Maisie curled up on her favorite spot on the couch with her ears perked, watching me curiously as I pulled out my cell phone to call The Mill.

"Thanks for calling The Mill. Lisa speaking. How can I help you?"

"Hey, it's me."

"What's up, boss?" Lisa asked.

"I don't have any afternoon classes to teach today, so I was thinking of taking the afternoon off. What do you think? Can you manage the floor on your own today?"

"Shit, you never take time off. Are you feeling okay?" she joked.

"I'm fine. I just have a few things to do."

"Sure thing. We got it covered over here. Take all the time you need."

"Thanks. The treadmills still need to be sanitized today, and the vitamin supplements were looking a little bare. You'll need to restock—"

"I know the drill. You have daily tasks lists posted all over the office. We'll get it done."

"I know," I laughed. "But I had to say it, anyway. Thanks, Lisa. I appreciate you covering for me."

Ending the call, I grabbed my laptop from the coffee table and sat on the couch next to Maisie. She curled into my side while I waited for the computer to power up. Hoping Google would give me a little insight into my mystery girl, I recalled a certain glittery gold font and typed the two names I'd once read, Ethan and Gianna Walker.

"Here goes nothing."

I pushed aside the thought I may be bordering on stalking and scrolled through the search results.

I learned they owned a home in a quiet suburb called Indian Hill. Good schools. Population 5,887. I found a few social media accounts for Val under the Gianna Walker name, but the profiles showed she hadn't been active in years. Other than that, I didn't find much else.

I continued to search until I saw Ethan's name show up in a link to the Cincinnati Police Department. I clicked on it and discovered her ex-husband was the chief of police.

Interesting.

I don't know what I expected him to do for a living, but I

never would have guessed he was a cop. I stared at the image of him wearing his dress blues. He was a good-looking guy with dark hair and a medium build. He hadn't changed much since I saw him last. Unexpectedly, a twinge of what I recognized as jealousy needled me. It was crazy, really. I was jealous of some guy who I'd barely even met.

"Why?" I asked aloud to the computer screen, but I knew the answer.

I was jealous because he got to spend years with the woman I was only able to dream about. Just thinking about him sharing her bed, being inside of her, and fucking her as her husband made me green with envy in the most indescribable way. I hated him despite barely knowing him. My brief encounter with her husband might not have given me much time to see what was beneath the surface, but the picture before me did. Staring at the image on the computer, I saw something I hadn't seen before. There was a cold, mean glint to his eyes. Something was off with him, but I couldn't quite place it.

The longer I stared, the more uneasy I began to feel. Instinct led me to believe there was something dark and sinister hiding behind those eyes. An innate need to protect Val from whatever demons she was running from was overwhelming. She was hiding her true identity for a reason and I had a feeling that reason was staring back at me through my computer screen.

14

Val (Gianna)

I spent the next few days exploring the three blocks around my apartment and getting a subway card. I found places to hide if need be—a twenty-four-hour diner that had a payphone, and a woman's shelter that was three minutes away on foot. I also occupied myself with trying to find a job, but I needed a job off the books, and it was slim pickings. I could walk dogs, clean houses, bartend, or waitress—as long as I didn't have to hand over a social security number Ethan could use to track me.

Until I found one, keeping myself busy had been a challenge. I hadn't been sleeping well and spent more time than not jumping at my own shadow during the day. Every little noise in the quiet apartment made my nerves stand on end. I knew I was being ridiculous, but I couldn't help it. It was the reason I found myself at the hardware store I'd stumbled across the day before.

The lock on the door to my apartment was a single doorknob lock that could easily be card swiped. Updating the security to my residence was a must if I had any hope of getting a peaceful night's sleep. However, as I stared at the stores racking filled with nuts, bolts, tools, and wooden boards, I realized I had no idea what I would need. I knew I wanted to add a deadbolt. After the way Ethan beat down the door at the hotel, I also wanted to create a barricade using a couple of boards with hinges I could raise and lower as needed. Nobody would break down my door again.

After selecting what I thought I'd need, I lugged the supplies back to my apartment. Oscar was leaving the building just as I was coming in.

"Whoa, little lady!" my landlord said in surprise. "Let me give you a hand with that."

Relieved to be free of some of the heavy burden, I passed off two, four-feet-long wood planks.

"Thanks."

"Does something need fixing? If so, you should have told me."

"Oh, it's fine. I just want to put an extra lock on the door," I explained. He looked at me skeptically, his eyes shifting to the things I purchased, but didn't comment. Instead, he carried the wood to my door and left me to it. Thirty minutes later, as I was struggling to screw the hinge for one of the planks into the wall, Oscar returned carrying a drill, a small metal case, and a baseball bat.

"What's this?" I asked.

"You'll have an easier go of it with a drill than that rinky-dink screwdriver you've got there. There are different sized drill bits in the case."

"Oh, wow! This is great Oscar. Thanks! I'll be sure to get it back to you later on today."

"Keep it. It's one of my older drills. I have plenty more where that came from."

"And the bat? What's that for?"

A hard look flashed hot across his face, then he smiled knowingly.

"Just in case your new lock fails. I mean, sure, you can take those fancy self-defense classes they offer at The Mill, but sometimes it's best to handle things the old-fashioned way," he said with a wink.

When he walked away, I stared slack-jawed until he rounded the corner and was out of sight. For the first time, I began to wonder how much Teddy had told Oscar. I didn't know if I should be worried or relieved that I had someone here in my corner.

I glanced down at the wood bat he'd left for me. I knew, without a shadow of a doubt, I'd keep the bat right next to my bed. I couldn't believe I hadn't thought about getting one before. His mention of self-defense classes sparked my interest, and I wondered if I should wander over to the gym. I looked at the mess of tools and gadgets surrounding me. I was halfway done with adding extra security to my door. When I was finished, I decided I'd check out the gym. Learning self-defense was never a bad idea.

And maybe—just maybe—I'd catch a glimpse of Derek Mills while I was there.

I PUSHED through the turn-style doors to The Mill. Bright fluorescent lighting gleamed on expensive workout equipment and the smell of sweat and rubber permeated the air. Sneakers pounding on treadmills, the thumping of a racquetball, and the motivational shouts from a spotter for a nearby weightlifter created high-octane energy.

Walking over to a stand that held various brochures advertising the offerings at the gym, I located the one pertaining to self-defense. I perused the information, pleased with what I read, then stopped short when I saw the price tag. There was no way I could afford it on my current budget. I closed the brochure and went to put it back on the stand but paused as I took in the picture of the female on the cover. She was in a fighting stance, appearing proud and confident. What struck me most about her was the fierce look in her eyes. I envied that look in ways I couldn't even begin to process.

A tap on my shoulder nearly made me jump out of my skin and brought me out of my reverie. When I spun around, Derek Mills stood before me looking apologetic.

"Shit!" I cursed, clutching my chest. "Don't sneak up on me like that!"

"Sorry, I didn't mean to. I called your name three times, but you must not have heard me."

"You did?"

"Your name *is* Val, right?" he joked. He was smiling but wore a peculiar look, almost as if he knew that wasn't my name. My stomach dropped. I'd need to get used to responding to a different name or risk blowing my cover.

"Yeah... Val. My name is Val," I told him, desperately trying to get used to the sound of my new name rolling off my tongue. Derek narrowed his eyes curiously, then relaxed into an easy smile.

"Well, Val, what brings you here? You ready to cash in on that free trial month?"

"I don't know yet. I was just looking over the brochures. Is the self-defense class included in the trial?"

"Everything you see listed is included. However, I should let you know that the self-defense class only meets twice a week. To get the full training benefits, you really need to take the class for three months."

My shoulders sagged at the mere thought of how much that would set me back.

"I'll have to think about it," I told him. "I'll definitely do the free trial, but I'm still relatively new to the city and need to find a job before I can commit to anything longer."

"Hmmm, maybe I can help you out. What kind of experience do you have?" His smile was easy, and he was standing just close enough for me to catch his scent. The subtle cologne he wore smelled aquatic and woody with just a hint of spice. It reminded me of being near a lake surrounded by evergreens.

"I hate to admit it, but it's not much—just waitressing and bartending for the most part."

"Actually, you're in luck. My sister and her husband own a restaurant called Camilla's. It's a trendy Italian place. My bother-in-law recently mentioned that he was looking for a good waitress. They do pretty well over there. The place is always hopping and the tips are good from what I hear."

"Where's the restaurant?" I asked, feeling a shred of hope for the first time since coming to this city.

"Little Italy," he told me. I pinched my brow together and tried to remember where that was. He must have sensed my question because he elaborated. "It's about a thirty-minute subway ride from here. I can show you if you have trouble figuring it out."

I nodded my head as I recalled the routes I'd studied on the New York City subway map.

"I think I can figure it out, but thanks. How can I get a hold of your brother-in-law?"

"His name is Christopher. Christopher Pastori. I can call him for you. But…" He trailed off, pinching his brows together, appearing concerned and hesitant at the same time.

"But what?" I prodded.

"Before I call him, I should probably mention one thing. This might sound weird, but I'm pretty sure the job would be off the books. I hope that's not a concern for you."

Off the books!

Derek had no idea how much that meant to me. I couldn't have planned it better myself. Still, I needed to make sure I wasn't stepping into something shady simply because it was convenient.

"Is there a reason I should be worried about it?"

"Nah. Christopher is a good guy. I have no idea why he does it that way," Derek admitted with a shrug. Then he laughed and shook his head. "The day my sister married an Italian was the day I stopped asking questions. I've seen enough episodes of the Sopranos to know better. I hope that's okay."

I didn't care if his brother-in-law was Al Capone himself, so long as the job kept me off the radar. An excited smile spread across my face.

"Then it's a yes—definitely yes! This is great! Oh my gosh, I could kiss you right now!" As soon as the words were out of my mouth, I was mortified. Derek's eyebrow shot to the ceiling and my cheeks flamed twenty shades of red. Trying to adapt a calmer disposition, so I didn't seem so embarrassingly desperate, I smiled awkwardly and explained my overzealousness. "I'm sorry. I've just been struggling with trying to find work and this couldn't have come at a better time."

"Don't sweat it," he assured, flashing me a crooked smile that made my insides flutter.

To my surprise, Derek pulled his phone from his pocket. I didn't think he'd actually call his brother-in-law right at that moment. As he dialed the phone, I practically bounced with anticipation and silently prayed for Christopher to answer the call.

"Chris! Hey, man! Are you still looking for a waitress at the restaurant?" There was a brief pause before Derek smiled and gave me a thumbs up. "Good, because I have the perfect girl for you."

15

Derek

I couldn't stop thinking about Val for the rest of the day. After I'd taken Maisie for her evening walk, I paced my apartment and tried to put together the pieces of the puzzle. The problem was, I didn't know where the damn pieces fit because I couldn't see the whole picture.

I'd given her an opportunity to reveal her real name but she didn't take it. That only added further confirmation to my theory about her hiding. Whatever her reasons, I would go along with it for however long she needed me to. In fact, I'd already committed to taking it one step further. I would help keep her secret safe—which is why I mentioned the job at Camilla's.

I knew Christopher would keep an eye on her if I told him I thought she was in danger and I could count on him to be discreet. That's also why I found myself jumping on the 'A' train to Little Italy at nine o'clock at night. I wanted to talk to him in person about Val.

Thirty-five minutes later, I got off at the Canal Street Station and headed southeast toward Mulberry Street. The dinner crowd at Camilla's should be winding down at this hour. Hopefully, that meant my sister had gone home for the night and I could chat with Christopher without her nosing around in my business. She'd want to know every little detail, and there was no way I could explain the whole situation with Val when I barely understood it myself.

Camilla's was quiet when I entered. Andrea Bocelli's *Con te partiro* could be heard playing softly overhead and only a few corner tables were occupied, the lingering patrons clearly making the most of the authentic atmosphere the place had to offer. My sister and her husband only served Italy's best cuisine in their restaurant, an old-fashioned Roman trattoria reimagined and brought to life in a modern city. Every time I came here and smelled the delicious, mouthwatering aroma of garlic and fresh bread wafting from the kitchen, I felt a surge of pride for all they'd accomplished.

"Derek! It's late for you to be coming by," Christopher greeted when he saw me approaching the mosaic tiled bar.

"Hey, Chris."

"Have a seat." He motioned to one of the wrought iron bar stools. "You hungry? I can have Antonio whip you up a bit of linguine with clam sauce, just how you like it."

I shook my head and smiled. If I ate pasta every time Christopher offered it to me, I'd go back to that chubby kid in middle school in a matter of weeks.

"Nah, I'm good. Thanks though. Is Isabella around?"

"You just missed her. She took off about twenty minutes ago."

I suppressed a sigh of relief to hear my sister had already left for the night.

"That's alright. I wanted to talk to you alone anyway."

"Oh?" He raised an eyebrow in surprise.

"Don't look at me like that. I mean, I love my sister but you know how she can be. I just don't want to play twenty questions with her right now."

"The only time Isabella peppers you with questions is if there's a girl involved," he pointed out. When I didn't answer, he leaned against the doorjamb to the kitchen, crossed his arms, and gave me a knowing nod. "So, this is about a girl."

"Sort of. It's the girl I called you about earlier, the one who needs a job."

"I gotta admit, I was a little surprised. You're not a big believer in calling in favors and usually keep friends separate from business matters. The phone call was out of character for you so I knew something had to be up." Christopher went behind the bar and ducked down below the counter. I could hear the clinking of glass, and when he stood, he had a couple of old fashioned lowball glasses and a bottle of Sambuca in hand. After pouring us both a drink, he slid a glass across the bar toward me.

"This situation is different."

"Let me guess… smoking hot chick from the gym who's having trouble paying her monthly dues? Or maybe a damsel in distress with a great rack that needed saving?" he harassed with a waggle of his eyebrows.

I glared at him.

"Seriously, man. What do you take me for?" I snarled, but Christopher knew my words carried no real heat. His smile remained, but when he spoke again, his tone was serious.

"Relax, brother. I'm only teasing you. For real… what's going on?"

I eyed him ruefully, trying to determine how much I wanted him to know. I knew who Val really was, but I wasn't comfortable revealing the truth to anyone else. It was her story to tell when she was ready. Hell, I didn't even know the story. All I knew were the ten million questions I had were driving me insane. Still, Christopher was a keen observer and he was smart. It would only be a matter of time before he cut through all the bullshit, so I may as well be as straight as possible with him.

"I met this girl about three years ago in Cincinnati. As I mentioned to you earlier on the phone, her name is Gi—" I stopped short at my near slip-up. Getting used to calling her by her new name was proving to be more challenging than I originally thought. "Her name is Val. Our meeting was brief. A fluke, really." I proceeded to give him an abbreviated version of our first meeting, including the exchange I witnessed between her and her husband.

"He roughed her up on their wedding day?" Christopher asked incredulously.

"I would call it more like rough handling, but definitely threatening. I remember thinking she looked scared back then. Now here we are, three years later, and she looks more terrified than ever. I think she's on the run, bro."

"From the husband?"

"Yeah."

Christopher let out a long, low whistle.

"That's a sticky situation. Domestics can get complicated in a real hurry. Please don't tell me you're dating this girl."

"No! I'm not dating her." *Yet.*

Yes, I wanted Val—I wanted her bad—but Christopher was right. Until I knew her whole situation, it would be wise to remain cautious. Then again, I never claimed to be a wise man.

Christopher scratched his chin between his thumb and forefinger contemplatively.

"So, you're not dating her, but something tells me you really like her. Am I right?"

"Well..." I trailed off, struggling to put my feelings into words. "Honestly, I barely know her, but yeah, I mean... I *do* really like her—a lot. There's something between us, and I'd like the opportunity to figure out what that something is. The thing is, she's skittish, like a nervous puppy or something. It's not anything she said, more her mannerisms—like she's always looking over her shoulder. And I mean that both literally and figuratively. I don't even think she realizes she's doing it half the time."

Christopher shook his head and leaned against the counter behind the bar.

"Do you know what I think?" he asked.

"What?"

"I think you should forget this girl and go find yourself a nice piece of tail. It's been too long since you last got laid."

"When I got laid last is none of your fucking business," I snapped, and he chuckled.

"Okay, fine, don't forget about her. How about this? Have you considered that maybe she's not running from her husband? Maybe she's in legal trouble. You said it yourself. You barely know her. She could be a criminal or something. Or maybe she's a scorned bride out for vengeance—perhaps she murdered her husband."

I pursed my lips and eyed him with annoyance. I was trying to be serious and he was making comparisons to *Kill Bill*.

"You've watched too many Tarantino flicks."

"It could happen," he said with a shrug.

"It's nothing like that, Chris. Do you honestly think I'd refer her to you for employment if I thought she was secretly a hardened criminal? I'm telling you, she's just a scared girl. I feel this innate need to protect her. It's weird. The problem is all the unknowns. I don't know what I need to protect her from."

Christopher topped off my half-empty glass of Sambuca and pushed a basket of crostini my way. I nodded my thanks for the refill and took a sip. Grabbing a crostini, I bit into it and chewed thoughtfully. Christopher stayed silent, knowing I was trying to work things out in my head. He was good like that. I was frustrated and concerned for so many reasons, but I couldn't pinpoint what was bothering me the most.

"What are you thinking, brother?" he eventually asked.

"Her behavior reminds me a lot of the women who attend my self-defense class for the first time. They're jumpy, always looking at the door in case they need to bolt. Val has that look, but there's more to her. I saw determination—the kind of raw grit you only see in people who've truly had enough. She's fragile yet so strong." I shook my head and ran a hand over my face. To him, I probably sounded like a head case. "Fuck, man. I don't even know if I'm making any sense right now."

"For a girl who you hardly know, she's managed to get you all twisted up," My brother-in-law shook his head with a look of complete bewilderment. "Are you sure she's hiding something? Maybe she's just a private person."

"No, I know it's not that."

"How do you know for sure?"

"Her name for one thing. She lied to me about it. You see, we never exchanged names during our conversation three years ago. I only knew it because of the sign that was outside the reception hall. Val, the name she's going by now, isn't really her name."

Christopher's dark brows pushed together in a frown.

"So, what is it then?"

I hesitated again. I'd only called her by name a handful of times and it was a conscious effort. It was going to be tough since I'd been calling her Gianna in my dreams for the better part of three years.

"I don't want to tell you her real name. If you hire her, I don't want you using it by mistake and spook her. Hell, even I have a rough time remembering to call her the new name."

"Fair enough. If she's trying to hide, I can see how a slip-up like that might cause her to bolt."

"Thanks for being cool about it. That's honestly the whole reason I came here tonight. I figured you'd appreciate a heads-up about why things may not add up during your interview with her."

"I'll do what I can for her, I promise. Just remember, secrets never stay hidden for long, Derek. If she is hiding something, you need to make sure you can handle the truth when it comes out."

"I know."

A quiet settled between us and we finished our Sambuca in silence. The last of the customers in the dining room filtered out and I could hear dishes banging around in the kitchen as the staff cleaned up for the night. When our glasses were empty, I stood to leave. Christopher came around the bar and slapped a hand on my shoulder.

"This *bella donna* must be something special for you to go through all of this trouble."

Christopher had no idea. Val could give Monica Bellucci a run for her money. She was captivating, so much so, I found myself paralyzed with want and desire at the mere sight of her. It was ridiculous, really. I'd fantasized about her so much over the past three years, it bordered on obsessive.

"She's fucking gorgeous, Chris. I've never known a more beautiful woman. She's in my head in ways I can't begin to explain. I've never felt like this before."

"*Merda*," he swore and shook his head. "There's going to be no dealing with Isabella. She's going to have a field day with this."

I groaned at the thought of my sister's likely interrogation.

"Don't I know it."

16

Val (Gianna)

It was a day for firsts. Things had been happening so fast, and I had a serious case of first day jitters. Everything was almost too good to be true, and I had to fight the urge to pinch myself. For the first time in a long time, I felt optimistic about the future. The stars were aligning and opportunities awaited me —and I had Derek Mills to thank for all of it.

After Derek called Christopher over a week ago, I'd interviewed and landed the job at Camilla's. Christopher and his wife, Isabella, seemed like decent enough people. Isabella was pleasant and extremely efficient, whereas Christopher's burliness and quick wit reminded me a lot of Teddy. Neither one of them asked too many questions, which I was thankful for, and we'd hit it off right away. I started work later that very same day. Now, I was a week into the job and was excited to get my first official week of pay and felt confident in my ability to afford the self-defense class beyond the free trial period. The first one was this morning.

Dressed in hand-me-down sweats and a tight-fitting tank, I

slipped into my Nikes and headed out with a feeling of excited anticipation. When I entered the room where the class was held, there were about a dozen other women sitting on a large mat in the center of the floor, doing various stretches. They looked like they knew what they were doing, which was intimidating. It meant I'd look all the more foolish if I failed. I looked around for the instructor, but it appeared as though he or she hadn't arrived yet. Following the lead of my classmates, I began to do some stretching of my own.

"Good morning, everyone! Who's ready to start kicking some ass?" asked a male voice. My head snapped up from my downward dog position I'd been in. Derek Mills stood in the front of the class. I hadn't realized *he* would be the instructor. "Most of you know the drill, but I'm going to be a little more thorough with explanations today since we have a new join. Ladies, please welcome Val." He pointed in my direction. All the women turned and murmured their greetings.

"Thank you," I said with a timid smile. It was daunting to learn I was the only new person in the class, but I didn't have much time to fret over it because Derek began speaking again.

"We're going to start with a quick warmup. I'll keep it simple today. Forty jumping jacks, run in place for two minutes, and eight squat thrusts. We'll do four reps of that combo." Unfolding the muscle-corded arms from across his broad chest, he walked over to a stereo system. Flipping a switch, the sounds of Maroon 5 filled the space. "Let's go on four. One. Two. Three. Four."

Like robots, we began jumping jacks in unison at his command. Derek did the exercises right along with us, and I couldn't help but admire his godlike appearance. The elastic band of his blue gym shorts rested securely around his hips, and his gray shirt was fitted, stretching tight across hard pectorals and bronzed biceps as he performed the routine.

Once we were through the warmup, Derek turned down the

music and faced the class. He didn't look like he broke a sweat, whereas I was huffing and puffing from the exertion.

"Ladies, please position yourself around the mat. I need a volunteer to help me demonstrate a new maneuver I'd like to teach you." A bunch of hands shot up so fast, I nearly snorted. Who wouldn't want to volunteer to be the student when the teacher looked like Derek Mills? "Ahhh, you ladies never disappoint. So many volunteers! But I think I'm going to break in the new girl today. What do you say, Val?"

"Me?" I questioned in surprise. "But I don't know how to do anything yet."

"That's exactly why I want you. I want to get rid of any preconceived notions you might have about self-defense. A lot of people think it involves nothing more than punches and kicks. However, I teach more than that, including how to anticipate an attack and how to avoid it. That's one of the things I want to teach today. You up for it?"

"Um... sure." I shrugged. "Why not?" I walked over to the middle of the mat, where he stood. Turning his attention to the class, he began to explain how to escape or defend a chokehold from the front.

"In this scenario, the attacker is trying to choke you, either pushing or knocking you backward. This attack needs to be countered quickly because you could hit your head if you fall while being pushed. In addition, if you land on the ground, you could have someone on top of you choking you."

I froze at his words, humiliation wrapping its slimy tentacles around my neck. Visions of myself, flat on my stomach on the kitchen floor, swirled in my subconscious until they became reality. I felt Ethan pounding into me from behind like a battering ram, relentless and unforgiving. Rooted to the spot, I was overcome by the visceral memories that tormented my dreams by night and cloaked me in shame by day.

Lost in a haze of these sordid memories, I completely tuned

out Derek's words. Because of that, I didn't anticipate his next move. When his hand reached up to wrap around my neck, his grip was soft and anything but violent. Nevertheless, the reaction he sparked from me was instant.

"No! Don't!"

Backing up, I instinctively slapped his hand away.

"Val, are you alright? I didn't mean—"

"I don't...I don't think I can do this. I appreciate the chance and the free trial but I have to go. This just isn't... it isn't for me."

I hurried to the side of the room to grab my things, completely aware of the sympathetic stares from the other women. They could stare all they want. They didn't know anything about me or about what I'd been through. Every last one of them could piss off for all I cared.

As I approached the doors that would take me back to my apartment, I heard Derek call out.

"Hang on! Wait! Let's talk about this."

I didn't stop moving. I just needed to get the hell out of there and go back to the safety of my apartment—where I could make sure the window latches were securely locked and the door was barricaded closed. I could barely breathe in the vast openness of the gym.

I need air.

That thought had me turning on my heel and heading in a different direction. Instead of exiting through the interior door that connected the apartment building to the gym, I headed for the main doors. I needed fresh, clean air before I suffocated.

When I stepped out onto the street, a crisp October breeze assaulted my senses and instantly cooled my overheated skin. Leaning against the exterior brick wall, I brought a hand to my chest, closed my eyes and began counting to ten. I inhaled and exhaled, my measured breaths calming the racing beats of my heart. I'd only made it to five when I heard Derek's hesitant voice.

"Val?" Slowly, I opened my eyes to meet his. Hazel irises the color of autumn stared back at me, the gold, green, and amber clouded with concern. "Just breathe. I think you're having a panic attack."

I closed my eyes again and continued to count.

Six. Seven. Eight. Nine. Ten.

Feeling relatively calmer, I lowered my hand down to my side and directed a measured stare at Derek.

"I'm sorry, Derek. I've been through..." I faltered and struggled to find the words. "I've been through some things. I can't explain—"

"You don't have to explain anything," he interrupted. "Many of the women in that room have been where you are. It's not my place to ask questions. Every single one of you has a reason for being in that class. That reason belongs to you and you alone. I'm sorry I made you uncomfortable. That wasn't my intent."

Natalia's words from long ago rang in my mind. *"There are other men out there—kind and good men—who wouldn't treat their wife this way."*

But I wasn't Gia anymore. I was Val—a broken shell of the woman I used to be before Ethan. Perhaps Derek was a kind and good man, but there was no way for me to know—and I sure as hell couldn't trust my judgment. Still, in my head, I knew Derek wasn't Ethan. It hadn't been Ethan's hand on my neck back there in the defense class but the hand of a man who was simply trying to help. I sighed and straightened.

"I know it wasn't your intent. I overreacted."

Relief showed plainly on his face.

"So, what do you say? Want to come back to class?"

My face flushed at the mere thought of going back into that room. Seeing all the sympathetic stares from the other women was just too embarrassing. It was as if they could see through to my soul and to all the ugliness of my past, questioning why I had stayed with my husband for so long.

I shook my head.

"I don't think so, Derek. Maybe I'll go back one day. I just don't think I'm ready."

He raked a hand through his hair and seemed to contemplate something.

"Look, you've got a lot of spark. I'm going to throw this out there for you to consider. I do personal training." My eyes widened and I began to shake my head again, but he held up his hand. "Hear me out. I teach the private self-defense lessons differently than I would a standard personal training session. They aren't one-on-one. I partner up with Hana, another trainer. I've found having another woman present helps put the trainee at ease. Hana and I demonstrate technique until the trainee is comfortable enough to jump in. We work together to figure out what your boundaries are."

Personal training?

I nearly laughed.

"That's a nice offer, but I'd never be able to afford personal training sessions."

"You'd get the same deal. The first month will be free. If you decide to go past that, we can negotiate a price that works for you. Remember, I'm the owner. I can do things like that," he added with a wink and flashed me a self-assured smile. He seemed sincere yet I found myself hesitating.

"You helped me find a job, and now you're offering me free, private self-defense classes. I don't want to sound unappreciative, but I can't help wondering what the catch is."

"No catch at all. New York is a tough crowd. We aren't really known for being the city of good neighbors, so I try to do my part in changing that bad rep by paying it forward now and again. Plus, I know I really messed up back there in the class. I shouldn't have pushed right away. Consider this my way of making it up to you."

He had me backed into a corner. I'd be foolish to pass up the offer yet I still felt uncertain.

"I don't have to do anything until I feel ready, right?"

His eyes softened, and a look of concern passed quickly over his features. Before I could decipher what that concern may have meant, it was replaced with a look of determination—as if I was a challenge he was prepared to meet head-on.

"Not until you're one hundred percent ready. There won't be any pressure. Scouts honor," he said, holding up three fingers. This time, I did laugh.

"Okay, boy scout. I'll try, but I'm not making any promises."

His smile was wide as he extended a hand to me.

"It's a deal then. See you tomorrow, say ten in the morning?"

"It's a deal."

17

Derek

I watched Val disappear through the entry door to her apartment building and felt like I had the weight of the world on my shoulders. If I had any questions about whether she was running from her husband, they were answered the minute she ran out of my defense class. She was, without a doubt, the victim of abuse. There was no other explanation.

I'd been teaching women's self-defense classes for nearly eight years. Every woman was different, but they all suffered long-lasting emotional effects. Through the years, I learned offering support to a survivor went well beyond teaching them physical defense maneuvers. It meant I had to be receptive and nonjudgmental about whatever symptoms of trauma they might have. I had to listen to when they were speaking and respond without judgment. I also had to be careful about asking too many questions, which could possibly cause the survivor to be afraid.

And most importantly, I'd learned that certain touches could trigger memories, comparable to PTSD, and be counterproductive to any defensive maneuver I was trying to teach. I knew better than to touch Val before knowing her triggers. I knew how important it was to discover things that could elicit a negative reaction before any physical contact. It was practically the number one fucking rule—never remind a survivor of any sort of unresolved trauma from their past.

Yet I did exactly that with Val.

I had purposely ignored the rules.

What kind of man did that make me?

I'm a selfish dick.

I wanted her close to me, and I'd put that above all else. I wanted to interact with her—to have her so near I'd be able to smell the scent of the shampoo she'd used that morning. I wanted to have my hands on her—on her shoulders, hips, and thighs—positioning her body in different defensive stances.

That didn't just make me selfish—it made me a sick fuck.

I thought back to what I was doing that may have provoked her adverse reaction. I'd had one hand on her arm, the other on her neck. Was she afraid to have her arms pinned? Or was it the chokehold that sent her reeling? I didn't know the answer but it was my job, as her personal defense trainer, to find out.

I shook my head, disgusted with myself, and went back to class. The questioning eyes of the other woman in the room met mine. They didn't voice their questions aloud—they knew better than to ask. They understood in ways I could only try to imagine. So, for the next hour, they followed my lead and we finished the class as scheduled.

Once the last of the women filtered out of the room, I went to my office, closed the door behind me, and sat down behind my desk. I had next week's schedule to prepare and a list of supplies that needed ordering. I moved the mouse to wake the computer, but before I could get to work, the screen on my cell phone lit up, catching my attention. I had three missed calls from my sister. That could only mean one thing—Christopher had finally spilled the beans about Val.

"Asshole barely held out for a week," I muttered.

Giving up on writing the schedule, I went over to the minibar in my office to make myself a cup of coffee. I would need caffeine to get through a conversation about Val with my sister, that much was certain. After adding a splash of cream to the dark roast, I returned to my desk. Rather than put off the inevitable any longer, I dialed Isabella's number and hit the send button. She answered after only two rings.

"Derek, I've been calling you all morning," she said by way of greeting.

"I teach classes in the morning. You know that."

"Hmm," she murmured. "So, how are things?"

"That's why you called me three times?" I countered.

"Well, no. I wanted to talk to you about the new girl, Val. I thought I'd let you know that she's working out really well. She's a fast learner."

I smiled to myself. She didn't call just to tell me that. My sister was fishing and I wasn't going to bite.

"That's really good to hear, Bells," I said, deliberately keeping my tone aloof.

"She had the menu memorized after only one shift, and she's always on time," Isabella went on. "Smart as a whip, that one. Where did you find her?"

I leaned back in my chair. Stretching an arm up to place a hand behind my head, I contemplated how long I was going to torment her.

"She lives in the building attached to The Mill."

"Which location? The one in Queens?" she probed. I couldn't help but smirk. What my sister really wanted to know was if Val lived near me.

"Yep."

"Ah, that's nice. Has she lived there long?"

"Not sure," I replied indifferently, prompting her to huff out an exasperated sigh.

"Oh, come on Derek! Are you going to make me beg? Spill it!"

"Spill what?" I asked innocently, barely containing my laughter.

"I can almost see that shit-eating grin of yours right now. You know what I'm talking about!" This time, I didn't hold back, laughing long and hard. When I finally quieted again, Isabella pouted. "I'm glad you find this funny. You used to tell me everything. Imagine my surprise when I found out you spoke to Christopher about her over a week ago, and I'd been left completely in the dark."

"Rat bastard couldn't keep his mouth shut for very long," I teased.

"Actually, it wasn't him, not really anyway. Julianna was working the dining room that night and she happened to mention you stopped in. When I asked Christopher why you were here... well, you know him. It didn't take much for him to tell me everything."

Yes, I knew Christopher—but I knew my sister even better. She was as stubborn as a mule. When she wanted something, there was no holding her back. I'd bet it took her less than thirty seconds to get Christopher to fold. He was always soft when it came to her.

"Honestly, Bells. There's not much to tell."

"Oh, now that's the biggest load of bullshit I've ever heard."

"It's a long story."

"Do I sound busy to you?"

"Okay, okay," I sighed. "I'll tell you everything I told Chris and you can be the judge."

I thought about the night I met Val in the courtyard of the hotel and how we talked about so much, yet hardly anything at all. The conversation had been easy and natural. So just as I did with Christopher, I went through the tale of how I met a beautiful runaway bride. However, I went into way more detail this time around because Isabella had twenty-seven questions for every one sentence. After forty-five minutes on the phone, my coffee cup was nearly empty, and she had been brought up to speed. I ended with what happened today in the self-defense class.

My sister gasped after I'd finished telling her everything.

"Oh, the poor girl! Whatever happened to her, it's important for her to know she's not alone. You know we'll keep an eye on her while she's working at the restaurant."

"I appreciate that."

My sister fell unusually silent for a long moment. I was about to ask her if she was still on the line when she finally spoke again.

"I feel like you've been looking for the right girl for as long as I can remember," she eventually said. There was no mistaking the consternation in my sister's voice.

"Maybe I finally found her. I just think our timing is off, that's all."

"Derek, how serious are you about Val?"

"Serious?" I paused just as I was bringing the coffee mug to my mouth to finish the last few drops. "What gave you the impression we were even together? We're just friends."

"Well, you and I know that won't be the case for long. She might not know it but I can tell you're really into her. It makes me nervous."

I blinked twice, not completely sure about what would make my sister so anxious.

"Why?"

"Because you tend to fall first and think later."

I rolled my eyes as understanding dawned. She was thinking about Cassandra, my last girlfriend. I'd fucked more woman than I could count in my lifetime, yet my sister wanted to zero in on the one woman who lasted more than a few weeks—and ended disastrously.

Cassandra was beautiful. She and I had hit it off really well in the beginning. I didn't fall for her per se, but we did get serious rather quickly. Two months into our relationship—and one Cavalier puppy named Maisie later—I realized she'd masterfully managed to hide how materialistic she was. She valued her designer purses above anything else, including me and the puppy who had a penchant for chewing overpriced leather bags. In the end, I kept the puppy, and she kept what was left of her Louis Vuitton collection.

"Look, this isn't like Cassandra. All she cared about was my bank account. I'm not sure what my relationship with her was. She was more in love with herself than me."

"And you didn't see that before deciding to get a dog with her?" she asked dryly.

"You love Maisie and you know it," I countered.

"She's adorable. Of course, I love her, but that's not my point."

"So, what is your point?"

"Look, Derek. I love you, and I'm not trying to give you a hard time. I'm just concerned. You're a good-looking guy, and you have money and a huge heart. You'll be an amazing catch for someone one day.

"Just not Val?"

My sister sighed, seeming to take a minute to collect her thoughts.

"I like Val, and she's a hard worker. She seems nice enough, but she clearly has some sort of past she's running from. She showed up to her interview with obviously dyed hair that looked like it was cropped short with kitchen shears. So far, she's worked three shifts at Camilla's, and not once did her clothes fit properly. To me, they look like stretched out hand-me-downs. And while none of that should matter on iota, it does when you combine her appearance with the way she behaves. She's always casting furtive glances at the door as if she expects the boogie man to come through it at any moment. If you come up on her unexpectedly, she startles easily. At the end of the night, when she counts her tips, she gets this strange look of excitement on her face—like she found the pot of gold at the end of a rainbow. I don't know… it's hard to explain without seeing it. She looks exhausted too. The bags under her eyes make me think the poor girl hasn't slept in weeks."

Knowing Isabella was never one to judge someone by their appearance made it hard for me to hear her describe the woman I only saw as beautiful, no matter how her hair or clothes looked. However, for my sister to say something, Val's struggles had to have been glaringly obvious, and I found myself momentarily speechless.

"What are you trying to say?"

"I'm saying you hardly know this girl. Anyone can see she's a bit of a train wreck—anyone except you, that is. I can't help but wondering… why her, Derek?"

I thought about Val's angelic smile—timid yet genuine and absolutely gorgeous. She didn't smile nearly enough and I wanted more than anything to rectify that. Then I thought about her laugh, and although I hadn't heard it recently, I could still pull it from memory. It was like warm honey pouring over me— thick, full-bodied, and sincere. And that shape… just the thought of her naked curves wrapped in my arms made for too many lonely nights, imagining what it would feel like to have her writhing in pleasure beneath me. She was practically a stranger, but I wanted her desperately in the most unexplainable ways.

"I don't know why, Bells—and she's not a train wreck. I know her better than you think. This is not just an infatuation. I…" I paused, hearing the defensiveness in my voice and adopted a softer tone. "No, you're right. I hardly know her, but at the same time, it's like we've known each other for years. I feel something for this girl. I've never connected with someone so quickly before. There's a spark between us I can't explain."

"I felt the same about Christopher. There was this

gravitational force, pulling us to the center until it felt like we were the only two people in the world. I get it, Derek—really, I do. But Christopher and I didn't come with baggage—unless, of course, you count his overbearing mother, who thinks she knows everything just because she's an Italian. I mean, really. She could drive anyone to drink. It's a miracle I don't go to bed with a bottle of Sambuca every night," she said with a laugh. I heard her release a long sigh, signaling that she had a lot more on her mind.

"Give it to me straight. What's really bugging you about my interest in Val?"

She huffed out a frustrated breath, and even though she wasn't right in front of me, I could picture her pinching the bridge of her nose like she always did when she was stressed.

"You're just like dad, Derek. When you love, you don't just love a little. You love with your whole heart. If you end up with Val, she'll be lucky to have you, but I think there's a lot about her you can't see from the outside. If she's an abuse survivor as we both suspect, you'd be wise to take things slow—no diving in headfirst with this one. For all you know, she may harbor extreme fears stemming from a bad experience. Think about what you know about Hana and all she went through. You've seen firsthand what catastrophic thinking looks like. That kind of mindset could lead Val to obsess over worst-case outcomes. I'm not saying that's going to happen with her, but I worry that she may unintentionally sabotage your relationship before it even starts. I don't want to see you get hurt in the process."

I frowned at my sister's assessment and pushed aside the nagging worry she could possibly be right. It may feel like she was constantly nosing into my business but she almost always gave sound advice.

"Are you trying to say I shouldn't pursue anything with her?"

"On the contrary, I don't think that at all. In fact, I think you absolutely should pursue her. If not, you'll be left wondering again—and you've already wondered about her for too many years. I just want to make sure you've thought it through. Who knows? Perhaps you're exactly what a girl like her needs. That spark you talked about? It's time to see if it was meant to turn into a flame."

18

Val (Gianna)

I absently spooned a bowl of lukewarm oatmeal and stared at the clock. I had two hours until my private training session. With each passing minute, my apprehension grew.

Not having much of an appetite, I dumped the contents of the bowl and went to get dressed. Throwing on the same sweats and tank top I'd only worn for a short time the day before, I gave myself a once over in the mirror. One thing was certain—I left much to be desired. My short hair was pulled into a pathetic little nub at the back of my head. One of these days I'd scrape together enough cash to get a proper haircut. The old clothes on my body didn't quite fit me right. They were too tight in some places, too baggy in others. Teddy's ex-wife was roughly my size —roughly being the keyword. While her shirts fit me across the shoulders, I was bustier, and everything pulled tight across the chest. Her hips were wider, which gave me a serious case of sag in the pants. It was no wonder I lacked any confidence—I looked like a ragamuffin.

I eyed up the cash tips I'd left on the bedside table the

night before and thought about the cute fitness clothing boutique three blocks away. My first week at Camilla's had gone remarkably well. While the tips weren't quite as good as the ones I'd received at Teddy's Tavern, I still managed to bring home three hundred last night. It was a start, and more than enough to get myself some new clothes for today.

I took in my appearance once again, then glanced back at the cash. I wouldn't need to spend it all, but perhaps a small splurge would make me feel better about the training session today. On impulse, I grabbed a few twenty-dollar bills and left the apartment before I could talk myself out of it.

WALKING into the gym felt completely different than it did the day before. The new workout clothes did wonders for my confidence. I was still nervous about what lay ahead, but the butterflies in my stomach had significantly calmed. I no longer compared them to a swarm of bees. I felt like a new woman, ready to conquer my first self-defense class.

Until I entered the training room.

Derek was already there, in the back of the room, talking quietly with a pretty Asian woman. I assumed she was the woman named Hana, who he mentioned the day before. They both looked in my direction when I cleared my throat.

"Here I am," I said with a timid shrug, laughing nervously. "Let's just hope today goes better than yesterday."

"I'm so glad you made it! Come on over and meet Hana, my training partner," Derek said. He was beaming, and if I wasn't mistaken, he also looked a little bit relieved.

Did he think I wouldn't show up?

If he had, I couldn't blame him. Up until the minute I walked through the door, I wasn't sure if I'd show up either.

The woman smiled warmly at me, then crossed the room to shake my hand.

"It's a pleasure to meet you."

"It's nice to meet you too, Hana." Her hand was small but the handshake was firm. Still, her tiny frame made me wonder how in the world she'd be able to defend herself against someone as tall and muscular as Derek.

"I was just talking to Derek about how to approach your sessions. Why don't we sit on the mats and we'll explain things? I thought it might be best if you knew what to expect before jumping right into watching Derek and me demonstrate."

"Sure, that sounds good."

The three of us moved to the center of the room and lowered down to the mat. Once seated comfortably, Derek began.

"I want to apologize again for yesterday. My defense classes have a sense of community. The people support and respect each other, so I tend to forget a newcomer hasn't had time to embrace that yet. I usually follow an order of steps, such as discovering a person's triggers before engaging in physical contact. I skipped ahead, and I'm very sorry."

I warmed to the sincerity in his voice. There was something about him I wasn't able to figure out. I wasn't sure if it was his friendliness, the way he looked, or a combination of both. I only knew I was drawn to him in an inexplicable way. I found his mere presence calming in ways I wasn't quite ready to confront.

"It's okay, Derek. Really. You don't need to apologize."

"Derek is the best. He taught me everything I know," Hana assured. "Self-defense training is not just about the physical act of learning how to protect yourself. We teach Krav Maga here. And yes, Krav Maga involves real kicking and hand-to-hand fighting. That's the core of self-defense, but I don't want you to be scared by that. Derek and I are here to teach you how to protect yourself from getting kicked and punched as well as how to use kicks and punches to deflect an attacker. If at any point you feel uncomfortable, all you have to do is say so, and we'll change course."

I nodded, reminding myself they were here to help me. Quitting before I even had a chance to learn anything would get me nowhere.

"Okay, I'll make sure to speak up this time. I won't run out like I did yesterday."

"I hope you don't, but if you need to, there's no judgment here. Our goal is to help you," she reiterated. "If you're ready, have a seat on one of the chairs against the wall. Derek and I will begin a basic demonstration."

Following her instructions, I stood and headed to the line of chairs as Derek and Hana positioned themselves in the center of the mat. Derek began to pace in a circle while Hana stood motionless.

"Krav Maga, when translated, means contact combat," he explained. "The technique has been proven to work in both military and in real-life situations. It also teaches you the psychological aspects of attacks, so you can be aware of threats and know how to defuse them before they happen."

Without warning, he reached out and grabbed Hana's neck from behind, but she was fast to react. She spun and was instantly free. I stared in awe, wishing I'd known how to do that so many times in the past.

"How did you do that?"

Derek smiled at my question.

"We'll show you. Slow motion this time, Hana. Let's walk it step-by-step." She moved back into position, and just like before, Derek's hands circled her neck. "With this particular attack, your defensive reaction needs to be quick. Hana, explain how you would get out of the choke."

"Using my shoulder, I'm going to lift my arm to dislodge his wrists from my throat. From there, I spin around and use my other hand to strike him in the center of the face. Most likely, the attacker won't be expecting it. That element of surprise dictates your next move. His natural body reactions will make him vulnerable to an attack to the groin or another attack to the face."

Her movements were slow and calculated, never actually making contact or causing harm to Derek in any way. It was hard to imagine their demonstration playing out in real life. As I narrowed my eyes and tried to envision it, Derek seemed to have read my mind.

"Very good, Hana. Why don't you go grab the protective gear, and we'll do this for real?" While she collected items from a cabinet in the corner, Derek turned to me. "You still with me?" I simply nodded. I didn't want to say more in case I chickened out when it was my turn. In reality, I was completely fascinated by what they were doing.

Derek and Hana sparred for the next twenty minutes, explaining everything they were doing for rest the of the training session. At times, I found it hard not to be distracted by Derek. The man was undeniably sexy but in an understated way, fit with well-defined muscles. As he stood in a fighting stance, it showed off his obvious physical prowess, which took up the entire room. He didn't seem to hold back when attacking Hana—at all—yet her tiny body somehow managed to kick his ass each and every time. It gave me confidence. Maybe—just maybe—I could actually do this one day.

As we neared the end of class, Hana turned to me.

"What do you think, Val? You ready to give it a shot?"

Caught by surprise, I blinked. I wasn't sure how to respond.

"Um, I suppose. Just no...no necks. I'm not ready for that."

I saw a look of dawning on Derek's face as if I'd given him some sort of insight. I couldn't process what it meant, as I was too distracted by nerves. I moved onto the mat and swallowed the lump that formed in my throat. Derek met me at the center and stopped when we were toe-to-toe. I could feel the heat from his exertion radiating off his body. His nearness sent my heart racing, causing blood to thrum loudly in my ears.

"Ahhh, Sparky, I don't think you're ready just yet," Derek said, snapping me back to reality. His voice was hushed—almost a whisper.

Did he just call me Sparky?

"Wh-what do you mean?" I stumbled, completely confused why I felt a blush creeping into my cheeks. I shook my head to clear it and focused on the lines of concern marring his features.

"I think the demonstration Hana and I gave you was enough for today. I promised you we'd go slow and I want to make sure I keep that promise. I don't want to spook you again by pushing you before you're truly ready."

Perhaps it was just my imagination, but I couldn't help but think there was a double meaning behind his words.

"Oh, I... I suppose."

"Maybe you can give it a go during the next session," he suggested and took a step back.

"Yeah, you're probably right. When do you want to meet next?"

"I teach the main self-defense class on Tuesdays and Thursdays. Let's meet on the off days—Monday, Wednesday, Friday. Same time work?"

I suppressed my disappointment at not seeing him for another forty-eight hours and gave myself a quick reprimand. Right now, I needed to focus on myself and learn how to stand on my own two feet. Getting all swoony over a man I barely knew was foolish and reckless.

"Yeah, that works. I'll see you Friday."

After collecting my things, I headed back to my apartment. On the way there, I thought of Natalia. I missed her more than I thought was imaginable. I wanted to talk to her and tell her about everything I was doing. I wanted to hear about the latest gossip from Teddy's Tavern and listen to her whine about

Teddy's latest grumblings. And more than anything—I wanted a friend.

My chest felt heavy. I planned to wait and only call her when I was sure it was safe, but I wondered if that day would ever come. Ethan was a madman, and I had to make sure my location stayed a secret. For all I knew, he managed to put a tap on her phone just like he had on ours. Or maybe he was tracing the location of incoming calls to her cell. I had no idea how far his capabilities and connections within the police department went —legal or illegal. That kind of technology was well out of my wheelhouse. Perhaps I was just paranoid, but I had to be cautious.

As I approached my apartment, I passed by the door of another tenant. There was box laying in front of their door—a delivery from a well-known online retailer. The sight of it caused my steps to slow as an idea slowly percolated in my mind.

That's it!

I finally figured out a way to contact Nat. I didn't just need to buy a pre-paid phone for me, I would need to get one for her as well. Newfound excitement overwhelmed me, and I ran the rest of the way to my apartment. Once inside, I quickly dumped my gym bag, grabbed my purse and headed back out the door. Splurging on a cab, I directed the cabbie to take me to the nearest telecommunications store.

Of course, as luck would have it, the store turned out to be only four blocks away.

I really need to get to know the area better.

I tossed a five-dollar bill at the driver, tried to ignore my irritation over the waste of cab fare, hurried out of the car, and anxiously went inside in search of a sales rep.

"Hello, can I help you, miss?" asked a pretty brunette with dark, almond-shaped eyes.

"Yes, actually, you can. I'd like to purchase two pre-paid cell phones please. One of them is for me, and the other is for a friend who lives out of town. Do you handle shipping here, or do I need to go to the post office?"

"We can do that for you here for a small fee," she replied. "All of our pre-paid phones are along that wall. Just pick out what you want and I can get it set up for you."

The world suddenly felt brighter. If all went well, I'd finally get to speak to my best friend again in just a matter of days.

I smiled broadly.

"Perfect."

19

Val (Gianna)

5 Weeks Later

I took a long swig from my water bottle, then tossed it in my gym bag. I had just completed my fifth week of self-defense classes with Derek and Hana and things were going relatively well—at least I thought they were. Any day where I didn't have flashbacks of the past was always a good one in my book. Today was one of those days. It took a few hard lessons, but I no longer had to watch Derek and Hana demonstrate before I felt comfortable trying something new. I took it head-on, listening to Hana's encouraging female voice and Derek's reassurances to master every defensive maneuver they threw at me. I felt good— stronger—both mentally and physically in ways I never had before.

As I was slipping my arms into the sleeves of a zip front sweatshirt, I glanced over at Derek. Hana had already left the room to go meet one of her other clients, so it was just him and me. Sweat made small strands of hair stick to his forehead. With his face still flushed from the effort put into my lesson, he grabbed a towel by the door and wiped the moisture from his face and neck.

When he stripped out of his t-shirt to pull on a hooded sweatshirt, I cast my eyes down and peered at him through lowered lashes, pretending like I didn't see the sculpted landscape of his chest and abdomen, the bronze color of his skin, or the lines of sinewy muscle in his arms. And his hands—hands that had touched me in more ways than one while he showed me different techniques during our training sessions. Although his touches were never inappropriate, he had awakened something inside me. If I wasn't aware of him before, I was now. With every passing lesson, I found myself way too cognizant of how mouthwatering, drop-dead gorgeous Derek Mills really was.

When he began to walk toward me, I busied myself with gathering my belongings, giving no indication he stirred feelings I didn't want to explore. I slung my bag over my shoulder and began to move past him.

"Leaving so soon, Sparky?"

I glanced up at him. I wasn't sure how I felt about the nickname he bestowed on me a few weeks prior. I only knew I felt little wings fluttering around my insides every time he said it.

"Shouldn't I be?"

"I guess so," he said with a shrug. "I just wanted to tell you something before you took off."

"Oh?"

"Yeah." He paused and eyed me in the most peculiar way. "Your determination to take instruction and learn is inspiring. You've come a long way in a very short time. You did really good today."

"Thanks."

He shifted his weight and cocked his head to one side.

"I've got to shoot over to the supplement supply shop to

replenish the protein powder for the smoothies. Want to come with me? It's only about a ten-minute walk."

Going outside still put me on edge and I only went out when absolutely necessary, and then only to places I was familiar with. I wondered if I'd ever get rid of the feeling of having to constantly look over my shoulder. I turned to look out the large floor-to-ceiling glass windows near the main entrance to the gym. It was broad daylight out and the streets were crowded with people. Knowing those things gave me a sense of security. Combined with my newfound confidence from the self-defense classes, I found myself smiling and nodding.

"Sure, why not?"

After securely locking my belongings in one of the gyms lockers, we walked out together. I made sure to keep ample distance between us, but on the crowded streets, touching was sometimes unavoidable, and his arm would occasionally brush mine. The mingling scent of sweat and his cologne billowed my way. It was intoxicating.

"Have you always lived in New York?" I asked, trying to ignore the heady smell.

"Born and raised. Brooklyn to be exact—Prospect Park area."

"I'm not familiar, but then again, I've only lived here for just shy of two months. I'm still trying to get to know the city," I admitted.

"I moved to Queens to be closer to the gym and to my parents. They had a house a couple of blocks over."

His voice sounded sad and I noticed his mention of his parents was past tense. I wanted to ask but didn't want to pry. Instead, I pressed my lips together and considered the surrounding area.

"This location is convenient," I observed. "Almost everything is within walking distance. I've been to many stores in the area to pick up essentials, but I haven't hit any of the restaurants yet. What do you recommend?"

"Delaney's if you want classic American bar food. Mario's if you want Italian, but don't tell Isabella I said that," he added with a wink. "There's also a good bakery on 31st that has a pretty kick-ass lunch menu. The Hatch has the best Manhattan clam chowder around, but that isn't really within walking distance. You'd have to head up to Flushing Bay for that. The Hatch does a really good dinner cruise too."

"A dinner cruise... hmmm. That could be fun. I've never been on a boat before."

"Really?" he asked, seeming genuinely surprised. He glanced down at me, and I could almost see the wheels spinning in his head. "Maybe I'll have to rectify that one day."

"Yeah, well..." I trailed off awkwardly. "Maybe one day. For now, I'll stick to the neighborhood restaurants. You told me who has the best food but what about coffee? Lattes are my guilty pleasure. There are chain places everywhere but I like to support local when I can."

"The best cup of coffee in the city is right here," he said, pointing to the maroon awning of a storefront about fifty feet ahead of us, with La Biga written in scrolling font. "It's family owned by the Gianfranco's. As big as New York is, I'm pretty sure everyone knows the family—especially Angelo, the founder. They have a few other locations in the city as well. Angelo's daughter and son-in-law run this one."

As we passed the front doors to the little coffee shop, I smelled the aroma of espresso and fresh pastries, and my stomach gave a low grumble, reminding me it was nearly lunchtime.

"I used to religiously drink coffee every morning. I feel like I haven't had a good cup in forever," I remarked.

"Do you want to grab a cup after I get these supplies ordered?"

"Oh, no. I didn't mean we had to...that is...I can't," I stuttered, thinking about my budget. I was doing okay, but every extra cent I had was being saved so I could pay back Teddy.

"Why not?"

"I don't have my wallet. It's back in my locker at the gym."

Derek laughed.

"It's only coffee. I can afford a few bucks. It'll be my treat."

"Oh, well...okay. If you insist," I said, albeit hesitantly. I really didn't want him to pay for my coffee, but I didn't have a reasonable excuse for saying no. Wallet or no wallet, the idea of explaining my very limited funds was awkward.

A few minutes later, we arrived at the supplement shop. Derek walked up to the customer service desk, placed his order, and was told it would be ready for him within the hour. The entire process took less than five minutes.

"Well, that was quick," I said as we walked out of the shop.

"That's why I like working with them. They're efficient and have a good product. I spent months searching for the right supplier. I needed a product I felt comfortable endorsing to my clients. Plant-based organic was a must, designed for people on the go, and formulated to fit their needs. I..." He stopped talking and gave me a sheepish grin. "Sorry. I'm probably boring the hell out of you. I geek out over shit like this."

"Not at all."

"You're lying," he teased with a wink. "It's okay though. We're just about to the coffee shop."

Entering La Biga, I was pleasantly surprised. The café was small, with a simple interior. The sound of espresso beans being ground and the voice of Frank Sinatra could be heard above the friendly chatter of the patrons. It was a quaint little place with multiple three-person tables and a craft coffee wall.

"This place is so charming!"

"Yeah, it kind of has that feeling of being home, you know? They have amazing pastries. Their *sfogliatella* is to die for."

"Their what?"

"*Sfogliatella*. Have you ever had it before?"

"Ah, no…can't say that I have," I said with a laugh, not even attempting to repeat back what he said.

"Oh, it's so good! I'm getting you one."

Once we ordered and received our drinks and pastries, we found an open table and sat down. I took a tentative sip of the tall, vanilla latte. I'd drink coffee in all its forms—flavored, black, with cream and sugar, extra foamy cappuccino, or poured over ice. Lattes were my weakness, but I didn't show prejudice as long as it was good—and this was fantastic. I sighed in appreciation over the first good cup I'd had in what seemed like forever. When I sampled the pastry, I nearly swooned. The melt-in-your-mouth, shell-shaped pastry was filled with some sort of orange-flavored ricotta and it really was to die for.

"Can I ask you something?"

"Maybe," I teased.

His lips twitched, but he didn't smile. Leaning back, he put his palms face down on the table.

"Feel free to slap me if I'm crossing a line."

I raised a brow. "Now, I'm afraid of what you want to ask."

His knee brushed mine under the table, and I quickly shifted away, pretending not to notice as I absently stirred the foamy top of my drink.

"I told you that your story is your business but I've never seen anyone go from being terrified to determined quite like you have. I'm trying to figure out your drive. If I understand it, maybe I can use it to help others in my group classes. What's your motivation for taking my classes?" His question was cautious but I could hear the innocent curiosity in it.

My breath stalled at the mere idea of Derek—or anyone else for that matter—finding out my motivations. If he knew what motivated me, he'd know about all the things Ethan did to me. I reached up to touch my throat—like Ethan's hand had—

shame wrapping around my neck like a boa constrictor, squeezing the life out of me. I shrugged, hoping the action would loosen the imaginative grip on my neck, struggling to find a simple explanation that wouldn't provoke further questioning.

"It's important I know how to defend myself. If I ever need to, that is. It's a big city. You never know what might be lurking in an ally," I said, keeping my tone even-keeled. It was a good enough explanation. I didn't need to make myself vulnerable, by saying anything more.

He nodded and sipped his café Americana while I nervously ripped my pastry into bite-size pieces over my plate.

"Why do you own a gym?" I asked, hoping to change the subject.

"Because I enjoy fitness," he responded matter-of-factly. "Believe it or not, I used to be a pretty chunky kid. The other kids in school picked on me a lot."

My eyes widened in surprise as I took in Derek's perfectly muscled shoulders that tapered down to a trim waistline. He looked perfect to me. In fact, everything about Derek was perfect —from the gentle way he looked at me to his patience teaching me in class. He was almost too perfect.

"I can't picture you as a chunky kid. I really find that hard to believe."

"It's no joke. Weight issues run in the family on my dad's side. I guess you could say I inherited the slower-than-average metabolism from him. My sister takes after my mom and is naturally thin. Still, she understood my struggle. She was a big motivator for me and helped out a lot. Her encouragement is why I started working out and eating better. I ended up going to college for physical therapy and worked at a gym part-time. After I graduated, I decided to venture into entrepreneurship rather than look for a job in my degree field, but New York is expensive—very expensive. Luckily for me, I was able to pull in a silent partner who believed in me. That's the guy I was meeting in Cincinnati when we first met."

"I remember," I murmured. I thought about how, even then, I was able to see the sharp contrasts between the stranger and my husband—Derek and his vulnerabilities versus Ethan and all of his arrogance.

"I understand the struggles of everyday people and I want to help them see their potential like I did. That was my focus when I started The Mill. I didn't want it to be all about bulking up or bodybuilding, although some clients are into that. I wanted The Mill to zero in on what it means to be healthy at all ages. We have programs for men, women, and children. We even have family programs where families can exercise together. I hired a nutritionist to consult with clients on diets that work for them. We began offering instructional classes, such as the self-defense class you took. I also brought on a full staff of personal trainers. When everything fell in line, I began considering expansion. Two years later, I opened my second location and recently added a third and fourth in other parts of the city."

"That amount of success is impressive for someone so young," I told him.

"How old do you think I am?" he asked with a laugh.

I flushed, hoping I wouldn't be too far off. I wasn't a very good judge of age.

"I don't know. Thirty maybe?"

"Close. I'm thirty-two. You? How old are you?"

"A woman never tells her age," I teased.

"Is that how it's going to be, Sparky?"

"You betcha. My lips are sealed," I said, emphasizing my words by pulling an imaginary zipper across my lips.

We talked for a close to an hour and by the time our coffee was finished, I didn't want to leave. It seemed as though he didn't either because we stayed long after that. I felt comfortable in his presence—at ease in a way I found difficult to grasp. Eventually, I shifted to signal I should get going. It was going on two in the afternoon and I was scheduled to work at four. If I wanted time to shower and change, I needed to get moving.

"I'm going to head back," I began. "I need to wash up and get ready for work."

Glancing at his watch, Derek nodded his agreement.

"Yeah. Those supplements were ready to go well over an hour ago. I'll walk you home then come back to grab them."

"You don't need to do that. No sense in going all the way back only to have to return this way for your order."

"It's not a big deal. Besides, I need to let Maisie out."

"Maisie?"

"Yeah, my pup. I normally stop home on my lunch hour to let her out but I ended up here with you instead. Her bladder is probably ready to burst," he joked.

He has a puppy? Of course, he does. And just when I thought he couldn't be any more perfect...

"Awww... I love puppies. Maybe I'll meet her one day, but not today. Seriously, Derek. No need to walk me back. Do what you need to do. I'll be fine."

Standing, Derek followed suit. He shoved his hands into the pockets of his gym shorts and rocked back on his heels.

"This was nice."

"Yeah, actually. It was," I agreed.

"Do it again? Maybe over dinner next time?"

If I wasn't mistaken, he seemed nervous. I realized I'd backed myself into a corner. The walls were closing in—his good looks, his warmth, the caring understanding, and thoughtfulness made a perfect square that was pressing in on me from all sides. He affected me in ways I never knew a man could. He always had—from the very first day we met. It was strange. By all normal standards, I barely knew him, yet my heart was singing a different tune, and I couldn't quite place it.

Until I could find the words on the tip of my tongue, I wasn't ready to act—far from it, actually.

I was broken—healing, but still broken.

Just under two months had passed since I'd left Ethan and I didn't know how to navigate my new terrain. The girl Derek met once upon a time—the girl with hopeful dreams and aspirations —was long gone. I didn't know how to get her back—deep down, I wasn't sure if I wanted her back. I was just starting to feel comfortable in this new skin and I needed time to sort out the new me before thinking about anything or anyone else. As much as I wanted to say yes to Derek, *I* needed to be my sole priority for a while.

Still, I couldn't help but wonder how different my life would have been had I met Derek before Ethan. Would I have been the woman Derek was searching for—the one who he once said he wanted to cherish? I didn't know, but I didn't want to believe our window of opportunity had closed. I only knew I couldn't step over that line right now... not yet. I needed more time.

Looking into those gorgeous hazel eyes, I focused on the tiny flecks of green that sparkled in anticipation. Reaching out, I touched his forearm, giving it a gentle squeeze, and the air began to fill with an affection neither of us dared to acknowledge. Bracing myself, I locked away my emotions and smiled.

"Ask me again in six months, Derek."

When I turned to walk away, I felt hopeful for the future. With every step I took toward home, my smile grew bigger— bigger than it had been in a long, long time.

20

Derek

Six months. That's how long I had to wait.

It was all I could think about as I sat on the couch with Maisie watching reruns of *Seinfeld*. I felt restless with impatience but understood why Val was putting me off. She needed to find herself again. I respected that, and I would wait for her.

She was worth it.

After all, I'd unknowingly been waiting three years for her. Hell, at times I wonder if I'd been waiting for her my whole life. Another six months was nothing. I'd fallen into her so quickly, wanting that easy, casual banter again—that connection and chemistry we'd shared on the very first day we met. All the missing pieces seemed to lock into place whenever we were together. The attraction shivered across the surface of every one of our conversations. I knew she felt it as well. I just had to make her see it. Whatever she was running from, she didn't have to run or be afraid with me. I'd keep her safe. And when she was ready,

I'd be there. Until then, I vowed to use every minute I had to earn her trust.

My cell phone buzzed in my pocket and I fished it out. Ryder Malone's name and number lit up the screen. I hadn't spoken with my friend and silent partner in a few weeks. I was sure he was calling to check on how things were going at the newest location we'd opened.

"Hey, Ryder."

"Derek! I haven't talked to you in a while. I wanted to check in on New York's most eligible bachelor. Any new, juicy articles published about you lately?"

"Don't even joke about it, man. If you sic that reporter on me ever again..." I warned.

Ryder laughed.

"I'm just yanking your chain. How are things going with The Mill Brooklyn?"

"Pretty good. I stopped in there a couple of days ago. Alyssa already has the place running like a well-oiled machine. She was a great hire." I paused, noticing the music and people chattering in the background for the first time. "Where are you? It sounds like a party."

"Vegas for a little R and R. I'm chilling by the pool at the moment. Happy hour is winding down, so I decided to give you a buzz. I honestly just realized the time difference. I hope I didn't call too late."

"No, it's cool. It's barely nine o'clock here."

"Good, good. You know me. Even in Vegas, I can't shut off work completely. I wanted to run through some numbers with you." He ran through cost scenarios and projections for the Brooklyn gym, but I was barely listening to him. I was too distracted, thinking of ways I could slowly convince Val to give me a chance—to give us a chance. So, when I showed little enthusiasm over the fantastic revenue stream we were experiencing, Ryder called me out on my lack of focus.

"Dude, I feel like you're barely listening. Did someone drop a barbell on your head?"

I laughed.

"Sorry, man. I've got some stuff on my mind. I didn't mean for it to be so obvious."

"Seriously. What's up? You sound really...I don't know... off."

"Do you remember when I came out to Cinci to see you a few years back? We were going over the contracts for The Mill and planning the grand opening."

"Sure, I remember."

"When I was there, I met this chick..." I stopped short, knowing my description was all wrong. Val was not just some random chick. "I met this woman at the hotel where I was staying."

"It's always a girl with you, isn't it?" he joked.

"Yeah, but this one is different. She moved to New York a couple of months ago and just so happens to live in the building across the street from me."

Ryder snorted.

"Let me guess—you're going to say it's fate or some other nonsense like that."

"Isn't it? I mean, what are the odds?"

"Pretty slim, I guess. Did you ask her out?"

"Yeah, but she's been through some shit."

"My friend, they've all been through some shit. And if they haven't been, they're bound to put *you* through some shit. I'm convinced all women have a little bit of crazy in them."

I laughed and thought about the long line of psychotic women Ryder had dated. He and I had been college roommates so I was there for every girl he paraded through our dorm room. Sometimes I wondered if it was really the women who had the issues, or if it was Ryder's wandering eye that drove them to madness.

"This girl ain't crazy," I assured.

"So what's the problem then?"

"Whatever she's been through is making her cautious. I asked her out to dinner earlier today. She told me to ask her again in six months."

"Whoa! Back up. If I'm not mistaken, that sounds an awful lot like you were moved to the 'I think it's better if we're just friends' zone, if you know what I mean."

I could see why Ryder thought that, but he didn't know about the connection I had with Val. The two of us weren't meant to be friends—there was way too much chemistry that couldn't be ignored.

"You're wrong. I'm telling you...there's just something about her."

"Well, then I suppose you have six months to win her over."

"And I will," I vowed. "So, anyway, enough about me. Let's get back to why you called. I swear I'll pay attention this time."

Changing topics, Ryder and I talked shop for the next thirty minutes. After I hung up, I glanced down at Maisie and ruffled her ears.

"What do you say, Miss Maisie? Ryder said I need to win over the girl. Want to help?" Maisie wagged her tail and scooched herself up so her paws were on my chest. When she gave a light lick to my face, I laughed. "I'll take that as a yes."

I only had one problem—I didn't know where to begin. I thought about everything I knew to be true about Val. I remembered her saying she liked daisies. Then again, she'd also said her husband used to buy them for her. She didn't need to be reminded of that asshole. It was probably best to skip flowers altogether.

I knew she liked vanilla lattes, and I got the impression she didn't treat herself to them very often. Perhaps I could start there. Bringing her coffee was a thoughtful gesture and not something that should make her feel pressured. Still, that didn't seem like it would be enough.

Leaning over, I opened the drawer of the end table next to the sofa and pulled out a piece of jewelry that I hadn't looked at in a long while—the earring lost by a runaway bride so many years ago. Holding it between my thumb and forefinger, I twisted it around and thought about the many times I'd stared at it, wondering what happened to the girl who got away. Now that she was back, I had to figure out how to keep her so I didn't lose her again.

Letting out a frustrated breath, I placed the earring back in the drawer, still not sure why I'd kept it all of this time. Just as I was about to close the drawer, a tattered paperback copy of *Awaken the Giant Within* by Tony Robbins caught my eye. I pulled it out and fanned the pages. I stopped at the dedication page and read the first couple of lines.

"Dedicated to the unlimited power that lies sleeping with you. Let it slumber no more."

I'D READ the book when I was thinking about venturing into entrepreneurship. I found Robbins to be a powerful communicator and a great authority on the subject of personal success. I had also found his creative psychology to be beneficial in more ways than one. He was a great life coach, and I often quoted him when trying to motivate clients at the gym who struggled with self-confidence.

I wondered if there was anything in the book that could help me with Val. She'd come a long way in her training sessions, but I could still see how she lacked confidence in her ability. I wanted her to see the spark that I saw—that burning fire deep in her belly that believed she was strong, beautiful, and capable.

In order to get her to see all the amazing things I did, I had to figure out what made her tick. I tapped my thumb against the cover of the book as I racked my brain in search of ideas. I quickly realized that I shouldn't be focusing on what I *did* know about her, but rather what I didn't know. What was her favorite color? What was her favorite movie or book? What did she like to do in her free time? The questions were endless. Knowing those little details would go a long way as I worked to earn her trust.

And her heart.

Maisie jumped down from her perch on the couch, went over to the front door, and began to scratch at it.

"Gotta go out, girl?"

Standing up, I grabbed a beer from the fridge, cracked it open, and met her at the door. Once her leash and harness were secure, I allowed her to lead the way to the elevator that would take us to the roof.

While Maisie sniffed around the fenced-in grassy patch for the perfect place to do her business, I took a seat on one of the Adirondack chairs available for tenants to use on nights such as these. The air was unusually warm for early November, but the slight breeze made for a perfect night outdoors. If the forecast was any indication, it was probably the last warm night of the year. Snow would be moving in soon, along with wind that would make the rooftop patio a miserable place to be.

Stretching my legs out, I took a long swig of the Five Boroughs hoppy lager. I looked out over the East River, past the Queensboro Bridge to the Empire State Building and the Chrysler Building. The skyline was alive with lights from the city that never sleeps, illuminating the deep purples and shades of blue left behind by the setting sun. The landscape made me think about the tourists who came to the Big Apple from all over the world. Val was still relatively new to the area. I wondered how far she'd ventured.

Perhaps she'd be interested in sightseeing?

We could explore the rich culture and history of the city, slowly getting to know each other while staying within the boundaries she set. Greenwich was always a fun place to visit. I wondered if she'd enjoy discovering the streets where Simon and Garfunkel made a name for themselves. Then there were the holidays to consider. Christmas in New York was like no place else. Would she enjoy seeing Bloomingdale's window displays or the tree in Rockefeller Center? Did she ice skate? Hell, I didn't even know if she liked Christmas.

I ran a frustrated hand through my hair just as Maisie made her way back to me, sitting down near my feet. Leaning down to scratch her behind her ears, she looked up at me with big black eyes, her tail wagging happily from my simple gesture of affection. She reminded me little things could make a big difference.

I was overthinking all this.

I was a simple guy with an uncomplicated life. I needed to make uncomplicated plans—and taking Val for a walk in Central Park with Maisie was as simple as it got. Pulling my phone from my pocket, I planned to call Val and see if she wanted to do exactly that this upcoming weekend. However, as I stared at the numbers on the screen, another realization came over me.

I didn't even have her damn phone number.

I looked at Maisie and frowned.

"Well, girl… it looks like we really have our work cut out for us."

PART V

BORN AGAIN

21

Ethan

Cincinnati, Ohio
Six Months Later

I gripped the wooden paddle that had once given me so much pleasure and stared down at the bloodied naked body of my beautiful dominatrix. Cynthia's lifeless body laid still, the blood from her wounds staining the pristine, white carpet of my West 4th Street condo.

She wasn't dead—at least not yet.

"It's your fault," I spat out. "You just had to ask too many questions."

"What happened to your wife, Ethan? Nobody has seen her in months. The Commissioner asked me about her. Why would he want to know where she is?"

Fuck her—which I did—and fuck the inept, my-daddy-got-me-the-job Police Commissioner Greyson. Why did they care about where Gianna was? Especially Cynthia. She was my mistress and should have no interest in my girl.

So many damned questions…
Now here we were.
I shook my head.
It was such a shame. I thought I'd have a little more time with this one.

The floral smell of Chantilly still lingered in the air as I tossed the paddle on the floor next to Cynthia's head. The room was finally peacefully silent, a stark contrast to what it had been only moments before. Of course, she had screamed—they all screamed.

I shouldn't relish in it.

But I did—just like I reveled in her pain.

It didn't matter how loud she cried out for help. Nobody could have possibly heard her as long as we were in this room. My mother made sure of that many years ago when we'd moved here after that unfortunate incident with Jenny in Salt Lake City. Looking around at the white, soundproof walls, I could almost picture my mother standing by the door, shaking her finger at me.

"Cry and scream all you want, my boy. Nobody will hear you. Only He can hear."

Then she would go and I would be alone.

When I first came to the White Room, I'd been eighteen years old. Long before spending time here, my mother tried to teach me the holy scriptures, but I'd been much too young and too head strong to truly understand. Societal influences were powerful—just as the lust I had for sweet, young Jenny had been powerful.

"That whosoever looketh on a woman to lust after her hath committed adultery with her already in his heart," I warned my mother, reciting from the Gospel of Matthew just as she had taught me. The lust-filled temptations I'd had for Jenny were potent and my resistance was weak. But my mother didn't heed my warnings. Instead, she advised me to avoid the girl and focus on my lessons.

But I didn't listen—it had already been too late. Lust had wrapped a leash around my neck, leading me to take what I had desperately wanted.

Then young Jenny died.

Her parents sought vengeance for the unknown man who had defiled and killed their sixteen-year-old daughter. I had wanted to repent and turn myself in to the authorities, but my mother wouldn't let me. Instead, we moved from our home in Salt Lake City and started anew in Cincinnati. She said my desires were the result of corruption that comes at all levels of society—it was a behavioral consequence of power and greed. The only way to escape it and fully embrace Him would be in the solidarity of the White Room.

So that's where she sent me.

Two years after stepping into the White Room for the first time, I finally began to understand my mothers' lessons, and I was never truly alone again. He was always with me in the windowless room where everything was white. A white comforter covered the white double mattress. A white dresser with drawers full of white sheets stood in the corner, with holy books wrapped in white dust jackets lined in a neat row on top of it. There were white lamps with bright, white lights.

So bright. All. The. Fucking. Time.

White carpet.

White frames that held no pictures hanging on the walls.

White, rubber chain links and shackles.

My mother loved white. She said it symbolized the purity and innocence she had been robbed of. The only thing marring all the white brilliance now was Cynthia's body.

"Oh, Cynthia, Mother will not be pleased."

I took one final glance at her mutilated face before closing the white door. I should kill her now and be done with it, but I couldn't just yet. I wasn't prepared. Had I known she was going to raise problems today, I would have planned things much differently. Now, I had to make a trip to Avondale to get what I needed. I would just have to hurry and make sure I was back before she woke up.

I walked down the hallway toward the front door. After lacing up a pair of Doc Martens, I grabbed my keys off the little table by the door and made my way to the elevator that would take me down to the lobby. When the metal elevator doors opened, I came face to face with Mr. Broderick, a building resident who lived on the second floor. He squinted at me for a moment before flashing a wide grin that revealed yellowing teeth. His eyebrows were bushy, and his nose hairs were in need of trimming, shooting out at weird angles from his nostrils. Disgusting. Someone needed to take him down the men's hygiene aisle at Kroger's and introduce him to Braun.

"Good evening, Ethan! Such a pleasant night out. Headed out to enjoy it?"

I really hated this guy.

He lived a boring life with his boring wife and boring fucking cat. He was practically blind and shouldn't have been outside after dark. He should have been indoors watching boring sitcoms, while sitting on what I was sure to be a boring couch.

But no, he just had to be blocking my path. I couldn't afford to waste time with his stupid chatter tonight. I wanted to shove him out of my way but I knew what my mother would say. *"Be steadfast, my boy. Be steadfast. Never show them who you really are. Your true self should only be shared with He who is Most High."*

I nodded and smiled politely at Mr. Broderick.

"Yes, sir! It is a nice night," I replied, using the voice I reserved for convincing people I was just like their favorite nephew. "I'm headed out to get a cone of fresh custard and maybe take a walk along the River." Like I would ever really walk along the Ohio River for fun. It was crowded with college kids who smoked too much weed while wearing their Mumford and Sons t-shirts. Fifteen years ago, it was Dave Matthews Band. Same shit, different name.

"I heard there was some trouble on the water a few nights back. You be careful now, son," Mr. Broderick warned.

I hated when he called me that. I was nobody's son.

"Sure thing, Mr. Broderick." I made to move past him, but he kept talking. There were sixty-four people living in this building, and somehow, I managed to avoid talking to all of them —except him.

"How's your mother doing? I haven't seen her in a while."

Of course, he hadn't seen her. She died over nine years ago— a fact Mr. Broderick never seemed to remember. *"Be steadfast, my boy. Be steadfast."*

"She's good," I lied, not wanting to explain her death to him for the forty-seventh time. "I have to run now, Mr. Broderick. I'll make sure to tell her you said hello." Not wasting any more time, I hurried past him toward the parking garage.

The drive to Avondale was short and uneventful. The gentle, arpeggiated harmonies of Beethoven's *Moonlight Sonata* soothed my agitation along the way. When I arrived at the apartment, I didn't even yell at the homeless man who was lying on the front steps—again. I didn't have time to waste with him either.

I went inside and grabbed what I needed. Disposing of Cynthia's body wouldn't be too difficult. I had an oversized, heavy-duty, duffle bag on wheels similar to the one's hockey players used for their equipment. Positioned the right way, Cynthia was just small enough to fit inside.

It was unfortunate she would have to die this way, but I knew the world would be better with one less lustful whore. Even if it wasn't His will, I took an oath when I became a police officer.

"On my honor, I will never betray my integrity, my character

*or the public trust. I will always have the courage to hold myself
and others accountable for our actions..."*

And hold her accountable I would.

After stuffing plastic sheeting, duct tape, and four
cinderblocks into the bag, I grabbed the long-handled iron I kept
in the closet behind the statue of the Blessed Mother and headed
back out to my car. Opening the trunk, I placed the large bag
inside. I kept the iron, one of my most prized possessions, with
me as I climbed back into the BMW.

Starting the ignition, I glanced down at the head of the
branding iron, resting across my lap. The chthonic serpent coiled
around the Tree of Knowledge starred back at me, a symbol of
sin and lust. Normally I would have used an industrial-strength
blow torch to heat the emblem at the tip, but lugging the bulky
contraption through the building of my condo might draw
attention. The gas range on my stove would have to do for today.
Cynthia, like all the rest, would only die after she was branded as
the whore she really was.

As I pulled away from the curb, my hands shook with
anticipation. I couldn't wait to press the hot iron on the skin
between Cynthia's navel and public bone, inhale the smell of
burning flesh covering her womb, and watch as she woke to the
excruciating pain.

That was the best part.

I grew hard thinking about the moment she comprehended
what was happening to her—when she finally realized she was
the reason for the fall of man. I'd seen it so many times before.

The understanding.

The fear.

The horror.

The shock of pain would wake her from unconsciousness just
long enough for me to choke the life from her whoring body,
then she'd lie with the fish at the bottom of the Ohio River. With

any luck, she'd be swept down to the waters of the Mississippi before summer came.

So many questions... she shouldn't have asked so many questions.

She should have been more like Gianna, and this wouldn't have happened. My girl wouldn't have pushed me like Cynthia did. My girl was soft and complacent, submissive in all the right ways. She had even stopped getting mad at me after I hit her. She understood my power. She knew I didn't mean to hurt her. My girl loved me—and I missed my girl. Oh, how I missed her.

She thought I didn't know where she was. Right. As if I would ever actually lose track of her. She thought she'd been so clever, but I'd had eyes on her almost from the moment she left for New York thanks to Teddy. Gianna had put too much faith in him. Her trusted ex-boss spilled his guts to Natalia, which made finding her all too easy.

"Gia is safe. She didn't want me to tell you but I know you'll worry. I'm taking her to New York. I've got a friend there who can help her out with an apartment and keep an eye on her."

Blah, blah, blah.

Natalia was a flake. Putting a tap on her phone had been a cakewalk. She never noticed because she never paid attention to anything. She was too busy putting hashtags all over social media.

Hashtag ridiculous.

While I'd never really paid much attention to her mundane conversations, I was glad I'd had the foresight to put the tap in place. It was worth listening to years of her meaningless ramblings because I eventually heard the conversation that mattered most—the one between her and Teddy that told me where to find my girl. All I had to do was track down one Oscar Tomasz, then finding Gianna had been simple.

Since then, I'd taken a few weekend trips to New York to

check on her. I'd immediately hated what she did to her hair. My girl used to have beautiful golden locks—but now? Now, she looked like a dirty little tomboy.

Still, I needed to see her again soon. Everything had been all wrong ever since the day she left. I tried to stay focused, to be steadfast as my mother taught me to be, but nothing felt right. I needed her with me again, so I could find balance.

In time, I would have her again. Gianna just needed to get over this phase. My girl knew we belonged together. This was just a fight. All couples have them. In the end, she couldn't resist me. She'd be back with me soon enough, and all would be okay again.

This, too, shall pass.

In no time at all, I was back on West 4th, and parking the BMW in my reserved space in the parking garage. Climbing out of the car, I decided to leave the bag in the trunk for the time being. I would return for it later.

Right now, all I needed was the iron.

The late hour meant the building was relatively quiet and I made it to my condo without seeing a single soul. Good. I didn't need any more run-ins with the Mr. Broderick's of the world.

After inserting my key into the lock, I opened the door and immediately noticed something was off. The tablecloth on the dining room table was uneven. It had shifted, almost as if someone had accidentally brushed against it. There was a small smudge near the corner—a reddish-brown stain—on the pristine, white linen.

Dried blood.

I glanced down the hallway. The white door for the White Room was open.

I thought I had closed it.

No, I had definitely closed it.

Rushing down the hall, I scrambled into the room.

Bloodstains remained on the white carpet, smearing across the nylon fibers, signaling someone had crawled across it—and Cynthia was gone.

22

Val (Gianna)

Queens, New York

With my eyes wide and mouth in the shape of an O, I leaned closer to the bathroom mirror and slowly applied black mascara root to tip. When I was finished, I stood up straight, blinked a few times, then sighed.

"Oh my God, Nat! What am I doing? I must be crazy—I am so not ready for this."

Exasperated, I tossed the mascara back into my makeup bag.

"You told Derek to ask you again in six months. I think it's romantic he remembered," Natalia said through the speaker of the phone propped up on the bathroom counter.

"I don't need romance. I thought I had that once and look where it got me."

"That was a long time ago. Besides, you already said yes. You can't bail on the guy now. You even bought a new outfit for the occasion. You've got this, girl."

"I know, and honestly, I don't want to bail. I'm just nervous, you know? What if I'm not ready? I mean, if he tries to kiss me or..." I trailed off, not wanting to let on how worried I was about freezing up during a moment of intimacy. Just the mere thought of taking that sort of plunge again made me anxious.

"Derek is not Ethan. You know that."

"I know, but..."

"No buts!" Natalia scolded. "Let's go through this again. Tell me the reasons for finally saying yes to a dinner with Derek."

"It was all the dog's fault. He tied a note to her collar, asking me out on a date. How could I possibly say no to Maisie's adorable puppy eyes?"

Natalia chuckled.

"He's definitely creative—I'll give him that much—but I'm serious. Why did you finally say yes?"

Thinking about all the tiny, yet significant, things Derek did, I smiled and bit my lower lip.

"He brought me vanilla lattes from La Biga because he just so happened to have walked by there—almost every single day," I added with a laugh. "It's too bad they aren't a publicly-traded company. I would have bought stock. His purchases alone would have made me rich!"

"Okay, what else?"

"He showed me all around the city so I could feel more comfortable with the area. He sends me motivational text messages on the mornings I'm scheduled to train with him."

"And?" she pushed.

I recalled the many times I caught him staring at me in appreciation when he thought I wasn't paying attention. The way he looked at me made me feel whole and incredibly feminine. It always made me smile, but I didn't need to tell Natalia all that. I knew where she was going with this.

"Look, Nat. I get what you're trying to do here. You have to understand the way I see things. Yes, I'm stronger and more confident now—more so than I've ever been before in my life, but I can't help but wonder if the coffee Derek bought for me so different from the daisies Ethan used to buy me? I allowed myself to be wooed once before, and it turned out to be a disaster. I know Derek is nothing like Ethan, but I'm allowed to be worried about the possibility of things going terribly wrong."

"And it might. Who knows? Life happens. But at least you're going into the evening, knowing you weren't pressured by some crazy, possessive guy. Derek respected your boundaries and honored your wishes about taking things slow. Don't forget that."

"What if he asks questions about my past?"

"Just tell him. What happened isn't your fault."

"It's more than that and you know it. For crying out loud, I can just hear myself now. Hi, my name is really Gia, not Val. And by the way, I'm legally married to a—"

"Stop over analyzing this. If he's worth it, he'll understand everything when you're ready to tell him. For tonight, go have fun. You deserve this, Gia." She paused and giggled. "Or should I say—Val?"

"Not funny, Nat. Not funny at all. I'm going to hang up now. He should be here any minute."

"Call me tomorrow. I want all the deets."

"I can't call tomorrow. I'm almost out of pre-paid minutes this month. It will have to wait until next week."

Now it was her turn to sigh.

"I'm so tired of this. I miss you. I wish I could come see you."

"Me too, Nat, me too. I just… I just don't think it's safe yet."

"I know," she agreed sadly. "I love you. Have a good time tonight."

"Love you, too."

I gave myself one last look before leaving the bathroom. Having finally spent money on a proper haircut and color, I fashioned the short style with soft beach waves and pinned it up loosely on the sides with two tiny clips. It was still dyed a dark brown but I'd asked the stylist to add a few lowlights to break up the solid. The overall look had grown on me and I didn't think I'd ever go back to blonde again.

I adjusted the straps of the burgundy silk tank top I'd purchased the day before. It showed off strong, toned arms from months of training with Derek and Hana. Skinny black ankle pants followed the long line down my legs to a pair of nude pumps that completed the outfit. I was satisfied with my appearance, and after spritzing a small amount of body spray over my neck and shoulders, I felt extremely feminine for the first time in a very long time. My reflection seemed to radiate confidence—and I didn't think it was the least bit arrogant to say I looked sexy as hell.

I smiled at my reflection.

"I'm ready for this."

Tossing my lipstick into my clutch purse, I snapped it closed just as a knock sounded at the door. I headed out to the family room and peered through the peephole to see Derek on the other side. Instantly, the bravado I had in the mirror just moments ago was gone, and my palms began to sweat. As I unbolted the door and lifted the wooden plank, I questioned why I was so nervous. I'd been training with Derek for months. Hardly a day went by when I didn't see him. Now, it felt like I didn't know him at all.

Wiping my sweaty palms on my pants, I opened the door and was greeted by Derek's huge smile. He wore dark blue jeans and a white button-up shirt that seemed tailor-made for him. The way it was cut, there was no disguising the slopes and valleys of the muscle underneath. One finger held a black sport coat slung over his right shoulder, while the opposite hand rested half inside his pants pocket. Trying not to gawk at his perfectly tapered waist, I brought my gaze up to his hard jaw and full lips, before moving to meet the bright hazel eyes staring down at me.

Instantly, my apprehension faded away. Nat was right, I

deserved this. We'd been dancing around this moment for months. I was more than ready.

"Hey, Sparky," he greeted.

Just those two little words sent my heart fluttering.

"I'm used to seeing you in gym gear. You clean up nice, Derek."

"I could say the same about you, but you do it better. Much better." He removed his hand from his pocket and reached for mine. Raising it to his lips, his smile broadened even more. "You look beautiful."

"Thank you," I appreciated with a nervous laugh. My face warmed until it felt like it was on fire—not from embarrassment, but from the heat of his gaze. I tucked a loose hair behind my ear just to have something to do.

"You ready to go?" he asked, extending his arm to me.

"Yeah, let me just grab a sweater." I grabbed a black cardigan hanging in the small closet behind the front door, then turned back to loop my hand around the crook of his elbow. Stepping through the front doors of the building onto the city streets, I glanced up at Derek curiously. "Where are we going?"

"Oh you're going to be one of those types," he teased and rolled his eyes.

"Those types? What's that supposed to mean?"

He laughed and shook his head, then surprised me by poking me lightly in the ribs.

"It means you're the type of person who can't just go with the flow."

"That's not my style. I like to know what's coming, that's all," I murmured. We stopped at a crosswalk, and I felt him looking down at me.

"I can tell. Trust me, I've waited a long time to properly take you out. Do you honestly think I'd screw it up?"

"Well, no. It's just that—"

"You'll like where I'm taking you. In my opinion,

McNuggets are completely underrated."

"McNuggets!" I laughed, the sound coming straight from my belly, full and throaty. "You are not taking me to McDonald's!" When his face remained impassive, my eyes widened, and I sobered. "Or are you?"

"That depends."

"On what?"

"If taking you to McDonald's means you'll laugh like that again, I'll call and cancel the dinner cruise reservations. I like hearing you laugh, Sparky. You should do it more often."

Not sure what to say about his compliment, I chose to back up and zero in on one point. "A dinner cruise?"

"If that's okay with you. We're having a warm spring, so I thought I'd take advantage of the nice weather. I mean, you did once tell me you thought going on a boat would be fun."

"I did, but that was over six months ago. I didn't expect you to remember."

He took my hand, brought it up to press against his heart, and leaned in close to my ear. My body tensed with awareness.

"There's not much, if anything, I'd forget about you," he whispered. He ran his nose along my cheek, and my breath hitched at the skin-to-skin contact.

I turned my head until there was barely an inch between our mouths. He cupped my face and used one finger to trace my lower lip. I didn't know how it happened, but our relationship went from moving at a snail's pace to sprinting to the finish line at a marathon in two seconds flat. I needed to put the brakes on.

"Derek…" I began.

"Don't worry. I'm not going to kiss you… yet. When I finally get to taste that pretty little mouth of yours, we won't be standing on a street corner." My mouth dropped open, but no words came out. I was rendered completely speechless. Derek laughed and tugged at my hand. "Our Uber just pulled up. Climb in, Sparky. I've got a whole night planned."

23

Derek

The patio for The Hatch was packed with people when we arrived. I was thankful I'd booked a dinner cruise rather than a table on the water at the infamous restaurant. For many New Yorkers, the city was at her best in the summer. The season called for evenings spent on rooftop bars and beaches. Gothamites worked hard and endured the long winters in order to make the most of the warmer months. If those warmer months came early, you could expect anything along the shoreline to be hopping.

Still, despite the crowd surge from the unexpected early spring, The Hatch lived up to its efficient reputation. Within minutes, we were escorted past the crowded restaurant toward the docks where The Hatch dinner cruise boat awaited.

I deliberately walked a few steps behind Val as the hostess led us to our table. I wanted a moment to appreciate the pure beauty of the woman I'd be dining with tonight without her noticing my discernible stare. At some point over the last six months, she'd transformed. She was no longer the scared woman who showed up for her first training class, wearing clothes that didn't fit and hair that stuck out at wild angles. Now, she was dressed in tight black pants that fit her like a glove, and her breasts swelled below the neckline of her silky tank, just giving a hint of what was underneath. She was sexy as all hell, but that wasn't what attracted me the most. Her confidence and inner strength were her most alluring qualities. She looked poised to conquer the world.

"This is really nice," Val said after we were seated. "Have you done this before?"

"I've been to the main restaurant many times, but I've only done the cruise once, years ago. I've wanted to do it again but always thought it was more for couples celebrating a special occasion, like an anniversary. I thought our first official date was as good an occasion as any, so here we are."

She smiled and cast her eyes down. It was hard to tell in the dim lighting but I thought I detected a slight blush spreading over her cheeks.

"What was the special occasion the last time?" she asked.

"I was here with Hana. She was celebrating her rebirth, so to speak."

"Oh?" Her brows pinched together in confusion and she nervously pushed a piece of hair behind her ear. "Did you guys…um…I didn't realize the two of you…"

She trailed off and I waited expectantly for her to continue. When she didn't, my eyes widened as the conclusion she'd drawn suddenly dawned. I had literally just said I thought the cruise was for romantic couples, then followed up by saying I'd been on the cruise before with Hana. I shook my head.

Smooth, Derek, real smooth.

"No, no, it's not like that. Hana and I never dated. We were only here that night because she wanted to celebrate her divorce, and I figured I'd treat her."

"I see," she replied slowly as if she wasn't quite buying my explanation.

I didn't like her blasé response.

What's going on in that pretty little head of hers?

She looked upset, not angry, but I thought there was a twinge of jealousy hiding beneath the surface. A part of me felt a little smug about the idea of her being jealous. It meant she cared enough. But another part of me knew I should squash whatever idea she might be cooking up before it potentially ruined our night. Besides, the thought of me being romantically involved with Hana was absurd. I had never once looked at her that way.

"Don't get lost in your head, Sparky. Hana and I go back years, and I can assure you, she is and always will be only a friend. In fact, the night we went on the cruise was awkward. We were clearly surrounded by couples while we were very much *not* that. I didn't realize how romantic the setting was until after we were already on board."

"It's okay if you dated her." She eyed me cautiously. "I mean, you had a life before you met me so it's totally understandable. I'll admit, though, I did feel a little uncomfortable for a minute there. Somehow, the thought of your ex-girlfriend training me is kind of weird," she said, then laughed.

"I suppose it would be," I agreed, and breathed a sigh of relief.

"How did you meet her?"

"She was a client of mine before I opened The Mill. She was the first person I gave private self-defense lessons to. Hana's ex-husband was abusive. She's a survivor, just like you. She attended a class I was teaching and later approached me about doing private training sessions. It's a long story, but it really came down to a scheduling thing. She couldn't go to the group classes without him finding out, so she scheduled her own lessons to hide what she was doing from him. During that time, I think she may have taught me more than I taught her," I added with a laugh. "The one-on-one interaction allowed me to understand her mental struggles as much as the physical ones. She inadvertently educated me about the psychological effects abusees can experience. As a result, she made me a better trainer."

I paused when the waitress walked up to go over the menu, grateful for the disruption. While I wanted to answer all of Val's questions, I didn't want to divulge too much and risk betraying Hana's confidences. Like all survivors, it was her story to tell, not mine.

After the waitress rattled off the daily specials and we placed our orders, I looked out the open windows to see the boat had slowly exited World's Fair Marina and was now headed into the deeper waters of Long Island Sound. Glancing back at Val, I noticed her gaze had followed mine. She was staring wistfully across the water, not seeming to focus on any one thing in particular.

"What are you thinking, Sparky?"

"I was just thinking about my mom. She always enjoyed spending time on the banks of the Ohio River. She would have loved this," she murmured. She had a faraway look on her face before focusing her attention back on me. "Speaking of parents... I've meant to ask you. Neither you nor your sister ever talks about your parents. I don't mean to pry, but the one time you did mention them, it seemed past tense."

An ache that never quite went away momentarily amplified in my chest at the thought of my parents. Val was a keen observer. She was right to notice that Isabella and I rarely mentioned them. It wasn't that we didn't want to—it was just too painful.

"My mom died of a brain aneurism seven years ago. It was very sudden. We were all devastated. One day she was here, and the next, she wasn't. Isabella took it really hard, but nobody took it quite as hard as my dad. My mother was his whole world, and he worshipped the ground she walked on. He died of a heart attack five months after Mom passed. The doctor said his weight was a big contributing factor, but my sister argued and said he died of a broken heart. He just couldn't bear to be without Mom any longer."

"I'm so sorry. That's both sad and sweet."

"I know. Losing a parent is hard, as I'm sure you know, but losing two so close together?" I paused as a thousand never spoken words passed between us, a gentle understanding that would never need to be voiced aloud. "To say it was a rough few years is putting it mildly. The only consolation was that neither one of them suffered."

The waitress arrived with our first course, effectively putting an end to the depressing topic, placing two piping hot bowls of Manhattan clam chowder in front of us.

"This smells delicious!" Val appreciated.

"It is, trust me. The Hatch is famous for it."

We ate the chunky tomato and clam broth in silence, neither one of us seeming to have a need to fill the space with idle chatter as we enjoyed the peaceful ambiance and gentle sway of the boat. Before long, the entrées were served. I'd ordered the miso-glazed cod with oyster mushrooms, while Val went for the jumbo lump crab cakes and sugar snap peas. Between bites, we took turns talking about various aspects of our week. She told me about her latest nightmarish customer at Camilla's, and I filled her in on the latest trick Maisie had learned. Last night, she'd mastered rolling over.

We talked about everything and nothing, savoring the meal as much as we did each other. Some might consider our conversations boring, but I considered it normal—so very normal and comfortable. Even though tonight was our first official date, I'd spent the last six months courting her in the most old-fashioned way. We got to know each other so well, conversations came easily now. I already knew her favorite color was purple, and that she like to read classic literature but considered Gillian Flynn and Clive Cussler her guilty pleasures. There was no awkwardness or first date jitters. As I continued to discover new things about her, I learned she was so much more than anything my imagination could conjure. We'd become friends before lovers, and perhaps that's what had been missing in all of my previous relationships.

Emotion scorched my throat as I began to realize something else.

I was falling in love with her.

Her deep blue eyes were my ocean, and I wanted to drown in her. I wanted to hold her for the rest of my life and never let her go.

However, as soon as the thoughts hit, they suffered a quick and painful death as another reality set in. I couldn't tell her how I felt anytime soon. She wasn't ready—not even close. She may have come to trust me over the past few months but she still didn't trust me enough to tell me one very basic thing—her true name. I contemplated whether I should bring it up but decided against it almost as soon as the thought came to mind. The evening was going great, and I wanted nothing to spoil our first official date. I'd waited months to get her to this point—I could bring up the subject of her name another time.

After our dinner plates were cleared, I reached across the table and took her hand in mine.

"There's live music up on deck. Do you dance?"

"It depends," she replied. One side of her mouth quirked up in a knowing smile.

"On what?"

"It depends on if I'm asked properly."

I grinned and stood. Walking to her side or the table, I made a grand sweeping gesture with my arm and bent at the waist.

"Sparky, may I have this dance?"

"Why, yes, I think you may."

24

Val (Gianna)

Pressing my palms down on the side rail of the boat, I closed my eyes and breathed deeply. The smell of the shore mingled with the mouthwatering aromas from dinner and the perfumed scents worn by the other guests on the dinner cruise. A pianist's notes intertwined with the content chatter of those wandering the main deck. Twinkling lights crisscrossed overhead like electric spaghetti, illuminating the moonless night with the city skyline sparkling in the distance.

To describe the evening as perfect would be an understatement. Enjoying Derek's company in such a tranquil setting was more than I could have asked for on a first date. Our conversation over dinner was an equal exchange, neither of us dominating the discussion, simply sharing pieces of ourselves in balanced harmony. It was as though he knew exactly what to do and say to put me at ease.

In his unassuming, patient way, Derek had gradually shown me what life could be like after Ethan. While we hadn't officially been dating over the past six months, I had seen him nearly every day. He'd shown me around the city, exploring all the touristy and not-so-touristy spots. We perused flea markets in China Town and watched the fireworks over Coney Island. Never once did he cross a line—a perfect boy scout through and through. He allowed a bond of friendship and trust to slowly develop, and through it all, I had more fun than I'd ever had before in my life.

Standing next to me, Derek took in the sights and sounds of the night. He was so close, his heat stroked my skin. I didn't know where things were going with us—if there was even an 'us' yet. I couldn't see past tonight, but that was perfectly okay. I didn't want to look ahead. The simple idea of knowing I could live again would make me forever grateful to the man standing beside me. He made me feel safe.

"It's such a nice night. This view is beautiful," I commented. Glancing up, I found him staring at me with an unreadable expression. "What? Why are you looking at me like that?"

His hand cupped my jaw and lifted my chin. I blinked disconcertedly at him. Coming into tonight, I hadn't prepared myself for how the simplest of touches would make me feel. I didn't know I would crave more of it from him. I wanted to lean into the warmth and allow it to dispel all the cold.

"Because you're more beautiful than the view."

The proverbial butterflies danced in my stomach again and I couldn't prevent a flush from blossoming over my cheeks. Thank God it was dark and he couldn't see.

"I'm sure you say that to all the girls who flock to your doorstep," I teased and looked away. The thought of him dating women before me caused an unexpected pang of jealousy.

"No, I don't, actually."

"Oh, come on! Looking like you do, I find that hard to believe."

"No, I mean, I don't have a revolving door for women, Sparky. Sure, I've had my share of one night stands just like the next person, but I'm not a fling sort of guy—at least not by choice. I was serious about all the women I dated, even if they weren't serious about me. And yes, I've told women they were beautiful before, but..." He trailed off. I looked back up at him, waiting for him to continue.

"But what?" I prompted.

"My answer is going to sound cliché."

"Try me."

"I've never told a woman they were beautiful and meant it like I do with you. You're different."

I raised a brow. "You're right. Very cliché."

He raked a frustrated hand through his hair and looked out over the water.

"I've watched you around the gym. If a male gets too close to you, I see how you visibly spook. You're good at covering it up, but it's there. You're very cautious—even with me. It's why I've kept Hana involved in our self-defense classes."

I frowned, completely perplexed about what this had to do with telling me—or any other woman—that they were beautiful.

"What does that have to do with anything?"

Turning to face me, he placed two cautious hands on my hips.

"There's always been this undercurrent between us I can't explain. You've kept me at arm's length for months now, and I've been patient. I don't know what your story is, but I hope you'll feel comfortable opening up to me one day. Until then, I don't want to say or do anything that might scare you off. And well...when I say you're beautiful, I don't mean it in a superficial way."

"What way do you mean it?"

My heart began to beat rapidly in my chest. I didn't know why I pushed him to continue. I was afraid his answer would somehow cause a seismic shift in how we were together, both as friends and—assuming I could make it there—as lovers.

"At the risk of sounding like a damn poet, I'll say it." He closed his eyes and sighed. "You're stunning. The beauty I see inside you is something I've never seen before in any other woman. You're strong and there's beauty in strength. But there's fear inside you, too, and I'm afraid that fear will hold you back from exploring this thing that's been growing between us."

I swallowed the lump in my throat, terrified to tell him his fears matched my own. Instead of responding right away, I flagged down a waitress who was walking around with a tray of bubbly champagne for guests to purchase. I fumbled in my purse for a twenty, but Derek beat me to it. After paying the waitress, he handed me a flute and kept one for himself. I downed mine in one long gulp. I wasn't a big drinker, so combined with the wine I'd had at dinner, the champagne went right to my head. I smiled weakly and shrugged.

"What can I say? It was good champagne."

"Talk to me, Sparky." Derek eyed me warily. "What's wrong?"

I stared at him, trying to articulate how I was feeling. I could tell him he made me feel safe, then immediately contradict that with all the reasons he terrified me. I could tell him the truth about being legally married, which could potentially shatter the fragile trust we had. I could share all the terrible things Ethan did to me, but that would bring me back to that final night—a night I wanted to bury forever.

Right now, I just wanted to be happy—to feel good. I wanted to be kissed and feel like a whole woman again but the idea of wanting a man again nearly choked me. I would love to give in and completely surrender—pretend I wasn't broken for just one moment—but Derek was right. I was afraid, and I wasn't sure if my body was capable of physical intimacy or pleasure anymore.

I had been attending group therapy sessions at Stone's Hope, a women's shelter not far from my apartment. The sessions made me see I wasn't alone. They stressed that there wasn't a miracle elixir to heal my pain. Only time could do that. I worried my mental scars ran much deeper than the physical ones. I'd relied too much on the shelter of my body to keep them safely hidden away, and I wasn't sure if I was ready to rip them open again. I took a deep breath and closed my eyes, inhaling his woody, spicy scent that was already so familiar. The only way for me to know any of the answers was to dive into the dark and murky waters to see if I could swim again. Opening my eyes, I looked deep into the depths of his.

"Why haven't you tried to kiss me?" I whispered.

"Is that what you want me to do?"

I blinked, not sure how to respond. I didn't expect him to counter with that.

"Well, er...yeah. I mean, we're on a date. Isn't that what comes next?"

He looked at me as if I was a mismatched puzzle and the pieces weren't quite fitting where they should.

"We've covered a lot of ground since you moved here. I know you're not ready for anything serious, and you want to go slow." He paused and set his glass down near his feet, then stood and snaked his arms around my waist. When he spoke again, his voice was hoarse and ragged, and his hazel eyes were a blazing inferno of desire. "You have to set the pace here, Sparky. I won't kiss you until you give me permission."

I thought back to the day he first tried to convince me to take a self-defense class. He promised not to push me to do anything until I was ready—and he'd been following that motto ever since.

"You really are a boy scout, aren't you?"

"I'm sorry?"

"I mean you're a good man, Derek. Almost too good to be true," I explained with a small smile.

He reached up and gently cupped my face, and his hazel eyes turned hypnotic—spellbinding and alluring. I could feel his warm breath mingling with mine as his thumb grazed my cheek. His other hand reached up to grip the nape of my neck and my heart began to pound. His lips were only inches away from mine but he didn't close the remaining gap. For a few moments, he simply looked at me.

"I want to kiss you," he stated, his voice husky and low.

"Then kiss me."

I could still feel his uncertainty—as if he thought I was a scared rabbit who could be spooked at a moment's notice. Perhaps I was, but I didn't want to wait to find out. I wanted to feel his lips on mine. Closing the small remaining gap between us, I pressed my mouth to his.

The moment our lips connected, I felt a current charge down my spine. Electric. Energizing. My tongue darted out to test the seam of his lips. He opened and allowed me to taste with savory, hungry licks, and I felt his gasp more than I heard it. Cupping the nape of my nape, he angled his head and deepened the kiss. Our lips grew urgent in frantic need, both of us terrified of breaking the electric thread holding us together.

The other people on the boat ceased to exist. We were in our own world, his kisses erasing away every kiss that came before. His tongue tangled with mine in a tentative exploration I felt all the way to the tips of my toes. I sifted my fingers through his misbehaving waves and my core tightened.

Kissing him made me realize this part of me—my desire—hadn't gone away forever. It had only been lying dormant—and Derek Mills had awakened it.

25

Val (Gianna)

Derek and I stood outside the door to my apartment, reluctant to have the night come to a close. Reaching into my purse, I pulled out my keys.

"Thank you for dinner," I told him.

"You're welcome. I had a nice time. I…" He hesitated, and I fiddled with the keyring as I waited for him to continue. Instead, his gaze flitted to my mouth, then back up to eyes. Wrapping his arms around my waist, he drew me in.

My heart stalled, and my tongue darted out to moisten my lips. I wanted this man to kiss me again more than anything. I hoped like hell he wasn't going to wait for me to give him permission this time around.

Heads bowed together, our breaths mingled as he slowly closed the distance, and the electricity sparked once again. Our mouths tangled and I couldn't get enough of him on my tongue. Aligning our bodies, he pulled me closer. He suckled my lips between his, then dipped his tongue in to taste mine. When his hand found the hem of my shirt, I moaned from the feel of his warm hand against the bare skin of my waist. My fingers curled at his nape and I contemplated inviting him inside.

However, before I could offer the invitation, the thumping bass from the dance club next door began to rattle the walls, effectively disrupting any thoughts I had about making a decision I would probably regret. Inviting Derek inside would only lead to one thing—the very thing I didn't think I was ready for. Reluctantly, I pulled my lips away but kept my forehead pressed to his as I looked down at my watch.

"Right on time," Derek said.

"What's right on time?"

"The music. It's ten o'clock on a Saturday. That's when Club Revolution opens its doors."

"It's also when the walls in the hallways begin to shake," I joked, pointing to one of the trembling light fixtures in the hallway. "I know it can't be helped, but I'm not sure I'll ever get used to it."

"I used to have an apartment here on the third floor. I moved across the street a couple of years ago when a bigger flat opened up, but I remember what it was like living in this building. The noise from the club is easier to ignore if you've been there. Whenever I heard the music, it made me want to pop in. The club is actually a pretty fun place."

"Is it?"

"Yeah. I mean, I'm sure the older residents of the building don't care much for the noise they make, but it's grown on me." He scratched his chin and cocked his head to one side contemplatively. "We should go together one weekend."

"How about next weekend?" I suggested, and one corner of his mouth tilted up in a knowing smile.

"Is this you asking me out on a second date, Sparky?"

"Maybe."

"Well, I might just have to say yes," he whispered.

He leaned in and pressed a feather-light kiss to my cheek

before stepping back. The space he vacated now felt cold and empty, but I knew it was time to call it a night.

"Goodnight, Derek."

"Goodnight, Sparky."

After I went inside and closed the door, I secured the deadbolt and lowered the wooden bar. Habitually, I walked around the apartment and double-checked all the window locks. Confident everything was buttoned up tight, I yawned and headed to my bedroom to change into pajamas. It was fairly early to go to sleep, but the idea of crawling under the covers with a good book seemed appealing.

Once I was dressed, I tossed my clothes from the day into the hamper and went to the bathroom to wash up. As I was removing the makeup from my face, something felt off. I stopped moving and stood perfectly still, taking in the sounds. The dance club music was a given. I could also hear the sounds of a neighbor's television that had obviously been turned up more than normal to be heard over the club music. Neither of those things was anything out of the ordinary.

"You're being ridiculous," I said aloud to the empty bathroom. Shaking off the feeling of unease, I resumed getting ready for bed. When I reached for the toothpaste, I froze. Icy fear snaked down my spine and goosebumps pebbled my skin. The toothpaste wasn't on the counter, where I always left it. It was a thing I did—deliberately not putting it away as if I was somehow giving Ethan a big 'fuck you' every time I left it out.

A whimper escaped my lips as I wrenched open the bathroom's vanity drawer. Resting in the drawer was the tube of mint paste. I shook my head. I didn't believe I'd put it there. There was no way I did.

Running to the bedroom, I grabbed the wooden baseball bat next to the bed and slowly stalked through the apartment, opening every closet door, looking under furniture and behind curtains. My heart thrummed wildly in my ears. I contemplated calling 911, then thought better of it. What would I say? I think my husband moved my toothpaste? Whoever was working dispatch would think I was crazy.

When I opened the oven door and realized I had a very real fear Ethan would jump out, I forced myself to come back down to earth. Slamming the oven door closed, I gave myself a verbal scolding.

"The oven? Get it together before you really do go crazy. There's nobody here."

More than likely, I had probably put it in the drawer myself. After all—I'd been conditioned to never, ever leave it sitting out.

Climbing onto the bed, I slipped under the covers and grabbed the latest Gillian Flynn release from my nightstand. I opened the book to where I'd left off and took a few calming breaths. I had simply overreacted. Everything was fine.

Nevertheless, I slept with the light on and the wooden bat pressed to my side.

SITTING IN THE GRASS, *I watch my mother dig in the dirt of our garden. The earth sifts through her fingers as she makes room for new life. She hands me a small, pointed shovel.*

"Here, Gia. Take this and start digging a narrow row for the impatiens."

"I still don't know why you refuse to plant daisies. The pink ones are so pretty and come back every year," I stubbornly argue.

"Daisies might be pretty, but they can't be trusted to do as you'd like. They'll be out of control within two years and take over the entire garden."

"Well, I don't care. When I have my own garden, I'm going to plant daisies."

"That's your prerogative. It's up to you to decide if you want

your flowers to have a shared space or if you want one flower to
control everything around it."

I look down at the tiny impatiens nestled in the dirt.

"Mom, do you think—" I freeze when I realize she's no
longer there. The air turns cold and my teeth start to chatter. I
stand, wrap my arms around myself, and call out. "Mom! Where
did you go?"

"She's dead, Gia. You only have me now," whispers a
familiar male voice. The hushed words come from somewhere
near my feet.

I look down to find the source of the voice but only see one
lonely daisy. I think of my mother's words about daisies taking
over and wonder how it got there. I reach down to pluck it from
the dirt, only for three more to push their way through the soil. I
pick those as well, but at least thirty more appear. Moving as
quickly as I can, I attempt to pull out the controlling flower
before it's too late. It's to no avail. In a matter of moments, I'm
surrounded by the suffocating plant growing taller and taller
around me.

The flowers stretch on for as far as the eye can see, their
stems and leaves intertwining through my arms and legs. I
struggle to break free and hear the male whisper again.

"You can't get away. I'll just keep coming back."

I recognize the voice now and I'm frozen in time, unable to
move as a flower angles toward me. Instead of seeing the sticky
bulb of the stigma, I see a face—his face—twisted in rage and
hurling volatile obscenities at me.

"You bitch! You'll never get away from me!"

"Let me go! Let me go!" I scream as loud as I can, tugging
at the powerful stems holding me in place.

I BOLTED UPRIGHT and fought against the restraints as tears
streamed down my face, overcome by pure, unadulterated panic.

It took me a solid two minutes to realize I'd only had a dream—or more accurately, a nightmare.

What I thought were flower stems wrapping around me was actually just my body tangled up in my own bedsheets. Flopping back down against the pillows, I took several deep breaths to calm my racing heart. Tears slipped over my cheeks, and I swiped them away in annoyance. Seeing my mother again—healthy and vibrant in her garden—was jarring.

"What the hell was that?" I yelled to the empty bedroom. Why was I dreaming about her now—especially in that context? Then there was the other part of the dream. It wasn't difficult recognizing the symbolism—the daisy, a controlling, overbearing flower, and Ethan, a controlling, overbearing husband. I loathed daisies now. They were never a way for Ethan to tell me he was looking out for me—it was a way to remind me he was always *watching* me.

It was just a dream. I'm in my own apartment. Ethan is not here.

Still, a part of me couldn't shake the feeling of being watched, and I knew I'd never get back to sleep. Wide awake, I stared at the ceiling, clutching the baseball bat until the sun finally began to rise.

26

Val (Gianna)

Feeling sluggish from lack of sleep, I took my time making breakfast. I kept it simple—a toasted bagel with cream cheese and a bowl of mixed berries. Sitting at the kitchen table, I thumbed through a magazine as I ate, hoping the mindless content of the pages would be a distraction from the crazy dream I had.

It didn't work, so I decided to head over The Mill and jump on one of the ellipticals. The gym would be quiet this time of the day. The early risers would be gone, ensuring an elliptical would be available for me to use. Derek usually took Sundays off, which would allow me a bit of solitude during my workout. It wasn't that I didn't want to see him, I just hoped a good, sweat-drenching routine without any distractions would help clear my head.

Thirty minutes later, my feet pushed through the final stride on the elliptical, and the sweat I'd been in search of dripped down the side of my face. I slowed my pace, grabbed the towel I had draped over the front of the machine, and wiped the sweat away. As I allowed my muscles to cool down, I turned my attention to one of the flat-screen televisions lining the wall in front of me. A twenty-four-hour news channel showed a picture of a man in a lab coat—a doctor I presumed. But it wasn't the picture of the doctor that caught my attention. It was the caption at the bottom of the screen.

DOMESTIC ABUSE WARNING SIGNS PRECEDED NEW YORK MURDER-SUICIDE

Stepping off the elliptical, I walked over to the television and turned up the volume so I could hear the news reporter over the music playing through the overhead speakers.

"A two-day nationwide manhunt for Dr. Thomas Jenkins has come to an end after his body was found in a ravine near his home with a self-inflicted gunshot wound to the head. Ballistics confirmed it was the same gun that killed thirty-one-year-old Julia Wheeler."

Images of a pretty blonde filled the television.

"Wheeler worked as a nurse at the Central New York General Hospital, the same hospital where Jenkins was the attending surgeon. According to friends, the two had been romantically involved until Wheeler broke it off a year prior. Hospital CCTV footage shows Jenkins luring Wheeler into a stairwell on Wednesday morning, where he shot her multiple times in the head and upper body. Wheeler was found after witnesses reported hearing shots just after nine a.m."

More images of the girl floated across the screen. I narrowed my eyes to look at her more closely. To the average person, she appeared to have been a happy woman, but I saw something else. There was a sadness in her eyes that was all too familiar—the same kind of sadness I saw in the bathroom mirror every single morning.

"Wheeler's friends have stated the relationship she shared

with the prominent surgeon was abusive. He allegedly stalked her and once held her captive in her home, wielding a gun. Wheeler had lived with Jenkins but left him because she believed he was having an affair with another woman. Jenkins refused to move on and put a global positioning system tracking device on her car to keep track of her movements. After Wheeler discovered the device, she filed a police report and tried to get an order of protection. Friends say Wheeler was dismissed by law enforcement officials despite the fact there had been several documented cases of abuse from Jenkins' ex-wife. Wheeler's friends believe the police ignored her complaints because Jenkins is the brother of the newly elected county sheriff. Channel 4 has reached out to the sheriff's office but they have so far declined to give a statement."

"Of course they covered up for their own! And now, a girl is dead because of it!" I ranted to no one in particular and shook my head in disgust.

Ignoring the curious glances thrown my way from a few nearby gym patrons, I scooped up my belongings and stormed back to my apartment. I was shaken and furious for the woman who was killed. Her story hit too close to home—it could have very easily been mine.

When I reached my apartment, I closed and barricaded the door. Pinching the bridge of my nose, I stared at the ceiling and went over all the precautions I had in place to ensure my safety, questioning if I was doing enough to protect myself. I was still afraid, and I hated that fact—hated the constant feeling of looking over my shoulder. Perhaps it was paranoia over the toothpaste incident last night, my nightmare, or the upsetting news I saw on the television about a girl I didn't even know— whatever it was had me pulling out my cell phone from the pocket of my sweatshirt.

"Nat," I said into the phone after my friend picked up.

"Hey, you! I didn't expect to hear from you today because

you said you were low on minutes. How did the date go? I need all the tea!"

"The date was great—and yes, I am low on minutes. I'll have to fill you in later as promised. Right now, I just need a favor."

"Sure, what's up?"

"I need you or Teddy to take a drive by my old house."

Natalia fell silent for the span of three heartbeats before speaking again.

"Um...for what?" I could already hear the alarm in her tone so I hesitated with my explanation of why I wanted her to do this.

"I need you to see if Ethan is there. I mean, I don't want you to go knocking on the door or anything. Just check to see if his car is there, lights are on...stuff like that."

"Did something happen? Do you think he's—"

"Everything is fine, Nat. It's probably nothing. I just had this weird dream last night, then I saw this thing on the news about a girl... I don't know. Call me crazy, but I just need you to do this so I can chill the fuck out."

"Are you sure that's the only reason?"

"I'm sure."

"Alright, alright. If it makes you feel better, I'll drive by sometime this week."

"Thanks, Nat. It's just so I can maintain sanity and nothing else. I promise."

At least I hoped it wasn't more than that.

27

Derek

I sat at the bar inside Camilla's and sipped a Peroni as I looked through the glass front windows. Despite the late hour, Mulberry Street was bustling with tourists, each one wanting to experience authentic pasta dishes, desserts, and trendy clothing stores in Lower Manhattan's Little Italy. Inside Camilla's, the dinner hour was coming to an end, and the restaurant crowd had begun to thin. Camilla's was one of the few restaurants in Little Italy to stop serving food after nine o'clock, which meant I could spend a little quiet time with Val at the end of her shift.

Val and Isabella were making final rounds to the tables of the remaining guests, and Christopher was wiping down everything behind the bar until it was sparkling clean. Seeming satisfied everything was to perfection, he tossed a dirty rag into a bin and headed toward me.

"This is the third night in a row you've graced us with your presence. I can't help but think it has something to do with one particular pretty waitress who works here," he said with a wink.

"You caught me," I said with a grin. I glanced where Val was talking to a restaurant patron on the opposite side of the restaurant. She handed them their check and moved on to the next table of guests. Her hips swayed as she weaved between tables, not even realizing how provocative her movements were. It was just the way her body naturally moved. No matter what her intentions were, desire still gripped me, and I suppressed a groan. Tearing my eyes away from that gorgeous body, I took another long swig of my beer.

"Things are going good with her then?" Christopher asked.

"I guess you could say that. I took her to dinner the other night. The weather has been warm, so we did The Hatch dinner cruise. We had a really nice time."

Before Christopher could pry any more, my sister sauntered over to us and took a seat on the wrought iron bar stool next to mine.

"You've barely taken your eyes off her since you got here, little brother," she said with a teasing punch to my shoulder. "Please tell me you've finally made a move to ask her out. I'm getting tired of watching you pine."

"Actually, he took her to dinner a few nights ago," Christopher answered for me. Isabella immediately turned away from me, all attention now on her husband.

"Really? Where did they go?" she asked Christopher, her eyes alight with excitement.

"He took her on a dinner cruise over at The Hatch."

"Oh, how romantic! What a great idea!" Isabella gushed.

"Yeah. I thought so too. Derek said the weather has been—"

"Yo! I'm sitting right here!" I laughed. I knew my sister would want all the details but before I could tell her more, Val headed our way. I smiled as she approached.

"You're all huddled up looking like cats who swallowed the canary," she joked. "What did I miss?"

"Nothing much. Only my sister and brother-in-law being

nosey," I told her as I placed a light kiss on her forehead. Out of the corner of my eye, I saw Isabella's beaming smile. I couldn't help wondering who was more excited about Val and me finally getting together—my sister or me. I shook my head and suppressed a grin.

"Val, if you want to visit with Derek, I'll finish up in the dining room," Isabella offered.

"Are you sure? I can—"

"I can handle it," my sister reiterated. Christopher conspicuously disappeared into the kitchen as Isabella slid down from her bar stool. Leaning in to peck me on the cheek, she whispered, "Take all the time you need."

As she walked away, I saw Val pass her a look of gratitude before silently mouthing, 'thank you.'

"Now, I feel like I missed something," I kidded. When Val only offered me a knowing look, my eyes widened in surprise. "What are you up to?"

"Nothing at all," she all too innocently denied. "Are you hungry?"

I eyed her suspiciously. Something was definitely going on. I wasn't sure what to think about this guileful side to her so I played along.

"I could be."

"Well, then, follow me this way, Mr. Mills. Your table awaits."

Once I was seated, Val brought me fresh bread and a plate of seasoned olive oil for dipping, then she disappeared through the door to the kitchen, leaving me relatively perplexed.

What in the hell was going on?

As the last customer exited the restaurant, Val reemerged from the kitchen. Christopher followed behind her and tossed a dish towel over his shoulder. Reaching into his pocket, he dropped a set of keys on the bar.

"The kitchen has been cleaned," I heard him say to her. "If

you make a mess, be sure to wipe everything down again. Isabella is already out back waiting for me. We're headed home. The front door is locked, just remember to lock up the rest of the place and set the alarm before you do."

"Will do, boss. Thanks."

To my surprise, my brother-in-law winked at her as if he was in on the secret, then turned to exit out the back door of the restaurant. Feeling more confounded than ever, I turned my attention to Val. She was now at my table, uncorking a wine bottle she'd procured from somewhere when I wasn't looking

"What was that all about?" I asked.

"What was what?"

"All that with Christopher just now and my sister earlier. What scheme have the three of you concocted?"

"Nothing," she denied again with an innocuous shrug. "Christopher has just been teaching me a few things in the kitchen, and I think I have a few of his recipes down pat."

"Is that so?"

"Yeah. I thought I'd try a few of them out on you tonight if that's okay."

I narrowed my eyes and studied her carefully as she poured the deep red Chianti into a bordeaux glass. I tried to get a read on what she was thinking, but her expression was guarded, and I got nothing. This had my sister written all over it—not that I minded. If it meant I got to be alone with Val, my sister could meddle all she wanted.

"Sounds good to me," I agreed casually as I accepted the glass she held out to me.

She walked away, only to return a few minutes later with a plate of *Insalata Caprese*. Rather than let me help myself to the appetizer, she used a serving fork to place a portion of the cheese and tomatoes onto a side dish for me. Then, to my surprise, she pulled out the chair next to me and sat down. Stabbing a small piece of mozzarella and tomato with my salad fork, she brought it to my lips and eyed me mischievously.

"Open," she commanded.

Allowing her to slip the fork between my lips, the tomato burst with flavor, and the cheese melted in my mouth. I pretended to contemplate the food, then nodded my head in approval as if I'd never had the dish before and was tasting it for the first time.

"It's very good. So, tell me... do you serve all of your customers this way?"

She bit the side of her cheek in the most endearing way, and I knew she was fighting back a smile.

"No, only you."

"Are you trying to impress me with your newfound skills?"

"Maybe," she replied coyly. The seconds ticked by as I scrutinized her, trying to find any sign of what her hidden agenda might be as she brought another forkful of mozzarella to my mouth. I had to admit, I was more than just a bit intrigued—I was fucking turned on.

I ate in silence, the two of us seldom breaking eye contact. This was quickly turning into the most erotic first course I'd ever eaten. Once my plate was clear, Val disappeared into the kitchen once more and returned with a plate of baked eggplant parmigiana. When she began to cut the eggplant into bite sized pieces, I placed my hand on her wrist to stop her.

"No, Sparky, let me."

Taking the fork and knife from her delicate fingers, I speared a small portion of what she had already cut and brought the fork to her lips. She opened automatically, chewing the breaded vegetable contemplatively as though she was critiquing her own skills in the kitchen. While she chewed, I refilled my wine glass and offered it to her.

"Thank you."

"I'm serious now. What is all of this?" I asked again.

"I guess this is my way of saying thank you for being so patient with me for the past six or so months. Is it working?" She slowly sipped the wine, eyeing me over the rim of the glass through lowered lashes. The elastic pull—always present when we were together—tightened the space between us. When her tongue darted out to swipe at the remnants of wine on her lips, I nearly groaned.

Fuck...what is this girl trying to do to me?

"Oh, it's working alright," I said, my voice sounding hoarse and husky, even to my own ears. My cock twitched. There was just something about the seductive side of Val that got my blood going. It took all the restraint I could manage not to bite her pouty lower lip or pick her up and lay her across the mosaic-tiled bar. I wanted to strip her down and use her body as a plate for her gourmet cooking. And when I was done, I would eat her for dessert.

Restraint. Don't push too fast.

The warning rang in my head, loud and intrusive. Still, there was no reason I couldn't test the waters just a little more—claim her mouth as mine then let her take the lead. I watched as she took another sip of wine and followed the gorgeous line of her throat as she swallowed. I saw the moment she realized I was studying her every move, and when her breath caught, any willpower I had was thrown to the wayside.

To hell with this.

I needed to taste her. It was an unexplainable need of epic proportions. Standing, I hauled her to her feet, wrapped my arms around her waist, and pulled her to my chest.

"Derek, what are you doing?" Shock registered in her eyes, and I realized I should give her a warning of some sort. I dipped my head to align my eyes with hers.

"I'm going to kiss you now, Sparky. Long and hard. I want you boneless in my arms."

"Oh, okay," she breathed. She tilted her head back and

released a small sigh, giving me all the permission I needed to kiss her senseless. I said a silent thanks to everything holy for giving me this moment—for giving me such a beautiful and complex woman. She was soft and fiery all at the same time, defining everything I'd desired for as long as I could remember.

Angling my head down to claim her mouth, I pushed my tongue past her waiting lips and devoured her. The press of our bodies was combustible, tempting the odds by sparking a match to gasoline-soaked timbers. She moaned and I could feel the burn, the vibration from her lips singeing a path straight to my groin. I worked my way down her neck, savoring the feel of her pulse hammering beneath her skin as I breathed in her scent. She smelled like strawberries and sunshine.

"You need to lead the way," I whispered. Nipping up her neck to her earlobe, she lolled her head to the side. I pulled her tighter against me, and she sighed her appreciation. "I don't want to push you too far, too fast. Tell me when to stop."

I caressed her back through her fitted black t-shirt, allowing my hands to move down to the curve of her hips. Pulling her body closer to mine, I captured her pouty, lower lip between my teeth and groaned.

God, she tastes divine.

My hands slid down to cup her ass and lifted her slightly until she was on her tiptoes. Her fingers burrowed into my hair, encouraging me to take more. Never before had I felt so desperate—so overcome with desire, I couldn't see straight. I moved my mouth back down to her neck, making love to the thrumming pulse beneath her skin.

"Oh, God, Derek," she whimpered, angling her head back to give me better access to the dip between her clavicle bones.

My hands roamed to cup her breasts through her shirt, and before I knew what I was doing, I was sitting on the chair, so my mouth was level with the swell of her breasts. I could see the hardened peaks of her nipples through her thin t-shirt and bra.

Flattening my palms against her back, I pulled her between my legs and leaned in to bite one taut nub through the material. I glanced up at her, and her gaze caught mine. The intimacy that passed between us was almost unbearable and I could barely think beyond the mesmerizing look in her eyes.

Finding the hem of her shirt, I slid my hands up and under, raising it high enough to reveal the pink, satin bra beneath. My lips found the smooth skin of her waist, eliciting tiny gasps from her with every sweep of my tongue. She felt like the softest of silks under my palms and her skin tasted like my own personal slice of heaven. When I came across a raised area at the base of her ribcage, I paused and angled my head back—a two-inch scar contrasted with the smooth, unblemished area surrounding it.

"What's this from?" I murmured. I traced the scar with my thumb as I kissed the marred skin and felt her body stiffen.

"Derek, please don't—" Whatever she was about to say was interrupted by a rattling noise near the front of the restaurant. She jumped back and straightened her shirt. Her cheeks flushed crimson as she stared at me with glazed eyes and swollen lips, her confusion evident in her eyes. "I need to go see what that noise was."

I glanced in the direction the sound had come from. Because of our position, the front of the restaurant was out of view, but I was still able to pinpoint the source of the incessant rattling.

"It was nothing. It just sounded like someone pulling on the door handle. Chris said it was locked. We're fine." I reached for her again, wanting to resume my slow exploration of her body, but the rattling noise continued. "Damn it," I cursed under my breath.

Val stepped back and hurried toward the front door. I shifted back in the chair to make more room in my pants for an erection that rivaled no others and waited for her to return. When she did, her face looked different. She no longer had the sultry look of a woman who'd just seduced me. Instead, she looked more like a timid baby deer who was learning how to walk for the first time.

"Sorry about that," she said awkwardly. "I don't know what it was. Nobody was at the door. We should probably get going, anyway. It's late."

"Wait." I reached out and grabbed her wrist.

"Derek...don't. Please," she begged. Her hand began to tremble.

Frustration coursed through me, unable to understand when the switch flipped—when the light in her eyes had suddenly gone out.

"Don't what?"

"I lost control for a minute there."

I chuckled lightly. "And is that a bad thing?"

"It's... um..." She trailed off and pulled her hand from mine, twisting her fingers nervously as she tried to find the right words to explain how she felt. "I'm not ready. I'm sorry if I made it seem like I was."

I stood and wrapped my arms around her. She didn't stiffen like I thought she might but she didn't return my embrace either —that stung something fierce.

"I had no intention of letting things go too far. Relax, Sparky. We can go as slow as you want," I tried to assure. Her body softened as she brought her arms around my waist, and I breathed a sigh of relief.

"You're too good to me," she murmured.

I pulled back to look her in the eyes.

"No. I've just been waiting for you for a long time. I'll do whatever I need to do as long as it means I get to be with you. You don't have to apologize for anything." I pressed my lips to her forehead to, hopefully, ease her fears. "Now, why don't I help you clear the table and get things cleaned up?"

"You don't have to do that. I can manage if you want to head home."

"I insist," I told her and began collecting dishes from the table. I brought what I could carry to the kitchen, turned on the faucet over the sink, and waited for the water to warm. Val came in with the remaining dishes and set them off to the side.

"Are you close with Isabella? As in, do you have a good relationship with her?"

"Yeah. I think so. Why do you ask?" I saw her shrug out of the corner of my eye as I sprayed hot water over the dishes to rinse them.

"I was just wondering. You seem close. I think it's kind of cool, actually."

"I guess..." I laughed. "If you think it's cool to have an older sibling who's constantly in your business."

"I'm serious. Watching your dynamic is interesting. I never had that growing up. You know... siblings, a big family. I'm kind of jealous," she admitted.

I eyed her curiously, pondering over where this line of talk was coming from.

"Nothing to be jealous of. Bells is kind of a mother hen. Sometimes, I wonder if she's trying to fill the void my mom left when she passed. As for the big family, it's really just me and my sister. We have aunts, uncles, and cousins who live out of state but we don't see them much." I paused when I caught sight of her bending over to put a bottle of olive oil away under a cabinet. I couldn't stop myself from looking at her ass if I tried—it was just too goddamn perfect. When she stood, I quickly cast my eyes away and continued with what I'd been saying. "I have to be honest, though. It's not like Bells and I feel like we're missing out on anything by not seeing our distant relatives. Christopher has more cousins than I can count. There's been plenty of family to go around ever since my sister married him."

"I know." She smiled her understanding. "I think every last one of them has been through the doors of Camilla's in over the past week," she joked.

Twenty minutes later, we had everything gleaming to meet Isabella and Christopher's standards.

"I think we cleaned up alright," I said as I looked at the surrounding area.

"Thanks for the help."

"Anytime, Sparky." I flashed her a wide smile as she prepared to lock up. "Let's skip the train. I'm going to call an Uber. It's faster this time of night."

"With the amount of money you spend on Ubers, you should just buy yourself a car," she teased.

"I have a car, a Jeep Wrangler. I just never use it unless I have to leave the city."

"I've never once known you to use it. It seems silly to have a car and not drive it."

"Not really. Off-street parking in New York is hard to come by. If you snag a spot, never move unless you absolutely have to."

Draping an arm over her shoulders, we walked to the corner of Mulberry and Grand Street. As we stood on the curb, waiting for the Uber to arrive, I felt a few raindrops hit my face. I looked up at the starless sky and smelled the air. Lighting flashed in the distance and I knew a storm was rolling in. Turning to face Val, I circled my arms around her waist and pulled her in.

"Thanks for tonight. It was unexpected and nice."

"Hmm… you're welcome," she murmured and pushed up on her toes to plant a light kiss on my lips. "Are we still hitting Club Revolution this weekend?"

"I'll do whatever you want if it means I get to see you."

I leaned down to kiss her again, this time applying a little more pressure. Her acceptance encouraged me to press deeper into her mouth—tasting, possessing. She met every stroke of my tongue as I pulled her in closer, crushing her torso against mine. My fingertips caressed the nape of her neck, gliding over the slope of her collarbone. I was drowning in sensation.

Holy hell...

What this woman did to me was unreal. The feel of her lips on mine rocked me to my very core. If a simple kiss made me feel that way, I could only imagine how she'd feel once I was inside her.

I heard a car pull up next to the curb and knew it was our Uber driver, but I didn't care. The skies could open up and rain pour down, and the driver could wait in his silver Toyota all night. I cared about none of it. I had no intention of ever removing my mouth from hers until she gave the signal. I could stay lost in her, just like this, all night long.

28

Ethan

New York City

I stood inside Ferrara Bakery with the bill of my Yankees hat pulled low. Blending in with a crowd circling like vultures for a taste of the famous nougat candy hadn't been too difficult. The location was the perfect vantage point for watching the doors to Camilla's. I could only hope that my little rouse worked, and Gianna and the good-for-nothing lowlife would be leaving soon.

I seriously didn't know who that guy thought he was. He looked familiar, but I couldn't quite place him. All I knew was his name was Derek.

Derek.

What kind of name was that anyway? Apparently, *Derek* thought he could put his hands on my girl—on my wife. Oh, yes, they had thought nobody was watching, but I saw them.

The little slut.

I saw everything.

Anybody walking by could have seen them through the small gap in the partially drawn curtains on the restaurant windows. It was as if she wanted me to see her.

Maybe she did.

After all, my girl liked to taunt me to make me do things I shouldn't. That had to have been her plan all along. It was a good thing I caused a distraction with the door. Who knows what would have happened if I hadn't thought ahead to the what-ifs? If I'd allowed things to go further, I might have had to kill her lover, and there was enough heat on me already. No, I didn't need the aggravation that came with staging an accident. I had more important things to do—like getting my girl back.

I should have come for her months ago. It wasn't until she seemed to take an interest in the musclehead that I felt the need to come here more often to intervene. I used the toothpaste just to fuck with her—to let her know I was watching. Her infatuation with Derek the Dope would go away soon enough and she'd be mine again. And if she didn't want me, I would deal with it, but I'd be damned if anyone else would have her.

It was past ten, and Ferrara's began closing up shop. I had little choice but to leave. When I stepped outside, I pushed past a small crowd of people who had gathered to listen to a man playing the accordion just outside the bakery. He was a heavy-set guy, wearing a red, white, and green Italian Gatsby hat. He pulled out on the instrument to suck air into it, reminding me of a harmonica. The high crescendos grated on my nerves, and I couldn't get away fast enough.

"Such a fucking cliché," I muttered.

Glancing at the windows of Camilla's, I saw the lights were still on. I pulled the bill of my baseball cap low and walked as inconspicuously as possible up and down the sidewalk across the street from the little Italian restaurant. With all the people bustling about, trying to beat the incoming storm, nobody paid me much notice. I felt a few raindrops and heard a distant rumble. Lightning lit up the sky and cast an eerie glow around the shops in Little Italy. The clouded skies meant no moon, and I could stay hidden easier, but rain could complicate things. I wasn't in the mood to get soaking wet while I waited for my girl and her lover.

Whore. Slut.

That's all they were, every last one of them—including Cynthia, my beautiful dominatrix. Such a pity. She was one temptation I should have refused—my very own Jezebel, seducing me with her sexual immorality. It was her fault I was in this mess, to begin with. I should have killed her the moment she started asking too many questions and saved myself the stress. I'd thought if I could teach her a lesson, she'd get in line

But Cynthia was no Gianna.

She didn't learn a thing. Instead, she continued asking questions until I could take it no more. After she escaped the White Room, she came after me like a rabid dog. She may have succeeded in getting me suspended, pending an investigation, but that was as far as she got. A buddy of mine at the precinct told me she was considering contacting the FBI. For some reason, she thought they would be of more help to her.

Fuck the FBI.

I could easily hide in plain sight from the likes of those self-righteous assholes. Hadn't my mother and I done exactly that after the little incident with the sixteen-year girl in Salt Lake City? I mean, how was I supposed to know she was only sixteen? Not that it mattered. That temptress deserved to die, too. She was just another whore.

After passing by the accordion player for the eighth time, I looked toward Camilla's again.

"Why the fuck haven't they left yet?" I said under my breath.

As soon as I uttered the words, Gianna and her new boy toy exited through the front door. I watched her fiddle with the lock for a moment before they walked hand in hand up the street.

Hand-in-fucking-hand.

Whore. Slut.

They stopped at the street corner and he put his arms around her. My fists clenched as I watched him kiss her—kiss my girl—as if she was his to have. The worst part was watching her kiss him back. I wasn't sure if she'd ever kissed me that way. Her small hands were in his hair, weaving through it like he was a fucking loom for her own personal tapestry. Painful nausea roiled in my stomach, and I felt the urge to vomit.

"Let marriage be held in honor among all, and let the marriage bed be undefiled, for God will judge the sexually immoral and adulterous."

Gianna was defiling our marriage bed—our sacred vows.

"May fire and sulfur rain from heaven and destroy you both," I quietly hissed.

An Uber pulled up to the curb next to them, but they took their sweet time getting in, too busy with their disgusting public display of affection. I couldn't help wondering where they were going after this. Stepping out to the street, I kept my head low and raised an arm to hail a cab. The rain was beginning to fall harder now, and I rushed to climb inside.

"I want you to follow that Uber," I told the cabbie, pointing to the silver Toyota my girl and the musclehead were getting into. The driver looked at me questioningly.

"Follow it?" he said in a heavy Indian accent.

Of course, I had to get a fucking godless Hindu for a driver. I wanted to scream.

"Be steadfast, my boy. Be steadfast."

I tamped down my impatience and passed a fifty-dollar bill through the seats. Offering him a wide grin, I did my best to fake sincerity.

"Yeah, they're friends of mine. We just decided to take separate cars. They wanted some alone time. You know how newlyweds can be," I explained with a shrug. The driver smiled and nodded knowingly.

"Ah, yes! Say no more. I understand completely."

Settling back into the seat, I stared through the windshield at the taillights of the Toyota as the cabbie pulled away from the curb. *Smooth Operator* was playing on the radio. I smiled a looked to my left, envisioning Gianna sitting beside me.

"It's the song from our first date, honey," I would have said to her. I reached out and wrapped my hand around the cold metal of the seat belt buckle, imagining it was my girl's hand in mine.

TWENTY MINUTES LATER, we crossed the Queensboro Bridge and Gianna's end destination was clear. She was going back to her apartment. The question was, would Derek be invited inside? I really hoped not. That could seriously infringe on my plans for the evening.

When we were two blocks away, I tapped the cab driver on the shoulder.

"You can let me out here."

"You don't want me to keep following the car?" he asked through the review mirror.

"No, I changed my mind. I don't feel like third-wheeling anymore tonight. I'm just going to call it a night," I replied, keeping my tone light. Thankfully, the cabbie didn't question it and pulled over to let me out.

After he drove away, I walked the remaining two blocks to Gianna's apartment building. Someone had left an umbrella near the base of their front steps, and I grabbed it. The rain had slowed to a drizzle, but the umbrella would help keep my cover. Increasing my pace, I jogged the rest of the way and arrived just as they were climbing out of the car.

Ducking behind the cover of a large conversion van, I

watched as they stood with their arms around each other, and again—more kissing. I was sure my girl and I never kissed that much. Jealousy and anger ravaged my soul, and I fought to control it. Resentment destroyed the fool, and jealousy killed the simple. I was neither simple nor a fool.

Eventually, the lovebirds separated. When Gianna walked into her building alone, I exhaled a sigh of relief. Dickwad Derek crossed the street and entered the adjacent building.

Interesting. I hadn't realized he lived there.

How convenient.

Making a split-second decision, I followed the path he'd taken inside. Once in the lobby, I was confronted with a bank of elevators. The neon number above one of the elevators ticked up, until eventually stopping on the fifth floor. Since I hadn't seen anyone else enter the building, I could only assume it was the elevator Derek the Douche had taken. I made to follow him but was stopped when I realized I needed a key to get the elevator to work.

Damnit.

I leaned against the wall, contemplating how long it might be until another tenant used an elevator. Once the doors opened, I could just slip inside. But then again, what if I needed a key to get back down? That could pose another problem.

Getting into his apartment might not be as easy as it was to get into Gianna's. Accessing her place had been simple. All I had to do was pose as a worker for the local gas company and tell Oscar Tomasz—aka Oscar the Grouch, the gullible-as-hell landlord—there was a gas leak. Of course, I wasn't so stupid as to ask for access to Gianna's apartment first. No. I was smarter than that. I'd worked undercover before, and convincing Oscar was child's play.

Still, if only Gianna knew the sacrifices I'd made to get to her. Enduring the smell of cat piss in Mrs. Trout's apartment for far too long hadn't been pleasant. Then there was the packrat in apartment nine B. I didn't know how anyone could live in such squalor.

But it was all worth it when Oscar finally opened the door for my girl's apartment only four days after she'd moved in. The wooden plank she'd later used to barricade the door was laughable. She should have checked her window locks better. Jerry-rigging the lock, so I could slip in and out of the window in her tiny dining room was like stealing candy from a baby.

And the utility closet off the hallway to the bedroom? It was as if that little nook behind the hot water tank was made just for me. I could hide there and still keep most areas of her apartment in full view.

I'd enjoyed myself immensely during my visits. The toothpaste prank had been fun. Watching her panic as she searched the apartment had given me a hard-on like no other. My girl, despite her adulterous ways, still appealed to my need for the flesh, and I'd no choice but to rub one out in my hiding spot behind the hot water tank.

Then there were the times when she wasn't home. I liked that even more because I could smell her sheets and stroke myself, remembering how good she'd once felt. Sometimes, I even thought about the others. Yes, Gianna had been my favorite by far, but Cynthia, Julia, Samantha, Michelle, Sarah—each was perfect in their own way.

Until they weren't.

Scowling, I pushed away from the wall and headed back into the rain. Thunder boomed in the distance, and I knew the city had yet to see the worst of the storm. Abandoning my original plan to climb through Gianna's dining room window to watch her sleep, I headed west toward 41st Avenue and hoped the wretched weather would hold out until I made it the six blocks to Queensboro Plaza. From there, I'd jump on the subway line that would take to my room in Willets Point.

The motel where I was staying at was a mice-infested, seedy

place that rented rooms for the night or by the hour. I was a far cry from my usual standards, but I didn't have a choice. I needed a place where I could stay off the radar, and nobody ever looked twice at the unsavory characters who frequented places like this. It was His will that I found such a location. He was testing me, and I knew I had to remain steadfast.

"Be steadfast, my boy. Be steadfast."

"He who has stood the test will receive the crown of life..." I repeated the verse from the Book of James quietly to myself as I inserted the keycard for my motel room door.

Once inside, I removed my shoes and damp clothing. Naked, I kneeled at the foot of the bed and bowed my head. I had much planning to do, and I would need His guidance to show me the way.

29

Val (Gianna)

Derek and I sat in a dimly lit corner booth draped in purple velvet at Club Revolution. His arm around me, he held me close, allowing me to snuggle into his shoulder. How I missed him since last seeing him was completely out of proportion with the time we'd known each other. I just him that morning during my self-defense class, yet it seemed like we'd been apart for days. I should have been alarmed, but for some reason, it felt right.

I sipped on a Lemon Drop martini while Derek favored a gin and tonic with a twist of lime. It felt good being out in this sort of setting. Derek had been right. This was a pretty hopping place. The last time I did anything like this was with Natalia during my pre-shitty days, as I'd come to dub them. After my slight panic attack over the toothpaste incident and the nightmare I'd had last weekend, I began mentally referring to my life before, during, and after Ethan as pre-shitty, shitty, and post-shitty to keep myself from thinking *his* name. I'm pretty sure a psychologist would have a field day with that, but whatever. It was helping to keep me sane, and that was all that mattered.

I glanced around at the sea of dancing people as the DJ transitioned to a new song. *Nothing to Lose* by Vassy began to play, and I tapped my foot in time to the beat. Her lyrics about starting from the bottom and rising up got to me in an unexpected way. She sang of independence, yet wanting love. The lyrics were emotional in a sad way, but they also gave me hope. Perhaps it was the martini running through my veins, but the song made me aware of something else as well.

I wanted Derek—I *really* wanted him—and that was perfectly okay.

I still wasn't sure why I froze up a few nights back at Camilla's. I'd analyzed my reactions for days afterward. Derek didn't deserve the mixed signals I was sending. He deserved better—so did I. It was okay for me to give in to my desires, and I was committed to doing exactly that going forward.

"Do you like this song?" Derek asked, pointing to my tapping foot.

"What's not to love about it?"

Smiling, he placed a chaste kiss to my forehead.

"Come on. Let's go dance then." Without giving me a chance to respond, Derek grabbed my hand and dragged me out onto the dance floor.

"Derek, what are you doing? I can't dance!"

"Sure you can, Sparky. You danced with me on the dinner cruise."

"But that was slow dancing. This is different. Trust me, I can't dance."

"Everyone can dance," he insisted, his laughter clear despite the loud music in the club.

"Not this girl. When I come to places like this, I people-watch. That's it."

Ignoring my protests, he pulled me close to his body. He pressed another quick kiss to my forehead, took my right hand in his, and flashed me a wicked, melt-worthy smile.

"Just follow my lead."

With his chest hard against mine, we began to move. His motions were effortless, making me appear to be a much better dancer than I actually was. He moved in a flawless rhythm, sexy and confident, before extending his arm to spin me around. Pulling my hips against him once more, long-dormant hormones came to life and sent sparks flying south. When the DJ transitioned and announced a throwback tune, Derek began to tease me with a slow, circular grind to the sexually charged lyrics of *Too Close* by Next.

Holy hell…who knew dancing could be so erotic?

After thirty minutes of hard dancing, sweat began to form on my brow. I glanced at Derek, and he was sweating as well, his hair falling in damp waves over his brow.

"Ready to get another drink?" I asked, wiping my forehead with the back of my hand.

"Sure."

Derek ordered me another Lemon Drop Martini but surprised me when he got himself a bottle of water.

"Water?"

"Yeah, I'm not much of a drinker. I usually stop at one," he explained.

I frowned in confusion.

"But you had a couple of drinks last weekend and had two glasses of wine the other night at Camilla's."

"I did. That's why I'm limiting myself today."

I rolled my eyes.

"Is this a 'my body is a temple' sort of thing?"

"No, Sparky. This is an 'I don't want to be under the influence of anything but you the next time I kiss you' sort of thing."

Oh, wow...

I licked my lips.

"Is that so?"

"Yes."

The deep timbre of his voice caused a shiver to course through me. There was no mistaking his unspoken promise as he turned my body until my back was pressed against his front. His hand splayed across my midsection, and we moved to Sia's electropop ballad of soaring synthesizers and militant drums. In my semi-buzzed state, I found myself shamelessly gyrating against him, needing to hang on to this moment—this feeling of being happy and free. I wanted to bury the shame and pretend I was a woman who didn't have a past, someone who wasn't always afraid of things that went bump in the night. I placed a hand over Derek's and squeezed as though I was hanging on for dear life. I never wanted this moment, no matter how inconsequential, to end.

Glancing down at my half-empty glass, I impulsively threw back the rest of the contents and placed the glass on the bar. Turning around to face Derek, I used the liquid courage to kiss him long and hard. The heat of his lips against mine spread like wildfire through my veins, and my heart hammered an erratic beat in my ears. He pulled my body tight to his and returned my kiss, his lips passionately pressing down on mine. When a passerby let out a loud wolf whistle, I felt Derek's lips turn up in a smile.

"What do you say we get out of here and go back to my apartment?" I suggested. Derek pulled away, his eyes dark and hungry yet hesitant.

"Your apartment?"

"Yes. I want to be with you."

He studied me for a long moment before nodding.

"Okay." He cupped my cheek and leaned in to kiss me once more, his tongue tracing the seam of my lips, coaxing them open.

Our tongues danced together for the briefest of moments before he pulled away. "But remember, you need to set the pace."

30

Val (Gianna)

I silently thanked the gods, the club was right next door. I didn't think we would have made it through a cab or subway ride back to my apartment. Derek and I crashed through the door in a tangle of lips and limbs. When Derek kicked the door closed behind us, I didn't even pause to barricade the door or check the windows. The only thing that mattered was him and his touch. I needed him like I never needed anything in my life.

Pinning me against my living room wall, he ravaged my mouth. His hand skimmed up my waist, under my shirt, and brushed over my ribs. Shivers raced down my spine, and heat crashed between my legs. The arousal was all-consuming.

"God... your skin. You feel so good," he murmured against my mouth, his voice low and husky. I pulled my shirt up and over my head with frantic need. He groaned and pushed down the cups of my bra to circle each nipple with the pads of his thumbs and forefingers. I gasped when he bent his head and latched on with his teeth, leisurely suckling each one and coaxing them to straining, aching peaks.

Needing to feel his skin under my palms, I reached for the hem of his shirt and removed it. I'd seen Derek shirtless many times before, but it felt as though I were seeing him for the first time. Appreciating the hard lines of honed muscle, I ran my hands over his rippled abdomen, hard chest, and strong shoulders. I closed my eyes and inhaled the scent of his skin, needing him more and more with every breath I took. He was intoxicating. His hands moved to the button of my jeans, scorching a path over my skin. I sharply sucked in a gulp of air and felt him hesitate.

"Is this okay?"

"Yes, Derek. Don't stop," I breathed.

Sliding the zipper down, his hand slipped under the waistband of my panties. When he made gentle contact with my already moist folds, I nearly collapsed from pleasure. It had been too long since I last surrendered to a man's touch. I didn't realize how much I needed this physical connection again to feel normal. My back arched, and I moaned.

When I pictured Derek and me together for the first time, I thought it might be shadowed with memories of that final night with Ethan and all the terrible nights before that. Instead, I was filled with an incredible sense of power, knowing I was about to give my body willingly. It was up to me to decide when I wanted to share it and when I didn't. I owned it—and we owned tonight.

He worked his finger gently through my swollen flesh and teased my clit, the repeated flicking motions caused me to squirm. Pushing one finger in, he flexed it against the heated walls just inside my entrance. When he pushed in another finger, my hands flew up to grip his hair, the buildup to my orgasm coming swift and sweet.

"Oh God," I moaned, convulsing around his fingers. I stiffened beneath his merciless hand and came quickly and unexpectedly. White-hot flames overtook me, blinding me in a surge of heat as I went over the edge. I shuddered as the climax rocketed through my body and nearly collapsed from the intensity.

Derek caught me, my body yielding against his hard lines as he carried me to the bedroom. Setting me down, I laid back on the mattress and practically purred as he worked my jeans and panties down my legs, leaving a trail of kisses along my thighs, calves, and ankles.

Still wearing his pants, he positioned himself above my almost-naked body, careful to balance his weight on his elbows, so he didn't crush me. Brushing a stray piece of hair from my forehead, he studied me as if he was waiting for me to give him permission before continuing.

"Are you sure you want this?" he eventually asked. I smiled at how thoughtful he was.

"Yes, I'm sure."

Cupping my cheek, his lips moved to meld with mine. I kissed him desperately, our tongues sliding deep, clashing, and tasting. He suckled down the line of my neck and reached behind me to unclasp my bra, his fingers fumbling with the clasp for a moment before I heard him curse under his breath.

"What's wrong?"

"The damn clasp. The way it happens in the movies is bullshit. These double hooks are a bitch when you can't see what you're doing."

I laughed. "Here. Let me."

"No, I want to take my time undressing you. Roll over."

I flipped onto my stomach, and deft fingers roamed up my sides before coming together to effortlessly unhook the back clasp of my bra. His hands slid down my arms to lower the straps, placing feather-light kisses along my spine as he went. Brushing away the wisps of hair at my neck, his tongue found my ear. Nibbling on my earlobe, the full weight of him pressed down against my back.

Immediately, I felt as if I were suffocating. I couldn't breathe —images of the past reared up and smacked me in the face.

The glint of a butcher knife.

The hard press of fingers against my throat.

The sound of pants dropping to the floor.

Ragged panting breaths drowning out desperate pleas.

And the pain...

"Get off me!" I screamed. "Get off, get off!"

Derek moved quickly, jumping off the bed with his hands raised.

"What is it? Did I do something wrong? Are you okay?"

My chest heaved and it took me a minute to process his words. When I saw his panicked expression, my eyes filled with angry tears. I was so sure—so *damn* sure—I could do this.

I was wrong.

Ethan shattered a part of me I would never be able to get back—not even with someone as kind and as tender as Derek. My anger turned to embarrassment.

"I'm sorry."

"Don't be sorry. Just tell me what's wrong." When I didn't answer right away, he pressed on. "Talk to me, Sparky."

I shook my head and covered my naked breasts with one arm, using my free hand to reach for the edge of the bed comforter. Pulling it around to cover my body, I had to fight off the trembling that threatened to take over. It wasn't fair for me to drag this man through all of my crap.

"I'm fucked up, Derek. That's what's wrong. You should just... just go home."

Getting up from the bed, I went into the living room wrapped in the bulky blanket. Derek followed close behind.

"Oh, hell no. You're going to tell me what just happened in there," he said, pointing back toward the bedroom.

"I already told you. There are things in my past that are too painful to talk about. Please don't ask me to."

"No, the way you screamed just now..." He trailed off and shook his head. He took a step forward as though he wanted to touch me, but then thought better of it. "This shell you keep yourself in... I don't understand why, after all of these months, you haven't opened up to me. I feel things for you, strong things I can't put into words because I know I'd risk scaring you off. If you feel anything for me at all, you'll help me understand why you're afraid to let me in."

"You think I don't feel, too? That's the problem, Derek! I feel everything too damn much! I feel all the good with you, but all the other shit keeps getting in my way! Welcome to my post-shitty life!"

"Your what?"

"Never mind," I muttered, shaking my head. "Look, I want to shut off those *other* feelings, but I can't!

"What other feelings? What are you trying to shut off?"

Tears stung the backs of my eyes, but I blinked them away. I wanted to run—to hide. My gaze flitted around the room for a place to escape—the closet, the bathroom—anywhere would do as long as I could shed these angry tears without having to see the sadness and pity in Derek's eyes.

"Please, just go. I'm really sorry, but I think it's for the best."

He stood there, staring at me for a long while. I could feel his penetrating gaze but I was afraid to look at him. If I did, I knew I would break. When he eventually spoke, his voice was near a whisper.

"I need to know what happened to you. I want the truth."

My eyes snapped up to meet his.

"You want the truth?" I bit out. It was on the tip of my tongue to shout out the iconic line from *A Few Good Men*. I stifled the maniacal laughter threatening to bubble past my lips. The reality was, I knew Derek could, in fact, handle the truth. It was me who didn't want to face it.

"Talk to me, Val."

I laughed bitterly at the use of my fake name, the realization of how screwed up this was truly hitting me for the first time. All of this pretending...and for what? Ethan would always have the power. I looked pointedly at Derek, my next words coming out hard and resentful.

"Okay, here's a truth for you, boy scout. My name is not Val Bonetti. It's Gianna Valentini."

31

Derek

I stood perfectly still. The look on her face said she expected me to be shocked, but all I felt was relief. I was tired of the charade, the hiding, and everything else in between. This was the moment of truth I'd been waiting for.

"Why don't you look surprised?" she asked with a frown.

I closed my eyes briefly and exhaled a long sigh.

"Because I'm not. I knew your name. I always did."

"What do you mean you always knew?" The words dragged hesitantly over her lips as she shook her head with disbelief.

Pinching the bridge of my nose, I looked up at the ceiling. It was time for me to come clean. When my eyes met hers again, I could see her genuine embarrassment, but I also saw a hint of betrayal. I had to make this right. I thought I'd been helping her by keeping her secret—by giving her the time she needed to deal with whatever it was she was battling—but seeing her face now made me realize how bad I may have screwed this up.

"Fuck, I didn't want it to be like this."

"Like what?" she demanded.

"Just wait here for a minute."

"Wait here? But you—"

"Val, Gianna or... whatever. Just trust me on this. Please. I need to run to my apartment real quick. Don't barricade this place up like Fort Knox while I'm gone. Give me five minutes and I'll be right back."

Without another word, I left her gaping after me and rushed across the street to my apartment. When I arrived, Maisie was bouncing around in her crate to be let out.

Shit.

I'd completely forgot she'd been alone for over five hours. She probably had to go out.

"I'm sorry, girl. I got too wrapped up with Val... I mean, Gianna, tonight, and I almost forgot about you."

Gianna.

I smiled to myself, enjoying the sound of her true name coming from my lips for the first time. Moving as fast as I could, so I didn't keep Gianna waiting for too long, I opened the end table drawer and pulled out the teardrop earring she'd lost on her wedding day. After stashing it into my pocket, I let Maisie out of her crate, grabbed her leash, and prayed the elevator to the rooftop patio would come quickly.

When we arrived on the roof, I rushed Maisie over to the grassy patch, running by a couple of people sitting in hand-in-hand on two of the Adirondack chairs. The man had his legs stretched out with his feet crossed at the ankles and quickly pulled them in as I hurried by.

"Dog really has to go, huh?" he laughed.

I glanced back as I opened the gated fence to usher Maisie inside.

"Yeah, I guess so." I recognized him as a client from The Mill. Normally, I would have taken a few minutes to engage with him, but I didn't want to get caught up in idle chatter. I just wanted Maisie to do her thing quickly, so I could get back to

Gianna—but of course, she had to take her sweet old time, sniffing out every square inch of grass first. I puffed out an impatient breath. "Come on, girl. Hurry it up!"

I glanced back at the couple while I waited. They had resumed their conversation, already disinterested in what Maisie was doing, too wrapped up in each other to be bothered with anything else. I couldn't blame them. The night was gorgeous. Upon another look around, I saw there were several other couples on the roof. One particular couple was sitting on a blanket, sharing a bottle of wine, while another strolled the perimeter, holding hands as they took in the spectacular view of the Queensboro Bridge. The thing I noticed most was how happy and content they all looked. I knew I could have the same with Gianna—no, I'd *had* that with Gianna.

I only hoped it wasn't too late to get it back.

I'd gone against my instincts, staying quiet about her secret. I should have confronted her about her name long ago instead of carrying on with a cloud of secrecy over our heads. There had been plenty of opportunities to push her for the truth, and I botched every one of them. It never should have come out when she was naked beneath me. I'd waited to feel all that glorious, silky skin under my palms for far too long, only for it to be ruined by a past neither of us had any control over.

It hurt to know it had come to this. She didn't feel she could trust me, and panic was the only thing that propelled her to reveal the truth. I couldn't help wondering, if she hadn't been triggered by what I could only assume was a terrible memory, would we still be living her lie?

After Maisie completed her business, the two of us headed back to the elevator. Rather than leave her home alone again, I decided it was best to bring her with me to Gianna's, so I didn't have to worry about coming back to tend to her before I was ready.

"You want to go see Gianna, girl?"

She hopped with excitement. I didn't think Gianna would mind having her there. She'd been in Maisie's company plenty of times when we were sightseeing outdoors, and they'd gotten along well. Still, at just under a year and a half old, she was still considered a puppy—and puppies chewed things. Wanting to be safe rather than sorry, I made a pit stop back to my apartment to grab a few chew toys and her crate. I had a feeling it was going to be a long night.

When I returned to Gianna's apartment, I found her sitting on the sofa, sipping a glass of ice water, still wrapped in the bed comforter. She looked up to see me coming through the door with an armful of puppy paraphernalia and one excited pup. I unhooked Maisie's leash and she bounded toward Gianna.

"Well, hello, Miss Maisie! I didn't expect to see you tonight," she said in surprise, then glanced up questioningly.

"I hope I'm not being too presumptuous. I thought we might be here for a while. This was just easier," I explained as I set up a spot for Maisie in the corner of the family room.

"It's fine. She's welcome here," she assured and lightly laughed when Maisie bounced off her lap and scampered down the hallway.

"Maisie, no!" I told her when I saw her scratching at a door. She whined, and I scooped her up, offering Gianna an apologetic look. "Sorry, new place. She just wants to check everything out."

"Not much to see there. It's just a utility closet for the electric panel and hot water tank."

Setting Maisie down inside her crate, she immediately began to chew on a marrow bone I'd placed inside. Not wanting to mince any more words and drag this out longer than necessary, I crossed the room in three long strides and sat down on the sofa next to Gianna. Extending my hand, I opened it to reveal a single teardrop rhinestone earring.

"Recognize this?"

She blinked and it took her more than a minute for the shape to familiarize itself in her memory.

"It looks like the same earrings I wore on my wedding day. I lost one, but—"

"It's yours," I interrupted. "As in, it's the very same earring you lost. I found it on the ground after you walked away that night. I went inside to return it to you but stopped when I saw you arguing with your husband just outside the doors to the reception."

Her eyes widened, the betrayal on her face all too clear.

"Have you been playing me for a fool this entire time?" she whispered.

It crushed me to see tears glossing her eyes, knowing she thought I'd deceived her in some way. I lifted my finger to her lips to silence her, determined to get everything I was thinking and feeling out in the open.

"You're not a fool. In fact, you have one of the brightest minds I know. I knew it from the minute we first met. I never stopped thinking about that day... about you. To me, you were the one who got away. I'd thought of so many questions to ask if I ever saw you again. When I finally had my opportunity in the hallway right outside here," I said, raising a hand to point toward her front door. "I thought this is it, here's my chance, but my mind came up blank. Just seeing your face again was like being struck by lightning. All that energy was back in a flash, and I could barely breathe. Over the past few months, that energy grew and grew. And now... now I can only focus on one thing—the very thing I've been holding back from telling you because I've been too afraid you'd bolt."

"What are you afraid to tell me?" she breathed in a hushed voice, so quiet, I barely heard her. Her eyes were wide as if she was terrified of my response. I didn't care. I could no longer suppress my feelings because of what her reaction might be. She had to know how deep my emotions ran.

"I'm falling in love with you."

32

Gianna

Feeling disconcerted, I waited for my breath to even out and my heart to slow. I still couldn't make head or tail out of what had happened in the bedroom with Derek just minutes earlier. Now here he sat on my sofa with an earring that brought back a flood of memories. I needed the rush of blood in my ears to quiet. I felt sick, my body wanting nothing more than to purge the bile brought on by recollections of the past.

Then there were Derek's words.

"I'm falling in love with you."

I tried to think beyond those words and what they could mean. What had begun on uneven ground was shaping up to be something so much more. I felt like I was being pushed, lost in a colossal storm of emotions, I wasn't ready to feel. I knew it was time to take a giant step back. If I didn't, I sensed it wouldn't be long before I slipped and fell from the ledge. I needed to focus on the present before looking toward the future. I had no idea how we accelerated so quickly to this point, although I had no doubt his words were genuine.

Without saying a word, I left him sitting on the sofa and went back to the bedroom to throw on yoga pants and an oversized sweater. Derek and I barely had a chance to be together, and we were already arguing. Whether it was his fault or mine, I didn't really know. I only knew I didn't want this. The path I was on was all too familiar. I'd already been down it. One fight would turn into another, then...

Not wanting to go there—not wanting to believe for one second Derek was anything like Ethan—I stalked from the bedroom and began to pace the living room. My emotions were going haywire, and I needed to calm down. I wasn't sure if I was sad, confused, or angry, perhaps a little of all three.

Derek sat in complete silence, almost as if he knew I was trying to sort out everything in my head before speaking. He had placed the earring on the coffee table, the reflective glimmer taunting me with repressed memories.

Derek had seen me arguing with Ethan.

I remembered that moment as clear as if it had happened yesterday. Instinctively, I began to rub the arm Ethan had grabbed, unable to take my eyes off the earring. The sight of it was mindboggling, bringing back the inappropriate emotions I'd felt about Derek, another man, on what should have been the happiest day of my life. I was conflicted about why he had kept the earring all this time. It was a possessive thing to do and something I ought to run from. Alarm bells should have been sounding... yet they weren't for some reason. Instead of worrying about it, I focused on getting answers to the bigger question.

"Okay, so that's my earring. That doesn't explain how you knew my real name."

"There was a sign just outside the door to the banquet hall with your name, as well as your husband's, written on it," he explained. "I didn't know your last name was Valentini, but I did know your real first name."

I thought back to my former life and recalled the black A-frame sign with gold, swirling writing.

"Walker is technically my last name. Valentini is my maiden name." My words sounded robotic, almost foreign to my own ears as I tried to process what he was saying. "Why did you lie and not let me know you knew my real name this whole time?"

"I prefer to think I omitted, not lied. Lying is what you did," he countered.

"That isn't fair."

"Isn't it? I've been patient for months, waiting for you to tell me your truth. I may have known one little detail, but you have to fill in the blanks—and I have a feeling there are a lot of them."

I stopped pacing, took in his earnest expression, and returned to my seat beside him on the couch. There was no malice in the way his eyes pleaded with me to open up—just patient understanding. Our time together thus far may have been short, but it felt as if we'd known each other for decades. He wasn't really the stranger I thought he was but familiar to me in ways that were unexplainable.

"I made up the name because I'm hiding from my abusive husband. I'm not divorced, and still very much legally married." He nodded his acceptance, almost as if he knew that all along. "Did you already know that, too?"

"That you're married still? No, but I suspected abuse. When I saw you the first time after you moved here, you introduced yourself as Val. Of course, I knew that wasn't your name and I almost called you out."

"Why didn't you?"

"Something in your eyes stopped me. You looked genuinely afraid—terrified, actually. I'd seen that look all too many times from the women taking my self-defense classes. Combine that with your shorter and darker hairstyle, I figured there was a reason for hiding your true identity. So, I let you keep your lie and told myself your story was none of my business. But then we got to know each other and..." He ran a hand through his sandy waves, trying to find the right words. "I wanted to say something so many times. At first, I kept quiet because I thought I'd spook you. I didn't want you to run. I started to call you Sparky for the spark and energy you threw into your defense classes but also because I didn't want to get used to calling you by the wrong name. I don't know if you noticed, but I rarely called you Val. Eventually, I came to realize it was about trust. You didn't trust me with your truth. I had to earn it. When we went on our first official date, I knew I had to say something, but how could I at that point?"

"What do you mean? That seems like as good of a time as any."

"How could I say I knew the truth because of an earring I failed to return, then kept for years. That sounds crazy—like a stalker cherishing a memento," he said with a light laugh. "That wasn't the case, but I knew how it would look. So, I decided to wait for you to tell me. But then tonight..."

He wasn't wrong. As soon as I found out he'd kept my earring, my thoughts instantly went to something controlling and possessive.

"So why did you keep the earring?"

"I don't know why I saved it. I've dated plenty of women over the years, but none of them ever felt right. The only explanation I can think of for holding on to your earring is that it reminded me of our very first conversation. It probably sounds nuts, but whenever I looked at it, it reminded me to hold out for that one person I could one day cherish." He paused, took my hand, and looked meaningfully at me. "I know we haven't been together long, but things feel different with you. I can't stop wondering if you're the person I was waiting for this whole time."

"Derek..."

"Talk to me, Sparky. If we want to have any shot at a true relationship, I need to know what happened to you so we can move forward. I don't know what triggered you earlier tonight. I only know I don't want risk doing something that might upset or hurt you in any way again."

"Damn it." I knew he had valid reasons for wanting to know what happened, but this wasn't only about building trust between the two of us—it was also about me. If I truly wanted to move on from Ethan, I had to admit certain things to myself. My group therapy leader at Stone's Hope told me it might help if I confided in someone I trusted.

Did I trust Derek enough to share my story with him?

I studied his features, memorizing every line, so I would be able to see how much my truth might forever scar him. I wasn't sure if I could summon the strength to give it to him. Pulling my hand from his, I stood and began to pace the room again. It was time to choose my path—either hide the scars that made up who I was or own them.

"You're right, I have to tell you. No... that's wrong. I don't *have* to tell you anything, but I *want* to trust you with this. I just need you to know it was a complicated situation. I'm not weak. Part of the reason I hesitated to tell you was I didn't want you to see me as the victim. I'm not the victim, Derek. I got away. Changing my name just allowed me to survive. I'm still me."

"I know that."

"I know I can seem closed off, untrusting even, but it's not what it seems like. That's just my way of making sure I can keep my independence and never lose myself to a man again."

He came to me and placed his hands on my hips, effectively stopping me from pacing.

"I know that, too," he said, reaching up to tuck a loose piece of hair behind my ear. When his finger softly stroked the side of my cheek, I leaned into his touch. For some reason, it gave me the courage to continue.

"You see, for years, I had nothing to call my own. Ethan saw to that. Everything my husband ever gave me was meant as a way to control me," I explained gravely.

Derek stopped stroking my cheek and leaned back to look at me.

"Have I ever done anything that made you feel like I was trying to control you?" he asked, his expression showing genuine concern.

I contemplated his words, then slowly shook my head.

"No, you haven't. You've actually done the complete opposite. You encourage me to just be me."

Seemingly satisfied I was speaking the truth, he nodded.

"Go on then," he encouraged patiently.

"Ethan was extremely controlling—that's putting it mildly— but I was partly to blame because I easily gave in to him right from the beginning. He was mentally and physically abusive, just not at first. It was a gradual thing that became worse over time. About two years into our marriage, I found out he had a mistress. Not realizing what Ethan was truly capable of, I confronted him about the affair. We argued. One thing led to another…" I paused, not wanting to relive the details of the first time Ethan beat me and the subsequent miscarriage. "You want to talk about *Sleeping with the Enemy*? Well, I lived it."

"What exactly did he do?"

I took a shaky breath, trying to gather enough courage to dispel my apprehension.

"Derek, I'm sorry, but I don't think you know how hard this is for me to talk about."

"Just take it one step at a time."

"And say what? That I stuck around for years and let him beat me? Do you want me to tell you about all the bruises and broken bones? How about the pain in my ankle that hurts every day because of a fracture that never healed properly? Or about how…" I stopped and swallowed the lump in my throat, trying to find the courage to continue. "The details about what he did to me that day are irrelevant now, just as the many days like it that followed."

His face paled, and I could see disbelief begin to set in.

"Christ, what the fuck did he do to you?"

"At some point over the years, I completely lost myself. It got to a point where I didn't even recognize myself in the mirror." As much as I didn't want to cry, I felt a tear slide down my cheek. Hastily wiping it away, I was annoyed at showing signs of weakness. Derek wrapped an arm around my shoulder and tried to pull me close. I shook my head and stepped away. I didn't want to be held at that moment. I found it easier to talk while I paced. Taking my cue for needed space, he stepped back and returned to his seat on the sofa.

"You don't have to tell me anymore if you don't want to," he stated. His voice wavered uncharacteristically, almost as if he was afraid to hear the rest.

"No, I have to get this out. For me," I told him. He nodded once, accepting my need to finish. For some reason, I was awash with humiliation. I knew I had nothing to be ashamed of, yet I was unable to meet his eyes while I told the ending of my tale. "It wasn't uncommon for Ethan to force himself on me."

"Are you saying he raped you? On multiple occasions?" His hand was clenched into a fist on his knee. If he wasn't sitting down, I was fairly positive he would have punched something.

"I didn't constitute it as rape at the time. In my mind, he was my husband, and I hadn't actually said no. Looking back on it now, I didn't say no because I was too afraid. After a beating, he'd feel bad about what he'd done. He'd say he wanted to make it up to me—to love me. I would cry the entire time, but I never once said no."

"Jesus Christ," Derek hissed. He ran his hands through his hair in a display of obvious frustration.

"There's more."

I paused, swallowed, and took a shaky breath.

Don't cry. Don't cry.

I didn't even notice I'd stopped pacing until I felt Derek's hand on my cheek. Using his thumb, he brushed away a tear I hadn't realized had fallen.

"I want to kill that mother fucker for hurting you," he whispered. "Please don't cry, Sparky. You don't have to continue. I don't need to know all the details—I only wanted to know what *not* to do so I didn't mistakenly trigger a bad memory."

I looked up into his eyes, so full of patience and understanding. A weaker version of myself might have folded right then and there, seeking the solitude of my mind to protect myself from the rest of the world, but I wasn't that person anymore—I couldn't afford to be that person anymore. I'd come too far to go back. Determination settled in my bones with a renewed confidence that turned my spine to steel.

"Ethan wanted children. I knew it would be irresponsible to bring a child into that environment, and I didn't want anything that would tie myself to him for the rest of my life. I knew I was going to leave him by that point; I just didn't know when. Anyway, I was on birth control, and he found out. He came at me. I tried to defend myself, but I was no match against him. He beat me, and..." I paused, struggling to get the rest out. "He choked me and defiled me... from... from behind in the worst possible way."

Uttering those words made me feel as if I was being ripped apart from the inside. The shame tore at my soul, and with it came tremendous pain. I also felt a certain amount of relief through the hurt, as if the weight of the entire world had been removed from my shoulders.

He took a step back and began to walk in tight circles, raking his hands through his hair, patrolling like a wild animal locked in a cage. Shaking his head, he stopped pacing to look at me.

"Are you saying he...that he...he anally raped you?"

I winced, hearing him verbalize the brutality I tried so hard to keep buried. I wanted to lie—to deny what had happened—terrified Derek would look at me differently and wouldn't want me anymore. I nodded reluctantly, knowing no matter how much I wanted to, I couldn't escape the vicious truth.

"Yes. That's why, when you pressed your weight down on my back, I lost it. I'm sorry. I didn't know I'd have that kind of reaction."

"You have nothing to be sorry about," he growled.

"I thought he would surely kill me that day. When he didn't, I realized I had to act. I know what you're probably going to ask —no, I didn't call the police. I couldn't. Ethan's a cop. The chances of someone helping me were slim to none. Not to mention, embarrassing him with a scandal would have been like signing my own death warrant. Instead, I got in touch with a few friends—Natalia, Teddy, and Ben. They saved me that day. There was a scene, but in the end, I got out. Without them, I'm not sure what would have happened. I'm only here today because of them. Hopefully, you'll get to meet them one day. They're the only family I have."

Derek pulled me close, and this time, I welcomed his embrace. His touch seeped a little bit of warmth into my blood, which seemed to be flowing arctic cold. Taking my chin in his hand, he turned my head back to look at him.

"Do not blame yourself," he said vehemently. "You're not just another victim. You're tougher than that. You got out. You're a survivor."

"I'm trying to be," I whispered. The truth was, baring my soul left me vulnerable in ways I'd never felt before.

"You should talk to somebody, maybe a professional counselor about what happened to you. You can't keep this all inside."

"I've been talking to people, although I've never revealed as much as I just did with you. A couple of months ago, I started attending group therapy sessions at Stone's Hope. Listening to the other women made me realize I wasn't alone, and I've found strength through them. They're the reason I had the courage to give you my truth tonight."

He pressed a kiss to my forehead and held it there for a long while. Tightening his arms around me, I felt the deep rise and fall of his strong chest.

"Do you trust me, Gianna?"

I looked up at him, liking the sound of my true name coming from his lips. I inwardly smiled when I realized what that meant.

No more Val.

No more hiding.

I could just be me again.

"Yes, why?"

"Because I want to show you something. Come with me." Taking my hand, he led me to the bedroom. Once we were there, he turned to face me and lifted my chin to meet his gaze. "If you'll let me, I want to show you what it feels like to be touched by someone who truly cares for you."

"Derek, I—"

He held up his hand to stop me.

"No sex. It's clear you're not ready for that yet, and that's perfectly okay. I won't pretend to understand how you feel, but I know your husband took something from you, and now you're afraid. Tonight, I just want to show you how to feel again. So, I'll ask you once more. Do you trust me?"

"I trust you."

33

Derek

I knew she had a story, knew it most likely contained violence, but never did I imagine the horrors she'd been through. I was sure she'd only scratched the surface of what he did to her. As she spoke, it was all I could do to keep the rage out of my voice when I whispered words of comfort. I meant what I said—I wanted to kill the mother fucker. Every time she said his name, I wanted to punch something. Knowing a monster like him had not only harmed her but touched her in the most intimate ways—he'd been inside her—brought a crippling pain to my chest. He deserved a long, slow, and painful death.

However, my wrath wasn't what she needed right now. Gianna, my beautifully broken Gianna, needed to know what it felt like to be loved and cherished.

I saw a lump move down her throat as if she were attempting to swallow her nerves. I reached for her hand, intent on bringing it up to cover my heart and offer words of assurances, but when I saw her gaze flit to where my grip held her tiny wrist, I froze. My hand looked so big wrapped around her delicate bones. I

wondered if it looked this small in her husband's grasp—
wondered why he didn't care enough to consider it, deciding to
use her as a punching bag instead.

I took a cautious step closer and held her gaze. Her eyes were
indecisive, and I had a fleeting thought she might throw me out.
Not wanting to give her another second of hesitation, I released
her hand, walked over to her closet, and began rifling through
her clothing in search of a robe of some kind.

"What are you doing?" she asked.

"I'm looking for a bathrobe. Do you have one?"

"Um, yeah. It's hanging on the hook behind the bedroom
door."

Turning in the direction she pointed, I crossed the room in a
few short strides to retrieve the thin, terrycloth robe.

"Please get undressed and put this on. When you're ready,
meet me in the bathroom."

One of her eyebrows quirked up in confusion, but I didn't
answer any of the unspoken questions. Exiting the bedroom, I
headed into the bathroom. Once there, I turned the faucet on over
the old-fashioned clawfoot tub and adjusted it until the
temperature was suitable for a bath. On the counter next to the
sink, I spotted a basket full of colorful, chalky looking balls.
Recognizing them as bath bombs from the years I'd shared an
apartment with my sister, I grabbed one and dropped it into the
now half-full tub. Little fizzies floated to the surface of the
water, and a sweet vanilla-strawberry scent began to fill the air.
A few minutes later, Gianna came into the bathroom just as I'd
asked, wearing nothing but her robe.

"I'm not sure what you have planned but I don't think both
of us can fit in the tub," she remarked wryly. Although she kept
her tone light, I could see the apprehension in her eyes.

"*We* aren't taking a bath. You are. Turn around."

Slowly, she turned until she was facing the tub and her back
was to me. Gliding my hands up her arms, I lightly squeezed her

shoulders in an attempt to loosen the tension I felt in them. Leaning in, I nudged her head to the side so I could trail kisses up the side of her neck. As I did, I slid my fingers under the lapels of her robe until it slid down her shoulders. She let out a little gasp.

"Derek, I—"

"Shhh…trust me." I pushed the robe down past her elbows until it ended up in a pool near her feet. "Climb into the tub, Sparky. Let me take care of you."

She took a hesitant step into the water, testing the temperature with her toes before getting all the way in. Watching her uncertain movements made me realize I'd never really studied a woman as I always seemed to study her. She was different in the most indescribable ways. She unraveled a part of me, altering me in a way that could never be undone. My mouth went dry, and my dick throbbed. Seeing her naked like this was almost too much. It killed me not to touch her, to keep my hands from running over her smooth curves and tight ass, but it wasn't the right time. I'd made a promise—no sex. I'd keep that promise, even if it destroyed me.

She wrapped her arms around her sides, appearing self-conscious for a moment before lowering herself into the water and positioning her body, so her back was to me. Once she was comfortably seated, I pulled my cell phone from my pocket and scrolled through Spotify for a suitable playlist. I wanted something calming yet sensual at the same time. After settling on something I thought would be appropriate, I glanced around the surfaces in the bathroom.

"Do you have any candles around here?" I asked.

"Um, yeah. There are a couple under the kitchen sink. I bought them over the winter after we had a power outage."

I quickly went to retrieve the candles. I had no idea where she kept anything else in the kitchen and had to rummage through the drawers for a few minutes before I could locate a book of matches. On impulse, I decided to lug one of the kitchen chairs into the bathroom. It would be better than kneeling on the floor for an indefinite time.

I paused when I felt a draft. The window on the other side of the table was cracked open, allowing the cool night air to flow into the room. Angling around the table, I quickly closed it, not wanting Gianna to catch a chill when she got out of the tub.

When I returned to the bathroom, I lit the candles, then positioned the chair by the edge of the tub and sat down. Gianna turned to give me a curious, yet almost angst-ridden, look.

"For someone who said no sex, you're certainly doing a good job setting the mood," she murmured.

"I don't need sex to be happy."

"I don't believe that for a minute," she scoffed.

I chuckled and reached for the loofa sponge she had hanging off the showerhead.

"Okay, fine. I'll admit, I want inside you more than anything. How could I not? But honestly, I feel like sex is just a formality for the true intimacy we already have. I'm satisfied being with you, regardless. What can I say? I guess I'm an old-fashioned guy."

I squeezed body wash into the sponge, worked it into a lather, and spread it over her back and shoulders. Using one finger, I traced a line down her back, sliding over the slight notches of her spine.

"Or maybe it's the boy scout in you."

"Nah. I've always been kind of a hopeless romantic. My sister says I get it from my dad. It might sound crazy, but I could never understand today's swipe-based dating scene," I mused, working my thumb around her shoulder blade to smooth out a knot of tension. "None of the girls I dated were honest about their relationship goals. They were either allergic to commitment, having one eye on the next swipe, or they wanted to get married after the first date. There was never any in-between. Modern dating is a hot mess, in my opinion."

Gianna nodded in agreement.

"My friend, Natalia, always said chivalry is lost. Too many prefer looking at a screen over making eye contact with a human being. I think you're a rare exception. I can count on one hand how many times you've texted me. You've always called or spoken to me in person."

"I would text you more, but you're always worried about going over your monthly allotment. You know," I added as an afterthought. "We could solve that problem if I added you to my cellphone plan."

There was no mistaking the way she stiffened beneath my palms.

"No. I'll get a better cellphone plan one day on my own... but thank you."

"Fair enough," I replied, thinking about what she'd said earlier about her husband controlling her. I now had an understanding why she wanted to maintain her independence, but that didn't mean I had to like it. As much as I wanted to make her life easier, I had to respect her decisions.

"I wonder if romance was hard for our grandparents and great-grandparents," she said, returning to our previous topic. She craned her neck to the side, allowing me to massage the tendons above her collarbone. "I mean, I don't want to glorify a time period with repressive gender roles and patriarchy, but I am curious if good, old-fashioned courting made things easier."

"It did for us."

"What do you mean?"

"Think about the six months we spent just being so-called friends. If that wasn't old-fashioned courting, I don't know what is."

"Hmmm... you might be on to something there." She fell silent for a while as I massaged her neck and shoulders, until eventually angling her head back to look at me. "Derek, can I ask you something?"

My fingers slid over a raised area near her shoulder, and I paused to look at it. The discoloration on her creamy skin was similar to what I'd seen on her abdomen that day at Camilla's—another scar. I pushed down the rage threatening to boil over and focused on her question.

"You can ask me anything."

"Why me?"

I carefully studied her face and tried to get a read on what she was thinking. Her eyes looked moist as if she was holding back tears. I had a thousand answers for her, but I wasn't sure if they would be too much for her to hear. My throat clogged with emotion. This woman owned my heart in more ways than one. Taking a chance, I wrapped my arms around her wet shoulders and pressed my lips lightly to her forehead. She didn't push me away, closing her eyes and melting against me.

"I think the bigger question is, why not you? After everything you've been through, nobody would blame you if you didn't want to be involved romantically with anyone ever again. I'm humbled by your strength, and I'm honored that you chose me. I'd be a fool to not want someone like you. When we first met, I knew there was something about you. I just didn't know what. Then you were gone, and there was this ache in my chest. I don't know if this will make sense, but it was akin to a phantom pain—as if a part of me was lost, even though it was never a part of me to begin with."

"It makes perfect sense," she replied softly. "I thought about you too. Our meeting should have been inconsequential, yet you were often the safe place in my head when things... when things were bad."

Her eyes glistened with tears as she reached up and pulled my head down. Our breaths mingled hesitantly as I waited for her to close the distance. When she did, our mouths melded in perfect harmony. Her tongue danced with mine in a perfect rhythm of temperance and desire. The kiss was sweet yet indescribably erotic.

"You're beautiful," I whispered against her mouth before running my tongue over her lips, demanding she open to me. I kissed her tenderly, passionately—desperately. I wanted to erase her horrors and give her something new to dream about.

With one hand still entwined in my hair, she used her other hand to grab hold of my wrist, pulling my arm to position it, so my soap-covered palm cupped one of her breasts. I nearly groaned as my fingers slid over her pebbled nipple. Pinching the hardened nub, I felt a shiver rock her body as she moaned. Trailing my mouth down the line of her neck, I tasted the divot near her collarbone and nipped along the curve of her shoulder.

"Derek…" she sighed. The sound of my name on her lips was like a fragmentary caress that ended in private agony. When she tried to turn and face me, I stopped her, keeping her back firmly against the side of the tub.

"No. Just stay still and relax."

I wanted to explore for just a little while longer and savor this sweet moment. When I brought my other hand around, so I could cup both breasts at the same time, I captured her startled cry with my mouth as I rolled the tight peaks between my fingers. Her back arched, searching for more. I complied, sliding one hand down the tight curve of her side, under the water, until my fingers reached the folds I'd barely had time to explore. I couldn't wait for the day I'd finally get to taste her—to explore every nook and crevice of her most intimate parts with my tongue—but for now, I would give her this.

I slid the pad of one finger gently over her clit. Her back bowed as an elicited gasp wrenched from her throat.

"Oh, God!"

As I parted her center and slowly sank one finger inside her heated well, a sharp hiss escaped me. She was so damn tight. I slid another finger in, stroking her inner walls while my thumb traced slow, leisurely circles over the pulsing bundle of nerves. Her soft, mewing sighs echoed through the steam-filled bathroom as she slowly built up to the most delicate climax I'd ever witnessed. It was only a matter of minutes before she began to clench around me.

"That's it. Let go," I whispered into her ear. "I want to feel you pulse around my fingers, for you to feel all the things I was meant to make you feel."

Her head lolled side to side as she pushed up against my hand. I pumped faster, deep and firm, searching for the release she so desperately wanted to give. I used my other hand to pull and pinch at one of her straining nipples. Her soft cries changed to breathless pleas as I drove her higher and higher. I felt her body stiffen and heard her sharp intake of breath. When she came, she screamed out my name, and it was the most magnificent fucking thing I'd ever heard.

My cock strained in my pants, and I thought I might come on the spot. I wanted nothing more than to pull her from the tub and fuck her senseless, right here on the floor. My need was so hot, I couldn't even think straight. This woman was turning me inside out.

But I could not give in to anything that might mess this up. I'd relaxed her body and her mind enough, she wasn't thinking straight. I didn't want her to have any regrets in the morning. That worry was the only thing that forced me to pull my fingers from the clutches of her body. I allowed my hands to linger over her lush, glorious tits for just a second longer before reining in my mad desire and resolving to do exactly as I'd promised.

Unwillingly tearing my mouth from hers, I cradled her upturned face between my palms. Seeing the expression of pure contentment on her face was more than enough for me for tonight—just being with her in any way would always be enough.

"Come on, Sparky. It's late. Let's get you to bed."

"Wait, what about—"

"Shhh…I made you a promise and I intend to keep it."

Her eyes searched mine, and a hurricane of emotion swirled in her eyes, the sea of blue thrashing like waves in a storm. After a few moments, her eyes cleared, and she nodded.

"You're right. Are you going to stay the night?" she asked quietly.

"Only if you want me to."

"Yes, I think I'd like that."

I helped Gianna out of the tub, then wrapped her in a towel. My arms banded tightly around her and I hauled her to my chest, lifting her petite body until she was cradled in my arms. Her warm hands slipped around my neck to hold on, even though I had no intention of ever letting her go. I kissed her softly, not removing my lips from hers until we entered the bedroom.

I slowly lowered her to the bed as if she might break—as if *we* might break. This moment was so fragile, and I didn't want to do anything that could shatter it. Casting my eyes around the room, I looked for a pair of pajamas or anything else she may sleep in. If I was spending the night, my will power was only so strong. There was no way I could keep my hands off her for an entire night if she was lying naked beside me in bed.

"Do you have pajamas somewhere?" I asked.

"Over there. On the chair in the corner. The pink sleep shirt."

I grabbed the shirt and stretched the hem to position it over her head.

"Arms up."

"You surprise me," she murmured. "I thought for sure I'd be sleeping naked."

"Oh, trust me, baby, I'd much rather you that way. I just don't trust myself to behave."

After she was dressed and under the covers, I went around the apartment to turn off all the lights. Maisie whimpered. She didn't like being left alone in her crate, in the dark, in a strange place. Scooping her up, I brought her into the bedroom with me and set her down on the floor next to the bed.

Stripping down until I was wearing only my boxers, I crawled into bed beside Gianna. She rolled onto her side and positioned her head in the crook of my arm. Using one finger, she traced small circles over my chest and abdomen. A few seconds later, I heard a brief scratching, and the bed shifted, signaling that Maisie had joined us.

"Is it okay if she's on the bed?" I asked. I felt the curve of Gianna's smile against my chest.

"She's fine."

I cocked my head to the side to get a look at her face. The curtains were drawn, but it wasn't completely dark. Streetlight filtered in through the crevices, and I could just make out the outline of her features. She looked sated, as though she couldn't imagine herself being anywhere else at that moment.

"If she annoys you during the night, just kick me to wake up and I'll take care of her."

I felt more than heard the low chuckle coming from Gianna's chest.

"I'm sure Maisie will be okay. Thank you for tonight," she whispered into the dark.

"You're welcome, beautiful."

We laid together in the quiet darkness. Maisie's gentle sigh from the foot of the bed told me she was content and settling in for the night—as though she was right where she belonged. I smiled to myself, sharing her sense of peace.

"I think I want to get a tattoo," Gianna revealed suddenly.

I quirked up an eyebrow in surprise, unsure of what prompted her announcement.

"That's, ah… random. What brought that on?"

"My bucket list. Maisie made me think of it. Natalia and I used to add things to it all the time. We just started writing things on a cocktail napkin one day, and it grew from there. It was a joke between us that wasn't really a joke," she explained, and I felt her shrug. "Having a dog one day was on my list."

I was intrigued to know she had made a bucket list. Knowing what she had on it might give me a bit more insight into the perfectly imperfect woman in my arms.

"What else was on it?"

"Oh, lots of things. Some things were silly, others not so much. Traveling, getting my college degree." She paused and I felt the arc of her smile against my chest once again. "Bungee jumping. Cage diving with sharks. There really was no rhyme or reason to the things on it."

I chuckled.

"Well, if getting a tattoo was on that list, I have to say, I'd much rather you do that over cage dive with sharks."

"Seriously, though, would you mind?" she asked.

"Would I mind what?" I really hoped she wasn't serious about jumping into a shark tank.

"If I got a tattoo." I felt her body stiffen beside me, and she sounded genuinely worried about my answer. It was absurd.

"Of course not. It's your body, Gianna. Do what you want."

"Ethan didn't like tattoos. He forbade me from getting one," she quietly remarked. Then it clicked. She was concerned I'd try to stop her from getting one too. I shouldn't have been surprised. Nothing was ever typical where she was concerned.

"Sparky, look at me." When she angled her head up, I could see unshed tears glimmering in the darkness. "I'm not him. I would never forbid you from doing something no more than I'd ever force you to do something you didn't want to do. I promise."

She reached up to cup my cheek. Her small hand was warm and soft, a stark contrast to the five o'clock shadow covering my jaw.

"Sometimes, I feel like you're a dream—like you're not

really here—and one day, I'm going to wake up to find I'm still stuck in hell."

"I'm not a dream. I'm really here and I'm not going anywhere. I'm yours to keep for as long as you'll have me," I whispered, never before giving voice to a more fervent truth. She had me under her spell, and I was all hers.

I gently stroked the top of her head. Her petite form cushioned against my body as she clung to my chest with her head buried in the crook of my arm. I didn't need to utter any more hushed words, and neither did she. The unspoken, silent tenderness seemed to convey more than words ever could. Before long, we were both pulled into a dreamless sleep.

34

Gianna

I turned on the faucet for the shower, adjusted the temp, and stripped out of the oversized t-shirt I'd slept in. As I was pulling it over my head, I paused to breathe in the scent. The shirt smelled like Derek, making me smile. Stepping in and pulling the shower curtain closed, I let the water stream over me as I scrubbed my hair and thought about last night.

Derek had created a tranquil, relaxing mood, and I loved the feeling of falling asleep in his strong arms. At some point during the night, I'd awaken to find him still next to me, one arm draped protectively over my hip. Maisie was at the foot of the bed, her gentle snores combined with Derek's even breathing, making me feel more content than I'd ever felt before in my life. At that moment, I had come to realize something.

I was falling for Derek Mills.

Recognizing that was shocking, to say the least. I wouldn't go so far as to say I was actually in love with him, but there was something strong there, I couldn't deny—a magnetic pull that had been present since the day we met. Over the past six months, that intensely charged current had only grown stronger. I could no longer imagine my days without him.

Wanting to make sure I saved hot water for Derek, I quickly washed and got out. I dried my body and wrapped my hair up in a separate towel on top of my head. The bathroom mirror was clouded with steam, and I used my hand to wipe it away.

Dropping the towel, I looked at my naked body in the mirror. I recalled a time when I would critique my reflection, judging all the flaws and imperfections, self-conscious if I was good enough for Ethan. Now when I looked at myself, I didn't critique my body like I used to. When I looked at it now, all I saw were the faint scars in the most random places—battle wounds that would forever symbolize Ethan's brutality. I wondered if Derek had noticed any of them last night.

Worry pricked at me. I was afraid he might judge me for staying with Ethan for so long—for allowing him to leave those scars in the first place. The way his hands had so reverently stroked my body last night said the complete opposite—he didn't judge me but made me feel cherished.

My gaze traveled back up to my face. My eyes had a twinkle to them that I'd never seen before. My cheeks were flushed, but I wasn't sure if it was from the heat of the shower or thoughts of Derek. My heart was doing an unfamiliar boom at the thought of walking out of this bathroom and seeing him in my bed. I now knew what that all meant. I wanted to erase whatever fears and hesitations I had last night—I wanted Derek in every sense of the word. I wanted to explore and try again.

Wrapping myself back up in the towel, I went to the bedroom. Derek was awake but still in bed, sitting up and shirtless, propped up by pillows, and looking at his phone. Maisie was curled up beside him, lazily gnawing on a rubber chew toy. He appeared extremely relaxed—at home, even. I tried to ignore the way the sheet slid down around his hips to reveal the beginning of the delectable "V" that would leave any woman swooning.

"Morning, Derek. Sorry if I woke you."

"Nah, you didn't wake me. I had to get up to feed and take this little bugger outside. Right, girl," he said, changing his voice to sound all cutesy when he addressed her. It was endearing to watch him with Maisie. The affection he lavished on his pup was enough to make any woman melt—and I wasn't immune.

"The shower is all yours. Towels are in the linen closet," I told him, trying to act as nonchalant as humanly possible.

He looked up at me, flashed a bright smile, then swung his legs over the side of the bed. Walking over to me, he kissed the tip of my nose. I savored the intoxicating scent of him and the wash of warmth I felt when he was so near.

"Thanks, beautiful. I'll make it quick, then cook us some breakfast."

After he disappeared into the bathroom, I sat on the edge of the bed and ran a comb through my cropped hair. I fingered the short ends and wondered if I'd ever have the long tresses again. My hair had been dyed dark brown and cut short for so many months now, I wondered if I'd recognize my old look—or if I even wanted to.

True to his word, Derek was out of the shower ten minutes later. I was sitting on the edge of the bed when he returned to the bedroom wearing nothing but a towel around his trim waist. Droplets of water rained down from his head, glistening on his shoulders and chest. He was a magnificent sight, and I sighed inwardly.

"God, you're perfect," I said, my words barely a whisper.

"What did you say?"

"You. You're perfect."

He flashed me a crooked grin and reached for the pants and shirt he'd been wearing the night before.

"I try," he teased. After he pulled on his shirt, he turned his back to me and unabashedly dropped his towel. I nearly groaned at the sight of his hard, tight ass as he stepped into his jeans.

Regaining my focus, I stood and went over to him.

"No, I'm serious. I don't think you realize what last night meant to me. The way you treated me was..." I trailed off, unable to formulate the words that would do the experience justice. "Look, I wish I could erase those years of my life, but I can't."

"Why would you want to erase them?" he asked and cocked his head to one side. Reaching up, he pushed a wet strand of hair from my forehead. "They taught you so much. You're stronger because of it—stronger than anyone I know. You picked yourself up off the ground and began anew. That takes more strength than you're giving yourself credit for. I said as much last night but I'll say it again now. You're the face of a true survivor."

Emotion choked me.

"Derek, I...I want to try again."

He stilled and looked at me with cautious eyes.

"What do you mean?"

"A part of me may always be broken, I've accepted that, but I also know there's life after Ethan, and I believe you'll be a part of that life. Everything is so messed up, and there are so many unknowns, but if there's one thing I can be sure of, it's you. I want to be with you. I can do this. I just need you to remember my limitations—not from behind and no hands near my throat, okay?"

He reached for me and pulled me against his body. His hold was steadfast, pinning me to his torso, eyes never once wavering from mine. My cheeks flushed crimson, and his striking hazel eyes darkened. I felt my heart rate accelerate even faster as I returned his gaze. I couldn't think beyond this mesmerizing moment. He was so close, his broad, wide palm pressed against the small of my back while the other cupped my chin. His Adam's apple bobbed as he swallowed deeply.

"Sparky, I need to make sure I understand you correctly. Are you saying you want to try having sex again?" His words were slow and deliberate.

"Yes," I whispered and brought my hands up to his chest. His shoulders were solid beneath the thin cotton of his t-shirt and I longed to touch his flesh.

"You don't need to prove anything to me. I can wait. Are you absolutely sure you want to do this?"

I smiled softly. He was almost too perfect—a boy scout in every sense of the word—always more concerned with my well-being than anything else.

"I'm sure."

I tucked my head down and stepped back, hiding from the scorching heat of his gaze. Without another word, I began to open the towel.

"Wait," Derek said, stopping me by placing his hands over mine. "Hold that thought."

Moving faster than I'd ever seen him move, he ran to the side of the bed to where Maisie was still chewing on her toy, scooped her up, and left the room. I heard the sound of a zipper and I could only assume he had put her in her crate in the living room. When he returned, I started laughing.

"Don't want an audience?" I teased.

"Not particularly. Now… where were we?"

His eyes were dark and full of promise. My heart pummeled me from the inside, rattling against my ribs. Bringing my hands back to the edges of the towel, I didn't hesitate as I let it slip from my body. The morning sunlight, filtered by the curtains that were drawn closed, suddenly seemed brighter than it had a moment before. The light made me feel exposed in ways I hadn't considered the previous night. In this light, he'd be able to see the imperfections on my body—the scars marking the evidence of former injuries, each one telling a story of where I'd been.

"Derek, let me—" I began, feeling the need to explain the marks.

"You're the most beautiful woman I've ever laid eyes on," he interrupted as his eyes traveled down every inch of me. His large hands reached out to splay over my hips and wrap around to my lower back. His touch was reverent as he pulled me close and allowed me to take the lead. Stepping backward, I guided us to the bed. The fabric of jeans brushed against the bare skin of my thighs as we lowered to the mattress. Propped up on one elbow, he used one hand to cup my face while the other journeyed south to grab my thigh and loop my leg around his hips.

"Sparky, I don't want you to be afraid," he murmured against my lips. "I might unknowingly do something wrong but I don't want it to spook you. I would never intentionally hurt you. So please, tell me again. Are you one hundred percent sure you're ready for this?"

Any reservations I may have had fell away at his words.

"I want you, Derek. All of you."

With a slight nudge to his shoulder, I coaxed him onto his back and straddled his legs. Slowly, I pulled his jeans down his thighs and exposed his growing length.

"What are you doing? You don't have to do th—" he began to protest.

"Shhh... I want to."

Not wanting to give in to a single moment of hesitation, I leaned down and ran my tongue around the smooth crown of his erection.

"Holy mother..." he groaned, giving me encouragement to take in a little more of him. I wrapped my lips around his head, circling my tongue around the tip. Opening my mouth wider, I took more of him inside. He was thick and soft on my tongue as I sucked, his ridges sliding back and forth over my lips.

He reached around and entwined both of his hands in my hair, thrusting himself deeper and forcing a steady rhythm. For a split second, I froze. Images of Ethan and the sick gratification he'd get out of forcing his cock into my mouth flashed in my mind. I glanced up at Derek's face, desperately needing to remember that the hands tangled in my hair were not the hands of a monster.

When my eyes met his, I saw nothing but pleasure and awe as he watched my mouth slide over his sleek shaft. His fingers moved to tenderly push my hair out of my face. This man wasn't a monster, but someone who was kind and gentle—someone who cherished me.

Suddenly filled with an overwhelming desire to please him, I opened my throat to further accept him, sucking and twisting my tongue around him. I pushed my head forward, taking him deep with my swallow, and held him there. I pulled back and did it again, but this time I adjusted my throat to take him even deeper.

"Shit! Gianna, stop!" he hissed, pulling back. His breathing was ragged, coming out in short successions. "I need to be able to last for you."

Without warning, he rolled until I was on my back. His mouth came down on mine, his tongue plunging deep as my hips reflexively rocked into him.

"Oh, God. Derek, I need you more than you know. I need this. Make me feel whole again."

He answered with a groan and worked his way down my neck. His teeth grazed over my nipples, nipping and suckling on the hardened peeks until I thought I might combust from the pleasure. Moving down my body, his tongue traced small circles over and around my belly button. His fingers lingered on a scar on my side, evidence of where a hard boot had once connected with tender flesh. I tensed briefly but relaxed when he reverently kissed the area as if he was trying to kiss my horrors away.

"Mother of God, you're gorgeous. The things I want to do to you... the things I want to make you feel..." Moving his lips, he placed open-mouthed kisses over my hips and the top of my thighs. "Open your legs. I want to see you... all of you."

After a brief moment of hesitation, I dropped my knees apart. He took them in each hand and raised them up, so I was completely exposed to him, staring hungrily for what seemed like an embarrassingly long while before moving down to position his head between my legs. His hands slowly slid over my legs, spreading my thighs impossibly wider before coming to rest just inches from my throbbing clit. Parting my folds with two fingers, he exposed the throbbing nub of desire. Drenched, I arched my back up in longing.

My teeth clenched as his tongue swept up my entrance, through my wet folds, and over my clit. He began lightly, teasing me, as he nipped and sucked my tender flesh. He probed my entrance with one, two, then three fingers, pushing in as his tongue became more aggressive. My hands balled into fists, every muscle in my body shuddering under his ruthless mouth. When his free hand moved up to pinch one of my nipples, I was lost. I bucked under him, my hips pushing upward to fuck his hand and mouth until I felt a tightening in my core. My legs stiffened, and my eyes rolled to the heavens. In a blinding white light, he pushed me over the edge, leaving me completely liquified and breathless beneath him.

I could barely move as he worked his way back up, leaving a trail of hot, open-mouthed kisses on my belly and the curves of my breasts. I could only lie there, my bones feeling like they'd been turned to Jell-O, as I enjoyed the last few flutters of my orgasm. I felt his weight shift, then heard the telltale sound of a condom foil wrapper being torn open. Raising my lids, my eyes connected with Derek's. He was settled between my thighs, his cock positioned just outside my entrance.

"Tell me one more time, Gia. Are you sure?"

My answer was instant.

"I've never been more sure of anything in my whole life."

With my hands braced on his shoulders, he pushed into the tight clutches of my body, moving in a slow and steady rhythm. Catching his face in my hands, I brought his head down and kissed him hard. I wanted him to know I was irrevocably and willingly his. I moaned against his lips, surrendering to the centripetal force. The intensity of the way he returned the kiss sent shockwaves through my system as he moved inside me.

He pushed deeper, and I tightened around him. His motions were determined, matching me thrust after thrust. I gripped his shoulders, and we moved together, his rippled muscles bunching beneath my palms. I kissed him again, and our breath mingled as our need for each other rose to a new height. When he unexpectedly broke away, his breathing was ragged as his hands flexed around my hips.

"You are beautiful and strong," he said, his voice thick with emotion. "I want to give you everything you need. I never want you to feel afraid, only safe and cherished."

The intensity of his words nearly leveled me. Emotion clogged my throat, and it suddenly felt like he wasn't close enough—I needed more of him.

"More," I breathed, wanting every sensation he could make me feel.

He shoved inside of me with a force that took my breath away, then withdrew, teasing me with his cock, before ruthlessly plunging back in. His eyes met mine, his gaze transfixed with a reverent intensity. Never before had I felt so close to someone—so connected.

"I'm almost there," I panted and tightened my legs around him. I trembled, losing more of myself with every passing moment. I became desperate, the promise of release all-consuming.

"Now, Gianna. Give it to me now!"

With one hard thrust, he plunged deeper. My sensitive tissues rippled and spasmed uncontrollably, his words sending me into a heart-pounding orgasm. Colors flashed before my eyes as the rush surged through me.

"Derek!" I cried out, unraveling around him, my body overwhelmed with the sensation of blinding white heat. I was mindless, writhing against him shamelessly as I split apart at the seams. My fingernails clawed at his back, pulling him closer. His body shuddered before he stilled, then his cock became impossibly harder, pulsing deliciously as his own climax burst forth.

35

Gianna

Thirty minutes later, Derek and I were still a tangle of limbs and sheets. I didn't want to move, wanting to extend the after-bliss of the most intense sexual experience of my life for as long as possible instead. I suspected Derek felt the same because every time I shifted, he'd groan and pull me tighter to his hard, warm body.

I didn't know what was happening between us and found my mind racing to keep up with my heart. He'd stumbled into my life at the most inopportune moment. I was building a new life here, and I meant what I said to him—I wanted him to be a part of that. There was only one thing truly holding me back from completely giving into my feelings for him—a marriage certificate. Filing for divorce meant returning to Cincinnati and seeing Ethan. I knew it was only a matter of time before I had to face my demon again. I had hoped to allow more time to pass, but I didn't want to live my life like this. I needed an exit strategy—one that didn't include hiding and would allow me to be free of Ethan once and for all.

I rolled onto my back and giggled when I heard Derek's stomach rumble.

"Worked up an appetite, did you?" I teased.

"You damn near killed me, woman. If I had known it would be that good, I might not have been so patient these past six months," he teased back. "But now we need sustenance. Do you have eggs in the fridge?"

"Yeah, I think so."

"Perfect. I'm going to make us some breakfast."

Disentangling himself from bedsheets, Derek stood. Foregoing his boxer briefs, he slid his jeans over lean, muscular legs and buttoned the fly. He didn't bother with a shirt, just tossed me a wink and sexy grin before disappearing into the kitchen. When I heard him rifling through my cabinets in search of ingredients and pots and pans, I knew I should get up to help him.

Dragging my sex-laden body from the bed, I went into the bathroom to get dressed. One look in the mirror and I cringed. My wet hair had long since dried and was sticking up in all directions. I wet a hairbrush and worked to smooth it out. As I combed through the snarled strands one yank at a time, a familiar feeling of trepidation came over me. It was the same sort of feeling I'd felt the other day when the toothpaste was out of place. Instinctively, I glanced down at the counter.

The toothpaste wasn't there.

My stomach sank. I knew I left it out. There's no way I'd accidentally put it away a second time—especially after what happened when it was out of place the last time. I yanked open the vanity drawer, and sure enough, the toothpaste was there, but what was worse—it had been rolled up from the bottom. I was one hundred percent sure I hadn't done that.

I placed a hand over my mouth and stifled a scream. Either someone was playing a very sick joke, or Ethan had been here. Nobody knew about his toothpaste obsession except me. If he had been here, when? I retraced my steps. The last time I'd used the toothpaste was last night before going to bed. That would mean he'd have been here between last night and... I felt all blood drain from my face as the realization dawned.

He might still be here now.

Fear seized my gut, and I ran to the kitchen. The pressure in my chest was so severe, I could barely breathe. Derek was at the counter cracking an egg into a bowl. When he saw me, his concern was immediate.

"Sparky, what's wrong? You look like you've seen a ghost."

"The toothpaste. Did you use it?"

Derek scratched his head, a perplexed look on his face.

"Uh, yeah. This morning actually. I hope you don't mind. I didn't use your toothbrush though. I just used my fing—"

"I don't care about that. I just need to know—did you put the toothpaste away in the drawer?"

"Maybe. To be honest, I don't remember."

"What about rolling the tube up from the bottom? Did you do that?"

His confused look transitioned to genuine concern. I was sure I sounded like a crazy person but I didn't have time to worry about it.

"No, I don't think I rolled it up...maybe. Gianna, Christ. It's only toothpaste. Why are you so upset?"

His placating tone reminded me of Natalia when I asked her to drive by my old house. It made me remember I hadn't heard back from her. Immediately, I snatched my cell phone up from the kitchen counter and dialed Natalia.

"Nat," I said once she picked up. "Did you ever do that drive by like I asked you to?"

"Good morning to you, too," she mumbled. "What the hell, Gia? It's not even eight o'clock yet... and it's a Sunday."

"I'm serious, Nat. Did you do it?"

"Yeah, I did it, but I couldn't tell if he was there—at least not until last night. All kinds of crazy shit happened. I would have called, but it was late. I planned to call you today about it."

"About what? What crazy shit?"

"Ethan. Apparently, he beat up some woman named Cynthia pretty good a few weeks back. She barely lived. Once she recovered, she went after him hard."

I glanced at Derek. His concerned expression was still there. I couldn't blame him after the way I was acting. He needed to understand. Moving the phone away from my ear, I put it on speaker.

"Nat, I'm with Derek. You're on speakerphone. Keep going. Cynthia was the name of Ethan's mistress. What do you mean she went after him hard?"

"Oooh, you're with Derek this early in the morning?"

I nearly rolled my eyes, becoming more and more impatient with each passing second.

"Nat, that's not important. Tell me what happened."

"Geesh, okay. Apparently, Cynthia is a prosecutor and she has even more pull than Ethan did. She pressed charges—her lawyers were on the television last night saying it was attempted murder. It was all over the local news. He was suspended from his job while an investigation took place. They had a warrant to search the house for some kind of club—or whatever it was he supposedly used to beat her. When they got there, they discovered a safe full of coke and about a half a million in cash. Ethan was nowhere to be found. There's a warrant out for his arrest."

Memories came in quick snapshots—the safe I didn't know the combination for, the duffle bags Ethan came home with, his ability to afford the expensive house in the upscale neighborhood, the expensive cars he always drove...

"And you didn't call me last night because it was late?" I accused as the implications of what all this could mean seeped in. I thought about what the news stations might be saying.

Memories of all the police functions I'd attended flashed in my mind. The officers, their wives...what would they think? Would they know Ethan had abused me, too? I could almost hear their accusations, wondering why I'd stayed for so long.

"I'm sorry! I had...I had company last night," Natalia explained.

In other words, she was getting laid. I huffed out a frustrated breath.

"Have they found him?" I asked.

"Not yet. The police are still looking for him. They're also looking for you."

"Me? Why me?"

"The news didn't say, but I'm guessing they want to question you about Ethan."

My stomach sank, not knowing which cops Ethan might still have in his corner.

"Have the police tried to contact you?"

"No, not yet. Why?"

"Nat, you can't tell them where I am."

"I would never!" Natalie said vehemently. "I don't trust them as far as I can throw them. I'm not sure if you can get the Cincinnati news stations in New York, but I just turned on our morning news. Ethan's picture is plastered all over the place. Apparently, they didn't catch him yet. Now that he's on the run, who knows what he'll do? You need to be careful, toots."

If Ethan lost his badge, there was no telling what his state of mind would be. That badge was his entire identity. Without it, I was sure he'd be more volatile than ever before. I truly believed it was the only thing that kept him from killing me, Teddy, Ben, and Natalia the night I escaped. A shiver of cold goosebumps raced down my spine.

"Alright. Thanks, Nat. I've got to go."

"You don't think he'd try to find you, do you?"

"I think he might have already. I really have to go. I'll call you later."

"Wait! What do you mean?"

I didn't answer, and ended the call. Running through the apartment, I opened every closet door, looking for potential hiding places. If Ethan was here... if he was watching Derek and me...the thought of him seeing me naked in Derek's arms this morning made me want to vomit.

The apartment wasn't that big, and it only took me a minute or so to realize Ethan wasn't there. Derek had been close on my heels during my search. Now that I was fairly certain Ethan wasn't here, I turned to him.

"You need to leave—we both need to leave. It's not safe here."

Going to my bedroom closet, I pulled out a large canvas bag and began throwing clothes into it. My mind raced through all the hiding places I'd mapped out when I first arrived in the city. My focus was singular, only able to see through the tunnel that would lead me to safety. I didn't even realize Derek had been peppering me with questions until I felt his hand touch my shoulder.

"Gianna, what's going on? What are you doing?"

"Packing," I replied automatically. "Every bone in my body is saying Ethan was here recently. I need to get out."

"What do you mean he was here? How do you know?"

"The toothpaste. He was fucking neurotic about it. Now please, Derek...you need to leave and I need to..." I hesitated, not sure what it was I needed at that moment. I only knew I had to run. "I need to get someplace safe."

"You're running," Derek asserted.

"Yes. Well, sort of."

He grabbed hold of my arm and turned me to face him. Planting one hand firmly on my shoulder, the other lifted to cup my cheek.

"No. I missed you for three long years. You were the piece of me I didn't know I was missing—the one who got away. You can't run again."

My heart was racing, ready to beat out of my chest. I wanted to give him the explanation he deserved, but there wasn't time. I had to act now.

"I have to leave, but I promise it won't be for long."

"Look, I know you're afraid, but let's be rational about this."

"Rational? Derek, you don't understand. It's not about fear. I won't shy away from being afraid. I can't. Fear is what kept me alive all of those years, and it has never failed me. But I trust my instincts more—and they're telling me to run."

"No," he repeated more forcefully. "I'm not letting you run."

"You're not letting me? After all you know about me, you have to know I'll never wait for a man to *let* me do anything ever again. I'm telling you I need to go—I have to take care of this—but I need a plan first. You asked me to trust you last night. Now, I'm asking you to trust me. Just give me a day, and I'll be in touch."

36

Derek

My feet hammered through my eighth mile on the treadmill. It didn't seem to matter how long or how far I ran, nothing could ease the tirade of emotions coursing through me ever since Gianna bolted out of her apartment the previous morning. I hadn't heard from her. I was agitated, pissed off, and worried beyond all belief. I didn't know if I was coming or going anymore.

The alarm on my sports watch sounded, alerting me that employees would be arriving at The Mill in thirty minutes. I impatiently stopped the treadmill and skipped my usual cool down. The gym opened for business at six in the morning. I wanted to be showered and locked in my office before I got pulled into a conversation with another human. At that moment, I didn't want to talk to anyone but Gianna.

The problem was, Gianna was gone, and I had no idea where to find her.

Grabbing a towel to wipe the sweat off my neck, I headed to the showers. After I stripped out of my t-shirt and shorts, I braced myself against the shower wall and let the water stream over me, I thought about everything that had happened over the past twenty-four hours.

I felt trapped with my hands tied behind my back, utterly helpless to protect Gianna from the monster from her past. I couldn't understand why she ran—why she wouldn't stay and let me help her. Was I that wrong about what we had together?

She was out there all alone, and only God knows what could happen to her.

After I towel dried and dressed, I left the locker room to seek the quiet confines of my office. Unfortunately, the front desk was already active with gym members. I must have taken longer in the shower than I thought. Clients were lined up to the door, each one holding out their membership cards so they could be scanned in. Lisa was behind the counter of the Nutrition Center, pulling supplements and fruit from the refrigerator for smoothie orders that would soon follow their workouts.

"Hey, boss," Lisa said cheerily when she saw me walking by.

She looked so happy—so normal. She was mentally healthy and whole, having never experienced the horrors Gianna had. Emotion scorched my throat as I thought about all Gianna had been through. It was all I could do to keep my shit together.

"Morning," I greeted without making eye contact. "I've got a bunch of stuff to do and don't want to be disturbed."

Through my peripheral, I saw the odd look she tossed at me, but I didn't stop moving until my office door was closed behind me. I turned the lock and leaned against the back of the door. Pinching the bridge of my nose, I paced the length of the room like a caged animal. I wracking my brain, trying to think of where Gianna could be and how I could possibly help her. Impulsively, I ripped my cell from the pocket of my shorts and dialed my sister.

"Derek, it's six-thirty in the morning," Isabella growled groggily. "This better be good."

"Have you heard from Gianna?" I asked without preamble.

"Gianna? Who's that?"

"Val. I mean Val. Have you heard from her?"

My sister, dazed from sleep, didn't think to question my slip-up. I wasn't sure if I was supposed to continue using Gianna's fake name. We never got to discuss that part before she ran out on me. Until I got the all-clear from her, I'd need to remember to be careful.

"No. She's scheduled off until Wednesday. Why?"

"You know how we've talked about her possibly being abused?"

"Yeah. What about it?"

"Well, she was—badly. It was her husband. Yesterday morning she took off because she thinks he found her."

"Wait. What?" my sister asked, suddenly sounding wide awake. "What do you mean he found her? Start from the beginning."

I gave Isabella a brief recap of everything Gianna had told me last night, leaving out only the most sordid details but saying enough for her to get the complete picture. Rehashing it all—giving voice to the story about the woman who I loved more and more with every passing moment—was debilitating.

Blinding, white-hot rage flashed as my brain scrambled to understand how anyone could even think to hurt Gianna. My eyes burned. I couldn't remember the last time I'd felt the sting of tears or if I'd ever had such a gripping tightness in my chest. I only wished I could take away everything that had happened to her.

"Isabella, she's the brightest, smartest, most beautiful..." Driving my hands into my hair, emotion clogged my throat as I paced tight circles around my office. "How could he... how could anyone... do that to her? I just want to protect her, but I don't know how to find her. What if she never comes back?"

"I've seen the way she looks at you, little brother. You've found your diamond in the rough. She'll be back."

"What if something happens to her before then? She shouldn't be alone."

My sister stayed silent for a moment. I took a few calming breaths while I waited, holding onto my sanity by a thread.

"Karma is a bitch, Derek. He'll get his due. Until then, you need to do everything in your power to help her—which means doing what she asks. She needs you now more than ever. I hate to say it, but she probably understands what he's capable of more than both of us combined."

37

Gianna

The support I'd received from my group therapy sessions was the reason I found myself on the doorstep of Stone's Hope, twenty-four hours after I'd abandoned Derek at my apartment. I'd spent the first day and night in a nearby hotel room, planning my course of action. However, memories of Ethan breaking down my hotel room door all those months ago niggled at my subconscious, causing the hairs on the back of my arms to rise on more than one occasion. It seemed as if it had happened a lifetime ago, yet the visions were as clear as if it happened only yesterday.

I'd barely slept a wink, jumping at the slightest noise, and quickly learned I couldn't stay in a hotel. Exhaustion was one luxury I couldn't afford if I wanted to keep my wits about me. Gathering my things, I'd checked out of the hotel just after sunrise and went to the one place I knew I could be truly safe—Stone's Hope. It wasn't only a place where women could receive counseling. It was also a shelter for those looking to escape their abusers. My only concern was whether they had a room for me. If not, I didn't know where I would go.

When I first started going to Stone's Hope for group therapy, I wasn't an active participant. I'd sit quietly, sipping on tea or nibble on a homemade dessert that always seemed to be present, listening to other women speak their truths. They taught me how abuse could be invisible and how many of us were living with secrets. It was staggering to learn that one in three women were victims of rape, physical violence, or stalking by an intimate partner in the United States alone.

The group of women who met each week was small, and eventually, I began to open up to them. There were only six of us plus the leader, Krystina Stone. We all knew each other intimately, so when I saw Krystina's familiar face when I walked through the door today, it was a relief.

Of all the women in the group, I related to her the most. While she hadn't been married to the person who abused her, he had been her longtime boyfriend. It wasn't until she met and married her very own prince charming, who just so happened to be the founder of Stone's Hope, did she finally open up publicly about what happened to her.

"Val! Fancy seeing you here today."

"Krystina!" I greeted with some surprise. Just as I had with Derek, the women in my counseling sessions were given my fake name. Until this mess with Ethan was sorted out, I would need to keep up the façade. "I didn't expect to see you here today, either. I thought you only came in on group therapy nights."

"That's normally the case. I had to stop by to drop off a check. We had a fundraising event last night, and I wanted to get the proceeds on the books as soon as possible. What are you doing here?" she asked.

"I... um... I need a room," I said hesitantly. When her eyebrows raised in surprise, I quickly explained. "It's not what you might be thinking. I didn't go back to my husband, but… but I think he found me. Until I know I'm safe, I can't go back home."

Krystina nodded her head in understanding.

"Say no more. I know you're familiar with how our therapy groups run, but I'm not sure if you know how the shelter works. Without having small kids, you can't get your own room. You'd be placed in the communal room with several other women. I'll need to check if there's a bed available. If there is, the longest you can stay is a few days."

"That's it?" I asked incredulously

"Well, yes. There are extenuating circumstances, but—"

"I think that might be me," I rushed in, desperate for more time. I quickly gave her the abbreviated story about Ethan. "So, you see, it's only a matter of time before the police pick him up. Once they do, I can leave and go back home. A few days stay might not be long enough depending on how quickly the police can flush him out."

"I see," she mused thoughtfully and tapped her finger on her chin. "Let me see what I can do about getting you an extended stay. You'll be required to help out—light dusting, vacuuming, etcetera."

"I don't mind that at all."

While Krystina spoke with someone at the registration desk, my mind raced. I didn't know the shelter had a restriction on the number of nights you could stay. When I thought about it, it made sense. They had to enact a policy to ensure people didn't take advantage. Even if Krystina was able to get me more time, I didn't know how much would be enough. What if Ethan was still a fugitive a month from now? I couldn't live this way forever. I would have to go back to my apartment, eventually.

Then there was the possibility of him getting off free and clear. It was crazy how I now felt like a one-woman cheering squad for the mistress I used to hate. If Cynthia's lawyers couldn't get him convicted, he'd be back to get me, eventually. There would be no stopping him. Sure, my self-defense classes might help, but I needed more assurances than that. I needed to be rid of Ethan forever.

A cold realization of what I might have to do began to creep in.

No.

My only intent was to hide until the authorities caught up to Ethan, but the more I thought about it, the more I came to see it might not work out like I was hoping. There was a very real possibility I'd be left with no other option than to take care of Ethan myself.

PART VI

TAKING IT BACK

38

Gianna

Three days later, I stood over Derek after having taken him down for the second time that day. I was beyond frustrated. Hana was an excellent trainer—small but mighty. She taught me a lot, but it wasn't enough. Taking down someone like her was a lot different from taking down a full-grown man who had the police academy and ground fighter training under his belt. I needed someone with brute strength—someone like Derek —to push me to the limit. He couldn't hold back at a time when I needed to be pushed.

The problem was it seemed as though Derek was afraid he was going to hurt me.

"Damnit!" My chest was heaving from exertion. "Stop going easy on me! That's not going to help me."

"I don't know what it is you want me to help you with! You won't tell me anything!" Derek snapped. He huffed out a frustrated breath and raked a hand through his hair. "I don't even know where you've been for the past three days. All I know is you call your friend, and she tells you your ex-husband—or should I say husband—is wanted for attempted murder, and now you think he's coming for you. You don't know if he is for sure, yet you ran off without telling me where you were going. Then you show up here yesterday, hell-bent on aggressive training. You've been practically begging me to kick your ass, but I can't do that. You know I can't."

"If you want to help me, that's exactly what you need to do —kick my ass."

"She's right, Derek," Hana chimed in. "You're going easy on her. If she's right and her husband is lurking around, you won't be able to help her if he attacks. She needs to be confident in her abilities to protect herself. What do you think about calling Xi?"

"No fucking way!"

"Who's Xi?" I asked.

"He's a fighter, not a trainer. We're not calling him," Derek reiterated.

"Then I'll go to another gym. I hear The Cage is pretty good at teaching people how to fight."

Derek threw me an exasperated look.

"That shithole over in the Bronx? That place is a meat market—a prime place for jugheads hyped up on roids to come at girls who look just like you. You want a real-life self-defense lesson? Oh, you'll get one alright—in the dingy parking lot behind their building. You won't even have to go looking."

I'd heard the stories about The Cage and had no intention of going to the seedy gym, but Derek didn't know that. My goal was to convince him to train me—properly train me.

"Well, if that's what it takes," I taunted.

Hana looked back and forth between the two of us and shook her head.

"I'm calling Xi," she announced, pulling her cell phone out of her gym bag. I tossed her an appreciative smile.

"Thanks."

"Oh, for fuck's sake... Fine!" Derek yelled and threw up his hands.

I listened to Hana speak in Japanese, presumably to Xi. I had no idea what she was saying, but when she hung up, she was smiling.

"I didn't know you spoke Japanese so fluently," I said.

"I was born here, but my parents are from Yokohama. I can speak the language, but only use it on occasion—like when I'm trying to keep secrets from Derek," she teased and looked pointedly at him. "Anyway, Xi is free now. He said he can meet us over at the boxing ring in fifteen minutes, then we can get started."

Derek scowled at her before turning to point a finger at me.

"I'm warning you. Xi isn't a teacher. He's an MMA fighter. He doesn't understand boundaries or limits. If something goes wrong, don't say—"

"I get it, Derek," I bit out. "If I get hurt, it's on me."

THE NEXT MORNING, I discovered the reason behind Derek's warning—felt it in the fibers of every single muscle in my body. Halfway through the session, Derek had stormed out in protest of what he thought was unnecessary roughness. It was true. Xi was no joke. He took me to task in the traditional boxing ring— which was exactly what I needed. I reminded myself of that as I stretched my calves for lesson number two.

"Back for more," Hana joked when she walked into the room. After dumping her bag in the corner, she joined me on the mat next to the ring. I just smiled weakly, trying not to look at the posters of fierce MMA fighters on the walls. Her grin turned into a frown. "Are you okay?"

"I don't know, Hana. I honestly don't know. Sometimes, I wonder if I'm only fooling myself."

"Are you sure you don't want to go to the police just in case? I mean, if your husband really is here, he doesn't have the pull in New York like he does—"

"No, Hana. No police. It won't make a bit of difference. There are good cops and bad cops, but I've yet to meet one who didn't hide behind the blue wall of silence. If there was a way for people to know who the bad cops are, they wouldn't *be* bad. I don't know who Ethan has paid off, so I can't trust any of them. Besides, even if the NYPD did help me, that wouldn't stop Ethan from coming for me. You and I both know that."

She sighed and shook her head.

"The shit women have to go through just isn't fair."

A silence passed between us, neither one of us needing to elaborate on how skewed the system was.

"I'm scared," I whispered, more to myself than to her.

Before she could respond, Derek came into the room with Xi following behind him. He nodded curtly, then walked over to the stereo system.

"Are you stretched?" Derek asked me.

"All set to go."

"Good. Go gear up. Xi is going to… well, he's going to try to kick your ass again today. But the keyword there is 'try.'" Looking pointedly at me, his face turned hard. "You aren't going to let him win today. Do you understand me?"

My eyes widened in surprise. Derek had never taken an authoritative tone with me—ever. As I tried to decide whether that had been the missing link to all this, I went to put on the protective gear.

Derek turned on the stereo, and angry, growling lyrics from Three Days Grace blasted through the speakers. Derek nodded his head at Hana and pointed to the door. Reacting to his silent message, she went and closed it.

With the music loud in my ears, I climbed up into the ring. Xi began by taking me through a series of drills, none like the self-defense moves I'd learned. He taught me how to respond to a first hit and how to initiate one. All were grueling once we got into it, and I hit the deck more times than I could count. After an hour, Xi took a step back.

"Are you ready to go at this for real now?" he asked, his Japanese accent thick in between pants.

"Yeah, let me just grab a quick drink."

Walking over to the corner of the ring, I took the water bottle Derek held out to me.

"I don't know what you're trying to prove here, Sparky. This is a bad idea," he warned. "Xi went easy on you yesterday. Are you sure you're ready for this?"

I ignored the sinking feeling in my stomach. I was still sore from yesterday, and my muscles were already wrought with exhaustion from today, but Derek didn't understand why I had to do this—why I had to be prepared. He was a man and I was a woman. As much as I cared for him and appreciated his many self-defense lessons, he would never truly comprehend how different our worlds were. Instead of showing any sort of concern, I just nodded and handed the bottle back to him.

"I'm ready."

Turning around to face Xi once more, I moved to the center of the ring. Without warning, he attacked. I was on my back in a matter of seconds with his body towering over me.

"This is bullshit!" Derek roared. "Enough of this!" He crossed the ring and placed a hand under my arm to help me up.

"No," I hissed and shrugged him off. Getting back to my feet on my own, I rounded on him. "You don't understand, Derek!"

"I don't understand what? I mean, come on! You expect me to sit back and watch you get pulverized by a man twice your size?" Gone was the authoritative tone he'd originally come in the room with. Now, all I heard was genuine concern and fear.

"Yeah, I do."

"Tell me one reason why I should allow this to continue."

DAKOTA WILLINK

"Because I need to be ready, damn you!" I shouted. "If Ethan comes for me again—and I know he will—I need to be ready. So, are you going to help me or not?"

Derek and I stared at each other, a battle of wills neither one of us was willing to surrender to. After a few moments, resignation settled into his shoulders.

"Fine," he spat out and moved back to the corner of the ring. "Xi, go again."

Once again, Xi came at me without warning. When I turned to face him, he was already there poised to clothesline me, but I anticipated his movements. Using my shorter height to my advantage, I easily ducked out of the way. Unfortunately, my triumph was short-lived. Before I could get my feet planted firmly once again, Xi turned and landed a blow to the side of my head. I had protective headgear on, but that didn't stop the ringing in my ears. The force of the blow sent me sideways, and I went down hard.

"That was a fucking cheap shot, Xi," I cursed.

"Not good enough, Gia!" Derek yelled. "This isn't like classroom lessons. Your attacker will always take the cheap shot. You need to anticipate and react accordingly. Get up and do it again!"

I scowled at Xi and got to my feet. I was pissed at his tactics to catch me unaware. In class, maneuvers were taught, and we'd practice accordingly. Sneak attacks hadn't been practiced at all. But Derek was right—real life wouldn't be anything like self-defense class.

I moved toward the center of the ring. I saw Hana moving along the far wall out of the corner of my eye and glanced her way. In that split second, Xi was on me like white on rice. With one swift kick, he swept my legs out from under me, and I went down again.

"Shit, Xi. What the—" I began, but Derek cut me off.

"I saw your eyes shift to Hana. You let yourself be distracted. Do it again!"

So, we did—and again, and again. Angry music raged on as I was repeatedly brought to my knees. I lost count of how many times I found myself flat on my back. Angry, rage-filled tears stung my eyes when Xi brought me down yet again.

Who was I kidding?

I'd never be able to handle myself if Ethan came at me. He'd win. He'd always win.

Suddenly, the music was silenced. Xi stood over me, and I closed my eyes, so he wouldn't see my tears. I expected Derek to yell again, but instead, I heard his quiet voice next to my ear.

"Keep your eyes closed. You need to learn to trust your instincts and see with more than your eyes. Tell me what you hear," he said. Doing as instructed, I listened to the sounds around me.

"I don't hear anything. Just some thumping coming from the racquetball courts."

"Wrong. Listen again."

Taking a deep breath, I trained my ears to pick up the slightest sounds around me.

Breathing.

I could hear Xi's labored breaths from taking me to task for the last hour.

Swish, swish, squeak.

There was a rustling of material, a sound I recognized it as the material of Hana's wind pants, followed by the scuff of a sneaker against the polished concrete floor.

"I hear Xi breathing. And Hana... her pants. She uncrossed her legs. Both of her feet are on the floor."

"Very good. Now, what do you smell."

I inhaled through my nose once... twice... three times.

"Vinyl from the mats. Rubber from the ring. Soap and sweat. Someone's deodorant... Xi's, I think."

"Now, tell me what you feel."

Keeping my eyes closed, I focused my attention on my body. "I feel my heart beating on my chest. My skin is sticky. My muscles—"

"No, Gia. That's not what I mean. Try again. What do you feel *inside*?" Derek asked again, emphasizing the last word. I shook my head, too embarrassed to say it out loud, but he was persistent. "How do you feel, Gia?"

"Weak," I admitted in a whisper.

"Lie still. Take a deep breath. Inhale, exhale, then do it again. Inhale. Exhale. In through the nose, out through the mouth." I did as he instructed, still sensing Xi hovering over me. I detected Derek moving closer until he was able to whisper directly into my ear. "You are not weak. You are not what he says you are. Tell yourself that."

"I am not weak. I am not what he says I am."

"You are smart and intelligent."

"I am smart and intelligent," I repeated, feeling somewhat silly.

"What happened is not your fault. You did not fail." When I didn't copy his words immediately, Derek's voice grew louder, and he barked, "Say it!"

"What happened is not my fault! I did not fail!"

"You are strong. You are enough. You are in charge."

"I am strong. I am enough. I am in charge."

"I am. Those are two very strong words. What you put after them can shape your reality. So, say it again… and say it like you mean it!" he ordered. I clenched my teeth as a sudden surge of adrenaline coursed through my body.

"I am strong! I am enough! I am in charge!"

"He can't hurt you anymore."

"He can't hurt me anymore!"

"Good, Sparky. That's good. Now breathe deep again and imagine this. You are down on the ground. You are at your weakest. That's what he wants—what he preys on. Will you let him strike?"

"No."

"What are you going to do?"

"I will attack first."

"And if he fights back?"

"It won't matter. I am going to be enough."

"How are you going to make sure of that?" Derek pushed.

A sound bubbled up, detonating from some place deep in my belly and erupting into something like a growl on my lips. Before Xi could even think about what he was about to do, I was up.

"Because my life is my own, and I'm going to take it back."

39

Derek

I watched Gianna zip up her gym bag then stand to rotate her neck to stretch the muscles. Every part of her had to hurt. As much as it killed me to know that, I knew the pain was a good thing. After four more failed attempts, she had finally taken Xi down. I was awed by her fierce determination.

"You did good, but you still have more to learn," I told her after Hana and Xi left the room. "You should break tomorrow and let your muscles relax."

She shook her head.

"I can't take a break and you know it."

I pursed my lips, annoyed by her stubbornness, but decided not to push the issue. Reaching into my pocket, I pulled out a small silver tube and handed it to her.

"Take this," I instructed and slipped the four-inch metal stick into her hand.

"What is it?"

"It's a kubotan."

"It looks like a penlight keychain."

"It's meant to look that way for discretion purposes. It has a small knife hidden inside. It's not really big enough to do any major damage, but if used properly, you could buy yourself precious seconds needed to get away from anyone who may be trying to harm you. It's a pretty common self-defense weapon. Technically, it's not legal, so don't go waving it around. I don't know Ethan but from what you've said, I think you should keep this on your person just in case. If you're alone, make sure to always have this at the ready. All you have to do is unscrew the tip, flip it around, and screw it back in."

I watched as she twisted it open and did as I instructed so the top became the handle. The hidden blade made a perfect, pocket-sized knife. She looked up at me and smiled.

"Uh, thanks, I guess. Hopefully I won't need to use it," she joked lightly.

"This isn't a laughing matter, Gia. I don't know what's going on in your head, but I need you to promise me that you'll be safe."

Wrapping her arms around my waist, she attempted to give me a reassuring squeeze.

"Trust me, Derek. I'm trying in every way I know how."

"Are you going to tell me where you're staying?" When she shook her head, I released a grunt of frustration. "I don't know why the hell you can't trust me. I don't see the need for all of this secrecy."

"Don't get mad. This isn't about whether or not I trust you. It's the police I don't trust. I can't rely on them to keep me safe. If you know where I am and they pressure you to tell them, it could get back to Ethan. Call me crazy, but I think of it as survival. I'm doing what I need to do. It's you who needs to trust me."

Not knowing where she was living was driving me absolutely insane. I'd barely slept in three days because of it. I suspected she might be at a woman's shelter, but I couldn't be sure. There were so many shelters around the city. If I started calling each one of them, I wouldn't get far. They did a good job of hiding women from abusers. If Ethan really was watching as she suspected, I needed to be on guard as well. Any attempt I made to find her could inadvertently tip him off to her location.

Pulling her closer, I squeezed her tight. I never wanted her to leave my side. I loved this fierce little woman with every fiber of my being and couldn't wait for the day I could tell her everything I felt for her. I wanted to protect her and keep her safe more than anything in the world. I understood her reasons for doing what she was doing, but that didn't mean I had to like it.

"I trust you. It's him I don't trust," I murmured into the top of her head. I made sure my tone was soft, but inside, I felt a raging beast fighting to be unleashed. I hated this—hated that he'd hurt her, hated that she was afraid, and most of all, I hated feeling helpless.

She looked up and placed a chaste kiss on lips.

"I have to go. I'll call you later tonight."

Reluctantly, I stepped back. It killed me to watch her leave the gym all alone. It was just after-dinner hour and still light outside. The streets would be crowded enough to keep her relatively safe, but that didn't stop me from worrying. Frustrated beyond all hell, I had a sudden urge to throw something. I had tried to keep calm, but after days of worrying about Gianna's safety, I was ready to snap.

I eyed the long punching bag in the corner of the room. Not bothering with boxing gloves, I stepped up to the bag and took a bare-fisted swing. Hitting the vinyl felt better than I expected. I'd never used a bag to work out my anger, but after the third strike, I could already feel how it was helping work through the swarm of emotions that pumped through my veins. I beat at the bag, over and over again, relishing the cathartic release with every blow.

I gave my girlfriend a pocketknife to protect herself—a fucking knife!

I didn't want to think about how seriously messed up that was. I spun around and struck the bag with a forceful back fist and tried to erase the memory of Gianna telling me what Ethan had done to her—all the reasons why she needed a knife and self-defense classes. I turned again and landed a punishing roundhouse kick, forcing the image of her fearful eyes when she thought he'd found her. I pulled Ethan's face from the deep recesses of my memory and imagined his bones and cartilage crunching beneath my fists as I inflicted another punch into the cylindrical bag.

Feral, violent thoughts consumed me. I didn't like feeling this way and knew I needed to calm this unfamiliar temper. Rage wasn't going to help Gianna—she'd already experienced enough rage from one man.

Taking a few calming breaths, I resumed working the bag at a more measured pace.

Snap. Two. Three. Four. Punch. Two. Three. Four. Kick. Two. Three. Four.

I counted the reps over and over again, using the tempo to calm the roiling anger. I let the punches flow freely, the snap keeping a steady pace as my feet moved effortlessly around the bag.

Thirty minutes later, I was drenched in sweat, and my knuckles were raw from repeatedly hitting the vinyl without the proper gear. However, my mind felt clearer. While still frustrated about the entire situation, I no longer felt as if I was about to lose control. With labored breaths, I stepped away from the bag and leaned down to brace my hands on my knees.

In general, I didn't consider myself an angry person who couldn't control his emotions. I took most problems in stride and allowed things to roll off my back. The fury I felt now came from some place deep within me—a place I hadn't known existed until now. I may have unwillingly committed to trusting Gianna with whatever it was she was doing, but there was no way in hell I would let this go on indefinitely. I'd waited too long to have her. Now that we were finally together, I'd be damned before I let some son of a bitch fuck it all up. Gianna deserved happiness, and I would do everything in my power to make sure she got it.

40

Derek

I unlocked the door to my apartment and ushered Maisie inside. We'd just come back from the roof after letting her out one last time for the night. She scampered over to her crate and curled up inside, and before I'd removed my sneakers, she was already fast asleep.

"Must be nice," I mumbled and shook my head. I'd barely slept in days. Making my way to the refrigerator to grab a bottle of water, I contemplated how easy it must be to live the life of a dog. Eat, sleep, poop. That was about it.

I twisted off the bottle cap and took a long swig. Mid swallow, a knock at the door sounded. I slowly pulled the plastic bottle from my lips and looked at the door. It was nearing midnight, and I typically didn't get late-night visitors.

The hairs on the back of my arms stood on end, and an icy chill crept up my spine. I wasn't one to spook easily, but I couldn't stop Gianna's fears from racing to the forefront of my mind. Grabbing a butcher knife from one of the drawers in the kitchen, I cautiously made my way to the door and peered through the peephole. A uniformed officer stood on the other side. That didn't ease my concern. I never put much thought into Gianna's theories about not trusting the police, but now... this uneasy feeling was making me think perhaps I should have.

I hooked the security chain on the door, hid the knife behind my back, and opened the door a crack.

"Derek Mills?" the officer asked.

"That's me."

"I'm Officer Ridley with the NYPD. Are you the owner of the gym across the street?"

"Um, yes. That's correct," I said, feeling somewhat perplexed.

"Unfortunately, there's been a break-in. Someone standing outside waiting to get into Club Revolution noticed something was off inside the gym and called it in."

I frowned. That didn't make sense. I should have been notified.

"What do you mean there was a break-in? Why didn't the alarm company call me?"

"It appears the alarm was disabled. The person who called it in also happens to live in this building. She's the one who told us you lived here. It's pretty bad. I'm here to ask you to come with me. We need to ask you a few questions and—"

"Hang on," I interrupted. I wasn't going to get to the bottom of this by talking through two inches of space. Momentarily closing the door, I tossed the butcher knife onto the couch. Just as I was about to remove the security chain from the door, I found myself hesitating. Moving quickly to the windows, I looked down at the street below. There was a line of people waiting to get into Club Revolution, extending all the way down the block. Three cop cars were positioned in front of The Mill, their lights flashing brightly into the night sky as the clubgoers looked on curiously. At least four armed officers stood talking to one another on the sidewalk.

Clearly, this wasn't some hoax concocted by Gianna's husband. This was the real deal.

Shit!

Hurrying back the door, I opened it and followed Officer Ridley down to The Mill, hoping and praying nothing of real value was taken.

"You said the break-in was bad. How much did they take?" I asked him as we exited my building. He paused at the curb and turned to face me. There was pity in his eyes.

"I don't know what, if anything, was taken. The vandalism is what makes it so bad. Do you have any enemies, Mr. Mills?"

I didn't respond as I mentally put together a possible scenario.

Vandalism. Nothing was taken. Enemies.

I had a sinking feeling I knew who was behind the break-in, but before I voiced my suspicions, I wanted to see how bad the damage was. Crossing the street, I walked through the main doors to The Mill. It was dark inside, the only light coming from the streetlights and the police cars. Still, at a quick glance, things looked in rough shape. Heading straight for the main desk, I hit the light switches on the wall.

I audibly gasped when the fluorescent lighting filled the space. I could barely believe what I was seeing.

Every single treadmill was destroyed. While replacing the slashed belts was easy enough, there would be no repairing the smashed NordicTrack touchscreens. The stationary bikes were all flipped on end, and the elastic cords from the rowing machines had been ripped from their wheels. However, the property destruction wasn't the reason for my shock.

Every wall had been vandalized with red spray paint, covering the white and gray surfaces with barely legible words and symbols I wasn't familiar with. The free-standing banner next to the front desk, once advertising yoga class offerings, had been shredded to ribbons. The frame for it was still intact, and the vandal had used a jump rope to fashion a noose from the top rail. Hanging from it was a large stuffed dog—one that very much resembled a Cavalier King Charles Spaniel.

Maisie.

A chill raced down my spine. I had to force myself to remember I'd just left her, and she was completely fine.

"Who would do such a thing?" I whispered to myself.

This wasn't some random act. It was clearly the work of a madman. I walked across the main floor, surveying the rest of the damage. The smoothie bar was in ruins. Blenders and tumblers had been tossed about, and everything was covered in smashed fruit and supplement powder. Every one of the bench presses was toppled over, and the weight bars had been strewn haphazardly across the main floor. I nearly tripped over one and stopped to pick it up. However, I paused when I noticed the angle was identical to the one lying in front of it. I stood and took another look at the weight bars. On second glance, they weren't tossed as carelessly as I'd thought. In fact, they looked like they formed a pattern.

I quickly headed toward the raised platform on the far-left side of the gym, skipping every other step until I reached the long row of ellipticals lining the railings. Looking down at the main floor, the arrangement of the barbells and weight bench bars clearly formed the shape of a cross.

What the fuck?

At this height, I could also see other areas of the gym more clearly. Through the wall of broken glass windows at the back of the gym, I was able to see the rooms with the racket ball court and the boxing ring where Gianna had been training just that morning. Written in red spray paint, the word 'wrath' defaced the vinyl floor of the ring.

Wrath?

I shifted my gaze to take a closer look at the spray-painted walls I'd seen when I first arrived. If I wasn't mistaken, two of the scrawled words spelled out 'lust' and 'greed.'

I heard a thumping on the stairs and looked over to see Pete Milano following the path I'd just taken up to the platform. Pete was a lieutenant with NYPD and a client at The Mill. Although I knew he was a cop, it was strange to see him in uniform. I was used to seeing him in sweatpants and his standard gray NYPD t-shirt.

"Pete," I greeted with a nod and accepted his offered handshake.

"Hey, man. Tough break. I came here as soon as the call came over the radio."

"This is brutal. I haven't even begun to wrap my head around it. There's just so much destruction."

"You ain't kidding. I was just talking to Detective Warhol. He said whoever it was cut the phone lines so the alarm company wasn't notified, then gained entry through the service door in the alley. The frame was chipped, and he found a heavy-duty paint scraping tool on the ground. Forensics will dust it for prints, and hopefully, we'll get a lead." He paused, glanced around at the damage again, then frowned. Raising a hand, he pointed down toward the barbells on the main floor. "Is that a cross?"

"Yeah, I'm pretty sure that's exactly what it is."

"This looks more like a hate crime than anything else. Do you know anyone who might do this?

"I think I have an idea," I stated wryly. "Although, the cross and the words spray-painted on the walls are throwing me off." I stared hard at the bright red, sloppily painted words, trying to recall if Gianna had ever mentioned Ethan being a religious fanatic.

"Throwing you off, how?"

"I'm dating this girl, and it's very possible her husband may have done this. His name is Ethan Walker. She left him a while back after he knocked her around one too many times," I told him, deliberately avoiding the horrific details out of respect for Gianna's privacy. "We recently found out the Cincinnati police are looking for him. She thinks he's here in New York. The thing is, I don't remember her saying he was some kind of religious extremist."

"Wait a minute. Did you say, Ethan Walker? He doesn't happen to be a cop, does he?"

"Yeah, actually, he is—or at least he was. I heard he was suspended from the job. Why do you ask?"

Pete let out a low whistle and shook his head.

"Shit, your girlfriend was married to *that* guy?"

I didn't bother to correct him that she was *still* married to him. Instead, I zeroed in on the fact he'd even heard of Ethan in the first place. I was fairly certain the NYPD didn't make a habit of knowing the business of the Cincinnati Police.

"Yeah, so. Why do you say it like that?"

"If we're talking about the same dude, the Cincinnati police aren't the only ones looking for him. He's a fucking nut job. I'm talking serial killer nuts. He had a secret apartment of sorts. It was weird—like a sadomasochist den. Now, all of this is making sense."

"What do you mean?"

"I saw pictures of the place. The imagery was a sadist's delight, and he seemed obsessed with the seven deadly sins."

"You saw pictures?" I was trying to piece together what he was saying and realized my questions kept coming fast and furious.

"Yeah, the FBI sent them over just a few days ago. It was like seeing pictures from the movie set for *Seven*—you know, that movie with Brad Pitt? Anyway, it was really messed up shit. An APB on this guy went out to precincts all across the country. I have to call my Captain. If you think this might have been done by Ethan Walker, the FBI is going to want to know."

41

Derek

Forty-five minutes later, I watched as the police taped off the exterior of my building and a forensic team bustled about warning everyone not to touch anything. I anxiously paced, holding Maisie in my arms. Considering everything, I didn't want to leave her alone. She whined and nervously licked my face, sensing my unease.

"I know, girl. Don't worry. I've got you."

I took in her big round eyes and black button nose. If anything had happened to her, I don't know what I would have done. If this lunatic was able to bypass my security system to get into The Mill, accessing my apartment would be a walk in the park. And if this was, in fact, Ethan who did this, I was terrified for Gianna's safety as well.

I'd tried to call her several times, but it went straight to voicemail. It was infuriating. While it wasn't unusual for her to have her phone off, I needed to know if she was okay. I'd already been questioned by Detective Warhol, but he wasn't forthcoming with any details about Ethan Walker. He told me I needed to stay put until the FBI arrived. I still didn't know why the FBI was involved, but from the looks of what was going on outside, I assumed I'd find out soon.

Two unmarked SUV's had just pulled up with blue lights flashing through the windshield, signaling they were the FBI. Hopefully, I'd finally get some answers to whatever the hell was going on.

Four people emerged from the vehicles. After talking to the responding officers for a moment, they split off in various directions, with the lone female agent heading straight for me. She was dressed in a sharp, navy pantsuit and carrying a briefcase.

"Derek Mills?" she asked as she approached, flashing her badge.

"That's me," I replied cautiously.

"I'm Agent Gregory, FBI. I work out of the New York field office, Division of Violent Crimes. Is there a place we can talk privately?"

"Yeah, sure, my office. Follow me."

I hadn't been inside my office yet and silently wondered if that had been destroyed as well. Unfortunately, whoever did this didn't show prejudice. Even though the office door had been locked, breaking through the hollow wooden door hadn't been difficult.

Once inside, I found the desk had been cleared of its contents. Everything was scattered all over the floor, including my six-thousand-dollar Apple desktop, lying face up with a coffee mug smashed into the middle of the screen. Fitness posters had been torn from the walls, and all the files from my filing cabinet had been torn up.

Fuck.

I had insurance that should cover the monetary costs of things, but there was no way to replace the hundreds of hours' worth of paperwork. Frustrated and pissed off, I kicked aside the debris to make a path to the small table and two chairs in the corner. I sat down, positioned Maisie on my lap, and motioned for the agent to have a seat across from me.

Not wasting time, Agent Gregory removed a laptop from her briefcase, fired it up, and turned the screen to face me. A picture of Ethan Walker stared back at me.

"Do you know this man?" she asked.

"Not really. I only met him once briefly three years ago, although we were never formally introduced." Before I could elaborate further, she clicked a button on the keyboard, and another image appeared. This one was of Gianna. The picture must have been an older one because her hair was still blond when it was taken.

"What about her?"

"That's the woman I'm seeing." The agent nodded her head knowingly as if pieces of the puzzle were starting to fall into place. "What is this all about? What does she have to do with the break-in."

"So, Gianna is still alive. Good. That gives me some relief, at least."

"Still alive?" I stared incredulously at Agent Gregory, waiting for her to elaborate.

"Yes. I think your girlfriend was the motive," she explained before turning the computer back toward her and clicking away on the keyboard again. "I've been profiling Ethan Walker for some time now, although I never had a name for him until now. He is the suspect in four homicides in Cincinnati, Cleveland, New York City, and Niagara Falls."

"Homicides?"

"Mr. Mills, I believe your girlfriend is in very real danger," she told me as she continued to type. "I need you to tell me everything you know and anything she might have told you about Ethan Walker. I'm also going to need to question her but

I've been unable to locate her. I'm hoping you can help me with that."

"Look, Agent Gregory, I already told you I don't personally know Ethan. The only time Gianna ever really spoke of him was a couple of days ago when she told me her history with him. He abused her terribly. She's terrified of him."

"She should be. He's a dangerous man."

"She also told me because of his influence, she's terrified of the police," I said pointedly. "She doesn't trust them to protect her. I understand why you want to talk to her, but when I consider her feelings about law enforcement, I'm hesitant to betray her trust. If what you suspect is true, and Ethan really did kill those other women, I need more assurances from you before I lead you to Gianna. What makes you so sure you can protect her?"

"I don't think you understand how dangerous Ethan Walker is. In all four homicide cases, the women went missing for long periods of time. Eventually, their bodies were found." Reaching down into her briefcase, she procured four pictures, each of a badly beaten woman. Purplish-black marks ringed their necks, showing clear evidence of strangulation. Unconsciously, I brought my hand to my throat and recalled Gianna's fear of having her neck touched on the first day she took my self-defense class.

"Jesus Christ," I whispered.

"My team was able to reconstruct the behavioral sequence for each homicide, trying to understand the modus operandi or method of committing the crime. The only reason we were able to connect the dots was because of Cynthia Dufresne, an attorney in Cincinnati. Ethan nearly killed her. She tried to tell the police what happened to her, but it fell on deaf ears. I can see why Gianna harbors so much mistrust," she added with a hint of distain. "Ms. Dufresne contacted her local FBI field office. I routinely read reports from other offices. When I read her case, the pieces started to fall into place, and I knew we finally had our guy. The crime signatures were exactly the same. Each woman was severely beaten with a club or cane of some sort, tied down, and branded with the emblem of a serpent. Then he strangled to them death. The only difference was that Cynthia lived, whereas the others did not. Her statement allowed us to get a search warrant for his home in Indian Hill. During the raid, we found paperwork showing he also had two other places of residence. These other pictures are from a raid we conducted on one of those residences." The look on her face was somber as she pushed aside the gruesome pictures of the dead women and turned the computer toward me.

The images on the screen were of rooms with painted black walls, decidedly gothic, and decorated with all kinds of instruments designed to inflict pain. The walls had been written on with red spray paint, the markings similar to what had been scrawled on the walls in The Mill. I couldn't help but recall what Pete Milano said about it being a sadist's delight as Agent Gregory clicked through image after image.

My eyes widened in shock when I saw the multiple corkboards, each one designated for pictures of at least ten different women. It was obvious the pictures were taken with a telephoto lens from a distance, signaling none of the women knew the shots were being taken. One of the boards was filled with images of Gianna.

"Four of these women have been found dead. They were the victims in the photographs I showed you. Other than Gianna, I can't say for certain if any of these other women are still alive. We're still trying to identify them," Agent Gregory said, pointing at the corkboards for each deceased woman. She continued to click through the images and showed me one where a shrine to the Virgin Mary had been erected. The small table on which the statue sat was littered with odd paraphernalia—a framed photo of an older woman, perfume bottles, candles, rosary beads, and scraps of paper. There was a large, fifty-gallon fish tank along the wall of what I presumed to be a living room of sorts. Inside the tank was a large snake.

"What's with his snake obsession?" I asked, remembering what she's said about the women being branded with a serpent.

"If I had to take a guess, based our profiling, Ethan is a radicalized Catholic who is obsessed with the seven deadly sins —lust, pride, greed, wrath, envy, gluttony, and sloth. While the cow traditionally symbolizes lust, in Catholicism, the serpent was the reason for the destruction of the Garden of Eden. The snake brought lust into the Garden when it tempted Eve to eat the apple from the Tree of Knowledge, and most likely reminds him about that. When he gives in to the temptation of lust, he punishes himself." Pausing, she clicked on another image. "This is a cattail whip found in the apartment. We believe he used it to flog himself as an act of penance."

"I can't believe this," I whispered as a chill raced down my spine. I sat back in my chair, horrified to know Gianna had been married to this man.

"BELIEVE IT," she said and reached into her briefcase to pull out another folder. "This is Ethan's file of employment from the Cincinnati Police Department. Everything in it has been fabricated, going all the way back to his degree from Bowling Green. We checked with the college. No one by the name of Ethan Walker ever attended there. He's a master manipulator—a sociopath in every sense of the word. So, do you see now why we need to find your girlfriend?"

"There's no way Gianna knew anything about this," I vehemently stated, but as I said the words, I remembered all of the questions I'd had on the day Gianna took off. I never completely understood the level of fear in her eyes. Too many things hadn't quite added up. Suddenly, everything calculated to one horrifying sum.

Gianna had kept so many secrets tight to her chest. It was possible she did know but was too embarrassed to tell me. As soon as the thought entered my mind, I dismissed it. Every bone in my body was telling me she never knew. She may have thought she knew him—enough so that she trained hard in case she was ever forced to handle him on her own—but she would never deliberately face him alone.

Or would she?

Just the idea of her facing this sadistic fucker one-on-one made my blood run cold. She needed to know exactly who her husband was before it was too late.

Grabbing my phone, I dialed Gianna's number. She had to know what she was up against. Maisie began to whine on my lap as I impatiently waited for Gianna to pick up. I rubbed the top of her head, not sure if I was trying to soothe her anxieties or my own.

The phone just rang and rang. And again, there was no answer.

42

Gianna

"Forty-seven, forty-eight, forty-nine—"

The sound of my cell phone vibrating interrupted my nightly regimen of two hundred crunches. In the shelter's shared bunk room, other women always eyed me curiously when I did these, but nobody asked questions. If they did, it would break an unspoken code. We all had our story, and not one of us owed another an explanation.

Reaching over to the small table next to my bed, I looked at the vibrating screen of the phone. Derek was calling.

"Hey, you," I greeted. "What's up?"

"Gianna, finally! Are you all right?" The alarm in his tone was apparent.

"Yeah, why wouldn't I be? Are you? What's going on?" A worrying silence fell on the other end of the line. "Derek?"

"I've been trying to reach you all night. Why didn't you answer any of my calls?"

I ignored the accusatory tone and focused on the underlying panic I heard in his voice.

"I left my phone in my room while I was…" I trailed off, unable to tell him that I was helping the other women in the shelter clean the common room. If I did, I'd reveal my location. "Does it matter? Derek, what's wrong?"

"There was a break-in at the gym tonight, probably right after we closed. Whoever broke in managed to bypass the alarm system. Club Revolution has some high-profile DJ there tonight and there was a huge line to get in—one that extended to the front of the gym. They saw something was up and called the police."

"Did they catch the person?"

"No. I'm here at The Mill with the police now. They're just wrapping up. The FBI just left."

"The FBI?"

"Jesus Christ, Gia… I don't even know how to tell you this."

Now, I was beginning to panic and gripped the phone tighter.

"Tell me what?"

"The gym was vandalized."

"Well, that's just stupid. I never understood why people feel the need to vandalize things. Breaking in and robbing the place is bad enough. Why wreck everything?"

"That's just it—this wasn't a robbery. Nothing appears to be taken. This was very deliberate."

A sinking feeling settled in my stomach.

"What do you mean?"

"I think you're right about Ethan being in New York. I think he did this. I just finished talking to the FBI about him."

Shivers raced down my spine, and I wondered if the time to confront Ethan was near. I'd only been hard training with Xi for two weeks. While I felt more prepared, I wished I'd had more time. Now, with Derek talking to the police—and apparently the FBI—it was only a matter of time before I was flushed out of my hiding place.

"The FBI doesn't get involved in local, petty crimes like vandalism. Why were you talking to them?" I asked.

"It had something to do with the Violent Crimes Division and criminal profiling. There are things... things you need to know. He's not who you think he is. Yes, he's a monster, but it's so much worse than you thought." He fell silent, and my heart began to beat rapidly in my chest. I'd never heard him sound like this before. He sounded genuinely terrified.

"What, Derek? Tell me."

"Four women are dead, Gia. The FBI thinks he killed them. I saw pictures of things... terrible things. He had an apartment with a bunch of corkboards covered with photos of the women he's stalking. There were pictures of you that looked like they were taken long before you ever met him. There was a weird shrine to the Virgin Mary and a fish tank with a snake. He uses a whip to punish himself, and—"

"Derek, stop." He was rambling and not making any sense. "I don't know what you're talking about. Who has an apartment with a snake? Ethan?"

"Yes!"

Derek continued at a more measured pace, recapping everything that happened from the moment a police officer had come to his door to tell him there'd been a break-in. The more he talked, the more I felt like I was living in an alternate reality.

Missing women.

Homicide.

Radicalized Catholic. The seven deadly sins. Shrines. Crosses.

Homicide.

Homicide.

Homicide.

Keywords replayed over and over again in my head as quick, shallow breaths chopped at my chest.

No, no, no!

While I heard what Derek was saying, it was as though he was speaking to someone else in another life. I knew Ethan to be among the most vile who walked the earth, but if what Derek said was true, what did that say about me? I'd been married to a serial killer and I didn't even know it. I staggered under the cumulative weight of his words.

Flashes of my life with Ethan assaulted me—sunset walks when we were dating, his marriage proposal, our wedding vows, moments of intimacy. All of it had been with a stranger. I'd shared my bed with a murderer. How could I have been so blind—to not know about this other life my own husband lived?

A part of me wanted to curl into a ball and deny what I was hearing. They say ignorance is bliss. Would I have been better not knowing any of this—not knowing that my husband was secretly a religious zealot who stalked and murdered women? I thought back to the many instances of abuse I'd experienced at Ethan's hand. I'd often wondered if he'd mentally kissed his knuckles before smashing them into my cheek. Now I knew he was reverently kissing a cross in the most twisted, hedonistic sort of way.

My stomach roiled, and I wanted to be sick. Oddly, I also felt a strong surge of guilt—guilty for surviving while so many others had died. If I'd had the courage to go to the police or the FBI like Cynthia had, could I have prevented any of those women from dying?

I tried not to contemplate the horrors they may have gone through and swallowed the bile welling in my throat. Sheer will was the only thing keeping the tremble out of my body as I finished listening to Derek.

"The FBI wants to talk to you. They want to offer you witness protection."

"Not a chance in hell," I immediately responded.

"Gianna, please," Derek begged. "I know you don't trust the

police, but you have to take my word about this. Talk to Agent
Gregory. She promised to keep you safe."

I sighed and pinched the bridge of my nose. A tension
headache was beginning to spread across my forehead, either
from keeping my jaw clenched for so long or from the surge of
adrenaline that always came with fear.

"This isn't about trusting them, Derek... at least now it isn't.
It's about not wanting to hide anymore. After I told you
everything, I finally felt there was hope—like I could have a real
shot at life after Ethan. I don't want to go backward. Witness
protection would do exactly that. What happens to me if some
hotshot lawyer manages to get him off on a technicality? I'd
have to stay hidden indefinitely, and I don't want to hide
anymore."

"Sparky, listen to me. The man is absolutely crazy. There's
no telling what he's capable of. You need the FBI's help. You
can't do this alone."

"Can't I?" I stated bitterly. "I survived Ethan on my own for
years, and I can do it again. I don't need the FBI."

"This is bullshit, and you know it," he snapped, his
frustration evident. "You can't possibly expect me to sit here and
do nothing. Where are you? I'm coming to get you."

Despite all of Derek's usual patience and understanding, this
was one thing he'd never understand. Ethan took everything
from me. Now, he was targeting Derek, and I'd be damned
before I'd let him take Derek away from me, too. If Ethan was
given the chance, I knew he'd kill Derek just as surely as he
would kill me.

My hand knotted into an angry fist. I couldn't take my
chances with the FBI and the broken system. It was time for me
to face Ethan—once and for all.

"I've got this. There are things I need to do, and arguing with
you isn't one of them. You need to trust me. Goodnight, Derek."

I heard him talking but I ended the call before I could make it out his words. It immediately started vibrating again with Derek's number lighting up the screen. I ignored the call and powered off the phone. A pang of guilt hit me for cutting him off, but it was for the best. I wasn't sure what the rest of the night was going to bring but knew he would be better off if I left him in the dark.

Plausible deniability.

I looked around the large room and across the row of cots. Lights out was at eleven. It was after midnight now, and all the women taking shelter for the night appeared to be sleeping. As quietly as I could, I reached under my cot and pulled out my canvas book bag. Inside were the clothes I'd grabbed in my mad dash to leave my apartment and a few other things I'd picked up over the past two weeks. I sat on the floor and unzipped the bag to lay out everything I would need—a change of clothes, a notebook and pen, baby oil, rings, and steel-toed boots. I stared at the items for a long while and tried to calm my mounting anxiety with long, deep breaths. I needed to have a clear head if I wanted to properly prepare for what lay ahead.

Once my racing heart returned to a normal rhythm, I picked up the paper and pen first and wrote out three identical letters of instruction. A few days ago, I had concocted a plan to blackmail Ethan into leaving me alone. Given everything Derek told me over the phone, I knew that plan was no longer going to work. Now it was more important the FBI had an arsenal of evidence to put Ethan away for life, but if something happened to me, they'd never have my contribution to their case.

When I was finished, I placed the letters in large manila envelopes I'd already had prepared and addressed. One envelope was addressed to Natalia, and another was addressed to Teddy. I planned to drop those off at the nearest USPS mailbox within the hour. The third envelope had Krystina Cole's name on it and went back inside the canvas bag. If all went well, I'd be back to retrieve it tomorrow. If not, I was certain someone in the shelter would find it and give it to her.

Looking down at the other items I'd removed from the bag, I continued on with my preparations. I had hoped it wouldn't come to this but knew it was my only way to be truly free again. Changing out of the jeans and bulky cowlneck sweater I'd been wearing, I slipped into a pair of black yoga pants and a tight-fitting tank top. Loose clothing was a liability that would make me vulnerable to an attacker if they tried to grab me.

After lacing up the steel-toed boots, I moved on to the baby oil. I flipped open the top and slathered it all over my neck and arms. I needed to be as slippery as an eel if I wanted a fighting chance at escaping a chokehold—one of Ethan's favorite pastimes was wringing my neck.

Using a pair of scissors, I sliced an old black t-shirt into two equal parts, then opened a Ziplock bag that held the eight chunky metal rings I'd purchased from a nearby dollar store. They were nothing but gaudy costume jewelry, but they'd do the trick. After slipping one on each finger, I wrapped my knuckles in the black t-shirt strips, leaving only the top portion of my fingers free.

Placing my discarded clothes and the half-empty bottle of oil in the bag, I made sure to position the envelope addressed to Krystina on top and zipped it closed. Sliding the bag back under the bed, I stood straight, slipped the kubotan Derek had given me into the hidden waistband pocket of my pants, and pulled on an oversized sweatshirt. Turning towards the exit, I squared my shoulders.

It was time to face the music.

THIRTY MINUTES LATER, I unlocked the door to my apartment and cautiously entered. Club Revolution was louder than usual tonight, the thump-thump of the bass matching the pulsing of the blood roaring in my ears. I struggled to block it out and had to really strain to hear any sounds of movement in the apartment.

When I didn't hear anything out of the ordinary, I immediately went to the bathroom to see if my suspicions were correct. The toothpaste was on the counter and exactly where I had left it, but the tube was rolled up tight from the bottom.

Ethan had most certainly been here.

Leaving the bathroom, I scanned the other visible areas. My gaze landed on a vase sitting on the center of the kitchen table. Pink daisies were perfectly arranged, the water crystal clear without an ounce of cloudiness. He was sending me a message. Ethan had not only been here—he'd been in here very recently—and if instinct served me right, he was still here. My already hammering heart began to pound double time.

As quietly as I could, I tiptoed to the kitchen. I removed all of the knives from the butcher block and hid them in the oven. Opening the drawer that held the other kitchen gadgets, such as the rolling pin and mallet, I removed any instruments that could potentially cause serious harm and hid those in the oven next to the knives.

After silently closing the oven door, I looked around the apartment for anything else I might need to stash away. I spotted the mop and broom and shoved those behind the refrigerator. For once I was thankful for the overhead lighting. That meant no lamps and avoidance of any blunt force trauma they could potentially cause.

Maybe I was a fool for thinking I could confront him—like the person who goes outside during a wicked thunderstorm and waits for lightning to strike. Ethan was the lightning and I had no insulator for protection. The only thing I had was myself and I was positioning to be the conductor.

But I knew this feeling.

I had felt it with every tick of the clock while I waited for Ethan to get home from work. Years of being married to him

DAKOTA WILLINK

taught me how to predict a coming storm. Yet as I pulled the sweatshirt I was wearing over my head and tossed it onto the sofa, I knew this time was different. This time I was truly prepared for it—prepared for him.

"Ethan, I know you're here." I fell silent and waited to hear a response or a sound—anything to signal he was near. When there was no reply, I continued talking. "It was you who vandalized the gym, wasn't it? No need to get Derek involved. He's a good guy and didn't deserve that." Still, no response. I would have to push him and get his temper riled up. Ethan was the jealous type, so I knew it wouldn't be too difficult.

"How long have you known I was in New York? Days? Weeks? Months? Were you here the morning I fucked Derek? Did you see him in my bed?" I taunted. If he was here, it wouldn't be much longer before he showed his face. "Derek's way better than you could ever hope to be. And I'm not just talking about in bed. He's kind and caring while you're nothing but a twisted, sadistic coward who gets off on beating women. Rumor has it that you killed a few of them too. You think it makes you strong, but you're wrong. You're the weakest man I know."

The old grandfather clock began to chime one o'clock and it was the most ominous sound I'd ever heard. A creak in the old floorboards made me jump. Panic sucked the air from my chest and I spun my head in the direction of the sound. Ethan was leaning against the doorjamb to the utility closet.

"Hello, Gia."

43

Gianna

I took in the sight of him. Ethan had always been well put together, but now... I'd never seen him look so unkempt. His hair was a mess, and his eyes were dark and wild, sunken into a face he clearly hadn't shaved for days. His appearance made me second guess my decision to confront him. He looked like a madman, and I truly had no idea what he was capable of.

My fight-or-flight instinct threatened to kick into overdrive. Fighting would be my only option if I wanted this to end. It's what I came here for. I squared my shoulders, not wanting to show an ounce of fear.

"So, when did you find out I was in New York?"

"I always knew where you were, Gia. I'll admit, I did lose you for a day or two, but I've had eyes on you ever since you moved into this place." He motioned to the space around him and grimaced at the threadbare sofa with disgust. "I didn't think you'd go back to slumming it."

He took a step closer.

"Yeah, well, I didn't have much of a choice. It might not be the Ritz, but I like it," I replied, inching backward and not taking my eyes off him for one second.

"You've proven to be resourceful. I'll give you that much. You even used your pussy to lure in a new man, as if he could actually replace me," he said in an eerily calm voice. "I've known all about Derek the Dickwad for quite some time too. And yes, I was here the day you spread your legs for him like a whore. I wanted you back with me, where you belonged, but not anymore—not after you let him use you. Oh, I heard how you came for him—how you screamed his name. From my spot behind the hot water tank, I watched you when you sucked him off. You always did give good head."

Although I suspected he'd been here after the fact, I never thought to check the utility closet. My stomach churned with an overwhelming urge to vomit. I didn't want to think about him putting a black stain on my relationship with Derek. What we had was pure and special—and real.

"You're a sick bastard!" I spat out.

"For out of the heart come evil thoughts, murder, adultery, sexual immorality, theft, false witness, slander. Matthew 15:19." He shook his head and tsked. "Your insolence is partly my fault. I should have taught you the good Word, and maybe we wouldn't be here right now."

I blinked, having no idea what he was talking about, but I was sure it was related to the psychotic things Derek had relayed to me.

"You're crazy."

He took another step in my direction, so he was only a few feet away. I brought my hands up in a defensive position, and he laughed.

"What is this? You wrapped your hands? I feel like we've already been through this, Gia. Haven't you learned anything? You can't fight me."

"Oh, no?"

In a swift move he never saw coming, my palm of my left hand connected with his nose. Just as quickly, my right hand followed and snapped a punch to his mouth. Staggering back, he lifted a hand to his lips. When he pulled it back, blood glistened on the tip of one finger. I smiled inwardly, knowing the split lip was the result of the rings I wore. Still, the vengeance I felt wasn't nearly enough to make up for all the times he'd done it to me.

"You're going to pay for that," he hissed.

"No, Ethan, I'm not."

"You really want to play this game? You know how it will end."

"I do—and it won't end well for you. I know all about Cynthia. I know about the FBI and your little masochistic den. I know all about the women you murdered. How much time do you think you'll get for all of that?"

"I have an alibi for everything. They have nothing on me."

Internally, I was shaking at the idea of him walking free, but I couldn't let him know that. I had to keep him talking and distracted.

"I wouldn't be so sure about that. I mean, you always could schmooze your way out of everything, but I don't think your charm will get you far this time. Maybe that's one of the reasons you're here. Am I a loose end you need to tie up? I can assure you, Ethan. I can't help the FBI. I was blindsided by your secret life. I have nothing to tell them. Apparently, I don't even know who you are. What's the point in trying to shut me up?"

"Shutting you up is something I should have done a long fucking time ago."

He lunged at me, but I was quick to sidestep his advance, and he stumbled past me. Spinning to face him once again, I watched as he tried to regain his balance.

"You see, here's the thing, Ethan. You've always underestimated me. In fact, you've underestimated women in general. You might have your cronies in the police department at your back, but you know nothing about women and their survival instincts. Perhaps Cynthia figured it out sooner than I did, but that doesn't mean I didn't learn eventually. Even if you get off scot-free in this FBI homicide investigation—which I doubt—I have other protections in place. I won't run and hide from you anymore. I've prepared three letters, two of which are already in the hands of the United States Postal Service. In fact, I dropped them in the mailbox before coming here tonight. If something happens to me, the recipients of those letters have been given instructions to turn the contents of the envelope over to the D.A. Even if you kill me, the truth about what you did to me will come out."

"You have no proof of anything. Your little letters will be your word against mine."

"And the word of several medical professionals. I have the medical records from the night I miscarried. I also have the results of a rape kit from the night I left you." To my instant gratification, genuine outrage began to show on his face. "That's right, Ethan. After you chased me from the hotel, I asked Teddy to bring me to a twenty-four-hour urgent care center. They accepted cash and the fake name I gave them, and I must say— they were extremely thorough. They took all kinds of x-rays. The doctors were shocked by the evidence of previous injuries that never properly healed."

"I would have known if you went to a hospital. I'm calling your bluff," he stated, twisting his lips into a menacing grin. "Then I'm going to kill you."

He took one step forward. I took one step back and shook my head.

"Nope, it's not a bluff. Oh, then there are the pictures the doc took. The bruises on my neck..." I let my words linger and tsked him. "That will be damning evidence. I mean, thanks to Cynthia, the FBI already has a shitload on you. This is just my little contribution."

There was that telltale angry tick in his jaw and I chanced a glance at his fists. They were opening and closing, a sure sign that he was about to attack.

"It doesn't matter. None of it matters. You may have your protections, but so do I. The FBI will never get to me. I'll disappear. Vanish. Poof. It will be like Ethan Walker never even existed. I did it once before, and I can do it again. My mother taught me exactly how to do it. She taught me everything I know."

For the first time tonight, he'd rattled me.

"What do you mean you did it before?"

"Ah, my girl. How easily I was able to fool you and everyone else. It was years ago. Some little slut in Salt Lake City overdosed on Rohypnol—you know, roofies? When the heat started to come down, Mother and I just picked up a new identity and started a new life in Cinci."

My brows pinched together as I tried to piece together what he was implying.

"What kind of new identity?"

He laughed, the high-pitched, maniacal sound a stark contrast to the deep bass booming from Club Revolution.

"As if Mother would actually name me Ethan. I was born Anthony Gallo, after St. Anthony, the patron saint of lost things. My mother named me that with the hopes of finding the faith she thought she'd lost after she was raped by the man whose seed created me. Born out of wedlock, she feared I would be damned. So, you see, *Val*," he said, emphasizing the name I'd once used. "You aren't the only one who can come up with a fake name."

His name is really Anthony?

I stood stock-still, barely able to process what the stranger before me was saying. I tried to remember the things he'd said about his mother, attempting to figure out if her religion was the reason he'd become the sick, twisted bastard he was today. When I saw him reach down toward his ankle, I forced myself to focus on the present. I knew he was going for the gun most likely secured there.

I was expecting that.

Just as he lifted the hem of his pants and removed it from the holster, I brought my leg around to kick him in the face. The heavy boots caused blood to spurt from his nose as he flew backward and sprawled on the ground. The gun skittered toward me and out of his reach. Moving quickly, I kicked it away and watched as it disappeared under the sofa. I couldn't have planned the guns landing place better if I'd tried.

Ethan scrambled back up to his feet and spit blood on the ground. His eyes flashed.

This was it—the final test to see if all of my training had been in vain.

"You fucking bitch!"

I didn't know who moved first—him or me. Whoever it was, I wasn't fast enough. A hard fist connected with my cheek, and I went hurling to the floor. I scrambled to my knees as Ethan gripped the top of my cropped hair. He yanked me roughly to my feet and smashed my head against the living room wall. Stars dotted my vision, and it was if I were thrown back in time. I remembered this feeling of pain blooming in my skull all too well.

Releasing my hair, he wrapped a hand around my neck. When it began to slip from the oil, he wrapped the other hand around like a manacle, squeezing until my vision began to darken, and I thought I might pass out. I remembered what this felt like—the panic, the hysteria—but shoved it down, focusing on my training. I'd survived this monster once when I had little more than my naïve self-declared bravado. This time, I'd survive because I knew that bravery was no longer false. I could feel it in my bones. I could survive this—I could survive him—and I would live to see another day.

My body shot adrenaline to every vital organ. Calling on my lessons with Derek, Hana, and Xi, I raised my right arm and twisted. Using all my strength, I tried to dislodge his wrists from my throat.

But it didn't work.

What I was taught—all of my defense lessons—didn't work.

He was too strong.

"No, Ethan. Please, don't do this!" I rasped.

"It's useless to try to fight me, Gia. How many times do I have to tell you that?" he growled.

"Please. I just want you to leave me alone. Go... go..." I coughed, struggling to gulp air. "Just go away."

"You're my girl, Gia. Mine. Not his. Not ever. Do you understand me?"

In a fit of rage, he let go of my throat, grabbed me by the roots of my hair again, and whipped me down to the ground. Along the way, my side smacked against the coffee table, and I could swear I heard a crack. Whether it was my ribs or the table, I couldn't be sure. My head, my cheek, my back—I hurt all over, and it was hard to tell where the pain stopped and started. The room tilted, my vision becoming hazy. I couldn't move, my body nothing but a lifeless heap on the floor.

He's finally going to kill me.

I was stupid to come here.

I laid there motionless with my eyes closed, knowing he was near because I could hear his ragged breaths. He was mumbling something that sounded like an incantation, but I tuned him out. In my mind, the words Derek had once made me say came into focus.

I am not weak.

I am not what he says I am.

I am smart and intelligent.

What happened is not my fault.

I did not fail.

I am strong. I am enough. I am in charge.

I am.

He can't hurt me anymore.

I couldn't let Ethan strike. I needed to fight. This was my life and I was going to take it back.

I am enough.

Drawing on the mental aspects of my self-defense training, I kept my eyes closed and listened to the sounds around me. I heard a hollow wood door opening and closing, signaling he had gone down into the hallway for some reason. There was a click-click that reminded me of the stove burner being lit. I tried to peer through partially closed lids to see what he was doing in the kitchen, but I couldn't tell from my angle on the living room floor. A few moments later, there was a strange burning smell, but I couldn't place it. Before I could think about how to investigate further, I heard the shuffle of his feet as he stalked closer.

I pinched my eyes closed tight. From the sound of his breathing, I knew he was hovering above me. He reached down and gripped my jaw with one large hand.

"I'm going to kill your boyfriend next, Gia. If I can't have you, neither can he. He never should have touched you, and now he has to pay. Perhaps I'll skin his fucking little dog alive while he watches as punishment," he hissed. "But first, I'm going to brand you and take what's mine one last time. My cock will be the last thing you ever feel on this earth. Because make no mistake—you will die tonight."

He wants to brand me?

I didn't know what kind of vile, sadistic shit he had planned but I could certainly imagine the worst. With my eyes still closed, I tried not to scream bloody murder as I heard the sound of his pants' buckle come undone. The only security I had was knowing I was fully clothed.

Instead of panicking, I focused on trying to retrieve the kubotan tucked into the side of my waistband without him seeing it. I peered at him, cracking my eyes open just enough to see that he wasn't paying one bit of attention to what I might be doing. He was too preoccupied with his lust, struggling to free his dick.

Then I saw why he was struggling. He was trying to do it one-handed while the other hand brandished a black iron pole with a flaming red tip.

Then it clicked.

The burning smell.

He literally meant physical branding—as if I was a cow, he was preparing to slaughter.

I swallowed back the bile welling in my throat as I slid the tiny knife from its hiding spot. Using my thumb and forefinger, I unscrewed the cap until I could pull it from its sheath. Keeping it hidden under my hip, I waited. When the zipping sound of his fly filled my ears, I knew I would only have seconds to act.

"Why do you do these things, Gia? I just wanted to love you. We were supposed to have babies, and I'd raise them and teach them in the White Room, just as mother taught me. I gave you everything but you had to fuck it all up," he muttered, almost whining, before stepping between my legs and lowering himself down to me. When he reached for the elastic waistband of my yoga pants, I swung my arm up with all of my might and felt the kubotan sink into flesh.

"Fuck!" Ethan roared, but I didn't stop. Pulling the knife out, I plunged it in a second time, then a third. He rolled off me, the hot iron clanging off to the side as he clutched his arm and blood-stained sleeve. "I can't believe you fucking stabbed me! I told you not to fight me, damn it!"

"I'm not fighting you, Ethan. This is self-defense!"

Not wasting a moment, I quickly got to my feet, but Ethan

was almost as quick. Lunging for me, he tripped over the corner of the area rug. It was like watching a scene in slow motion. With arms flailing as he went down, his head smacked the corner of the coffee table, and his body sprawled to the floor. He laid there unconscious and unmoving.

Knowing I didn't have a moment to waste, I ran as fast as I could to the bedroom to retrieve the bat. If I hesitated even for a second, I knew I'd never be able to do what needed to be done. If I ever wanted to truly be free, there was no other option.

I had to kill him.

If I didn't, he would surely kill me—something I'd always known, but I never truly believed this moment would come to fruition.

When I returned to the living room, I hoisted the bat over my head, preparing to throw all of my strength behind the swing. However, the expression on Ethan's face made me pause. His body was perfectly still, and his eyes...they were open and vacant as if he was already...

"Ethan?" I hesitantly whispered.

Standing over him, I watched the stain of blood grow larger and larger on the carpet. It was coming from an unseen wound on his head. Using the toe of my boot, I gave him a slight nudge.

Nothing.

Cautiously, I squatted down to press my fingers to his neck. There was no pulse or intake of breath, no rise and fall to his chest. He wasn't screaming at me, calling me names, or threatening me with things I knew he'd one day make good on.

He was just still.

And quiet... so very quiet.

Ethan was dead.

For the first time since meeting him, I was surrounded by the sound of silence.

Slowly, I stood. With the wooden bat in hand, I moved like a zombie toward my bedroom. Once there, I returned the bat to its proper place, then removed the material wrapped around my hands. Slipping the bulky rings from each finger, I balled them up in the material and shoved it in my sports bra. It was the best I could do until I could one day dispose of it all. Self-defense, even with the kubotan, was one thing, but there could be no evidence of intent.

After swapping out my boots for a pair of sneakers, I went into the bathroom and washed the baby oil from my arms and neck, then pulled on an oversized sweatshirt. Going back to the living room, I sat on the floor next to Ethan.

Tears began to stream down my face. I didn't cry because he was dead but from the relief of knowing it was finally over. My chest heaved with sobs that came from deep in my core. I gave myself over to it, feeling all the hurt, betrayal, and anger. I mourned the fantasy of a man I thought I loved, finally saying goodbye to a part of my life that would never, ever be forgotten.

Wiping my tears from my face, I pulled out my cell phone and dialed 9-1-1.

"9-1-1. What's your emergency?"

"Hello. My name is Gianna Valentini. My husband...he's dead."

44

Gianna

Queens, New York
1 week later

I exited Grand Central Terminal and headed outside to catch a cab. My skin prickled with goosebumps from the wind blowing off the East River as I waved my arm to signal a taxi.

"Where to, Miss?" the cab driver asked.

"The Mill Fitness Center in Queens."

The driver pulled away from the curb, and I looked out the window at the passing streets. It seemed like I moved to this city a lifetime ago, even though it had been less than a year. Perhaps it was the stress of being on the run and looking over my shoulder every single day that made my time here seem endless. I couldn't be sure. I only knew that after being away from New York for only a week, I had learned one thing.

I was no longer that girl who hated city living. Somewhere along the way, Queens, the underrated borough in the city that never sleeps, had become my home. It was a place for the culturally diverse and the working class—a place where I finally discovered who I really was. It would take me a lifetime to experience all the cuisines and cultures that resided in the borough, many of which Derek tried to show me when he was "old-fashioned courting" me. I'd fallen in love with Queens, just as I'd fallen in love with him. I couldn't imagine living anywhere else.

When the cab pulled up in front of The Mill, I paid the driver and stepped out onto the pavement. My hands were clammy from anxious jitters, so I wiped them on my jeans. I was a nervous wreck about facing Derek. I hadn't spoken to him since the night of Ethan's death. When we spoke that night, police had been everywhere. There was no mistaking the questioning look in Derek's eyes as I willingly climbed into the back of a police car. He'd been wondering if I had killed Ethan.

Technically, I didn't—but I would have if it came down to it. Somewhere in my subconscious, I knew I'd been secretly planning to do exactly that. It would have been premeditated. Did Derek know that, too? When he saw me today, I worried if he'd still look at me the same.

Walking inside, I took stock of the gym, and my heart sank. Derek had reopened for business, but there were still large areas roped off where the damage had yet to be repaired. He hadn't exaggerated when he called me the night of the break-in to describe everything Ethan had done. The place was literally an absolute mess.

I spotted Derek standing outside his office door, talking to an older man wearing a yellow hard hat. The man was pointing at one of the broken glass panels for the racquetball court, and I assumed he was a contractor here to repair the damages. Derek turned his head slightly and spotted me walking in his direction. His eyes widened in surprise, and he smiled a cheek-splitting grin. Quickly excusing himself, he closed the distance between us in three long, powerful strides.

He pulled me into his embrace, hugging me so tightly, I could barely breathe. I didn't mind. The warm feel of his body against mine and the scent of his aquatic, woodsy cologne completed my homecoming. After a few moments, I pulled back and peered at him through lowered lashes.

"Hey," I said quietly.

He touched the side of my face and my hair, almost as if he were testing to see if I was real.

"Sparky, where have you been? I was so…" He seemed at a loss for words before abruptly pulling me tight to his chest once more. Stroking my head, he whispered in my ear, "It doesn't matter where you were. I'm just glad you're back. God, I was so worried. When you didn't answer my calls, and I didn't know how to find you… The last time I saw you, you were being escorted to the police station."

"I'm sorry about that. Really, I am. I went back to Cincinnati. I just needed time alone to work out some things on my own."

"Such as?

"Derek, I…" I pulled back slightly to look at him. "When I'm with you, I feel too much. I had to eliminate that distraction —if that makes any sense."

"Sort of, I think," he said with a light chuckle. "But go on."

"It's over, Derek. I don't have to worry about Ethan anymore."

"I know that, but…" Raking a hand through his hair, worry lines marred his beautiful face. "Shit, Gianna. This past week has been the scariest in my life. Between me, Isabella, Christopher… we've all been freaking out, wondering what happened to you. The police wouldn't give me a damn thing. Can you at least tell me a little about what the hell went down that day?"

"Your training happened. Your words." I took a step back, held out my arm, and shifted my sleeve up. On the underside of my wrist, the words 'I Am' had been tattooed in a cursive font.

The skin surrounding the ink was still shiny and pink, not yet completely healed.

"You got a tattoo."

"I had it done a few days ago when I was in Cinci. It was a spur-of-the-moment thing, but I think it's fitting. These were the words you made me say. I remembered them, and you saved me."

"I saved you? Are you trying to say…"

"If you think I killed him, I didn't. I want to be clear about that before it becomes an elephant in the room. But… I would have done it if I had to," I added in a whisper.

"But you didn't. Even if you had, nobody would blame you. That son of a bitch deserved to die. I wanted to kill him myself." The venom in his voice caused me to shiver. "What else happened?"

I squeezed my eyes shut as I recalled the deafening crack of Ethan's head connecting with the coffee table, the pool of blood, and my tears of relief.

"There was a fight. He said some things… He really was a complete stranger to me. His name wasn't even Ethan Walker. For four years, my life was nothing but a lie. His name was Anthony Gallo."

"You're joking, right?"

I shook my head.

"I wish I was. He came after me, but I fought him off. He tripped, went down hard, and hit his head on the corner of a table. He died almost instantly. The police and the FBI easily deduced self-defense, and I've been cleared of any wrongdoing," I assured. The clanking of weight machines in the background caused me to pause as I remembered where we were. I looked around at the people in the gym. Clients were busy with their workout as employees and contractors bustled about. Nobody seemed to be paying much attention to us, but that didn't mean we couldn't be overheard. "There's more to the story, but that's it in a nutshell. I don't really want to get into it here. Okay?"

"Okay," he agreed, nodding. "Why don't we take a walk to La Biga, grab a coffee, and chat on the way."

"That sounds like a perfect idea."

Derek took my hand, and we began the short walk to the little coffee shop that had quickly become one of my favorite places in Queens.

"I like the tattoo. And you're right—it is fitting. But I doubt you went all the way back to Cincinnati just for a tattoo. Are you going to tell me what else you were doing there?" he asked as we waited for the traffic light to turn, so we could cross the street.

"After I told the FBI Ethan's real name, it opened up a whole new can of worms. Agent Gregory was able to track down who his mother was. Apparently, she had a history of mental illness and was in and out of psychiatric institutions throughout her twenties. There's a police record in Salt Lake City of her claiming she was raped, but there was no follow-up. Her history picks back up nine months later when Ethan—or rather, Anthony—was born. His birth records proved he wasn't lying about his real name. It brought the legality of our marriage into question and complicated who was next of kin. His supposed 'big family' was really just people he knew from the police department. I never knew they weren't really his cousins. There was no blood relation at all. God, I was so stupid..." I trailed off, thinking about how easily I believed everything he told me.

"Not stupid," Derek stated vehemently. "The guy was a sociopath. You can't blame yourself for his manipulations."

"Maybe." I shrugged. "Maybe not. At the very least, I should have questioned things. If I hadn't ignored the red flags, maybe things would have happened differently. I suppose it doesn't matter now. I can't change the past, which is basically what the lawyer said."

"Lawyer?"

"Yes. I had to meet with a lawyer about the estate. Ultimately, I left it up to him to work out the legalities, but I did get the opportunity to go through my old house. The FBI was with me to supervise and approve anything I wanted to take out. They said something about preserving evidence after they found the bodies of five other women Ethan had photographs of. So far, they've tallied nine women." I forced myself to swallow the emotional guilt welling in my throat. I wondered if I'd ever get over the guilt of living when so many others had died.

If only I had gone to the authorities sooner, maybe...

There were so many what-ifs, I would go crazy if I didn't stop thinking about them.

Derek's grip on my hand tightened, almost as if he knew what I was thinking.

"Like I said, the son of a bitch deserved to die. None of this is your fault."

I returned his squeeze, taking comfort from his words.

"Apparently, he had mementos from the places he'd disposed of their bodies. He had the items hidden in the safe in the house —the house I lived in for years," I spat out in disgust, unable to believe there had been evidence of such gruesome murders right under my nose for years.

Our conversation died once we arrived at La Biga. The coffee shop, as usual, was bustling, and there was no way to talk without raising our voices several octaves. While we waited for our to-go beverages, I watched Derek out of the corner of my eye. After the emotional week, I wanted to take a moment to appreciate him—to appreciate the man I was choosing to be with. He was gorgeous and always made me a little weak in the knees. His stance was confident yet easy, with one hand inside the pocket of his gym shorts. Wide shoulders bulged beneath the red t-shirt that seemed molded to his skin, accentuating the hard-muscled pectorals no shirt could ever hope to conceal. I didn't think I'd ever tire of looking at him.

After we collected our drink orders, we exited the coffee shop. Derek kept throwing cautious glances my way as if I were a mirage that would disappear at any moment. I needed to keep talking and assure him I wasn't going to run anymore—I was here to stay.

"The FBI showed me the pictures you told me about," I said as we walked aimlessly with no destination in mind. "The ones of his apartment in Avondale. You have to believe me, I had no idea."

"I never thought you did," he replied automatically.

His unwavering loyalty and faith in me brought a small smile to my face.

"When I was at the house, I was surprised to see Ethan had kept all of my stuff. At first, I didn't know what to do with it. I hadn't made up my mind whether I was going to stay in Cincinnati or come back to New York."

Derek stopped walking and turned to take my chin between his thumb and forefinger, angling my head up to meet his gaze.

"Sparky, if you've never listened to a thing I've said before, I need you to hear me now. I've already thought about this long and hard. Whether you choose New York or Cincinnati, I will follow you. Ethan controlled your life for too long. It's time for you to do you without all the strings attached. Wherever you decide to go or whatever you decide to do, I'll be more than happy to let you lead me to the ends of the earth. You've earned… " He stopped contemplatively. "No, that's the wrong word. Deserve is more accurate. You deserve someone to follow you. You know that, right?"

I smiled and thought about a conversation I'd had with Natalia while I was in Cincinnati. She thought I'd wasted enough time on a 'slow burn' relationship with Derek—her words, not mine. She reminded me that love could be healthy and told me to explore what Derek and I had. She was right, although she didn't have to work too hard to convince me. I already knew where my heart was.

I smiled and rested my head against his strong chest.

"I do know that. Just like I know, I deserve to be happy. That's why I came back. It didn't take me long to realize my happiness was in New York because that's where you were. I planned to rent a moving truck and bring some things back here —like the couch, so I could replace the old one I'm currently using. But..." I hesitated, not sure how to articulate my feelings.

"But what?" Derek prodded, leaning back to look at me.

"I didn't want anything—not the couch, not any of my old clothes or jewelry. The only thing I took was a small cedarwood box that had mementos of my mom. Taking anything else would have reminded me of that part of my life. I want to forget all of it, Derek. I want to start over, old couch and all. I have a new life here in Queens, and I want to focus on that. I never want to be dependent on a man again, but with you..." I needed him to understand in a way I'd never needed him to understand me before.

There were many pieces of my past I never wanted to give voice to—secrets I would take to my grave because I couldn't bear looking at the completed puzzle—but how I felt about Derek wasn't going to be a part of that jigsaw. Today, I would begin creating a new picture.

"What is it, Sparky?" he prompted.

"Being away made me realize how much I need you in my life... no... how much I *want* you in my life. I love you, Derek, and I was hoping maybe—just maybe—you might be on the same page. What do you say, boy scout? Me, you, Maisie? Want to start over and give this a real chance? No more secrets. No more Val. Just me, Gianna Valentini."

He tilted my chin up and forced me to look into those gorgeous hazel eyes. The tiny flecks of green sparkled as his gaze intensified. I blushed from the powerful wave of deep emotion and looked down.

He chuckled.

"I love the way you lower those long lashes when you're embarrassed."

I snapped my head up to look at him again.

"I'm not embarrassed."

That just made him laugh more.

"I love that, too—the way your tiny shoulders stiffen with indignation when you're offended."

I pursed my lips in a frown and quirked up a brow.

"You still haven't answered my question," I pointed out.

Instead of answering me, he went to toss his near-empty coffee cup in a trash can by the side of the road. When he returned to me, something intense had swallowed his easy humor from a moment before. He placed his hands on my hips and turned me to face him, so we were toe-to-toe. Everything around us seemed to fade away. All the people and cars passing by were nothing more than a backdrop. The only thing I was aware of was the tall, sandy-haired, and broad-shouldered man before me. His gaze was penetrating.

"I love you, Gianna. I love you with everything that I am. We all have demons, but it's up to us when we choose to face them. You confronted yours and managed to stand strong in the end. Your story is a testament to getting back up. I'm proud of you. You inspire me, and I am honored you're choosing me to share your life."

My mouth tilted up on one side.

"So, is that a yes?"

He reached up to graze the side of my cheek ever so softly with his knuckles. His eyes glimmered with a barrage of emotions—affection, desire, and longing, but most of all, I saw love.

"It's definitely a yes."

My breath caught, and all the air seemed to dissipate from my lungs as if I'd been swept away by a fierce undercurrent. I was drowning, and Derek was my ocean. Our breaths mingled together as his arms circled my lower back and pulled me to him. He was so strong in the way he held me as he brought his lips down to meet mine. I surrendered to the kiss, knowing I didn't have to lose a piece of myself to find love. I could accept his without reservation, freely and completely.

Independence and love could coexist as long as I allowed it.

THE END

Thank you for reading *The Sound of Silence*! I hope you enjoyed Gianna's story of survival! If you enjoyed this book, you might like *The Stone Series*, a *USA Today* bestseller. Keep turning the pages for an excerpt from this sexy, billionaire romance!

BLURB:

Bound by need. Entwined in secrets...

Krystina
I had dreams and aspirations, none of which included a man by my side. Been there, done that. Then I forgot my cellphone, and all of my carefully laid plans went to hell.
He wasn't supposed to be there when I fell. I wasn't supposed to get lost in a sea of sapphire blue when he helped me up. And he wasn't supposed to be Alexander Stone, the New York billionaire real estate tycoon.

I saw the dark promises in his eyes when he looked at me. But the shadows of my past haunted me, making me afraid to explore the possibilities I could never before have imagined.

Alexander

I was used to getting what I wanted. I understood the value of finesse and patience to achieve the desired result. But a chance run-in with Krystina Cole quickly turned my world upside down.

She was strong, determined, devastatingly beautiful—and stubborn as hell. Her quick wit and firecracker attitude was the complete opposite of what I wanted in a woman. But I still wanted to claim her. Tame her. Make her mine.

And I always get what I want.

Heart of Stone is the first book in Krystina & Alexander's epic love story. It's the beginning of the steamy and unforgettable series by *USA Today* Bestselling Author Dakota Willink.

Start reading on Amazon, Apple Books, Barnes & Noble, Nook, Google Play, or wherever books are sold.

A Note From The Author

Dear Readers,

I hope you enjoyed reading *The Sound of Silence*. This book was inspired by a piece I wrote for *Nevertheless We Persisted: Me Too*, a special audiobook collection of essays and poems from people who are survivors of sexual discrimination and abuse. While *The Sound of Silence* is fiction, there are many truths to it —not in the actual storyline per se, but reflective in our way of life. For too long, victims have been silent. Some remain quiet because of shame, others because of fear. Silence also comes from societal pressures that convince victims their story is not real, valid, or important.

I realize parts of this book were not always easy to read—just as the life of a victim is not easy to endure. I spoke to many abuse survivors while writing this book, seeking their input to ensure Gianna's story was nothing short of authentic. While being married to a radicalized serial killer is far from reality, the story of her abuse isn't.

The women I interviewed told me about their experiences, and I will forever be grateful to them for their brutal honesty. These brave women shared stories of put downs which, eventually, turned into full blown criticisms from their partner. Soon after, the control would start. They were questioned, had no personal space, and endured unrealistic demands. Then came the mistreatment, cruelty, and abuse. It was often so subtle, by the time it was noticed, it was too late. More often than not, the women were made to feel it was somehow their fault. The feelings of confusion, bewilderment, and fear were so powerful, they no longer recognized their way out.

During my conversations, I came to realize one very important fact. Every woman I know has been victim of harassment, abuse, or violence of some kind. I want all the women out there to know, me too.

People often say, "Why doesn't she just leave?" The reality is, it's not the easiest thing to do. No relationship is ever black and white. Then there are those who indirectly suggest the woman provoked an abuser by saying, "Well, what did she do?" Trust me when I say—no woman 'asks for it.' For too long, victims have been told to be quiet, to feel ashamed, and are forced to shoulder the blame and suffer in silence.

This is wrong.

On average, twenty-four people per minute are victims of rape, physical violence or stalking by an intimate partner in the United States. Nearly one in ten women in the U.S. have been raped by an intimate partner, while one in six have experienced stalking victimization in which they felt fearful or believed they or someone close to them would be harmed or killed. Those are staggering numbers.

To the strong women who shared their truths with me, thank you. I salute your bravery, resilience, and capacity to love. You are beautiful, capable, and worthy. You are magnificent and strong—and more powerful than you can imagine.

If you or someone you know is a victim of abuse, please call the National Domestic Violence Hotline at 1−800−799−SAFE.

SUBSCRIBE TO DAKOTA'S NEWSLETTER

My newsletter goes out twice a month (sometimes less). It's packed with new content, sales on signed paperbacks and Angel Book Boxes from my online store, and giveaways. Don't miss out! I value your email address and promise to NEVER spam you.

SUBSCRIBE HERE: https://dakotawillink.com/subscribe

BOOKS & BOXED WINE CONFESSIONS

Want fun stuff and sneak peek excerpts from Dakota?
Join Books & Boxed Wine Confessions and get the inside scoop!
Fans in this interactive reader Facebook group are the first to know the latest news!

JOIN HERE: https://www.facebook.com/groups/
1635080436793794

MUSIC PLAYLIST

Thank you to the musical talents who influenced and inspired *The Sound of Silence*. Their creativity helped me bring this story to life.

"Smooth Operator" by Sade *(The Ultimate Collection)*
"Perfect Duet" by Ed Sheeran & Beyoncé *(Perfect Duet)*
"My Soul I" by Anna Leone *(Wandered Away)*
"I Feel Like I'm Drowning" by Two Feet *(A 20 Something Fuck)*
"Preach" by John Legend *(Preach)*
"When the Party's Over" by Billie Eilish *(When We All Fall Asleep, Where Do We Go?)*
"Troubled - Stripped" by Halsey *(Room 93)*
"Howling" by Cathedrals *(Howling)*
"Con te partirò" by Andrea Bocelli *(Bocelli, remastered)*
"Moves Like Jagger: by Maroon 5 & Christina Aguilera *(Hands All Over)*
"I've Got You Under My Skin" by Frank Sinatra *(Ultimate Sinatra)*
"Moonlight Sonata" by Ludwig van Beethoven, Luke Woodapple *(Peaceful Moments)*
"When Yo Were Young" by Benjamin Francis Leftwich *(When You Were Young)*
"Nothin To Lose" by VASSY *(Nothing To Lose)*
"Too Close" by Next *(Rated Next)*
"Chandelier" by Sia *(1000 Forms of Fear)*
"Love Song" by Lana Del Rey *(Norman Fucking Rockwell!)*
"Take Me Under" by Three Days Grace *(Three Days Grace)*
"The Sound of Silence" by Pentatonix *(The Sound of Silence)*

LISTEN ON SPOTIFY

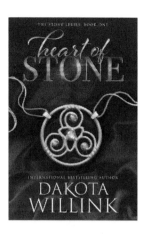

Excerpt from HEART OF STONE
by Dakota Willink

Traffic was terrible upon entering the financial district, but we still made good time. For once, I was thankful for the fearless and reckless driving of a New York City cabbie, despite the fact my knuckles were white from hanging on to the seat so tightly.

When the cab reached our destination, it screeched to a halt. I paid the driver and stepped out onto the pavement. I looked up apprehensively at the impressive structure towering before me. There was a large sign above the main entrance that read Cornerstone Tower in silver lettering. A sleek ornamental spire soared high above the building, piercing a stray passing cloud.

The sheer size of the place was intimidating, and I found my steps toward the revolving glass doors to be somewhat hesitant. I tilted my head from side to side, stretching my neck like a boxer headed into the ring.

I need to relax. I've got this.

However, as much as I tried to talk myself down, I was still a nervous wreck when I walked through the main doors. I knew my career opportunities in New York were starting to run out. If I wanted to stay in the city, it was vital for me to ace this interview.

The vestibule was large, and it took me a moment to locate the security desk. A man wearing an official-looking uniform sat behind a polished mahogany wood counter. He was looking at the security monitors and didn't notice my arrival.

I cleared my throat and said, "Excuse me, sir. My name is Krystina Cole. I have an appointment with Laura Kaufman today at nine o'clock."

The security guard glanced up at me before looking down at a logbook on the desk. He ran his finger over the page until he located my name.

"Yes, Miss Cole. Just take the elevator to the fiftieth floor. Ms. Kaufman is expecting you," he said with a kind smile. He pointed down a corridor to his left. "The elevators are just down that hall."

"Thank you."

I made my way across the blue-veined marble floors to the bank of elevators. When I reached them, I typed the floor number into the keypad.

Here goes nothing.

The doors slid open, and I stepped inside. My ears popped as the elevator climbed higher and higher. When the lift finally reached its destination, a lavish waiting area came into view.

The room was furnished with several slate gray leather sofas. They were contemporary in style and positioned in a U shape off to my right. A low glass table sat in the middle of the sofas, displaying some sort of small stone sculpture. Eclectic artwork in varying shades of grays and blues adorned the stark white walls.

When I looked to my left, an attractive woman in a killer designer suit stood up from behind a desk. Her suit was vibrant emerald green, and it hugged every one of her flawless curves. Her makeup was impeccable, and not a single strand of her angled bob was out of place. She looked professional yet exceedingly sexy at the same time. When she walked around the desk to where I was standing, matching six-inch green stilettos came into view.

I would kill myself if I ever tried to walk in shoes like that.

I was suddenly very self-conscious of my modest navy-blue jacket and skirt.

"You must be Krystina Cole. I'm Laura Kaufman." She smiled and extended a perfectly manicured hand to me.

"It's nice to meet you, Ms. Kaufman," I replied as I shook her hand. She appeared to be in her early thirties, younger than I had anticipated based on our brief phone conversation. Her voice was so gentle and sweet, and I had pictured her to be the grandmotherly type. I couldn't have been more wrong.

"Please, call me Laura. Just one moment, please." She walked back behind her desk and pressed a button on the desktop phone. "Excuse me, sir. Miss Cole has arrived for her interview. Shall I bring her to your office? Or would you prefer the conference room?"

"Come to the conference room, Laura. I'm just finishing up with something," said a male voice from the speaker.

Laura turned back to me, "If you follow me this way, I'll bring you to Mr. Stone now."

Mr. Stone?

My eyes widened in surprise upon hearing the name.

No way. It can't be the same guy. Mr. Blue Eyes. Mr. Keep-me-up-all-night-dreaming-of-sapphire. Impossible.

Then the light bulb went on, a blinding glare that almost knocked me flat on my ass, as I remembered all of the things I knew about Alexander Stone.

Stone Enterprise. Stoneworks Foundation.

My stomach dropped as panic began to set in. The building I stood in was called Cornerstone Tower. And I was about to interview for a position at Turning Stone Advertising.

It has to be the same Mr. Stone. How can I be so ridiculously obtuse?

I cursed quietly under my breath, knowing the intelligent thing to do would be to leave immediately.

If I can't figure out what one plus one is, I'm obviously unfit for the job.

"Forgive me, Ms. Kaufman, but I assumed I would be interviewing with you," I said with a wobbly smile, scrambling to think of a way out of the situation.

"I'm sorry?" She looked confused by my statement.

"I, um…" I stuttered as I tried to think of something —*anything* that might prevent me from coming face to face with Alexander Stone again. "I didn't realize I'd be interviewing with Mr. Stone. I assumed since you were a large company, you would have an HR department to handle your hiring," I explained, not able to come up with anything better. I could only hope this actually *was* a large company.

Realization dawned on Laura's face.

"Mr. Stone must be considering you for an important position, or else that would normally be the case. Our human resources department usually handles the initial applicant screening. However, Mr. Stone personally conducts all of the interviews for high potential candidates," she clarified with a smile.

High potential?

My palms began to sweat as I silently followed the strawberry blond Laura to the conference room. Her subtle red hair was a reminder of all the articles I had read online about Alexander Stone's preference for redheads.

But surely that can't be a prerequisite for working for him? Or can it?

My stomach constricted into a nervous knot. Everything about the situation was terribly wrong. Not only was I a fool for not connecting the dots, but I also had the wrong hair color for the job.

Someone like Alexander Stone would want to hire someone

competent and witty—not someone whose tongue got stuck to the roof of her mouth every time he was near. This was a disaster in the making. He was too *distracting*, nothing but sex and sin and every girl's spiciest fantasy. I couldn't imagine the thought of going through an entire job interview with him.

I felt like I was walking through a tunnel, my nerves gradually taking over every rational part of me. Apprehension caused my steps to lag slowly behind Laura as she walked to the door at the end of the corridor.

I toyed with the idea of bolting right then and there, but my window of time for a quick exit had ended. We had reached the conference room. I took a deep breath and made a conscious effort to still my fidgeting hands.

Keep it together—it's a job interview. I'm overreacting.

Feeling only slightly more composed, I stepped through the door Laura held open for me.

Maybe it's not even the same Mr. Stone.

But it was.

One-click HEART OF STONE now!

ABOUT THE AUTHOR

 Dakota Willink is an award-winning *USA Today* Bestselling Author from New York. She loves writing about damaged heroes who fall in love with sassy and independent females. Her books are character-driven, emotional, and sexy, yet written with a flare that keeps them real. With a wide range of published books, a magazine publication, and the *Leave Me Breathless World* under her belt, Dakota's imagination is constantly spinning new ideas.

Dakota often says she survived her first publishing with coffee and wine. She's an unabashed *Star Wars* fanatic and still dreams of getting her letter from Hogwarts one day. Her daily routines usually include rocking Lululemon yoga pants, putting on lipstick, and obsessing over Excel spreadsheets. Two spoiled Cavaliers are her furry writing companions who bring her regular smiles. She enjoys traveling with her husband and debating social and economic issues with her politically savvy Generation Z son and daughter.

Dakota's favorite book genres include contemporary or dark romance, political & psychological thrillers, and autobiographies. Visit www.dakotawillink.com for more information for current news, book signing information, and upcoming releases.

AWARDS, ACCOLADES, AND OTHER PROJECTS

The Stone Series is Dakota's first published book series. It has been recognized for various awards and bestseller lists, including *USA Today* and the *Readers' Favorite* 2017 Gold Medal in Romance, and has since been translated into multiple languages internationally.

The *Fade Into You* series (formally known as the *Cadence* duet) was a finalist in the *HEAR Now Festival Independent Audiobook Awards*.

In addition, Dakota has written under the alternate pen name, Marie Christy. Under this name, she has written and published a children's book for charity titled, *And I Smile*. Also writing as Marie Christy, she was a contributor to the Blunder Woman Productions project, *Nevertheless We Persisted: Me Too*, a 2019 *Audie Award* Finalist and *Earphones Awards* Winner. This project inspired Dakota to write *The Sound of Silence*, a dark romantic suspense novel that tackles the realities of domestic abuse.

Dakota Willink is the founder of Dragonfly Ink Publishing, whose mission is to promote a common passion for reading by partnering with like-minded authors and industry professionals. Through this company, Dakota has assisted and published multiple authors, created the *Leave Me Breathless World,* published a romance literary magazine called *Love & Lace Inkorporated*, hosted ALLURE Audiobook Con, and sponsored various charity anthologies.

For inquiries about film or TV rights, please email Dakota@ dakotawillink.com.

Printed in Great Britain
by Amazon